WHISPER OF THE DARKSONG

LISA CASSIDY

TATE HOUSE

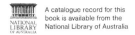 A catalogue record for this
book is available from the
National Library of Australia

National Library of Australia Cataloguing-in-Publication entry

Creator: Cassidy, Lisa, 2022 - author.

Title: Whisper of the Darksong

ISBN (ebook): 978-1-922533-06-7

ISBN (print): 978-1-922533-07-4

Subjects: Young Adult fantasy

Series: Heir to the Darkmage

First published 2022 by Tate House

Cover artwork and design by Jeff Brown Graphics

Map artwork by Chaim Holtjer

This one is for Tara.

CHAPTER I

L ira stared fixedly at the manacles around her wrists. Time seemed to slow to a crawl as her Taliath guard took a key from his pocket, slid it into the lock, and turned it. Behind him, two more Taliath watched carefully. To them, her expression would appear distant, but inside she waged war. Her body was rigid with the force of her internal struggle, her heart thundering as she wrestled with herself.

Longing battling with reason. Anger with the need for patience.

In a second, a heartbeat, she could set the guards alight, use her telekinesis to grab the nearest one's keys, unlock the cell door, and leave. That's all it would take. A single moment and she could be walking free down the hall.

But then her manacles opened, the sharp click snapping the moment. Lira blinked. Took a steadying breath. The guard yanked the metal off her wrists—clearly wanting to move away from her as quickly as possible—but Lira barely registered the sting as she withdrew her hands from the slot in the bars. She'd grown accustomed to the pain.

Even if it had been unbearable agony, Lira still wouldn't have made a sound. She never showed an ounce of expression to any of her guards. It was one of her rules.

The three Taliath left without a word, the manacles clanking all the way back down the long hallway to the single door at the end that they closed behind them.

As soon as they were gone, Lira let out a long breath, body shuddering with the adrenalin reserves that flooded through her. She fought this same internal battle every single day: desperate fight-or-flight versus rational understanding. It would be foolish to try to fight her way free unless she had a good chance of succeeding.

Three times Lira had attempted to escape from this prison.

Three times she'd failed.

But she'd gotten a little further each time. Learned a little more. Lost herself to despair with each failure before dragging herself out of the darkness and starting to plan all over again.

One thing Lira Astor had learned behind these walls was the value of patience. Determination she had in endless supply, but without patience, she would never escape. Without patience, one day the depression and despair would hold her down and never let her resurface.

She'd come to hate the word with a fierce passion but learn it she did. It was the key to her survival. And Lira was nothing if not a survivor.

After her first escape attempt, when she'd made it through the door at the end of the hall before being overwhelmed, they'd added two heavily armed Tregayan soldiers to her Taliath escort whenever she was taken from her cell. This occurred daily for her allotment of fresh air and sunlight in a small yard, three times weekly to bathe, and when necessary to see the prison's healer.

Her second thwarted escape had killed both soldiers, disabled the Taliath, and gotten her down two levels—not to mention taught her more about the layout of the prison. That one had earned her the manacles for every trip out of her cell.

She had been surprised to find the restraints were made from normal iron. She'd expected them to use bindings made from the melted-down remnants of the Hunter medallions the Mage Council had recovered after the war with the Darkmage—the lock on her cell door was, and it seemed an obvious thing to use in a prison designed for holding mages. Early in her sentence, she'd thought about asking why, but had decided it wasn't worth giving the guards her attention. Or betraying her interest.

Perhaps Lucinda and the Shadowcouncil had stolen the medallions from the council at some point? But Lira had long theorised that the Shadowcouncil had found a way to bind razak blood with metal, thereby providing the medallions worn by their Shiven warriors—designed and trained in the same mould as Shakar's Hunters.

The Shadowcouncil ... fury stirred within at the thought of what they'd done to her, and Lira ruthlessly forced all thoughts of them aside. Not dwelling on the corrosive bitterness inside her was another key to maintaining her sanity.

In her third escape attempt, Lira had taken brutal advantage of their assumption that the Taliath and their backup guards would be enough to subdue her should she break free of the manacles, that they'd be on her before her telekinetic magic could unlock them. That time, she'd almost reached the front entrance of the building that housed the prison. Almost. That had marked Lira's first visit to the prison healer, and it had been several weeks before the broken bones and other assorted injures had healed.

After that, they'd added two more Taliath to her guard escort and started locking her ankles in manacles as well. Not only that, but they changed the locking mechanism on both sets—complex ones that would take upwards of an hour for her to pick with her magic. Her telekinesis could probably still rip them off, but it would take a significant amount of magical energy, probably everything she had in one concentrated burst. And she'd need her magic to get farther than just her cell door. Especially if she managed to get *out* of the prison.

So, every single day, Lira probed the locks with her telekinesis, learning their inner workings, getting closer and closer to the solution.

Two more Taliath to deal with in addition to being unable to run freely *did* pose a stronger impediment to escape. Not to mention that the daily rubbing of rough metal edges on her bare wrists and ankles left reddened raw skin that had, over the months, turned into calloused scarring. The prison healer worked only on serious illness or injury—prisoners were left to deal with minor cuts, bruises, or illnesses on their own—so those scars marked her forever now.

A door somewhere else on her level, out of sight, slammed, pulling her sharply from her thoughts. Lira blinked, giving herself a little shake. That happened often, the drifting of her mind. She tried to keep herself in the present as much as possible, but that was hard when one day bled into another without any obvious passing of the time apart from the gradual shifting of the seasons outside her window.

Once the echoes of the slamming door died away, she turned and faced the interior of her cell. Morning sunlight filled the small space. She'd just had her weekly bath, and her damp hair dripped down the back of her neck, the shorter ends curling around her ears and forehead. The limited sunlight she received had changed the colour of her hair from light brown to a darker shade, and her skin had turned sickly pale. She might almost pass for Shiven now, if it weren't for her grandfather's pale blue eyes.

Now the day stretched before her, long and unending. And another day after that.

And then another. And another.

Just over two years down. The rest of her life to go.

Her spirit quailed at that thought, teetered on the edge of complete despair before she took hold of herself. A deep breath in. Out. Another.

Settled, she lowered herself to the floor and began her morning routine. She performed the same movements every day, stretching out every muscle in her body slowly and deliberately, keeping herself as limber as possible. Ready.

Strength exercises came next—push-ups, sit-ups, squats—over and over until the sun reached the apex of the sky outside. No matter how tedious, how boring, how tired and sore her muscles became, she pushed through. No matter how much sweat slicked her skin or how she hated every second of it. She made herself continue until she filled that time. *Anything* was better than simply staring at the walls—she'd learned she would lose herself if she gave in to that.

This ruthless routine to fill time and pass the days was how she'd kept herself sane. But it was a constant battle, and some days she came perilously close to losing.

At midday, the door would open at the end of the hall, and the steady footsteps of a Taliath guard would echo down the corridor. She rarely saw the same face more than once a fortnight, and the guard would always stand several steps away from the bars of Lira's cell until she backed up to the window. Once she was at a safe distance, the guard would shove a tray of food through the inch-high gap under the bars, his or her eyes fixed on Lira the entire time.

That measure had been instituted after her first attempt at escape involved leaping out as the guard was in the process of opening the door to bring her tray in, shoving it hard into his body and sending him staggering away before she fled down the hall.

Now Lira watched, a little smile on her face, as today's Taliath backed up as quickly as she could after leaving the tray of food, then walked away with too-fast strides.

She waited for the door at the end of the hall to close and then sat to eat her food slowly, deliberately, taking up more time from the day. Once finished, she moved to her small desk and read the latest parchment she'd requested.

Prisoners weren't treated badly in Carhall, not under the new Mage Council led by Tarrick Tylender and founded by Alyx Egalion. They were able to request reading material from the great library nearby in Centre Square and given parchment, quills, and ink when they wanted. The guards were silent, distant, but never cruel.

Even after Lira's escape attempts, they'd continued allowing her access to the library. She could never settle on how she felt about that. Contempt for their softness, or grudging respect for their refusal to lower themselves to the level of those they'd imprisoned. Maybe it was both.

But the mage prisoners were never allowed to use magic outside their cells. And the most dangerous ones were always guarded by a

Taliath immune to their magic whenever they were allowed out. Or three Taliath now, in Lira's case.

What the council might *not* have realised was that no Taliath was immune to Lira's fire magic—a secret she held close. If they hadn't already guessed, they eventually would, given they had to have figured out by now it had been her that had burned the razak to ashes at DarkSkull Hall. But either way, it was the best advantage she had over them, and she was reluctant to squander it until it was critically necessary.

While she could burn a Taliath, her flame magic quickly depleted her energy levels, and Taliath were warriors with a speed, skill, and strength that she simply couldn't match. She might succeed in burning one, *maybe* two, before they were on her, but not all three. And by careful memorisation of faces, and noting the resistance she'd encountered during her escape attempts, she estimated there were at least fifteen Taliath rotating through the prison, though it was impossible to know exactly how many there were on duty at any one time.

Even more importantly, if she killed a Taliath with magic—thereby proving the extent of the danger she posed to the council—more stringent measures would be implemented that would probably make getting out impossible. Not to mention how afraid it would make them of her. Even if she did manage to break free, they would never stop hunting her.

None of the escape plans she'd tried so far had worked, but each time she'd gotten further than the time before, a fact she held on to whenever the inevitable wave of despair came to try and claim her again.

A little smile flickered at her mouth. She doubted any prisoner had ever tested the prison's defences so thoroughly.

And she would keep testing them until they broke. Lira had absolutely no intention of remaining inside this cell for the rest of her life.

Which brought her back to figuring out her next plan ... such as it was. There was no hope of banding together with other imprisoned mages, combining magical strength to try and escape, as Lira was kept isolated from everyone else in the prison. Her window was too high to jump out of, even if she could melt the bars outside it with her fire magic. And there was no way of getting a message outside even if she had someone to write to, someone who would help her. Which she did not.

She closed her eyes; the smile faded as quickly as it had come, smothered by the wave of despair threatening to rise again. As hard as she'd tried, she still hadn't succeeded. And nobody was coming to save her. Nobody ever would.

Spending over two years in prison had proved to Lira that, despite foolishly hoping otherwise, she remained utterly alone in the world. The quill trembled in her hand as that gaping void in her chest opened up, and it took several minutes to battle it away. Even then, the heaviness still hung over her.

She used focus as a weapon to fight it, a ruthless focus on escape. She continued reading, scrawling notes as she went, until her eyes glazed over with boredom—no matter how hard she'd studied at Temari to catch up with her classmates, Lira would never be a scholar. Then, she spent the hours until dusk practicing her magic.

There were limits to what she could do inside this small cell. She certainly couldn't use large amounts of magic without drawing the attention of the guards. Every single day she cursed the fact she hadn't inherited her grandfather's depth of magical power—with that, she could have brought the walls of the prison down around her and simply walked out.

Instead she practised subtlety and skill, honing control over her magical abilities, which now numbered three. Her third ability—a result of the razak-blood injections she'd been given during her kidnapping by the Shadowcouncil—had broken out only a few weeks into her sentence.

Liquid and gas were two forms of matter that telekinetics could not manipulate—she'd sat in classes at Temari where one of the masters had explained the common theories on why this was the case, but she'd quickly grown bored and now couldn't remember any of it.

But one afternoon, a snap of temper had resulted in the water inside the cup on her lunch tray suddenly exploding into the air.

Lira's anger had died in a blink and she'd leapt out of her chair to stare at the droplets all over the floor.

She'd made water move.

Now, each day, Lira played with the cup of water delivered to her cell with every meal—frustration always gnawing at her to have so little to experiment on. She had no idea how strong her ability was, or how much water she could manipulate at one time, but at least she could practice her control.

The more she practised, the more she realised that she could *sense* the water too, when she focused. At night, she'd lay on her narrow cot and sense the water flowing through the pipes in the kitchens, drawn from a deep underground well nearby. When she focused and summoned more magic, she could sense the water in nearby buildings too.

Months and years on, Lira hungered for more magic, for *powerful* magic, but she didn't know enough about this ability yet to decide whether it would be useful.

But it was something.

Finally, in the hour before dinner, she allowed herself to stare out the window and watch the life of Carhall unfold below. The prison sat on the northern side of Centre Square, a stone's throw from the domed Mage Council building on the western end. Her window looked out over the gleaming square and the streets beyond its southern edge, and her cell's floor was high enough that she could just see over the Carhall outer city walls toward the haze of distant hills to the south.

If she watched too long, despair would claim her. But for the short periods she allowed herself, it gave her an all-too-brief escape from the confines of her cell. And as she watched the world outside carry on without her, she let it reinforce her determination to escape. She would be free. And when she was...

A cold smile spread over her face at the thought. She'd been planning for that. Meticulously.

There were many scores to settle.

CHAPTER 2

On the evening of her next bathing day, Lira watched with interest as a cloud of dust rising above the southern walls resolved into a large party of riders racing towards the city. As they approached the gates, the high outer wall hid them from sight, but it wasn't long before they came into view riding through the eastern gate into Centre Square.

She craned her neck to the left to try and get a better view. Three of the riders wore blue Mage Council cloaks, but the rest sat their horses with the rigidly straight backs of cavalrymen and wore the Rionnan Blue Guard hats. Despite the usual crowds thronging Centre Square, they moved through it with reckless haste. Lira's gaze narrowed in curiosity. They must bring some urgent news from Alistriem.

She watched their progress as they headed straight for the council building, close enough now that she could make out their faces. All of them grim. Once there, the mages dismounted, walking with hurried strides up the steps and into the domed building. The Bluecoats milled for a moment, before the majority wheeled away and headed back toward the gates, leaving a handful behind.

The mages still hadn't reappeared by the time Lira's dinner arrived, the Bluecoats still waiting patiently at the bottom of the steps.

The sight lingered with her for several days. Even such a small change to the monotony of her routine was something to be feasted on.

Two weeks later, or possibly three, as Lira dressed in preparation for the arrival of three Taliath to take her to her scheduled bath, she heard the door open at the end of the hall. Instantly she stilled—it was too early. And instead of the heavy tread of the guards and clanking of the manacles hanging from their hands, there was silence.

Her gaze narrowed. There hadn't been a change to her routine once since her arrival.

Wariness spreading quickly through her, she crossed to the bars and craned her head to stare down the hallway. Someone had come through the door at the end, but they weren't dressed as a guard, wore no mage cloak, and didn't carry a Taliath sword.

Her sweeping gaze took this in with a single glance and then moved to the person's face.

She froze.

He hadn't spotted her yet, his expression a curious mix of determined and despairing as his gaze roved the cells lining the hall, presumably looking for hers. She didn't move, didn't blink, not willing to draw his attention to the fact he was being watched. She wanted time to think, to prepare, but her mind was a frozen muddle.

What was Tarion Caverlock doing here?

Lira took a breath. Used the time he spent hesitating to push away any emotion roused at the sight of someone she'd once learned to call friend. Someone she'd once trusted with her life. Someone she'd once really, really liked. More than she'd ever admit to herself. Anger surged then, white-hot fury, stronger than she'd expected. Her magic flared with it, and it took another moment to wrestle it back under control. The anger remained, though, undaunted by her efforts. Her fingers curled white-knuckled at her sides.

He must have been stalling rather than genuinely looking for where to go, because after a moment he gave himself a little shake and began walking straight towards her cell with long, graceful, strides.

He didn't wear the blue cloak of a mage who'd passed his Trials, and she couldn't spot a mage staff or any other weapon on him. His black hair was cut far shorter and more neatly than she remembered, the dark colour a sharp contrast with his fair Shiven skin. Her criminal eye noted that his breeches, tunic, and boots were of expensive material and well-tailored, making him look every inch a young lord. But he didn't carry the air of arrogance or superiority those of his ilk usually did; in fact, he seemed almost uncomfortable, as if his clothes didn't fit quite right, no matter how fine they looked.

Over two years had passed. He should be a council warrior mage by now. Lira stuck on that oddity for a moment, realised that was foolish, and focused her attention on watching him, fighting her surging anger, and readying herself for whatever was coming.

As he walked, his hazel eyes remained determinedly on the floor, even though he seemed to know where he was going. When he finally lifted his gaze and spotted her, their eyes met in a single, charged moment.

His stride faltered briefly, but then he kept coming. Lira stayed where she was, half a pace away from the bars of her cell, utterly still. Her nails dug deep into the skin of her palms. The silence drew out, long and heavy with tension, until he came to a halt before her. He didn't wait for her to back away before coming so close, and his expression was shuttered, the sadness he'd been wearing when she first saw him carefully erased.

"Tarion Caverlock," she greeted him, eyes narrowed. Her voice was chilly, even saying his name threatening her tenuous hold on her fury. "My first visitor in over two years. How delightful."

"Lira." His voice was rough, and there were shadows under his eyes. Was his Shiven skin even whiter than she remembered, or was it just the lighting in the hallway? After saying her name, he came to a halt, and silence filled the corridor. His expressionless mask hadn't held up long.

"Still painfully shy then," she remarked. "It's good to know some things don't change."

He still said nothing, gaze dropping to the floor.

Her jaw clenched and her mouth curled into a silent snarl. Was he really just going to stand there and stare at the ground? The last time she'd seen Tarion Caverlock, she'd been leaving him behind in Alistriem after discovering the experiments Underground had done on him had turned him into a violent killer ... a physical change outside of his control.

It hadn't been long after that everything had gone so horribly wrong. And not once had Tarion or any of her other supposed friends lifted a finger to help her or speak out on her behalf. Or even come to see her, to get her side of her story. "Why are you here, Tarion?" She didn't bother to keep the anger from her voice.

He took a long breath, straightened his shoulders, and lifted his gaze to meet hers again. The shuttered reserve was back. "I don't have long." He glanced towards the closed door. "One of Caria's friends got me in, but she's not on duty much longer. If anyone else sees me here, it will be reported."

"That's a problem for you, not me." She stared at him, waiting.

After a beat, he spoke again. "I need your help."

She huffed a bitterly amused breath, astonishment quickly followed by a flash of rage. This time it broke through her control, and she spat, "Go away, Tarion."

"Lira, I'm serious. I wouldn't be here if—" He stepped forward, gripped the bars with his hands. "I'm sorry for what happened to you. I'm sorry you're in here. There was nothing we could do."

She stared at his hands. He was so close. Close enough to grab, to burn, to send flying into the opposite wall. It wouldn't get her out of this cell, but it would feel delightfully satisfying to get *some* kind of vengeance on one of those who'd betrayed her so thoroughly.

Her fingers twitched, almost of their own accord, gaze fixed on his fingers. She took a half step forward...

"Lira?"

His voice snapped her from the almost trance she'd fallen into, and when she looked up, his eyes widened dramatically at the desire to make him hurt that must have been written all over her face. He didn't move though.

After a moment, she turned her back on him and went to stand by the window. Her heart galloped in her chest. "You should go before the guards come. I'm due for my weekly bath."

"My parents are gone. Taken." His voice was low, raw.

Lira fought the urge to turn around. She'd found an equilibrium in here—a way to survive. And this was very much threatening to ruin it. His mere presence was bringing back too much of the past. "So what?"

"I want you to help me find them."

A beat of silence while Lira processed that, tried to figure out what he really wanted. Once she was confident she could control herself, she turned and leaned back against the wall by the window. "I'm in prison, in case you hadn't noticed." Anger laced her words despite her attempts at composure. "I couldn't help you darn a sock, even if I wanted to. Which I don't. You and the entire Mage Council can go to rotting hells for all I care, and your parents along with it."

Tarion wore the storm of her words without flinching, then took a breath and met her gaze. "If you agree to help me, I can get you out of here."

"You and what army?" she scoffed.

"I can get you out," he repeated.

Lira laughed, low and bitter. "You're going to let Shakar's heir out of prison and loose on the world? You *are* desperate."

"I know you're not—"

"No you don't!" She crossed the room in quick strides, pressing her face as close to his through the bars as she could despite the height difference. Every inch of her itched to *hurl* her magic at him. "You don't know who I am anymore. You left me here to rot."

"Don't tell me you don't want to get out of here." He refused to look away, hazel eyes unflinching on hers.

He was determined. Far more so than the shy boy she remembered who could barely look anyone in the eye when speaking, who couldn't handle disagreeing with anyone let alone engaging in a verbal argument. Tarion had grown some steel in the intervening years. Either that or he was so desperate he'd forgotten his reserve.

She cocked her head. "You must really be desperate, to even *consider* letting me out of this cage."

The quiet menace in her voice couldn't have escaped him, but he forged ahead anyway, the only evidence of his despair the white-knuckled grip of his hands on the bars. "We get you out, you help us find my parents, and then you're free to do whatever you want. That's the deal."

"Now it's a *we*?" She latched instantly onto the change in wording.

He said nothing.

The battle of wills lasted a moment, then she conceded. "Why do you need *my* help exactly?" She didn't want to be curious. Didn't want to feel a flicker of hope of escape. She'd fought so hard to maintain an even-keeled state of mind that would allow her to survive this place, had struggled back from despair more than once, and here he was, threatening to destroy it in a single conversation. Damn him.

Tarion's jaw clenched. "I think Underground has them."

That name rippled through Lira like a blade to her kidneys, painful and raw. Her response was instinctive, the words out before she thought them through. "They're gone."

"That's what everyone thinks."

She shifted back from the bars and crossed her arms over her chest. "I was their leader, didn't you hear? I think I'd know if they were still around."

"There's no time for this," he said sharply, shifting from foot to foot. "The next guard shift will arrive any moment. Do you agree to my deal? I can explain everything once you're out."

"It boggles my mind that you think I would trust you after what happened." She shook her head. "For all I know this is some kind of test, or trap."

"You don't know it's not." His jaw tightened. "But what are your other options? Stay here for the rest of your life?"

She studied him. He was obviously desperate. He knew her well enough to know she'd never go for this, never be willing to trust him. Which meant he was probably telling the truth and believed he had no other option but to seek her help. Her eyes narrowed. "What exactly are you offering here? You break me out of this place, I help you find your parents, and then I'm allowed to leave freely?"

"Yes."

"You don't have the authority for that. You're already lying to me."

"Once you help us find my parents, I won't try and bring you back here. I'll let you walk away. I can't control what the council will do, but *I* will do nothing, and I won't tell them where you've gone." Tarion held her gaze. "I swear it."

The Tarion she'd once known was too honourable to break his word on something this important. But that same Tarion had left her to rot in prison. And two years was a long time. Even if he did keep his word, the Mage Council would never let her go; she wasn't foolish enough to think otherwise, no matter who she rescued. But all she needed was to be out from these walls. Once that happened ... she wouldn't ever let them get close enough to her to catch her again.

Her gaze narrowed. "Who's 'us'?" Before even considering saying yes, she needed to know who else he was referring to ... who else would be another potential betrayal.

"You'll find out when we're out of this place."

"No deal."

"I won't compromise them, because I don't trust you any more than you trust me right now. For all I know you could go tattling to the guards as soon as I walk out."

"You always were a smart one." She considered him with grudging respect. "You give me your word that once we're out, you'll tell me everything. That after I help you find your parents, you'll let me walk free?"

"I swear it."

Lira wavered. It might take longer to break out on her own, but she'd only have to trust herself; there was less chance of compromise that way. As it was, she wasn't even sure she could hold herself back from tearing him to pieces if she got free.

Stalling, she asked, "Why aren't you a mage?"

He blinked at the sharp change in subject. "What?"

"You look like Lord Tarion Caverlock of Rionn, not a council warrior mage. Why?"

He frowned, like he thought she was asking a silly question. "I never became a mage."

She scoffed. "What, someone turned off your magic?"

He held out both arms, through the bars, the cuffs of his tunic riding up to reveal a narrow circlet of metal fitted snugly around each wrist. She flinched away from the sense of dissonance they gave her. "What are they?"

"Agree to my deal." He pulled his hands back through the bars and crossed his arms over his chest. "And I'll tell you."

She eyed him thoughtfully. In the end it came down to one thing ... she wanted out. Desperately enough to take the risk of trusting him to make that happen sooner. She hoped she wasn't making a terrible mistake.

A moment later, she stuck her hand through the bars. "Deal."

Relief slumped his shoulders, even though he tried to hide it. He didn't even hesitate to take her hand and shake it, which was either extremely brave or extremely foolish. She was once again tempted to yank him hard against the bars, set fire to his tunic, make him hurt.

But escape was what she wanted more than anything else in the world, and so she used her hard-won focus and patience to wrestle that urge under control. Barely. And let his hand go.

He stepped away from the bars, glanced down the hallway. "Be ready tomorrow tonight. Whatever happens, just go with it."

She arched an eyebrow. "So soon?"

"Caria can only do so much. And I made sure everything else was ready before talking to you. If we don't move quickly then we'll lose the opportunity."

She whistled. "You're cutting it fine, Tarion."

Without a word, Tarion turned and strode down the hall to the closed door. It opened at his knock, and he disappeared.

Lira wasn't sure what to feel once he'd gone. It was hard to parse out emotion beyond the blinding anger and bitterness his sudden appearance had caused, but she couldn't entirely ignore the hope building in her chest. All she needed was an opportunity to get outside these walls...

Her thoughts turned to planning what came after he got her out. The best option was to use Tarion to get out and clear of the prison, then abandon him and make her own way. She could get clear of Carhall and the pursuit and freedom would be hers. They'd never catch her again.

Except ... he thought Underground was behind his parent's disappearance.

Fury flickered inside her again.

She had a score to settle with the people who'd put her in here. Lucinda, the deadly spider who'd controlled the entire web of Underground, but also Greyson, her loyal cell leader, and the rest of the Shadowcouncil. Those who had set Lira up so perfectly for the Mage Council to lock her away. *If* Tarion was right and they'd somehow managed to kidnap a mage of the higher order and her Taliath husband, then finding Tarion's parents would mean finding Underground.

And Lira hungered for revenge. She wanted to see them burn by her own hand.

Once that was done, Lucinda and all remnants of her group utterly destroyed, then she'd think about what to do with the Mage Council ... those that had taken Underground's word over hers and locked her away for the rest of her life for something she hadn't done.

Lira began pacing. Her gaze fell on the desk, where a neat pile of notes she'd been making for herself sat. There'd be no sleep tonight.

She had too much planning to do.

CHAPTER 3

It started with a brawl.

Lira lingered longer at her window the evening after Tarion's visit, past her dinner arriving. Ready. While her gaze roved Centre Square below, every one of her other senses was attuned to the corridor outside her cell.

As dusk bathed the city in an orange glow, Lira's gaze caught on a group of off-duty Bluecoats—some of them still wearing their distinctive coats, unbuttoned—crossing Centre Square in the company of a roughly equal number of Tregayan militia. As they neared the building housing the prison, their casual, good-natured body language turned stiff, unfriendly, their laughter disappearing.

As suddenly as a match striking, one of the militia threw a punch. Two Bluecoats responded with angry shouts, and before long there were upwards of twenty soldiers fighting outside the prison. Even from several floors up, the shouting and cursing was loud enough that Lira could hear it.

The brawl quickly drew the attention of not only the guards posted at the front of the prison building, but also those guarding the nearest gates into Centre Square. The melee grew substantially bigger as neither Bluecoats nor militia responded to the guards' attempts to quell their brawl, instead only drawing them into the fighting.

It was all fists and foreheads and boots, though. No weapons. If nothing else, this fact convinced Lira that the brawl was Tarion's diversion.

She turned from the window, gave her cell a final scan to make sure there wasn't anything she should take with her, or anything she didn't want the guards stumbling over once she was gone. The collection of notes she'd made for herself over time she'd burned earlier that afternoon. There was nothing left behind to betray the project she'd been working on for the past two years but a neat pile of ash sitting in the centre of the desktop.

Confident there was nothing to give her intentions away, she took a deep breath, summoned enough magic to be ready to use at an instant, then waited. The patience she'd painstakingly forced herself to learn now helped quell the furious fluttering of anticipatory nerves in the pit of her stomach.

Within minutes, the door at the end of her corridor opened—far more quietly than usual—and soft footfalls headed towards her cell. Tarion came into view, key in hand. He wore plain, dark clothing and a mask covering his face.

"A brawl is rather elaborate. Why didn't you just use your magic to transport us both out of here?" she asked.

"The foundations of the exterior walls of the building are lined with melted-down Hunter medallions. It's not enough to affect magic use inside the building, but enough to stop it passing through the walls—I believe the idea was to prevent any mage with telepathic magic being able to communicate in or out of the prison, but it also stops me."

It was a logical answer, but Tarion's eyes flickered to his wrists as he spoke, telling her it wasn't the full truth. Whatever. As long as he got her out of this cell she wasn't going to quibble about the method. "It wouldn't stop a mage with flying ability either," she noted.

"Fortunately no mage alive apart from my mother has that ability."

That you know of. Lira glanced down the hall—the door stood open, nobody visible beyond it—then back at him. "All we need to do then is get *outside* the exterior walls of this building, and you can teleport us away?"

Tarion finished with the lock and swung the door open. "Yes. I can only go a short distance while carrying someone, but it should be enough to get us outside the walls of Centre Square, and then we run."

Lira stepped out into the hall, searching for threats, finding none. A smile curled at her mouth, the first stirrings of freedom rising through her, waking the thrill that had always lived in the pit of her stomach but had been dormant too long. It drowned whatever remaining doubts she had about relying on Tarion to escape. "What do you plan to do about the guards between here and the exit?"

"The brawl outside will draw in most of those on the ground floor. Caria will keep the route we need to take clear as long as she can. I estimate we have a half hour, no more, and probably less."

Not bad. "Well planned, Tarion. The mask is a nice touch too. If this all goes to hell, I get all the blame, and they'll never know who you are."

He didn't appear to hear her; his eyes were dark with worry as he closed and re-locked the cell. "We should hurry. If even one thing goes wrong, we'll be in trouble."

She gestured. "In that case, lead on."

Tarion headed down the hallway with long, quick strides. Lira followed but hesitated at the half-open door. He'd said they had half an hour ... it wouldn't take that long to get down to an exit. "Wait."

"What?" His voice was tight with impatience.

"Is Greyson being held here?"

Puzzlement flicked in his eyes. "Underground's Karonan cell leader?"

"Yes, him."

"He's here. Why do—"

Anticipation leapt in Lira. "Take me to him."

Frustrated exasperation filled his voice. "We don't have time for that. If we don't go now, we won't make it out."

She didn't budge. "Either you make time, or I go and look for him on my own and you can leave. Your choice."

"I thought you wanted to escape!"

"I do, *after* I talk to Greyson." She was confident that with the brawl outside, in addition to Caria's intervention, even if they were seen trying to escape that she could handle whatever guards remained. Especially with Tarion's help.

His tone became uncharacteristically snappish, "What, do you want to help him escape too? Make some sort of plan with him before you leave?"

"What I want with Greyson is my business," she said calmly. "As I said, either take me to him, or leave me and make your own way. Standing here arguing is only wasting precious time."

She was banking on the fact that he couldn't cut and run now, not after going to so much effort to get her out. Not when he was so desperate to find his parents. So she was unsurprised when he gave in with a curt, "He's on the ground level with other non-mage prisoners."

She walked through the door. "Well we have to go down anyway, right? Let's move, mage-prince."

Greyson's cell sat in a row of identical cells, in the eastern wing of the ground floor. Similar to the one on Lira's level, the entrance to the long hall was guarded by a steel door and a table where guards normally sat. Tonight the chairs around the table were empty—their occupants presumably drawn by the ruckus outside the front entrance barely metres away. Judging from the cursing and shouting coming down the hall, the brawl was still going strong. Good.

Tarion's key opened this door too, and he hurried her inside, casting anxious glances back toward the empty guard desk. "Third cell on the right. Hurry!"

She gave him a suspicious glance. "How do you know exactly where he is?"

"That's my business," he said shortly.

She shrugged, putting the question aside to follow up on later. They didn't have long before her escape would be in jeopardy. She'd have to get this done quickly.

Greyson was seated at the desk in his cell, reading by lamplight. It was almost double the size of hers, with a wider bed, comfortable armchair, and carpeted floor. They'd approached quietly, and it was dark in the corridor, so he was unaware of their presence. At the sight of him, looking so comfortable, anger lit up inside Lira. She savoured it, let it slide through her and spark her magic.

Tarion's next words answered her unasked question. "Due to his cooperation with the Mage Council, he was given a comfortable cell and more privileges than most prisoners."

Cooperation. Her lip curled. The only thing he'd cooperated with were the Shadowcouncil's orders to frame Lira and have her imprisoned for the rest of her life. The anger surged inside her.

"So he's in for the rest of his life too?" she murmured, gaze not moving from the older man.

A quick shake of his head. "Just ten years. Lira, Caria won't be able to keep our route clear much longer. We could already be compromised."

Ten years. While she'd been given life. The fury burned hotter as Lira stepped up to the bars of the cell. Greyson spotted the movement in the corner of his eye and turned, shock flaring over his face when he saw who it was. Unease followed quickly on its heels. "Lira?"

"Greyson," she said. "Nice cell you've got here. Maybe it's just me, but I would have asked for a hell of a lot more in return for selling out Shakar's heir."

He rose from his chair, slowly, every movement careful, wary. "I don't know what they told you but—"

"Save it." She cut him off. "I know what you did and I don't have the time or interest to debate it with you. I'd just like to know one thing. Why?"

"I followed the Shadowcouncil's orders. Surely you've guessed that already? Everything we did was on their orders," he said. "Absolute loyalty, Lira. It was that or failure for our cause."

"You didn't think your cause had failed when every one of your members was arrested and thrown into prison? It seems pretty dead to me."

"Loyalty to the end," he said, conviction in his face and voice. "It's the only way. There were bigger plans at work, I know it. We will see victory one day."

Lira frowned, something about his words ringing oddly. "Always the loyal soldier," she murmured. "You didn't even know what those 'bigger plans' were when you agreed to sacrifice yourself, did you?"

"What's happening?" He moved closer to the bars, eyes narrowing when he spotted Tarion hovering further back in the shadows. "Are you escaping?"

"I am."

Hope bloomed on his face. "And you've come to bring me with you? They're still out there, aren't they? It's not really over. It was just a feint? Some kind of—"

"Lira, I don't care what you say, I'm not letting this man out," Tarion snapped. "And if we don't go right now, we're not getting out either."

"No, Greyson." Lira ignored Tarion, her gaze locked on the Karonan cell leader. She might have hesitated, stayed her hand ... if he'd known anything useful to tell her. But it was clear he knew nothing, that he'd been a willing pawn in Underground's larger game. "There is no hope, and it *is* all over. I'm just here to kill you before I leave."

He blanched, eyes darkening with shock and fear. "What do you mean. You can't..." His words died away as he registered the look on her face. Understood how serious she was.

"You sold out the heir to the Darkmage and expected no consequences? More fool you." Lira lifted her right hand slowly, smiled at the fear on his face, then clicked her fingers. White-hot flame edged in violet surrounded Greyson in a rush.

He started screaming a second later. The scent of burning flesh filled the air.

Lira waited, not looking away once, until he burned to a pile of ash—it didn't take long—then she turned back to Tarion, who was staring at her, his horror obvious despite the mask, one hand over his mouth and nose. The other prisoners in the row had heard the screams and were crowding to the front of their cells, yelling and demanding to know what was happening.

The guards would hear it sooner rather than later. They'd best hurry.

Lira looked at Tarion. "We can go now."

CHAPTER 4

"What did you..." Tarion was looking at her as if he didn't recognise her, which gave her a jolt of smug satisfaction. Good. The sooner he stopped thinking he knew her, the better.

"You can spend time being horrified later. Right now we move, or you can take up residence in the cell next to mine upstairs." When that didn't seem to do the trick, she prompted coldly, "Your parents?"

Even then he wavered. She considered taking him out, going it alone ... but then he gave a shaky nod. Without saying anything, he turned on his heel and strode off, shoulders tense, hands curled into fists. They were halfway across the guards' room outside Greyson's cell block, heading for the left-most door, when running feet and crisp shouting sounded behind them.

Heading their way.

Someone had heard either Greyson's screams or the ruckus of his fellow prisoners. Tarion yanked the door open and dived through it, Lira slipping through the gap behind him just as the other entrance to the room opened. Sprinting, they both skidded around the first turn they came to.

Once they were around the corner, they paused, backs to the wall, catching their breath. Lira looked at Tarion. "Which way now, mage-prince?"

He hesitated again, his gaze flickering to her and then quickly away, over and over.

"Bit late now for doubts. I'm halfway out, Tarion. Either finish the job properly or you've got nobody to help find your parents."

He shook himself, resolve returning to his features. "This was the way Caria—"

The sound of a door opening cut off his response, the sound of several pairs of feet heading their way following immediately after. Tarion took off at another run and Lira didn't hesitate to follow. The route his sister had cleared for them—a tangle of narrow back hallways—remained clear.

Pursuit still sounded behind them, but far enough back to suggest their pursuers didn't know where Lira was, if they'd even figured out she was the one who'd gotten free. They both winced when a strident alarm pealed through the building.

"They've either found Greyson's remains or noticed you're not in your cell." Tarion was tense. "We've got seconds before they lock down every exit in this place."

"How far is the exit we're heading for?"

"Run faster."

Lira gritted her teeth and did her best. Her lungs burned from the unaccustomed exertion, though the rest of her was holding up well thanks to years of daily exercises.

Two guards were already converging on the side door that appeared to be Tarion's goal as they came flying around a sharp turn. There was no time to stop or backtrack before the guards saw them. Two men, both armed, neither Taliath.

Lira didn't hesitate. Her telekinetic magic swept out like a lasso, wrapping around both men and sending them flying backwards. Magic flared hot and alive in her blood, let fully loose for the first time in too long. The men hit the ground hard. One's head cracked against the tile, and he stayed down. By the time the second one was able to scramble back to his feet, drawing a sword, she and Tarion had reached the door.

He pushed it open, and the moment she followed him through—into what looked like a small delivery courtyard—she slammed it closed behind her so the guard couldn't see what happened next. Then, Tarion wrapped an arm around her waist and summoned his magic.

Her vision blurred; nausea rose in her stomach. When her vision cleared, she found herself standing in a dark and empty street, the walls of Centre Square visible a few blocks away. She stumbled, still off balance and fighting back the magic that was surging in her blood, wanting to explode everywhere.

Tarion stepped away from her with amusing speed. After a second, he tore the mask from his face, tossed it aside, then crossed to where a small cloth-wrapped bundle sat nestled under a section of broken drainpipe. His shoulders relaxed visibly as he unrolled it to reveal two narrow metal bracelets that he instantly snapped around each of his wrists.

"What *are* those?" she asked.

He ignored her, dragging out a duffel that had been hidden inside the drainpipe, and quickly unbuckling it. A moment later he threw a mound of cloth her way. She caught it, finding it was a long cloak made of fine velvet. He was already pulling a tunic out of the bag and dragging it on over his dark shirt. It had gold-embossed buttons and fine lace stitched into its cuffs and hem. Apart from his sweaty skin, he now looked more young lord than night thief.

She put the cloak on. Being seen wandering around the city in prison clothing would be a dead giveaway, but it made her already heated body far too warm, and she grimaced in distaste as the heavy cloth settled over her shoulders.

"What in all magical hells was that?" He rounded on her, fists clenched. She didn't need to be able to see his face properly in the dim light to know it was drawn in anger.

"We escaped."

"You murdered a man in cold blood."

"I did."

He stared at her, thrown. "And you have nothing to say about that?"

"What exactly would you like me to say?" she enquired.

"Maybe a good reason as to why you did it?"

"You just want to make yourself feel better about breaking me out of prison. It was all well and good when you were helping your parents, but now I've just made things complicated. Now I might be a danger to others. And if I hurt someone out here, that's on you, right?" She crossed her arms. "I have no interest in salving your conscience, Tarion."

Before he could say anything, the sound of voices calling out drifted on the night breeze. Light flared from the direction of the Centre Square gates. Multiple pinpoints of light indicating searchers with torches.

Tarion swore under his breath. He was clearly uncertain. Lira was about to turn and flee on her own—his delay was increasing the odds of them getting caught—when he let out a long breath and straightened his shoulders. "Follow me," he said tersely, and set off at a quick walk.

"Why are we walking? Can't you just keep jumping us farther and farther away?"

He said nothing, only kept walking. She would have preferred to pause a moment, get a feel of the night air, an indication of any pursuit nearby before rushing anywhere, but something told her he wouldn't listen if she told him to stop. Swallowing an irritated sigh, she went after him.

They moved quickly through the streets leading away from Centre Square. The air was warm, the stench of a nearby gutter awful, but she breathed it in deeply anyway, savouring it like the smoke of a cinnamon cigar.

She was free.

Her heartbeat quickened in her chest, magic leaping inside her veins. She fought the urge to abandon Tarion now, to turn and simply vanish into one of the alleyways, never to be seen again. But that wasn't the smart move—she was still too close to the council buildings, and she didn't know Carhall like she'd known Dirinan. On her own, and without resources, she'd be unlikely to make it far out of the city with the inevitable pursuit that would come.

Not to mention Tarion could be her way to Underground. It was worth hanging around to see if that was the case. If it turned out he wasn't, she'd abandon him then.

They jogged for over an hour through quiet streets, slowing to a swift walk when they reached more crowded areas. Lira cursed the years spent inside a cell that meant her stamina for running was woefully absent. Still, she pushed through her burning lungs and wobbly legs.

Tarion at least seemed to have a good sense of where he was going, pausing only once or twice to check the direction they were heading in before continuing.

It soon became clear that rather than heading in any particular direction, he was moving in a circular, zig-zagging route, presumably ensuring they weren't being followed or otherwise noticed before going to their real destination.

Neither of them spoke. He shot her the occasional worried look. She ignored him. She didn't care what Tarion thought of her actions, how guilty he felt about breaking her out. It made no difference to anything.

She was just glad Greyson was dead.

Lucinda and whatever remained of Underground would be next. And that felt good.

While they wound farther and farther away from Centre Square and the jail, Lira thought over the escape carefully to make sure she hadn't missed anything that would see her caught. Tarion's magic was a significant advantage. It meant the pursuit wouldn't have any idea which way she'd gone, even once they spoke to the guards she'd attacked and learned she'd escaped via the delivery courtyard. The authorities would have to search methodically, street by street, for her. The city gates would be closed soon, though. She hoped Tarion and his 'friends' had a plan for that.

Eventually, Tarion's pace slowed, and he became noticeably more watchful. Lira followed suit, all her old instincts clicking into place. She scanned their surroundings to ensure nobody was paying them undue attention. If he was leading her to some sort of safehouse or rendezvous point, she didn't want anyone reporting their presence to the inevitable searchers when they arrived.

They'd circled through what appeared to be the poorer area of the city, before doubling back to the area south of Centre Square where the streets had become cleaner, the houses bigger and nicer. Now, after lingering on an empty corner for several seconds, Tarion led them out of the narrow street they were in and into a busy thoroughfare.

Buildings on either side loomed high enough to cut out any moonlight from above, but the street was well lit by regularly placed streetlamps.

The doors set into stone walls—everything in Carhall seemed to have been constructed from stone, unlike Karonan or Dirinan—were ornate, polished, expensive. Lira followed Tarion to a building at the end of the street that sat on the corner of a crossroads, where he took the steps at the front without pause and strode through the open front doors.

It was an inn. An expensive one. Inside, the entry foyer contained chairs huddled around small tables, with a polished bar running along the wall to the right. The servants were neatly attired and unobtrusive. Tarion passed all of it, heading straight for the sweeping staircase directly opposite the doors. Lira followed, keeping her cloak pulled close around her and doing her best not to look like a street rat. In a place like this, that would draw attention fast. People would remember, too.

They went up one flight of stairs—her shoulders relaxing once they were out of sight of those in the entry foyer—then down a thickly carpeted hallway to the double doors at the end of it. Tarion stopped at the door, knocked three times, paused, then knocked twice more.

A long pause followed, Lira shifting from foot to foot in impatience, before a soft voice called for them to enter. Tarion pushed his way in, and after only a moment's hesitation, Lira followed. He quickly closed the door behind them.

The room inside was palatial. Plush carpeting, velvet drapes, a stone hearth, and several comfortable armchairs. A door on the left side of the room led into what appeared to be an equally large bedroom.

All of this Lira cased in a single sweeping glance, before she settled her attention on the well-dressed young man in the opposite side of the room. At their entrance, he turned from where he'd clearly been looking out the window.

It was Garan Egalion.

CHAPTER 5

Garan's face was as grim as his father's had ever looked. Like Tarion, he wore rich nobleman's attire rather than the blue cloak of a mage who'd passed his Trials.

All at once, the identity of Tarion's 'friends' became clear. Lira's stomach sank. She really should have guessed. Wished it had turned out to be anyone else. Strangers that she didn't know, people who didn't touch a painful nerve of bitterness and anger that tainted the delight of being free of that rotted prison.

Outside, in the streets, her anger at Tarion had been a manageable thing. But now, inside a too-small room and faced with another betrayer, it rose again. "Garan Egalion. What a surprise," she said, fighting to keep her voice even.

He ignored her. "What happened, Tar? You took far longer than you were supposed to."

"We had a little trouble on the way out," Tarion mumbled. "They know she's escaped."

Garan's face tightened. "I thought the plan was to get her out without anyone noticing so the search wouldn't start until morning, *after* we'd left," he said flatly.

"It *was* the plan, until Lira decided to murder Greyson in his cell on the way out. The screams of him burning alive drew some attention." An edge of ire made Tarion's voice more audible this time.

The same expression of horror Tarion had been wearing since leaving the prison filled Garan's as he finally turned to look at her. She stayed light on her feet, prepared to bolt out the door in a heartbeat if things went badly. She'd already noted that Tarion hadn't locked it behind them.

It didn't bode well that they apparently didn't seem to have a plan beyond getting her to this inn. The trapped sensation deepened, and she tried to calm her breathing but had little success. Sweat beaded on her forehead. Escape was supposed to feel good, liberating, not like this ... like not having enough air.

"Did anyone see you?" Garan snapped at Tarion.

Tarion shrugged. "I don't think so."

"You don't *think* so? Tarion, if you were seen, we're done. Instead of finding your parents, we'll be locked up alongside Lira."

"They didn't see him," Lira finally spoke, frustrated with Tarion's lack of assertiveness. "He was masked, and he teleported us from a small side courtyard when nobody was watching. But they might wonder how we got over the wall of the courtyard so quickly. It was high and didn't look particularly easy to climb."

"So they won't know it's you straight away, but you'll probably come under suspicion soon, especially when they find out we're both in the city. Not to mention once they put all that together with the fact that Caria is currently posted to Carhall." Garan let out a long breath, worry written all over him as he stared at his cousin. "We can't leave tonight as planned, now. The city gates will be locked down."

"And Caria will be drawn into the search," Tarion said quietly. "She can't afford to draw suspicion to herself by refusing, or suddenly disappearing. We'll be lucky if the search doesn't reach the inn by midday. We need to be gone by then."

"Even if they open the gates in the morning, they'll thoroughly search everyone leaving. Hiding Lira in our carriage won't work anymore." Garan ran a hand through his hair, looking genuinely frightened. "Tar, we're in a bad spot."

"I know," Tarion mumbled, staring at the floor.

A thick silence filled the room.

Disgusted, Lira shook her head. "The two of you seriously thought breaking me out, hiding me in a carriage, and then just idly trundling out of the city was going to work? Not only that, you didn't even plan for something going wrong?"

"It would have been a solid plan if you hadn't murdered a man on your way out," Garan snarled.

"You promised to help me escape," she said evenly. "So you'd best do that or else I might get ideas about burning you too."

Garan paled, almost took a step back. The uncertainty in his expression told her he wasn't sure if she was serious.

"Even if we get out of the city, we need a plan for where to go. We can't keep fleeing blindly," Tarion said quietly, ignoring Lira's comment.

"Isn't that why *she's* here?" Garan was studiously *not* looking in Lira's direction, instead lifting his eyebrows at Tarion.

"You want *me* to come up with a plan?" Lira drawled, hiding her unease. "That's a shame. I assumed you'd gotten me out so I could devour some small children. And I was so looking forward to it, too."

"Oh, you're going to play the victim card?" Garan finally looked at her, indignance written all over his face. "You? After betraying all of us and proving to be a traitor to the council."

"Garan, that's not—" Tarion began.

"Isn't it?" Garan met his stony look with one of his own. "You're going to tell me that with a straight face after she just murdered a man in cold blood by burning him alive in his cell?"

Their exchange had all the weariness of a battle that had taken place over and over again. She huffed a bitter laugh, equal parts annoyed and darkly amused. "I don't know what they've told you about me, but I don't have telepathic *or* psychic powers. If you want me to come up with a 'plan', you'll need to tell me what it's for. And don't say 'rescue Tarion's parents' without giving over any more information."

Garan spoke when Tarion stayed quiet. "Uncle Dash and Aunt Alyx were taken from Alistriem three weeks ago during an official visit to King Cayr—Uncle Dash was there to participate in some trade negotiations along with a delegation sent by Leader Astohar. There's no trace of what happened to them."

Interesting. She'd been mulling on this since Tarion had told her about it, and now obtaining more pieces of the puzzle was a nice distraction from her wariness, her constant urge to run from the room. "They were staying in a room in the Alistriem palace?"

"Yes."

Even more curious. That palace housed the king of Rionn and his family—it was the most protected building in Rionn. Not to mention the king's wife was a Taliath too. Lira tried to ignore the hope creeping through her, that this already sounded very much like Underground. "Caverlock is Astohar's military general. What was he doing participating in trade negotiations?" she asked.

"King Cayr is offering a subsidy for Bluecoat training of the Shiven army, *if* Leader Astohar agrees to some of his terms on import tariffs," Garan said. "And before you ask, Aunt Alyx travelled with him in a personal capacity. She spent most of her time with my parents and Tarion and me, actually. We hadn't seen each other in a while."

Lira nodded. "Next question. How do you know they're still alive?"

Tarion flinched. Garan only looked more thunderous, but answered, "No bodies have been recovered, and a thorough search is ongoing. But just like when we were taken, nobody knows where to even start looking."

"And you want *me* to find them where everybody else seems to have failed?"

"Tarion wants your help to find them, yes," Garan said. Now that he was with his cousin, Tarion seemed content to fade into the background and look troubled while Garan spoke for him. She rolled her eyes in Tarion's direction. He didn't notice.

"What is it exactly you think I can do?" It was a genuine question. She still didn't see how she was so important to this that they'd risked their lives and futures on breaking Lira Astor out of prison. She was missing something. She didn't like it.

"The Mage Council, in addition to King Cayr and King Mastaran of Tregaya, have instituted a massive search and are devoting an army of resources to finding them," Garan explained. "There's nothing we can add to what they're doing, but Tarion thinks Underground took them, and I think he might be right—the method of kidnap is strikingly similar to what happened to us. You know more about Underground than anyone. We want to search from that angle."

She let out a breath. "Fine. If you want my advice, you'll need to give me a moment to think on what you've just told me. In the meantime, you still need to figure out how you're getting us out of this city."

"I have an idea," Tarion said. Lira abruptly realised he hadn't been letting Garan speak for him; he'd been quietly figuring out what to do about their predicament. "Someone who might be able to help."

Garan's eyebrows shot skywards. "You want to draw someone *else* into this mess? Tar, you've already exposed Caria—the moment they figure out your involvement, they'll—"

Lira cut over him, "I didn't sign on for bringing strangers into this."

Tarion lifted a hand, as if to hold them both at bay. "Caria can't help us any further. She's smart, Garan, and can look after herself. But the two of us can't get Lira out of the city by ourselves now the alarm has been raised. So we need help. It's either that or we give up now."

Garan hesitated. "Lira has a point. Given what we've done, trusting a stranger to help could get us caught just as easily as trying to get out of the city on our own."

"This isn't a stranger." Tarion was already turning for the door. "And we can trust them. I'll be back soon."

"I'm starting to regret ever agreeing to this," Lira muttered as the door closed behind him.

"Then leave," Garan said flatly, turning away from her and dropping into the chair by the fire. "Tarion's the only one who wants you here."

She almost did. Sitting idly in this room while the net closed around her wasn't appealing in the slightest. Being in a confined space with a man who'd pretended friendship before betraying her was even less appealing.

But he and Tarion had resources. And influence. Lira wasn't getting through those gates on her own, and she didn't know the streets of Carhall well enough to evade the search for any length of time. Fighting her way out would draw far too much attention.

For now she'd stay. And be ready to flee at an instant if things turned the wrong way.

The weight in her chest grew heavy again.

This didn't feel like freedom at all.

CHAPTER 6

Roughly an hour passed, maybe a little more. Lira stood at the window the entire time, watchful gaze studying the street, looking for any indication of danger. As the night deepened into the early hours, the traffic below slowed, came to an almost halt.

Garan didn't speak a word the entire time, and neither did she. The tension in the room was palpable.

When the door clicked open, Lira was spinning before the sound had even registered, hand reaching for the knife she'd once always worn and clutching at air instead. But it was just Tarion.

Another young man followed him in. He wore the blue cloak of a council mage but had pushed it back off his shoulders in the warmth of the night.

Lorin Hester

Lira whistled. "How exciting. A reunion of the combat patrol that never was. Did you happen to dig up Fari while you were out too?"

None of them laughed. Or smiled. Lira's hands clenched and unclenched, the familiar tightness descending over her chest. Her body was poised to flee in an instant if necessary.

There were too many people in the room, now; she could trust none of them. And the way Garan was looking at Lorin and Tarion, the doubt about this venture written all over his face ... it was hard to ignore the feeling of being trapped, to quell the urge to fight her way out and run.

"Lorin?" Garan rose from the chair. "I didn't know you were in Carhall."

"Garan. I imagine you didn't. We haven't exactly stayed in touch since you graduated Temari." Lorin gave him a quick nod, then his gaze settled on Lira. His mouth quirked in an almost smile. "You've gotten yourselves into quite the mess."

"Stop looking so suspicious, Lira." Tarion spoke. "I explained everything to Lorin. I asked for his help, and he agreed. He's here with me rather than reporting us to the council."

"And how do we know he didn't do that so he could learn more about what you're up to and *then* report us to the council?" Lira enquired.

"You understand what you risked, telling him?" Garan's jaw was set, entire focus on his cousin.

"You agreed to help me find my parents, Garan," Tarion said quietly but firmly. "This is the only way. Lorin is a friend."

"He *was* your friend. Years ago," Lira pointed out.

Lorin spoke into the silence that followed, haughty expression firmly in place. "I gave Tarion my word that I would not betray him to the council."

Garan lifted a hand to rub his eyes, as if exhausted, then seemed to concede. "In that case, you have my gratitude, Lorin. How can you help us?"

Lorin threw Lira a quick, opaque glance before turning his attention to Garan. He'd been a gangly first-year initiate the last time she'd seen him. Now, he'd be eighteen years old, full grown. He towered over all of them, Shiven features set in a haughty glower, bare arms ropey with muscle. "The city gates are locked down. Search parties are moving through the streets north and east of Centre Square. They'll increase the number of searchers as soon as dawn arrives. I estimate they'll be here by mid-morning."

Garan let out a breath. "It's as bad as we thought then."

At a look from Tarion, Lorin nodded. "I can clear your way through the gates early tomorrow. Not too early that it looks odd, but before the searchers reach this area of the city. But before I do that, I'd like to know what comes next. Where do we go after leaving Carhall?"

"*We?*" Garan asked.

"Once I help you, I can't go back to the council. How long do you think it will take for them to put together reports of me helping Garan Egalion and Tarion Caverlock leave the city with Lira's escape?"

"Then we'll figure out another way," Tarion said immediately. "I don't want to compromise you too."

"It's a bit late for that," Garan said darkly.

"He's right," Lorin said. "I've given my word to help, so let's get on with it."

All eyes shifted to Lira.

She shrugged. "I have questions first. Why haven't you told the Mage Council your theory about Underground, get their army of resources to look in Underground's direction?"

"We tried that," Tarion said.

Garan's mouth tightened in disapproval. "The Magor-lier laughed in our faces."

"Oh, I'm sure he did." A wide smile crossed Lira's face. Now she *was* amused. "Well, at least that tells you Tarion is probably right."

"Explain," Garan snapped.

Lira bridled. "How about you go jump in a rotting pile of fish carcasses."

"Lira, please." Tarion stepped in. "You gave your word you would help us."

"I agreed to help you find your parents, not to take orders like a good little soldier," she retorted. *And only as long as it serves my purposes.* "What is it you think I know about Underground that will help you, even if you are right about them taking your parents?"

"Do we really need to spell it out? You worked with them for years," Garan said, jaw clenching.

Lira stilled. "If you're suggesting that you believe the Mage Council's account of my actions, then you're fools for breaking me out."

"Trust me, I'm fully aware of that," Garan said through gritted teeth. Even Tarion's expression had flooded with guilt. Tarion must have really worked hard to convince his cousin to help. It didn't necessarily surprise her—she'd seen firsthand how much he loved his parents.

But why had Lorin agreed to assist with this poorly-thought-out plan? He was risking his entire life by doing it. She glanced at the door. Swallowed. Tried to loosen her rigid muscles.

Lorin broke the silence again. "If the Mage Council's account is inaccurate, perhaps you could enlighten us as to the real story?"

"If you wanted to hear my side of things, you should have come to talk to me years ago. I don't owe you a thing." She turned for the door but checked the urge to leave and slam it in their faces. They had no proof Underground had done anything, but hearing their account of what had happened to Egalion and Caverlock had Lira's instincts stirring.

"Then don't explain, but you agreed to help," Tarion said in that quiet way of his. "I know your word is good, Lira."

It wasn't. If this wasn't a lead to Underground, she'd be gone before they even noticed. But they didn't have to know that. Lira took a steadying breath, tried to relax her shoulders. If she was going to stay, she needed to work with them, not fight them on everything. "Fine. Here's a bit of information you *don't* know. Your precious Magor-lier was working with Underground. It was after I found that out that I was thrown in prison. If he laughed you out of his presence, it probably means there's something to your theory."

They all stared at her, varying looks of disbelief on their faces. She shrugged. They could believe her or not. She had no intention of begging or trying to make them understand. The time for that was gone. Already she felt disgusted with herself when she remembered back to that night—how she'd begged Tarrick and Dawn to believe her, how she'd almost broken down before Dawn after Tarrick had left.

Never again.

Garan gave Tarion a look, like *you really think this level of crazy is helpful?* but then took a breath, one hand rising to rub his forehead as if he were doing his best not to argue.

Lorin asked, "Underground were wiped out by the council at the time you were arrested, Lira. How could the group have pulled off something like this?"

"Because they never really went away." Tarion's voice was once again firm. He seemed able to challenge the others when it came to finding his parents. "Who else on this continent has a demonstrated ability to capture mages and Taliath without leaving a trace? What if they've spent these last two years rebuilding? Or even worse, their destruction was only a sham, designed to lull us into a false sense of security."

"That's my bet," Lira offered, a little shiver going through her. She'd had years to think about this, to research, to try and figure out the many questions she still had about the group. "They organised to have me locked away for life and made a show of being destroyed by sacrificing all their unimportant pieces. Let me guess, nobody ever caught Lucinda, or any of the other Shadowcouncil members? Anyone with actual mage ability?"

Their uncomfortable silence was her answer.

Garan's gaze met Lira's, challenging. "They never caught the Darkhand, either."

"My point exactly." Lira smiled, cold and triumphant. For a brief moment everything in her loosened and she felt relaxed, buoyant. Ahrin was free.

But then the reality of that sank in, and with it came a gut-wrenching despair. The Mage Council had imprisoned Shakar's heir; there was no way word of that hadn't spread far and wide. Ahrin had to know by now what had happened to Lira. If she hadn't been caught too, that meant...

The smile faded; her breath hitched. Ahrin had left her in prison to rot.

For a moment, Lira was close to falling into that gaping emptiness inside her, but she fought bitterly with herself until she was able to lock that feeling away again. None but Tarion seemed to notice, and he said nothing, his gaze leaving her face as if to give her privacy.

"Their name is gone," Lorin said grimly. "Nobody uses it anymore. But the unrest they incited continues. It died down for almost a year after the arrests before the strikes started again. They've spread from Shivasa to Tregaya, and there are indications it's beginning in Rionn. Dealing with it is taking up increasing amounts of the council's time."

More silence. Lira said nothing. Eventually Garan broke it, his gaze settling on Lira. "Back to the reason we're here. You know more about Underground than anyone. Where should we start looking?"

Lira considered him for a long moment. It was becoming clear they truly did believe she knew something that would help them, but it was a desperate gamble that hadn't been well thought through. Worse, it didn't seem like they knew anything more about Underground's current activities that might help her.

But they weren't entirely wrong. Lira had done a lot of reading in jail. She'd been researching a number of topics—though she'd been careful to vary her requests for books and parchment so that nobody would figure out what she was doing—and had the beginnings of a theory ... or at least a place to look that might lead to real answers about Lucinda and the Shadowcouncil.

It was tenuous, but it was somewhere to start. The question now was whether to cut Tarion and the others loose to go her own way or use them to get her where she needed to go.

"Lira?" Lorin pushed.

Lira made a quick decision—for now it seemed smarter to use their help. Survival and staying free had to be her priority. Lucinda wasn't going to be an easy quarry to hunt down, and Garan and Tarion had resources she didn't. The moment they became a liability she could cut them loose.

She looked at Garan. "Is Finn A'ndreas still a master at Temari Hall?"

"Yes, but why—"

"And is Councillor Duneskal still posted to Karonan?"

"Yes, he is, but—" Garan tried again.

"Then we need to go to Karonan."

"Why?" Tarion asked.

"I'll tell you when we get there." She wasn't going to trust them with any more information than she had to. Also, if she were honest, her theory was flimsy. Perhaps even a product of desperate boredom—something to fight the despair while she'd been locked up. Now she was out, it was already feeling less solid than it had.

Still ... even if her theory was no more than a product of her imagination, there was something else in Karonan. An address that had been locked in her memory, niggling at her, for the past two years.

Tarion stepped closer, his gaze searching hers. "Are you sure about this?"

She looked away. She'd once been won over by his sincerity, the way he wore his heart on his sleeve, how deeply he cared for his family. Not anymore. Tarion was nothing more than a means to an end. She wouldn't allow herself to care again.

Lira shrugged. "Not in the slightest. But I have no other leads to offer you. It's this or we camp out here in your fancy room until someone has a better idea."

Garan looked at her for a long moment, then slowly nodded, pushing off the wall. "If you betray us, Lira, we—"

"Oh please." She snorted. "If you're going to threaten me, then do it properly. I could handle all of you without breaking a sweat and you know it."

"We're fully trained warrior mages now," Lorin said proudly.

Garan's gaze flicked to Tarion at his words, then just as quickly flicked away. So Tarion hadn't passed his Trials. Interesting.

"You and Garan are council-trained mages," she said coldly. "While I'm the heir to the Darkmage. I could burn you all where you stand before you moved an inch toward me. I've done it before and I'm more than willing to do it again. Tarion's seen that firsthand. Are you willing to kill so ruthlessly?" She let the words fill the silence, waited until their gazes dropped. "I didn't think so."

After a long pause, Lorin spoke. "We were friends once, Lira."

"Maybe. Then I got locked up in prison for two years for no other reason than who my grandfather was," Lira said. "I was facing spending the rest of my life in that place. Friendship never got me anywhere but betrayal—"

"You dare talk about betrayal!" Garan rounded on her, green eyes snapping in fury. "You left us on that roof in Aranan and walked off hand in hand with your lover. You put our lives in danger by being with us that night and then you abandoned us to our fate. That's not friendship."

"I was spying for your precious council," Lira hissed, violet light flaring around her hands as her magic slipped the bounds of her control.

He blanched, stepping back half a pace. She could practically see him mentally denying her words.

Lorin intervened. "We need to make everything look normal to anyone paying attention to us tonight. All of us being gathered in here so late will look odd. We don't want to help the council make the connection between us and Lira's escape any sooner than is necessary."

Lira snorted, looked at Tarion. "Getting his help was the first halfway smart thing you've done since you came up with your ridiculous plan."

Tarion ignored her. "You can still leave now, Lorin. I won't ask you to—"

"I'm not here for you or Garan, much as I respect what we once all went through together," he said simply. "I'm only standing here now, a warrior mage, because of Lira. She saved my life and my leg. That's why I'm here, to repay that debt."

Yet he was risking his life as a mage—the only thing he'd ever wanted—by doing any of this. Her doubt deepened, but she kept it to herself. It wasn't like she trusted Garan or Tarion either.

Lira addressed all of them as she spoke, lying through her teeth. "We made a deal. I'll stick to it, but only because I want my freedom. I hope that's clear."

"It's crystal clear." Garan pointed at the door, voice hard and dismissive. "The first door on the left is yours. Be up at dawn. We'll leave as soon as there's enough traffic on the streets that we won't stand out."

"I'll leave now, return to my apartment, just in case a messenger from the council comes to check on me," Lorin said.

"Lorin, is there a way you could get a message to Caria?" Tarion asked, anxiety lacing his voice. "To let her know things went awry and that there's a good chance she'll be exposed."

"I'll do my best," he said gravely. "And I'll return here early tomorrow morning to escort you through the gates."

Lira followed Lorin out the door without a word, pausing only to scan the hall outside to ensure nobody was out there to see her. She was sweating as she pushed open the door to her much smaller room. Now that she was alone, no longer having to put up a front, her stomach heaved. She scrambled to the bed, yanked out the chamber pot, and emptied her stomach.

Greyson's face flashed into her mind. His screams echoed in her thoughts. Garan's look of contempt replaced Greyson's terror. Her stomach continued convulsing even after there was nothing left, just empty, dry, retches.

Eventually, finally done, she staggered back to her feet and pulled off all her clothes before climbing into the bed, trying to push everything out of her head so that she could get some rest.

But sleep never came. Instead, she lay there and planned.

She would make sure that Lucinda never saw her coming. And when Lira found her, she would burn too, just like Greyson.

CHAPTER 7

The following morning, Garan had his carriage brought around to the back of the inn after he and Tarion made a show of enjoying a leisurely breakfast in the main room. Once it was ready, Lira took the back stairs, wearing a hooded cloak. Garan and Lorin engaged the stable hands in conversation while Tarion sneaked Lira into the carriage.

Garan joined them a moment later. Lorin mounted his horse and rode alongside the carriage. As soon as they were out of sight of the inn, Garan leaned down and opened a hidden compartment under his seat.

Without a word, Lira curled up inside it, the door closing as soon as she was comfortable. The carriage moved at a steady pace for some time, the sounds of clopping hooves and a busy city street filtering through and calming Lira's tension. Nothing seemed out of place.

Eventually, though, the carriage slowed and then came to a halt.

The wait grew interminable, and Lira grew increasingly uncomfortable in the tight space. Her stomach turned from the stale air and the rocking of the carriage every time it lurched forward a short distance.

She began to hear the stentorian shouts of the guards on the gates as they instructed each vehicle or person moving through to stop and be subjected to a search. The tension in her shoulders tightened to rigidity.

When it was their turn, Garan opened the window to his side of the carriage and spoke in his usual charming way, "Lord Garan Egalion. Is there a problem?"

"Yes, sir, we're under orders to search every person and vehicle leaving the city."

"Why?" He sounded puzzled.

"A prisoner escape, sir. We won't be long. If I could ask you and your companion to please step out of the carriage?"

"Surely this isn't necessary? I'm the son of Rionn's lord-mage—I think I can be trusted not to smuggle an escaped prisoner out of Carhall." Garan was convincingly incredulous, and Lira began to relax a little.

"I'm sorry, sir, but we have our orders. We won't take long."

There was a hesitation from above. Sweat trickled down Lira's spine—the compartment she was hidden in wouldn't stand up to much scrutiny.

Before Garan's hesitation could become suspicious, he heaved a sigh. The carriage rocked as he and Tarion moved to leave, but before they could step out, Lorin's haughty Shiven voice sounded nearby.

"I'm Mage Warrior Lorin Hester. These men are cleared to leave. Let them through, please."

"Warrior Hester." It was clear the guard recognised him. "They're with you?"

"They are. And we're on urgent business. I understand you have orders, Norrin, but we can't afford the delay. I'll vouch for them."

If Lira hadn't been so anxious, she would have smiled in enjoyment. Where the word of a privileged foreign lord hadn't been enough to get by Tregayan militia, that of an official Mage Council warrior most definitely was.

"Very good, Warrior Hester. Lord Egalion, you're free to go through."

The carriage lurched into welcome movement.

Lira's relief at getting through the gates faded quickly. Lorin had just destroyed his mage career, and even Garan and Tarion wouldn't escape without some consequences for what they were doing.

They were risking a lot for Tarion's parents. And Lira didn't buy for a second Lorin's claims he was here for her. Until she understood his motives better, she would have to keep an extra close eye on him.

But all of that paled in comparison for what would happen to Lira if they were caught. The idea of going back to that cell—now that she was free of it—was a horror that tightened her chest so fiercely she almost couldn't breathe for a moment.

Once through the gates, the carriage picked up speed, trundling along the main road out of Carhall to the south. Lira's stomach settled and she fell into a light doze. She woke when the horses slowed, then came to a halt. The carriage rocked as Tarion and Garan climbed out, then eventually Tarion slid aside the panel in front of her face and reached out a hand in to help her out.

She spurned the hand, scrambling out with relief, but almost falling out of the carriage door when her cramped legs didn't cooperate the way she wanted them to. He didn't laugh and she gave him a grudging nod for it. The carriage had been pulled over to the side of the road, sunlit forest surrounding it on either side. For the moment the area was empty, nobody coming in either direction.

"Come on." Garan set off into the trees.

"You're going to leave that here?" she asked, pointing at the carriage.

"We can't use it any longer. As soon as the council figures out what happened, they'll be looking for it everywhere."

She shrugged and followed them. They didn't walk far before arriving at a clearing where three horses grazed, loosely tethered to one of the trees. Bulging saddlebags were attached to the saddles on their backs. Tarion was already mounting. Lira hefted an inwards sigh. She hadn't ridden in two years and hadn't been particularly proficient at it before that.

She was going to be very sore in a few hours' time.

"We'll head east first," Garan said, swinging himself easily into the saddle. "Once they find the carriage, they'll look for tracks. We want to lead them away from our intended destination."

As much as she already hated taking orders from him, it was a good idea, and so Lira didn't disagree as she climbed onto her horse, a bay mare—as expected, she felt awkward, uncomfortable. The mare turned her head, giving Lira a look of deep scepticism. When she tightened the reins in an attempt to demonstrate control, the mare simply stood there, uninterested.

"Her name's Ariel. She's a little grumpy, but steady and strong," Tarion told her quietly. "I know you haven't ridden in a while."

She ignored him and masked her discomfort with irritation, pointing at Lorin's cloak. "Are you seriously going to keep wearing that?"

"It gives us cover if we pass any checkpoints on the road," Garan said. "As does the way Tarion and I are dressed."

"Unless they recognise you," she said.

"It will be a little while before they figure out we were involved in your escape, and until then we can use it." Garan spurred his horse. "Let's get moving."

So proud of their achievements. So loyal to their precious council. Bitterness burned in Lira's gut.

They headed east for the remainder of the day, moving through thick forest where they could. At dusk, they crossed a swift-flowing river and turned southwest. When night fell, they kept on, though the horses had slowed to a trot. Lira's thighs burned, arms aching from her battle for control with her mare. Ariel's reluctance to comply with Lira's instructions had not abated. It seemed she did not appreciate moving faster than a trot, or the reins being held too tightly.

"The whole world is going to be looking for me once they realise I'm gone," she remarked, breaking a silence that had held for several hours. The tension in it was making her itch and she could no longer hold back the compulsion to break it. "At least, the half of the world that *isn't* looking for Egalion and Caverlock."

"We know," Garan said.

His stony expression suggested he had no interest in discussing that further, so Lira turned to Lorin. "Why are you helping them? I get they want to rescue their family, but why are you risking imprisonment and maybe even death for helping me escape? You know those two will avoid the most serious consequences for breaking me out."

"I told you why," Lorin said simply.

She snorted.

He lifted a haughty eyebrow when she snorted again. "You don't believe me?"

"No, I don't."

"And when have I ever lied to you?"

Her mouth thinned and she shot him a glare. "How should I know?"

He shrugged. "I don't care whether you believe me or not. It doesn't change anything."

"I have a question, if you really want to talk," Garan said suddenly. "How did Ahrin Vensis manage to escape the council when you didn't?"

Lira's breath caught at the name. Her hesitation must have been obvious to all of them, so with ruthless brute force she shoved aside the reaction his words caused in her and managed, "It was me Underground were looking to frame, not her. And I'm not answering any more questions on the subject."

She wanted to ask them what they knew about Ahrin, whether they'd heard anything at all, even rumour, about what had happened to her. If Ahrin had held to her agreement with Lira, she would have come to Karonan after making sure Underground didn't suspect her of being involved with Lira's escape from Shadowfall Island. She would have looked for a message from Lira that never came. And instead of a message, she would have seen the council dismantle Underground after Lucinda sacrificed Greyson and the other cell leaders.

She would have left. Lira knew Ahrin well enough to know that the Darkhand's survival instinct would have had her cutting Lira loose and going to ground until she figured out her next play to get back on top, regain power and influence. If things had gone well, she would have taken Underground's coin with her. If not, she'd be starting from scratch. She'd be a long way away from any council outpost now. They'd never catch her.

She'd stayed free because she hadn't come back for Lira. She swallowed.

"She's probably the one who took your parents, Tarion," Lorin said soberly, startling Lira from her thoughts.

Lira wanted to disagree on principle. But when Ahrin hadn't found Lira in Karonan, had she decided to go back to what remained of the Shadowcouncil? Maybe she'd become involved in whatever long-term plan Lucinda had going on.

Because Lira was certain of one thing—Underground had orchestrated everything that had happened. They hadn't been beaten; they'd made a strategic withdrawal, probably because at some point they'd learned that Lira was spying for the council and that Ahrin wasn't the loyal soldier they'd thought she was. When she wasn't furiously and bitterly angry, Lira had to admire how Lucinda had turned an almost crushing loss into such a victory.

Lira had *almost* had her ... but then she'd been had in turn.

"We know the Darkhand led the team that took us from Temari Hall," Lorin added, tight anger lacing his voice. "I'd be surprised if she wasn't involved."

Tarion glanced at Lira briefly, troubled. Garan caught the look. "Still sure it was a good idea to break Lira out? That giving her the chance to reunite her with her evil girlfriend is the best plan?"

"Enough!" Tarion spoke with unusual firmness. "All we need is for Lira to get us to Underground. I don't care what happens after that."

"Then you're an idiot," Lira observed mildly.

"No he's not," Garan said just as mildly. "His mother is the most powerful mage in the world. Underground won't get the drop on her a second time. Once she's free, the council will burn what's left of Lucinda and her people."

No they wouldn't, and not only because Lira was going to get there first. Underground controlled the Magor-lier. She didn't say that, though. They hadn't believed her when she'd said it back at the inn and she had no proof to offer.

Talk faded again and unease slithered beneath her skin. She hated constant chatter, but ever since escaping, silence felt heavy, gave her too much time to think, to dwell. It reminded her too much of the silence of her cell. Of her utter aloneness in the world.

She tried concentrating on breathing the cool, rich air, feeling it whisper across the skin on her face. Focused on the soreness in her leg and arm muscles. It helped, but not for long. Too quickly the heaviness descended again.

There had been darker moments, despite her determination to escape, when she'd genuinely believed she'd never be free again. Never leave that cell she'd spent over two years pacing.

She'd thought getting out would feel different. Like a weight she'd barely managed to carry for years had been lifted from her shoulders.

Except it didn't. She tried to focus on the fact that no matter what happened next, right now, in this moment, she was free. She was breathing fresh air and listening to the sounds of the forest around her. But she couldn't hold onto it. She was so desperately afraid of having to go behind bars again, so unable to trust that she wouldn't, she *couldn't*, let herself relax into freedom.

So she kept it buried, kept her expectations, her hopes minimal, her aim to get from one hour to another, staying free. She would use Tarion and the others to get her to Underground, and she would ruin them.

And then she'd figure out a way to make sure the council never imprisoned her again.

Then maybe she'd feel truly free.

CHAPTER 8

I t took over two weeks of long days of riding to reach their destination. From Carhall they struck out through the hilly southwestern region of Tregaya, relying heavily on the maps Garan had brought with him to navigate their way through the rural roads and villages.

They never entered a village or town as a group; usually Lorin, wearing his mage cloak and purporting to be on Mage Council business, would enter alone to refresh their supplies and try to get a sense of how far news of Lira's escape had reached.

Lira thought it too much of a risk—all it would take would be council notices travelling ahead of them via messenger bird or telepath for Lorin's description to be known to the villagers—but all three young men were confident the risk was low.

"The council is already stretched in the search for Councillor Egalion and her husband," Lorin said one cold night as they huddled around a fire. "It will take them time to put all the pieces of your escape together."

"Tarrick Tylender will be far more interested in catching me than Alyx Egalion," Lira said. "I'd put money on him re-distributing resources to look for me."

"Even if that were true," Garan said, rolling his eyes, "they don't know in which direction we headed or where we're trying to get to. Besides, we need supplies. It's worth the risk."

"Lira might be right though," Tarion mumbled. In the firelight the shadows under his eyes were even more pronounced than usual. "Uncle

Tarrick aside, the council will be terrified that Shakar's heir is on the loose."

"Not to mention," Lira added, "by sending in Lorin with his cloak every time we need supplies or news, the council will be able to track us like a damned beacon once they do figure out his involvement."

"Once we cross into Shivasa we'll stay away from all the towns and villages," Garan said, conceding the point with a reluctant nod. "That way they won't be able to track us beyond the border."

"We're going to have trouble actually crossing the border," Lorin said. "The council has Taliath and mages stationed at every major border crossing on the continent. Telepaths at many of them too."

Lira narrowed her eyes at him. "You seem to know a lot for a mage warrior who's barely passed his Trials and must be pretty low down in the pecking order."

Lorin shrugged. "When I heard about the kidnapping, of course I was interested. Tarion and Garan were my friends. Not to mention the similarities with our kidnapping. Given I was on assignment in Carhall, it was easy to keep myself informed."

"I thought you'd all lost touch." She lifted an eyebrow.

"We all did, after you…" Garan shifted uncomfortably. "Except for Tar and me, anyway."

Lira shifted her attention back to Lorin. "What assignment were you on, exactly?"

"Guard duty at the council dome."

She burst out in a chuckle at the sour look on his face. "Typical posting for a penniless Shiven mage with no mageblood heritage to speak of. I'd bet a thousand gold pieces neither Garan nor Tarion would have been given that assignment if they'd graduated as council mages."

"I'll earn my way to more meaningful work," Lorin said with quiet patience.

"Not now you won't," she said sharply.

He said nothing, but his jaw tightened. After a moment, Garan glanced over at him, saying quietly, "Tar and I will do what we can for you, Lorin."

"My parents will intercede on your behalf," Tarion said. "All we need do is find them and bring them home."

The look on Lorin's face suggested he believed that no more than Lira did.

As Lorin had warned, they faced a significant delay after approaching the Shiven border, where they encountered bristling guard checkpoints even on the smaller roads through.

It forced them into a much longer overland route to avoid the roads. Either a telepath mage had already broadcast news of Lira's escape—the most likely option—or it was a reaction to the kidnap of Egalion and Caverlock. Maybe it was both. But eventually they crossed the border in an isolated northern area under cover of a night-time storm. Once over, they turned farther south, deeper into the country.

It wasn't an enjoyable journey. Lira's companions made little effort to speak to her beyond what was strictly necessary and didn't talk much amongst themselves either, conversation having faded to almost nothing by the second week. It made for tedious, wearying days in the saddle and uncomfortable rest at night. They were only a couple of months out from winter, which meant the weather was already becoming unbearably cold.

Unwilling to risk a fire at night, they switched to resting during the day, huddled together in cloaks and blankets while one of them stood watch. Lira forgot what it felt like to feel truly warm. Nights were a misery of sludging through cold and snow, the horses as unhappy as the riders. Lira grew almost affectionate towards Ariel's side-eye whenever Lira went to mount her for the night's ride.

Tarion seemed to suffer the cold most. He shivered almost constantly, and he didn't eat or sleep much when they did stop. She wondered if he'd caught a fever from the bad weather but didn't ask. She didn't care if he was sick.

Lorin was the lone member of the group who seemed to enjoy the trip, the grim look on his face having lightened several shades as each day passed. Lira wondered at the cause of it. Why such a loyal council mage didn't seem more worried about having abandoned his post indefinitely.

When his eyes brightened as they eventually approached the eastern shore of the frozen lake surrounding Karonan, she wondered if it came down to the simple fact this journey had brought him home to Shivasa.

Even Lira felt a stirring of familiarity, if not pleasure, at the sight of the city. Built right in the middle of a sprawling lake so large it was impossible to see the other side from one bank, the capital of Shivasa was attached to land by four causeways reaching out on each point of a compass; north, south, east, and west.

On the northern shore of the lake, situated within a walled compound barely a stone's throw from the northern causeway, was Temari Hall, its signature tower stretching high above the surrounding forest.

"If your plan is to stroll into Temari Hall and ask for a meeting with Uncle Finn, I don't think it's going to work very well." Garan spoke for the first time in hours as they brought their horses to a halt within sight of the eastern lakeshore. Not far distant, down a short rise to their left, horses, carts, and carriages moved in both directions along the main road leading to the eastern causeway. Snatches of conversation, the creak of carts, and the clopping of horses' hooves drifted up to them on the ice-cold air.

She gave him a scathing look. "The plan is to get inside the city first. I assume that's not going to be easy?"

Lorin nodded, pointing to the causeway. "The traffic heading into the city is pretty light this time of the morning, but it looks to be already slowing up. I'm confident guards will be searching everyone coming in."

"We'll need to split up to enter the city so nobody notices us arriving as a group," Lira said. Lorin had already coached them on the details they needed to get past the guards. "There used to be an abandoned house a few blocks southeast from the northern causeway." She explained its location in more detail. "We'll meet there once we're inside."

"At which point you'll tell us why we're here?" Garan lifted an eyebrow. "I assume we're supposed to trust you and not suspect that the minute we split up you'll abandon us and run for the hills."

"If I was planning to run for the hills, I certainly would have done it before enduring that miserable last fortnight traipsing over the country freezing my rotted carcass off with you," she said. "But how about you and I go in together, so you can keep an extra close eye on me?"

He nodded, happy with that arrangement.

She fought not to roll her eyes. "Good. We'll take the eastern causeway. Tarion, you and Lorin will go in via the south. Leave your horses at one of the public stables—they'll stand out in the area of the city where we're going. And I highly recommend taking off that damned mage cloak and concealing your mage staffs. It will only make you noticeable, not to mention if the council gets wind we're here, all this will be over pretty quickly. That city is full of mages and well-trained soldiers."

"And if the abandoned house you last knew of two years ago is no longer abandoned?" Tarion enquired. Lorin was already shrugging off his cloak and tucking it inside his saddlebag.

"Then linger nearby to wait for us, without looking suspicious if possible, and we'll come up with something else." Having no patience for further debate, Lira kicked Ariel forward and left them to follow her if they chose.

Garan didn't hesitate before coming after her. And she couldn't help but be reluctantly impressed by his willingness to put aside his ire at her when he said quietly, "Do you think my clothing makes me stand out too much for where we're going?"

She looked him up and down. "I know it's cold, but could you lose the tunic; those buttons alone mark you as wealthy. If the council has figured out you helped me escape and gotten word ahead of us, guards will be looking for two lordlings and a council mage. Untuck your shirt. The rumpled state of your clothes, stubble, and messy hair should do the rest."

He complied without complaint, tucking the tunic into his saddlebags. He'd already concealed his staff under his saddle.

Although Lira was on high alert for anything out of place—the last time she'd entered this city she'd been lured into an ambush by the council—nobody looked at her or Garan askance as they joined the traffic heading along the eastern causeway.

"You look different," he remarked as they were slowed up by a heavy cart in front of them, breaking what had been a relatively comfortable silence.

"Is that right?" Her gaze was ahead, her attention focused on making sure the slow cart wasn't the lead in to some sort of elaborate ambush. It looked legitimate enough. The thing was piled high with bulging sacks and the horse driving it was clearly labouring. Not far ahead, the forward movement had slowed considerably anyway.

"I suppose maybe this was always you; you just hid it from us like everything else."

She cut him a look. "Ah, so I was a master of deception and manipulation? I see."

"You always seemed so angry about the fact everyone looked at you and saw the Darkmage ... I believed that anger." He was frowning. "So I can't understand why you would ever want to join Underground."

"I did it because I was asked to."

"You're an impeccable liar, Lira Astor. Maybe that's true. But don't tell me you were ever loyal to the Mage Council, or that you had any motive outside looking out for yourself."

She shrugged. "If you recall, I did keep trying to tell you all that. I never lied to you, Garan. It was you who refused to believe me and kept casting me in the role of some kind of hero because that's what *you* wanted from me."

"Our mistake. We won't make it again." A hint of bitterness edged his voice.

Her betrayal had upset him, hurt him even. Good. Once that might have bothered her, but maybe now he'd finally learned how different reality was from his insulated noble-born existence.

Garan didn't speak again.

Soon after, they approached the gates—the six guards posted there were split into teams of two searching each cart, rider, and carriage before allowing it into the city.

Garan did most of the speaking once it was their turn, explaining to the guard that he and his sister were travelling from the farm they worked on to visit family in the city. Lorin's knowledge of the surrounding area meant the name of the farm he gave was legitimate and known for having a large number of local workers. When he then rattled off the name of the street their family supposedly lived on—one Lorin also knew from experience was where most of the city's itinerant farm workers lived in family groups—the guards' bored expressions only deepened, and they were quickly waved on.

Once clear of the sight of the gates, Lira led them to the public stable she'd described to the others. She gave Ariel a farewell pat—which was completely ignored—then waited at a distance while Garan took both horses in and paid the grooms. Once he emerged, she set off, leading him through the tangle of busy city streets towards their destination.

The bustle of people and carts and horses, the multitude of strong smells, the lack of personal space ... when someone brushed against her while hurrying past, Lira's breathing quickened and sweat pooled at the base of her spine. Her hands curled into fists at her sides. She'd forgotten how crowded and loud cities were. For a while Lira concentrated on simply breathing through the anxiety, refusing to allow Garan to see her distress.

Eventually, though, the sensory overload eased, and her muscles relaxed, leaving only the dull echoes of a headache throbbing at her temples. By the time they reached her destination, helped by the exertion of the long walk, she felt almost back to normal.

Fortunately, the house she'd described to the others remained abandoned. Less fortunately, something had died in it since the last time she'd been there and the rotting stench pervading the entire place was enough to make her stomach heave. She wasn't as desensitised as she'd once been to foul smells, a weakness that brought back some of her earlier anxiety.

A thorough look through all of the rooms showed signs that squatters were still using it at night, and some of the debris left by human occupants looked recent enough that she suspected they wouldn't be alone the coming night.

"We'll take this one." She chose a room on the ground floor that had a sound section of floor and roof but allowed them a window exit if needed. "If anyone comes, you protect this space as ours, but let them go wherever else they want in the house. Don't use magic except as a last resort—word of a mage in the area will spread like wildfire."

Garan crossed his arms over his chest. "And where will you be?"

"Our supplies are almost gone. I'm going to forage for more. I won't be too long, and unless they ran into trouble, the others should be here soon."

"You're the one that speaks street, Lira." He let out an uneasy breath. "Wouldn't it be better if you stayed to protect our patch or whatever and *I'll* go out for supplies?"

"I can stay unnoticed moving around; you can't. Besides, your store of coin is getting low and I'd rather keep that for emergencies."

"The problem is, I don't trust you. Tarion might believe that you're going to hold to your word and help us, but I don't, not for a second." He ran a hand through his hair, clearly agitated. "You've moved us into *your* territory, ground that you're comfortable and familiar with. You've got the leverage and the advantage."

"All true," she said evenly. "But if you want my help, then we do things my way. I'm not ever putting myself at your mercy again. So either take it or leave it."

He smiled bleakly. "Between you and Tarion, you've backed me into a corner where I've really got no way out but to keep acceding to the both of you. Go on then, do what you want."

"You're here, Garan Egalion, because you chose to help your cousin. Don't blame me for the predicament you find yourself in. It is still within your power to walk away."

He said nothing to that. His gaze was on the ground now, shoulders hunched. Part of her was glad to see him so beaten, but she couldn't afford for his despair to lead to apathy while she was gone. So she gave him a bolstering smile. "You'll be fine. I doubt anyone will come along till after dark anyway."

Unexpectedly, he let out a huff. "You're going to go and steal things, aren't you?"

She shrugged. "Wouldn't you prefer not to know? That way your hero-complex won't start itching uncomfortably."

He didn't laugh, instead merely shrugging and turning away as she left the room. Unbothered, she pushed Garan Egalion out of her thoughts. Finally, for the first time since being released from her cell, she was alone.

CHAPTER 9

Several blocks away, Lira spent an enjoyable hour pickpocketing at a busy marketplace. The day had warmed a little and she enjoyed the pressure-free time doing nothing but knocking the rust off the skills she'd learned as a child and soaking in her freedom. For a short time, the tightness in her chest eased, and she allowed herself to just be in the moment rather than worrying about what came next.

Once she had enough coin, she purchased food and water to last them a few days and headed back to the house, ensuring she wasn't followed. By the time she arrived, Lorin and Tarion were there, crowded with Garan into the room she'd chosen.

"Any trouble?" she asked, placing the supplies she'd bought on the ground in the centre of the room, her appetite stirring at the delicious smells wafting from it. For a moment it masked the horrible rotting scent emanating through the place.

She'd hoped some of Garan's suspicion might have faded on proof that she'd always intended to return, but he merely gave her a searching glance before turning away. Neither Tarion nor Lorin looked surprised to see her. She wasn't sure which response she preferred.

"None." Garan helped himself to food, just beating out Lorin, who scowled at him.

"No issues for us getting through the city gates either," Lorin added. "We tailed a large group of performers entering the city, and the guards assumed we were with them. Didn't even need to use our cover."

"I was surprised it worked so well, actually." Tarion frowned. "I suspect either word hasn't reached Karonan yet of Lira's escape, or they don't think she's heading this way."

Conversation stopped briefly as everyone sat around the food, helped themselves, and ate hungrily. Tarion took less than the others, and as far as Lira could tell, was picking at it rather than eating.

"We can't stay at this location more than a day or two," Lira said after swallowing a mouthful of grilled bread and beef. "Squatters will be here later tonight for a roof over their heads to sleep. They'll note our presence and word will get around that there are new arrivals in the area."

"Then maybe you should tell us what we're doing here, so that we can accomplish it and leave," Garan said pointedly.

Lira nodded but finished her mouthful before she shifted, trying to settle more comfortably on the hard floor. "I don't have any clear answers as to why Underground might have taken Egalion and Caverlock or where they'd have taken them. But there were always oddities with the group that never quite made sense to me, and I think shedding some light on those might put us on the right path to finding them. *If* they are still in existence as Tarion believes."

Garan snorted. "What in all magic does that actually mean?"

"The Shadowcouncil were very interested in something Finn A'ndreas was working on," Lira said. "That's why Lucinda placed Ahrin at Temari, to get close to him and find out as much as she could about what he was doing." The mention of the Darkhand's name rippled through her in a shiver of pain, but she ignored it and forged on.

"What was it they were so interested in?" Tarion asked, puzzled.

"They wouldn't say." Lira let those words lie for a moment. "Ahrin was the Darkhand, the most trusted of all the Shadowcouncil's operatives, so the fact they wouldn't give her any more detail tells me that whatever it was, it was highly sensitive."

"Uncle Finn's been working on the mystery of Rotherburn for years now." Garan shook his head, clearly annoyed. "That's his major piece of research work outside his teaching duties at Temari. Why in all magical hells would Underground care about that? Lira, if you've dragged us here on some kind of—"

"I've been thinking about it a lot," she interrupted him, "and I think A'ndreas must have been working on something else, something secret, for the council. Right before we were kidnapped, Greyson tasked me with stealing a letter from Councillor Duneskal to A'ndreas. I can't say for certain, but I got the distinct sense they weren't just testing me ... they really wanted that letter."

"And did you steal it for them?" Lorin lifted an eyebrow.

"I did."

Garan looked at her in disbelief. "And? What did it say?"

"It was Duneskal summarising some research work he'd done for A'ndreas in Carhall." She lifted a hand. "No, the topic of the research wasn't mentioned, but at the time I assumed it related to Rotherburn and dismissed it as unimportant. I've since reconsidered."

Tarion ran a hand through his hair, the metal bracelet on his wrist glinting in the firelight as the sleeve of his tunic fell back. "That's why we're in the city instead of sneaking into Temari Hall. You want to get at Councillor Duneskal."

"Exactly. We can hide ourselves in this big city, but not inside an academy full of mages and Taliath. And instinct tells me Duneskal will be a much easier target to extract information from than Finn A'ndreas."

Lorin's eyes widened. "You're actually going to *talk* to him?"

"The only other option is breaking into Duneskal's office and reading every single piece of parchment in there in the hopes of finding more about whatever the two of them were working on," Lira said. "Or doing the same inside A'ndreas' office in Temari Hall. That will take too long."

"The minute Councillor Duneskal sees you he'll call the guards and lock you away again. Then he'll toss us in right along with you," Garan pointed out.

"Right. So we need to plan our approach carefully, make sure we get what we need from him on our first attempt, then have a quick way out."

Lorin lifted a hand. "To be clear, you're basically talking about kidnapping a Mage Council member?"

"Not kidnapping. If we do it right, we don't have to move him anywhere. We'll just have a nice chat with him in his office."

"This is insane." Garan crossed his arms and looked at Tarion. "Breaking Lira out in some last-ditch attempt to help your parents is one thing, but I'm not abetting more crimes that will see me in prison right alongside her for the rest of my life. Not when I don't believe this is going to help you find Aunt Alyx and Uncle Dash."

"I don't need you or Lorin for this," Lira said coolly. "Just Tarion."

He gave her a startled look. "Why me?"

"You can get me inside wherever I need to go without anybody seeing us. I don't need anyone's help talking to Duneskal." She shrugged.

Tarion's gaze dropped to the floor. "I can't get you in."

She glared at him. "Why in rotted hells not? You moved me out of the prison back in Carhall just fine."

"That was an exception. It's the first and only time I've used magic in years. I don't use it anymore."

A thick, awkward silence fell over the group. Everybody looked away from Tarion to investigate various corners of the room.

"Somebody explain this to me, now," she snapped.

"The bracelets on Tar's wrists are made from old Hunter medallions," Garan said quietly. "They cut off his access to magic ... which includes the ability to transform into..." He trailed off.

Lira couldn't believe her ears. "*That* was the solution to what happened to him? Lock up his magic for the rest of his life? You cannot be serious."

Garan wouldn't meet her eyes. Lorin looked pained.

"And you agreed to that?" She stared at Tarion, but he wouldn't meet her gaze.

"I don't want to hurt people, Lira. It was the safest solution," he mumbled. "I wear these willingly."

Frustration burned inside her, even though she wasn't sure why she cared. "That's the stupidest thing I've ever heard. You need to learn to control it, not just turn it off."

"I *can't* control it." He spoke through gritted teeth, hands curled into fists.

"Have you ever tried?" she demanded. "I—"

"Lira, enough!" Garan said in that commanding tone of his. "You were right when you said you had no obligation to explain yourself to us, but the same is true in reverse. Leave off."

She bristled but couldn't argue with his logic. What did she care anyway? Tarion could live the rest of his life without magic if that's what he chose. It didn't affect her.

"It's not all bad anyway." Garan tossed a little smile Tarion's way. "He and Sesha are formally betrothed now. King Cayr approved the match."

"Only because Mama pressured him into it." A matching smile crossed Tarion's face, but it didn't last long. It flickered and died like a flame exposed to a gust of wind.

Garan cleared his throat and looked at Lira. "Can you do it without his magic?"

Lira ignored him and looked at Tarion. "You were willing to use your magic to break me out so that I could help find your parents. This is no different."

"There was no other way then," he said.

"There isn't now, either. It'll be a lot riskier if I try this without your magic, and there will be a much higher chance of all of us getting caught—which won't just affect you but Lorin and your cousin too." She rose to her feet. "I'll leave you to think on that. Either way, if we're going to do this, I need to go out and scout the area. I'll be back by dawn, but I suggest you set a watch. This isn't a nice neighbourhood."

"Really? I hadn't noticed." Garan poked glumly at the dirty patch on the floor beside her.

"And if something happens and you don't come back?" Lorin enquired.

"Then you're on your own, and you won't have to worry about being executed for kidnapping mage councillors."

Tarion caught her at the back door—she didn't want too much observable movement coming in and out of the front of the house—before she could step out into the night, but he seemed hesitant. "Spit it out or let me go," she said in irritation.

"Uncle Finn ... Rotherburn, whatever he was doing with Duneskal, they weren't the only things he was investigating, Lira."

She lifted an eyebrow.

"He is trying to track down your father."

There was a moment's thick silence. She hadn't thought about her father in years, not since that night she'd... "Yes, I know. I overheard your parents talking about it when we were in Alistriem after the ambush at DarkSkull, remember?"

"He didn't stop after you were imprisoned." Tarion hesitated again. "And he's become very interested in your mother, too."

"Why? She's long dead."

"I don't know. But—"

She waved him off. "Underground weren't spying on your uncle because he was curious about my father, Tarion."

"How do you know that for sure?"

"Because finding him doesn't give them anything useful. He wasn't the Darkmage's heir ... my mother was. And he didn't even know that."

He lifted his hands in the air in surrender. "Fine. I'm just trying to make sure you know all the facts. Stay safe out there."

Not bothering to respond, she walked away, quickly disappearing into the night. Her father had never been a relevant figure in her life. That wasn't going to change. She had more important things to focus on.

Like getting in front of Councillor Rawlin Duneskal and making him tell her everything he knew.

CHAPTER 10

After leaving Tarion, Lira slipped through the ramshackle fence at the boundary of the yard and into the street beyond before stilling.

A cool breeze whipped up, sending leaves rustling over the packed dirt of the street, but nothing else stirred in the shadows. Confident nobody was watching, Lira set off, footsteps quiet but confident, all senses alert.

Travelling the familiar dark alleys to the tailor's shop that had once been the location of Greyson's Underground meetings, it felt as if no time had passed at all. The area was as dark and quiet as she remembered, the only sounds the whistle of the breeze and the scuffle of rats and other night-time foragers. She stood in the shadows across from the shop's entrance for a long time. Nothing moved inside that she could tell. No lights were on. There wasn't much foot traffic either.

Several quick strides carried her across the street to the front door. She popped the lock in seconds and stepped inside before closing it quickly after her, using a quick touch of telekinetic magic to re-engage the lock.

Judging from the stock filling the shelves and draped over racks, not to mention the lack of dust, the shop was still operating, but nobody emerged from the dark interior to challenge her as she slipped through to the back room that held the basement entry. Here were the scuff marks on the floor she remembered.

She lifted the trapdoor to darkness and stepped down onto the narrow stairs, closing it behind her before summoning enough magic to create a ball of flickering flame above her right shoulder—large enough to see by.

Dust lay thick on the steps and floor of the basement. No footprints were visible, nothing breaking the layer of dust. Rickety chairs, stools, and crates sat scattered across the space just as she remembered, only messier, many turned over—no doubt the result of the Mage Council searchers after Greyson's arrest. She wondered what had happened to the rest of the cell members, whether they'd been let free with a warning, or still languished in jail.

The cellar had an empty, abandoned air about it. Lira's steps took her to the middle of the room. She didn't know why she'd come. If Underground continued to exist, the chances of them still using this place were miniscule.

The space had been full, the last time she'd been here, Greyson telling her he was glad to see her. The memory of him was vivid, quickly followed by the sound of his screams echoing in her ears. Hurriedly, she forced those horrible last sounds out of her mind, ignoring the twist of nausea in her stomach.

Questions, long simmering, swirled through her thoughts. Had he known at that last meeting that she was a spy, or had that knowledge come later? When exactly had he and Lucinda begun setting Lira up to take the fall?

Ahrin.

The Darkhand had been at that meeting too.

Lira slowly sank into a crouch, elbows resting on her knees, head hanging down.

Tears pricked at her eyes, the ache in her chest so fierce that it took her breath away. Every single day Lira had missed Ahrin with a longing that simply wouldn't let go despite the increasing passage of time.

Ahrin had chosen survival. She would have told Lira to do the same had their positions been reversed. But that hadn't stopped Lira from hoping that there might be one person in the world that cared enough to try and help her.

It was a stupid, foolish wanting, something she knew better than to feel.

Just as stupid as sitting here feeling sorry for herself.

There was nothing to be found here. Underground was long gone. Ahrin was in the past, best forgotten about. Except for one thing—

The address the Darkhand had given her just before everything had gone to pieces.

"There's something you should have ... I don't know if it will still be there, but once you're back in Karonan, go check it out. Be careful. They might have guards." The words resonated through Lira's thoughts in Ahrin's crisp voice, as clear as if the woman were standing right beside her.

Leaving the ghosts of the past behind her, Lira exited the tailor's shop, not bothering to waste time trying to erase her boot prints in the dust. Judging by the lack of other prints, Lira would be long gone before the traces of her presence were discovered.

She cut swiftly across the city, sticking to the back streets where she could, just another shadowy denizen of the night. An hour's walk brought her to the warehouse district. The address that Ahrin had written down the night they'd parted on Shadowfall Island was for a warehouse set amongst a block of them that were designed for storage of expensive stock.

When she reached the one she was looking for, Lira had to keep moving rather than linger and study it—the streets outside these warehouses were well-lit and patrolled heavily by city guards.

Her trained gaze quickly cased the sturdy warehouse doors, secured with bolts and locks, as she passed by, though. Bars covered the visible windows too.

Lira circled around and retraced her steps a few blocks to a less-secure area of warehousing where there were no guards and the streets were dark. It didn't take long for her to locate a warehouse with a set of exterior stairs that carried her almost all the way to its top. From there, a quick shimmy up a rusted drainpipe brought her onto the roof itself.

A cool breeze rustled through her hair and clothes as she crouched there, going still. Nothing moved. The roof was entirely empty. After waiting a few more moments to be sure, Lira rose to her feet, padding across the roof to its farther edge. A glance down showed an empty alley below. A short jump carried her over to the next roof.

In this way, Lira made her way steadily towards the one she wanted. The roof of her target warehouse was empty and dark, but she had to wait a long time before the street below was briefly clear of patrolling guards to make the jump over without the risk of being spotted. Once there she found the roof access heavily padlocked. It took several minutes of working the complicated mechanism with her telekinesis, but then Lira was inside and padding down a cramped stairwell.

At the bottom a narrow metal gallery looked down over a wide-open space in the centre, with mirroring floors of open corridors lining all four walls. Doors led off the corridors at regular intervals—individual storage rooms, she assumed. The concrete surface at the ground floor was well-lit by multiple torches. A single guard lazily patrolled the square, not looking up once in the time Lira watched him.

The address Ahrin had given her had included not only the warehouse location, but two numbers separated by a dash. *4-13-*. Making a guess that the four meant the fourth level, Lira turned and padded silently along the gangway looking for the stairs heading down.

Just one level of steps, and she reached the first row of red doors. Each had a number painted on it in white. Ensuring she kept glancing over the railing of the gangway to keep an eye on the guard, it didn't take long to make her way to number thirteen. The lock on this door was even more complicated and had been made from metal that voided mage power. At least it proved this was probably the right room—Underground seemed to have extensive access to that kind of metal.

With an internal sigh, Lira crouched, pulled out the lockpicks she'd purchased earlier that day, and set to work.

When the lock finally clicked open, she gave herself a mental pat on the back, then cautiously pushed the door open. A small space lay beyond, lit only by a narrow window high in the wall—too narrow for even a child to slip through. Two solid metal bars lined it anyway.

It was empty apart from a single table in the middle of the room. A black cloth lay draped over a long, narrow, object lying on its surface. Lira slipped inside, pulled the door closed behind her, and went to investigate.

A careful study of the table and its immediate surrounds revealed no obvious traps, though she wouldn't have put it past Lucinda to leave one, so she stepped warily closer. Her breath escaped in a gasp when she pulled off the cloth, letting it fall unheeded to the floor.

A Taliath blade lay there, a plainly tooled sheath placed beside it.

The blade had been forged from some unidentifiable dark metal, dark charcoal in colour rather than the silver of most swords. And its hilt and cross guard ... carved from onyx so dark it drank in the light around it. There was little ornamentation, no jewels or designs carved into it, but it was stunning in its simplicity.

A weapon made to kill and nothing more.

She knew. Before she even reached out to close her fingers around the hilt, she knew why Ahrin had sent her here. They'd clearly been keeping it here waiting for the day they were going to use Lira to take up the mantle of her grandfather. Had Lucinda not had an opportunity to grab it before fleeing?

Her gaze drank in the blade. Another gasp escaped her as she touched the cool hilt; the echoes of her grandfather's magic leapt out to greet hers—like calling to like.

Violet light flared through the room, her magic flaring out of her control.

This was why Underground had gone to the remains of DarkSkull Hall in the first place. To dig up Shakar's Taliath sword from the ruins of where he'd made his final stand against Alyx Egalion.

Lira lifted the blade from the table. It was too heavy for her, and too long for someone of her small stature, but she felt kinship with it in a way she never had with anything before ... or at least not since her mother had died.

She swung it clumsily, and the blade made a whisper of sound, almost a melody, as it cut through the air. Her fingers closed more tightly around the grip, her eyes closing as she swung it again to hear that melody.

For the first time in her life, Lira Astor felt the echoes of her grandfather.

And it felt like home.

She went back over the roofs, the sword bundled in the cloth and tucked awkwardly under one arm. Eschewing the drainpipe with only one free hand, she used a controlled burst of telekinesis to slow her jump down to the top of the exterior stairs.

By then she was sweaty and sore from lugging her package, and she welcomed the break as she waited at the bottom of the stairs to ensure the street remained empty. The cloud cover from earlier had cleared, so despite the lack of street lamps here, she could still see well enough in a watery moonlight.

Then, readjusting the heavy weight of the sword, she set off at a quick walk, her plan to cut through a different part of the city before re-joining the others at the abandoned house.

But she'd barely taken six strides when *something* prickled across her instincts. Her reaction was instantaneous. She slowed, turned, and slid into the shadows inside the opposite warehouse's entry overhang before going utterly still. When nothing immediately leapt at her, she carefully placed the sword on the ground, freeing her hands in case she had to fight.

Then, she waited.

Nothing stirred, and after a few long moments of silence, Lira began to wonder if she was being paranoid. But then something moved farther down the street to her right. Several more heartbeats passed before she could make anything out in the gloom, then the movement resolved into two tall figures heading in her direction. They walked casually, but there was something about the way they were looking around that spoke of intent.

Lira had not seen any guards in this part of the warehouse district—that was why she'd entered the roofs from here. There were no bars, brothels, or late-opening shops in this area of the city either. No reason for any normal citizen to be roaming these streets after midnight.

Lira slowed her breathing even further and sank into a crouch, making herself as small as possible and letting the night shroud her like a perfectly tailored cloak. Whoever it was would have to literally stumble over her to know she was there.

They were both men, she saw as they came closer, tall and broad shouldered like most Shiven, but moving with the lithe grace of warriors. Lira caught the features of one of them when he turned her way, his Shiven skin cast pure white in the silvery moonlight.

She froze, heart stilling in her chest before it began to beat rapidly.

It was Shiasta, one of the Shiven Hunters found by Shadowcouncil and trained on Shadowfall Island. One of the warriors Lira had gotten to know during her time there. And he and his companion were coming from the direction of the external stairs she'd just descended.

Lira didn't believe in coincidences that big.

Somehow, Underground had known Lira might come for what was being kept inside the warehouse, and Shiasta and his companion had been stationed in the area, watching as she went up and came back down. That was why Lucinda had left it there. Either that, or they'd picked her up somewhere else in the city and followed her here.

Rotted stinking fish carcasses. Either way, the Hunters had done a good enough job that her razor-sharp instincts hadn't tripped until they got too close. Fear and annoyance thrummed through Lira in equal measure.

They hadn't tried to stop her taking what was inside, though. Which meant they had another purpose ... her guess was that they planned to follow her, let her lead them back to the others.

Their presence here also meant the Shadowcouncil knew she was out of prison, and they'd known of her escape quickly enough to send Hunters to be in Karonan when she arrived. A little thrill ran down her spine—they'd probably sent Hunters to Dirinan and other places she might go, too.

Lira remained perfectly still, her breathing shallow, holding down on her magic so that it didn't betray her in a flare of violet light. As they came closer, she kept her gaze averted so that she wouldn't trip *their* well-honed instincts.

Shiasta and his companion passed by without pausing, continuing on down the street. Once they were out of sight, she took a deep breath and straightened, peering in the direction they'd gone.

She briefly debated following them, finding out where they were staying, how many of them were in Karonan. But if they knew about the warehouse, then chances were good they knew about the abandoned house where she'd once hidden her change of clothes for attending Underground meetings.

Which meant once they realised they'd lost her—and that wouldn't take long—they could be going there next.

Swearing under her breath, Lira turned and ran in the opposite direction, back through the dark streets, sacrificing stealth for speed. Despite her weary legs, hope stirred in her chest, along with a hot and seductive thrill of anticipation that gave her an endless burst of energy.

Underground was still alive and well, and they were looking for her in Karonan.

Lira was going to turn the hunter into the hunted.

CHAPTER 11

S lipping back through the fence at the rear of the house, Lira dug around in the bushes until finding the old duffel she'd once hidden there. It was covered in dirt but otherwise untouched, though the clothes in it were musty and beginning to rot. She tossed the clothes aside and opened the bag as wide as it would go. Her grandfather's sword *just* fit inside it. Re-buckling the bag, she shoved it as far back into the thickest section of bush as she could, then headed for the house.

Urgency thrummed at her as she stepped inside. Readying her magic, she padded down the interior hallway, instincts alert for anything out of place. They were deep into the early hours, though, and even the squatters appeared to be sleeping.

As she approached the front room where they'd set up, Lorin's tall figure stepped out of the doorway, staff ready, free hand raised. The moment he recognised her, he lowered the staff. "You took a while," he murmured.

She ignored him, pushing past and into the room. "Everyone up!" she said loudly enough that it would wake them without her voice carrying too far. She reinforced the words with a brief kick to both of the snoring bodies.

"What's going on?" Lorin asked, keeping his attention on the corridor outside.

"It's not safe to stay here any longer."

"Why?" Tarion asked, rubbing sleep from his eyes with one hand while shoving the blanket off himself with the other. He looked gaunt in the faint light.

"I'll explain once we're clear, but we have to go now."

Garan eyed her suspiciously. "What did you do?"

"Do as I ask or not. Up to you." Lira gathered up her saddlebag of belongings and slung it over her shoulder. "But I'm leaving now."

When Tarion rose without a word and began gathering his things, Garan gave a heavy sigh and followed suit. Lorin was already buckling up his saddlebag. Leaving them to it, she headed down to the front doorway to wait restlessly, keeping an eye on the street. If Shiasta and his friend had moved fast and come straight here, they could be only moments away.

She shifted from foot to foot, the trapped sensation increasing until the others came padding quietly down the hall, bags over their shoulders.

"There's an inn a block to the east of the public stables where we left the horses—the Feather Duster," she told Garan. "Get us a room there. Its clientele arrives at all hours, so you won't look out of place as long as you keep those mage cloaks and staffs hidden away in your bags. It's close to the horses and the eastern causeway in case we need to leave fast. I'll meet you soon."

"I suppose there's no point asking what you're going to do?" He lifted an eyebrow, then crossed his arms over his chest when Lira merely stared at him.

"Garan, please," Tarion said quietly.

Garan gave his cousin a look, then shook his head. "Fine, we'll go."

Once they were all clear, Lira went to retrieve the bag with her grandfather's sword, then headed back inside. Light footfalls took her all the way up the mostly functional stairs to the top level. Once there, she twisted through an opening in one of the broken windows and climbed up to the roof, trying not to lose her balance and fall as the heavy saddlebag and duffel swung precariously from her shoulders.

She dumped the bags when she reached the roof and crept towards the front-facing edge. Before reaching it, she dropped to her stomach and crawled forward until she could look down over the street at the front of the property.

Then, she waited.

Her heartbeat sounded loudly in her ears, but as she lay still and quiet, her body relaxed into the darkness. Up here, she was in a position of advantage, with room to move.

Barely a handful of minutes had passed when the shadows at the far end of the street stirred, then resolved into the walking figures of Shiasta and his companion. A little smile curled at Lira's mouth.

They were moving more quickly than before, no pretence this time, with intent. Maybe they realised they'd spooked her.

They paused out front of the house, making sure they were alone before slipping inside. Lira rose quietly to her feet and padded back across the roof before dropping to her stomach again. Just as she crawled into place, Shiasta and his friend exited the back of the house.

She held her breath while they searched the yard—including a search of the bushes along the back fence. Shiasta watched while his companion pulled out the clothes she'd cast aside. The two of them exchanged a few words, then the second searched even more thoroughly through the bushes.

Lira cursed under her breath. Underground had known so much about her—even down to the specific spot she'd hidden her change of clothes for meetings.

Eventually the two Hunters returned to the house empty handed. They must have searched the house, too, because after Lira re-positioned with a view of the front, she was waiting a long time before they reappeared, heading back down the street. Lira waited only until they were out of sight of the roof before rising and climbing back into the house. She sprinted down the stairs and out the front, heading in the direction they'd gone.

But they'd already vanished, disappearing into the dark and empty warren of streets. She circled the area multiple times with no luck.

Rotted carcasses. She'd forgotten how good they were, these trained Hunters the Shadowcouncil had found and recruited. She'd been fortunate that her instincts were sharp enough to have picked them up at all tonight ... and even then, it hadn't been until after she'd been in and out of the warehouse. She'd walked right into their trap.

A pang of sorrow rippled through her. These warriors were supposed to be hers, raised and conditioned to fight for her grandfather—and now for his heir. She'd liked Shiasta and his unit, had missed them even, during her time in prison. She hated that Underground was using her people for their own ends.

Still, she couldn't let that softness risk her safety. She'd have to be even more on guard now. Shiasta knew she was in Karonan, which meant he might call in reinforcements to search the city for her. She couldn't afford to linger in the city much longer.

Being caught by the council meant a return to imprisonment, a terrifying enough reality. But being caught by Underground, rather than finding and destroying them on her terms? Well ... Lucinda had already proven more than a match for Lira when she had the advantage.

Lira couldn't afford to let that happen again.

Lira went back to the house, collected her saddlebag and her grandfather's sword, then circled back to the Feather Duster. By then she was exhausted, trudging on weary legs, shoulders aching, fighting a yawn with every step. The moment she spotted Lorin waiting for her in the shadows out front, however, she straightened her shoulders and carefully scraped all weariness from her expression.

By now it was close to dawn, and blue light was already filling the shadows of the street. He didn't demand any answers straight away, merely guided her up a single flight of stairs to a room three doors along.

Tarion and Garan waited in there, a single lamp lit on a side table, each seated on one of the two narrow beds. She quickly dumped the duffel bag in the corner and dropped her saddlebag over it, hoping they'd be more curious about what was going on than why she was now carrying an extra bag.

"Everything okay?" Garan asked.

"Yes and no." She sat in the room's only chair gratefully, legs and arms welcoming the respite. Lorin took up a position by the door. "Tarion was right. Underground is still alive. And they know I'm in the city."

Garan looked genuinely surprised. Lorin expressionless. Tarion let his head fall back against the wall with a soft thump, pure relief filling his face. All the risks he'd taken hadn't been for nothing after all. They gave him a moment, then Garan asked Lira, "How do you know?"

"I went out earlier to poke around some old Underground locations," she explained vaguely. "See if there were any signs of the group still being active. All but one were abandoned."

"And the one that wasn't?" Lorin asked, a little frown on his face.

"I recognised two of their operatives watching the place. They tried to tail me away from it, but I shook them. I figured they might be going to the abandoned house next. They showed up not long after you left—my plan was to tail them in return, but they lost me too. They're good."

"Hold up." Tarion was paying close attention now. "That house was an Underground location?"

"No, it's where I hid a change of clothes that I wore to Underground meetings. I couldn't exactly show up to those things in my apprentice robe and mage staff."

"So you'd change there before and after meetings?" he pressed.

"Yes."

"Then how did they know to go looking for you there?"

"I..." She hesitated. "I don't remember telling them, but it's clear Lucinda knew far more about me than I thought she did."

Tarion didn't seem convinced. "Did you ever feel like you were being followed before or after meetings? Seems like that's something you would have picked up pretty quickly."

"No, I didn't," she admitted. "But what does it matter? They clearly knew about the house because they went there looking for me."

"Lira's right," Garan interrupted, cutting off Tarion as he was about to speak again. "If Underground knows we're here, we can't stay much longer—not unless Lira's chat with Councillor Duneskal gives us information that indicates Aunt Alyx and Uncle Dash might be here in the city. If that's the case, we'll cross that bridge then, but otherwise we should be ready to leave straight after."

"Not to mention," she said, "the council searchers looking for us will track us into Shivasa sooner rather than later, if they haven't already. Karonan is about to become the least safe place in the world for us. We move on Duneskal tonight."

"You still haven't explained how you're going to do that," Lorin said when nobody else spoke.

Lira looked at Tarion, lifted an eyebrow.

His jaw clenched, but then he gave a sharp nod.

"Good. Tarion will transport me into Duneskal's office inside the council building at the end of the day when there should be fewer people around—you *have* been there before?" She waited for his nod before continuing. "He'll stand lookout at the door while I talk to the councillor."

"What happens when he sounds the alarm?" Garan asked.

"He won't."

"You sound very confident of that."

"I am."

Garan let out a huff of frustration. "And what if he's already gone from his office by the time you teleport in there?"

"Then we'll watch for him to arrive the next morning and go in then." She lifted a hand to cut him off as he went to speak. "Yes, I know, there will be more people around at that time, but if we linger here too long we might never get out. I don't think we could afford to wait another full day."

There was a long silence then, all of them clearly thinking it over. Eventually Lorin spoke. "Wouldn't it be easier to go to his house, late at night? There will be fewer guards there, and if I remember correctly, he's unmarried, no children. Nobody to accidentally trip over."

Tarion replied before Lira had to. "I've visited the councillor at his office once. But I've never been to his house. Garan, do you know where he lives?"

"No." Garan shook his head. "We could trail him from his office, but—"

"That will take days—time we can't afford." Lorin nodded.

"Exactly." The presence of Hunters in the city was a ticking bomb. Shiasta would find her sooner rather than later. "Besides, the information we're after is likely to be in his office, not at his residence. Knowing him, he's probably going to weasel around and pretend not to remember things. If we catch him at home, he can claim the information I'm after is at his office. Dragging him back through the streets to the office isn't a viable solution, and we won't have an opportunity to talk to him a second time. We only have one shot."

Lorin shrugged and finally sat down, stretching out his long legs. "You and Tarion go in, chat to Duneskal, then leave the same way. Then what?"

"We make sure Duneskal isn't capable of sounding the alarm when we leave—" Lira turned a fierce glare on Garan as he opened his mouth. "No, I'm not going to kill him, not unless I have to. Murdering a mage councillor will bring far too much heat. But we do need to give ourselves time to return here, where you and Lorin will be waiting with the horses, and leave the city. A good old-fashioned knocking out should do."

"You think *assaulting* a mage councillor won't bring heat?" Garan muttered, but there was no fire to it. "These operatives you saw. How much of a danger are they to us?"

"They don't have magic, but they're well-trained fighters." Lira chose not to mention their medallions, which would make Garan and Lorin's mage abilities useless in a fight. "Tarion could handle them, but not you or Lorin, not one on one."

"We should get some rest. It could be a while before we're able to sleep again," Lorin said sensibly. "Even if all goes well tonight and we get out of the city, we'll need to ride a good long distance before stopping."

There seemed to be general agreement to this, and everyone busied themselves stretching out and getting comfortable. Lira stayed near the door, curled up in her blankets against her saddlebag.

"Stop looking so worried, Garan," Tarion murmured sleepily. "We're not going to be fighting anyone. If it comes to that, our mission is already a failure. The goal here is *sneaking*. You know, the thing Lira excels at."

Garan said something in reply, but Lira tuned it out. She turned to face the wall, grateful when someone blew out the lamp so that the room was cast into darkness.

She couldn't stop thinking about Shiasta or ignore the nagging urge to go and find him. She felt responsible for him and his warriors, she had from the moment she'd met them, since she'd understood what they were. What Ahrin was.

Lira promised herself that once she'd dealt with Lucinda, she'd find all the Hunters and make them hers, give them a proper place in the world. With that thought reassuring her, she slipped into sleep.

CHAPTER 12

The Mage Council offices in Karonan took up half a block directly across from the northern boundary of where Shivasa's government offices sprawled over multiple city blocks—where the leader of Shivasa ran his country. Immediately to the west of the council offices sat matching grey buildings housing the army command and their central barracks.

Not the easiest area to sneak into with the intent of accosting a mage councillor.

Lira shifted uncomfortably as she watched the main entrance from across the street and a block down. A half-hour walk of the area had given her a good sense of its layout, but she was uneasy anyway.

Despite her confidence when outlining her intentions to the others, she knew it was a bad idea to go in without a proper plan, without spending at least a week watching her mark and learning Duneskal's habits. How the guards patrolled. When shift change happened. How quickly they noticed or responded to suspicious behaviour nearby.

Instead, she was gambling on Duneskal working at least until dusk, when the dimming light would give her and Tarion some cover. She also had no idea how many guards watched the offices or how many other workers would be in the vicinity of Duneskal's office at this time of day.

There were too many variables. Too much risk. It drastically increased her chances of being caught. At that thought, the thrill stirred in the base of her stomach, the heady rush of danger and death banishing fear of consequences.

She was teetering on the edge of giving into it when Tarion appeared at her side—they'd deliberately travelled separately via different routes. She'd been half worried that he wouldn't show ... but she shouldn't have doubted. It was clear he would do anything for his parents.

"You've been in there before?" she asked him. They'd already spoken of this, but she was trying to remove the look of deep concern on his face by re-focusing his attention on the details.

A tense nod.

"And you know the layout well enough that you can get us directly into his office?"

He flicked her an annoyed look. "I said I could."

"Then let's go. Follow my lead, and whatever you do, don't hesitate or look nervous. We can't afford to draw attention." Lira pushed away from the wall she'd been casually leaning against, and—hands in pockets—strolled down the street separating the government block from the council offices.

Tarion loped at her side, shoulders hunched, eyes downward. She didn't like how recognisable the son of Alyx Egalion would be to those who frequented this part of the city, but wearing a hood drawn low over his face here would only arouse suspicion. They reached a narrow side street between two stone buildings Lira had noticed in her scouting, and she turned into it, relaxing slightly as the dim space enclosed them.

There they lingered, walking at a painfully slow stroll, until the handful of other pedestrians using the alley to cut between offices had emptied out. Lira immediately turned, pointing back to where several unruly weeds had grown up through the cracks in the stone along the edge of one building. Tarion nodded and reached for his bracelets.

When he hesitated, Lira let out an annoyed huff, snapping, "Someone could be along any moment."

His shoulders tensed, but he unlocked both bracelets and crouched to conceal them beneath the weeds. Once they were off, he didn't hesitate any longer. He wrapped an arm around Lira, and instantly her vision blurred, stomach lurching.

She'd barely gasped in a breath before her vision cleared and she found herself standing in a richly appointed room, directly in front of a large, ornate desk. A crackling fire made a soothing harmony with the scratching of the quill being used by the room's occupant.

Duneskal registered their presence a second later.

He leapt upwards, reaching for his staff with his left hand and sending a heavy book from his desk flying at them with a quick gesture of his right. Lira couldn't help but be impressed. Duneskal was a telekinetic mage like her, and his reflexes were commendable.

They just weren't as good as hers.

Lira and Tarion moved as one—Lira summoning a quick burst of magic to set the flying book alight while Tarion swung gracefully toward the office door and closed it before anyone outside could see what was happening.

Frozen halfway to his feet, Duneskal stared, wide-eyed, at the ashes of what had once been his book drifting lazily to the floor. Lira took advantage of his distraction, using another burst of magic to yank the staff from his hand and call it to her own. The wood was warm under her grip, but the residue of its owner's magic made her itch.

"Not a word," she snapped as the mage councillor opened his mouth, presumably to yell for help. "Or it will be you in ashes."

"You wouldn't dare—" Duneskal's arrogant words cut off as the sleeve of his tunic burst into violet-edged white flame. Swearing, he ripped off the tunic and stamped out the flames. She watched in amusement. The urge to strengthen the flames, to overwhelm his ability to put them out, flickered inside her, but after only a brief hesitation, she forced herself to ignore it. She needed this man alive.

"Now," she said evenly, once he was done stamping, "sit down. All I want is a conversation."

Duneskal slowly resumed his seat, watching her the whole time. Thwarted fury twisted his features. She could practically see his mind racing, trying to figure out how he could call for help, raise the alarm somehow.

"Tarion?" she asked, not moving her gaze from the councillor.

"All clear out there." He remained by the door, ready in case anyone tried to come through. "Looks like his clerk has gone home for the day—the desk outside is empty."

"What do you think you're doing, Tarion Caverlock?" Duneskal snapped. "Did you have a hand in breaking her out of jail? If so, you've clearly lost your mind, but it's not too late to fix things."

"Like Lira said. We're just here for a conversation." Tarion's voice was calm, almost flat. He remained with his back to the councillor, attention firmly outside the door.

Duneskal looked between them before his gaze finally settled on Lira, a supercilious look replacing the anger and fear. "I don't know what you think you're going to achieve by this."

Lira shrugged. "I have questions. You're going to answer them. Then we're going to go our separate ways."

He snorted. "You're going straight back to prison."

"I'm curious." She cocked her head. "When did you receive word of my escape?"

"Hours after it happened. We have a telepath mage stationed here."

"And did the message tell you what I did to the Underground cell leader you had imprisoned there on my way out?"

Sweat sheened on his forehead at her words—the first hint of any fear or discomfort he might be feeling—but he merely nodded.

"Good. So you know I'm not issuing empty threats. You tell me what I want to know, and I walk out of here without harming a hair on your head. If you don't..." She poked at the book's ashes with her toe. "Clear?"

His gaze narrowed. "Tarion Caverlock is not going to stand there and watch while you murder a mage councillor, a close friend and ally of his parents. Your threats are empty, Lira Astor."

"Tarion? Maybe you should scout outside, see how many guards or workers are still around," Lira said casually. "Leave us to our conversation."

She didn't look around but heard the door open behind her, and then close softly. Duneskal swallowed, his skin now several shades paler. "What could you possibly want from me?"

"Before I was imprisoned, you were helping Finn A'ndreas with something he was working on. I want to know what the two of you were doing, and if your work is still going on."

Duneskal blinked. Frowned. "Why in all magical—"

"No questions. Just answers."

"A'ndreas is trying to figure out what happened in Rotherburn decades ago—the reason the kingdom and all its people seemed to have vanished without a trace." Duneskal's lack of interest in this was apparent. "If you ask me, there are far more valuable things he could be spending his time on. The man is clever, but seriously, I—"

She cut him off with an impatient, "That's all he wanted your help on?"

"I just said that, didn't I?"

"There's nothing else he's asked you to do these past few years?"

"No."

Lira frowned. She sensed Duneskal was telling the truth—there was no hesitation or prevaricating in his answers. He clearly thought this information was unimportant, so had no qualms over giving it to her. "What did he want you to do exactly?"

"He wanted documents from the council's archive in Carhall—removing them from the library there requires council permission. I signed off on it for him."

"What documents did he want?"

"I barely paid attention at the time and have absolutely no recollection now. Burn me all you like, but I didn't care enough to remember, and those memories aren't going to magically reappear while I'm screaming in pain." Some of Duneskal's fear was fading, the arrogance returning to his voice.

"How many times did you do this for him?"

"Twice. I found the information he wanted, summarised it in a letter, and sent it to him. Then he wanted the originals, so I collected them for him on my next trip to Carhall. After that I told him to do his own research work."

Damn. That was the letter Lira had stolen from A'ndreas' office and handed to Greyson. There had been nothing in there that had seemed interesting to her then. Just old notes. Duneskal wasn't telling her anything new.

"There was absolutely no council business that you and A'ndreas worked on a few years ago? Something to do with Underground ... something discreet, secretive?"

"With A'ndreas?" Duneskal rolled his eyes. "He's not a council member, and all he does is bury himself in old books and teach healing. He's basically useless."

"What about his investigation into my father's identity?" she asked sharply.

He scoffed. "Another rabbit hole he got lost in. Nobody's ever going to find your father—there's nothing to go on. And I personally consider A'ndreas' theory that he's somehow involved in Underground half-baked and unlikely."

Lira hesitated. It all sounded like the truth, and though Duneskal was afraid of her, there was an underlying bemusement to every response he'd given that suggested he had no idea why she was asking these questions. She detected no hint that he was trying to hide anything. Her theory was wrong. There had been no secret council project.

Rotted hells. Which left her firmly at a dead end. Maybe there was something she could salvage from this conversation, though. "Tell me about the council search for me. Where are they looking?"

He smiled thinly. "They know you're in Shivasa."

"And what are they doing about it?"

He hesitated, opened his mouth as if he were about to pompously refuse to answer, but just as she moved to click her fingers, he swallowed and shifted in his chair, lifting his hands in a conciliatory gesture. "I don't know exactly because I'm not involved in organising the search. But I got orders this morning to have mages and Taliath deployed at every entrance to the city to watch for you."

Relief shimmered in her chest—they'd just gotten inside the city in time. "Where else?"

His jaw tightened but he responded after a moment's thought. "Villages in the north that were known to be affiliated with your grandfather. And Dirinan, though parts of that city are practically lawless now and it won't do much good."

That made sense, again suggesting he was telling the truth.

"You haven't asked me about your friends." He cocked his head, sneering at her. "Or are you trying to protect their involvement? We know all about Lorin Hester and Garan Egalion helping you, so don't bother."

Lira let out a genuine snort of amusement. "I don't have friends, and I honestly couldn't care less if your council captures them, or what you do with them. I only care about my own survival."

"A true heir to Shakar Astor." Duneskal smirked. "What exactly is your plan? Keep running until we eventually catch up to you and put you back in prison? You have to know that's an inevitability."

"If you say so." Lira shrugged, glad when her vision shimmered and Tarion reappeared in the room. He gave her a single nod, indicating all was well.

Duneskal's gaze shifted to Tarion. "As soon as you're gone, I'll call in every mage and soldier I can lay my hands on. Neither of you are getting out of this city, but you can still fix this, Tarion. Help me bring her in."

"All I want is to find my parents," Tarion said calmly. "Once that is done, I will hand myself in."

"And you think *she* can help?" Duneskal had forgotten his fear in the depth of his incredulity. "You've lost your mind from grief."

"Oh?" Lira asked coolly. "Because the Mage Council has done so well in finding them. How exactly are you helping your 'trusted friends and allies' from this comfortable office?"

Duneskal's face tightened.

"That's what I thought," she said in contempt. "Don't judge Tarion for something you're not even bothered enough to do yourself."

"We should go," Tarion said in a murmur. "Unless you need anything more from him?"

"Yes, I—" Lira froze, catching something on Duneskal's face, a quick look of triumph.

Rotted carcasses.

Suddenly Duneskal's willingness to answer questions reframed themselves in a new light. He'd been stalling, holding them here ... she was suddenly certain of it.

Tarion stiffened. "Lira? What is it?"

"What did you do?" she snapped at the councillor.

He merely smiled at her.

Running feet sounded outside, coming in their direction. Snarling, Lira turned to Tarion, "They're coming. Get us out of here now!"

He hesitated. "Do we knock him out?"

"There's no point now. Hurry, Tarion!"

"Wait!" Duneskal shot up from his chair, but it was too late.

Tarion wrapped an arm around her waist, the world blurred, and the councillor's coolly arrogant face vanished from sight.

CHAPTER 13

There was already loud shouting coming from the direction of the council offices when they materialised back in the alley. The alarm had been well and truly raised. Tarion nonetheless immediately snapped his bracelets back on. "What happened?"

"Duneskal was stalling—he raised the alarm somehow. Rotted hells I missed it." She swore, furious at Duneskal and herself.

"Then we need to run."

"You need to take those damned bracelets back off and get us clear of this area."

"I can't do that and take the bracelets with me. I won't leave them behind. We run."

She gave him a look but didn't waste time arguing—mages and soldiers would be spreading out to look for them already. They jogged down the alley, only to almost run straight into a unit of Shiven soldiers accompanied by a warrior mage. Abruptly, they changed direction, diving into a busy thoroughfare.

Fortunately the evening streets were full of people, mostly workers leaving to head home or to a bar to enjoy an ale or two. And Duneskal's searchers wouldn't know in which direction they'd gone. Still ... they weren't getting through the city gates now. They'd be locked up tight before Lira and Tarion got anywhere near the inn where Garan and Lorin waited.

They were trapped in Karonan.

Lira swore. Tried to focus on the most immediate problem first. "Have you got your mental shields up?" she snapped at Tarion as she made sure to reinforce her own. Taught by the most powerful telepath mage alive, Lira's were impregnable when she focused.

"Telepaths can't find me while I'm wearing these," he said calmly, lifting his wrists. "You think that's how he raised the alarm?"

"He's not a telepath, and the odds of a telepath contacting him right as we were talking to him are slim, but I can't think of a better explanation. He didn't move from that desk the whole time. I think we just got very unlucky."

Tarion glanced at her. "If that's the case, they'll struggle to track us now that we're clear, but..."

"Garan's always had a lazy mental shield and Lorin doesn't know to be wary. If the telepath is strong..."

"They'll find them," Tarion said with grim certainty. "Magical hells. We have to get to them first or they'll be captured."

That inn was where her grandfather's sword, not to mention all her supplies, were. She couldn't abandon either, which meant she couldn't abandon Garan and Lorin. Stinking fish carcasses!

They both increased their pace but couldn't move too quickly or they'd look out of place amidst other pedestrians. Lira slowed them as they approached the Feather Duster. Nothing looked out of place. No mage warriors were visible, no soldiers or city guards.

"Maybe it wasn't a telepath," Tarion murmured.

"Or at least not a strong one," she said. "Let's hurry. If we've gotten lucky, then we tell Garan and Lorin to focus on their shielding and we relocate somewhere safer."

Inside the Feather Duster, she and Tarion went straight up the back stairs to their room.

"What happened?" Garan asked the moment they opened the door, clearly reading the looks on their faces.

"Duneskal sounded the alarm somehow—we think a telepath," Tarion blurted. "Get your shields up now! Both of you."

Garan paled but closed his eyes and took a deep breath. Lorin did the same. Lira scanned the room—their saddlebags were buckled up, everything waited neat and ready. The inn was on the opposite side of the city from the government quarter, but Lira fully expected the entire city's detachment of mages and warriors would already be spreading throughout the city, and if a telepath was leading them, they could already be on their way to the inn.

"Let's go," she snapped, picking up her duffel and saddlebags.

"Where?" Garan was admirably calm. "We won't make it out of the city gates now."

"Another inn, a long way from here. We hunker down there, give ourselves time and space to come up with a plan. You and Lorin concentrate on holding your shields; Tarion and I will lead the way and watch out for danger."

Without waiting for a response—honestly, she'd be just as happy if they refused to follow her—she turned and hauled open the door.

There Fari Dirsk stood, shoulders square, arms crossed over her chest.

Lira moved, magic already flaring to life, a snarl ripping from her, but Tarion was faster. He wrapped an arm around her, yanking her sideways before her magic could leap out to engulf Fari in flame. Unprepared for his attack, she stumbled, and they both crashed to the ground in a tangle of limbs and bags.

By the time she furiously shoved him off her and regained her feet, flame flaring to life in both hands, Fari had entered the room and Garan was slumped, unconscious, in the corner. That sight was just incongruous enough to stay Lira's hand.

"What—" Lira started, but Fari cut her off.

"Lord-Mage Dawn A'ndreas is in the city, and she's had a telepathic lock on Garan since Duneskal raised the alarm. He's her son, he can't shield against her, even if he was good at it," she said crisply. "I knocked him out to break the connection, but they're already on the way. If you want to get out of the city, you'll have to come with me right now."

"Shouldn't you knock Lorin out too?" Tarion asked.

Lorin opened his mouth to protest, but Fari shook her head. "You can't carry both of them, so we'll have to rely on Lord-Mage A'ndreas not knowing Lorin well enough to be able to recognise his mind while it's shielded."

There was a moment of stunned silence, then Fari unfolded her arms and clapped her hands. "Now means now!"

Lorin and Tarion glanced at each other, then moved over to Garan's prone form, hauling him up between them, one of Garan's arms slung around each of their shoulders. Both men grunted from the strain.

Fari lifted an eyebrow at Lira when she didn't follow.

Lira shook her head. "You think I'm going to trust you, just like that? You're bait in the trap, Fari Dirsk."

Fari shrugged. "Then stay. I'm here to help them, not you."

She turned and walked out. Lorin and Tarion followed, Tarion throwing a look at Lira over his shoulder. "You gave me your word."

"I didn't give my word to walk straight into a trap."

His face tightened, but he didn't stop. In a moment, the door swung closed behind them.

It was in the moment after the door swung shut that Lira realised Fari hadn't been wearing a mage cloak—instead she'd been wearing traditional Shiven shirt and breeches, with healer's guild patches decorating the arms of her winter jacket. Then she ran through her chances of getting out of Karonan without help. And thought about how Fari hadn't made any effort to get Lira to come with them.

"Rotted shitting carcasses," she swore aloud.

And she ran after them.

Fari was shepherding them out the back door of the inn when Lira caught up, bags slung over each shoulder. She didn't look surprised to see Lira appear, and merely said, "Follow me and stay quiet."

Lira half expected to walk out the door into an ambush of mage warriors and Taliath, but the street was empty. Fari turned left, slowing her pace so that Lorin and Tarion could keep up. A few curious glances came their way, but as soon as they saw the patches on Fari's arm, the glances turned to amusement or scorn.

Just another drunk being taken to the healing centre.

The walk was a little too long for Lira's comfort—she felt extremely vulnerable every moment they were on the open streets—and for Lorin's and Tarion's fading strength. But eventually Fari steered them through a few narrower streets that led to an alley at the back of one of the city's healing centres.

She opened the back door without hesitation, then waited for them to walk in before closing it and gesturing down a set of steps to their immediate right. "Quick, before someone sees you."

A dim hallway at the base of the steps led away to left and right. Fari steered them to the left, taking them all the way to the end before unlocking the door there and waving them through.

Lira hesitated before going inside, but it just looked like an old storeroom, dusty and unused.

"Nobody comes down here," Fari said as she closed the door behind them. "So we're safe for now."

"They'll find us anywhere eventually if Dawn A'ndreas is here. We have to get out of the city," Lira rounded on her.

"I can get you out, but not until morning," she said calmly, going over to check on Garan. At Tarion's worried look, she smiled. "He's fine, just getting a good rest."

"Why in rotted hells are you helping us?" Lira demanded. "And why aren't you a mage?"

Fari lifted an eyebrow. "I'm sorry, at what point did I indicate a willingness to happily answer all your high-handed demands."

Lira's lip curled, her anger turning her words to ice. "I trust you no more than I trust them, and as far as I'm concerned you turned up at an awfully convenient moment. You explain, to my satisfaction, how you're not betraying me, or I will burn you where you stand."

Fari paled, taking a step back and looking genuinely afraid. Lira tried to ignore the guilt she felt at that. Fari had betrayed her just as thoroughly as everyone in this room—and she most, of all of them, had pretended to be Lira's friend.

Tarion stepped toward the healer. "Lira, enough. If Fari wanted to betray us, she wouldn't have brought us here."

"Stay out of this." Lira lifted her hand. "I'm not messing around."

"I'm not a mage because I failed my Trials," Fari said flatly. "I work here. I was at Temari Hall—part of a usual weekly lesson with Master A'ndreas—when his sister arrived. I overheard their conversation and came to help."

"Why?"

Fari's eyes glittered. "That's all you're getting, Lira Astor. Burn me or not, it's up to you, but none of you are getting out of this city without me."

"It's rather convoluted if this is a trap," Tarion pointed out. "They had us back at the inn—why use Fari to draw us here? And even if they did, why weren't they waiting here to grab us?"

All good points. But at least she could trust Tarion and Garan's desire to find Egalion and her husband, even if she couldn't trust them with anything else. Lorin's addition to the group had been a complication, and Fari showing up ... that was now two people whose motives she didn't understand. Two people she couldn't turn her back on.

But for the moment she had no better choice.

So she shrugged and lowered her hands. Fari snorted, then turned to face the others, hands on hips. "Somebody better tell me what's going on, right now."

By the time Tarion had relayed the full story to Fari, and no mages had come bursting through the door to capture them, Lira decided Fari could be trusted. For now. So she filled them all in on her conversation with Duneskal.

"Are you sure he was telling the truth?" Lorin asked.

"I'm as sure as I can be," Lira said.

"So much for that theory." Tarion ran a hand through his hair, a look of despair on his face. "Uncle Finn isn't working on some secret project for the council. Maybe I'm wrong about Underground being behind this," he said miserably. "Maybe we should just give ourselves in and help the council with their search."

Fari rolled her eyes. "Giving yourself up won't help with anything. At worst, you'll be sharing Lira's cell in prison. At best, you'll be expelled from the council and kept under close watch. You're lucky I came to help your sorry behinds or you'd be on your way there already."

"Why did you?" Tarion asked quietly. "You don't owe us anything. If you help us leave the city tomorrow, you'll be in just as much trouble as the rest of us."

Fari was silent a long moment, contemplating her hands as if they held the secrets to the universe. "Councillor Egalion was the only councillor who voted that I should pass my Trials. She fought to convince the others."

"But Uncle Tarrick overruled her," Tarion said, his head coming up as if just remembering. "The Tylender-Dirsk family rivalry."

"And when that happened, you spoke to Master A'ndreas and asked him to keep teaching me so I could help the non-mage healers here. And Garan sent me enough money to make sure I could afford somewhere to live until I started getting wages because my family cut me off."

For a moment Lira was almost warmed by this, but in an instant, it turned into corrosive anger. "It's nice to know you and Garan looked out for some of your friends," she said coldly.

"I wasn't a murdering traitor, so there is that," Fari said.

Lira merely looked way. She wasn't any more inclined to defend herself to Fari than she was to the others.

"Back to the original conversation. Fari is right," Lorin said gravely. "If you want to keep looking for your parents, Tarion, we have to stay free."

A heavy silence descended.

"Lorin, Fari, I can't ask you to do any more," Tarion said. "If you leave now, we'll tell the council you had nothing to do with this and it was all me and Garan."

"That won't work, and you know it. If Lord-Mage A'ndreas has been in Garan's head, then she knows everything." Lorin shrugged. "If we can't leave till morning, it's probably a good idea to get some rest."

"Aunt Dawn doesn't know about your involvement, Fari," Tarion said quietly.

Fari hesitated, glancing between them all before lingering on Lira for a long moment. Lira scowled in response. For some reason, that made Fari smile and shrug, "I made my decision already. It's too late to back out now. I'll get us out of the city tomorrow, but then what?"

They all looked at Lira. She shook her head. "With Dawn A'ndreas in the city, I'm not telling any of you a thing. We have to assume she's already read everything Garan knew. Once we're clear of the city, I'll tell you my plan."

She just hoped by then she'd actually *have* a plan.

CHAPTER 14

The day's activity in the healing centre above was already beginning by the time Fari came to fetch them. Footsteps overhead, the occasional thump, one man crying out in pain—it all filtered down through the ceiling.

When Fari opened the door, they were all tense, with only Garan slumbering peacefully in the corner. "I've got everything ready to go, but Lira, I'm going to need your help."

"With what?" she asked suspiciously.

"A diversion," Fari said. "The guards on the city gates are accustomed to seeing me—or the other healers here—escorting patients who are particularly unwell over to Temari Hall to receive treatment from Master A'ndreas and his apprentices."

Tarion brightened. "That's how you're getting us out."

"Right. You, Garan, and Lira are going to be patients in the back of our transport cart, and Lorin will be my driver, given he looks like a local. You'll all be wearing these." Fari tossed them each a cloth mask. "My story will be that I'm taking you to Master A'ndreas because I'm worried you have a highly infectious fever and want a second opinion."

"But getting us all into the cart unseen will be impossible with everyone wandering around up there, so you need a diversion," Lira said, impressed by the woman's carefully thought-out plan. "I can do that."

"Good. The cart is drawn up by the entrance we came in last night—it's kept there for emergencies during the day. Lira, we'll wait for you to start the diversion, then get Garan into the cart. Any questions?"

There were none.

"Then let's move." Fari opened the door for them.

"You gonna tell us what that is at any point?" Tarion asked Lira as she slung her saddlebag over her shoulder then bent to pick up the duffel holding Shakar's sword. Her shoulders groaned in complaint.

"Maybe." She shrugged and headed for the door.

At the base of the stairs, Fari waved Lira up. Glad that she didn't have to trust this plan to anything but her own skills and instincts, Lira nodded without hesitation.

The hall at the top of the stairs was momentarily clear, so she turned back to wave Fari and the others up, then put down her bags. Carefully, she padded along the hall to where it ended at another, wider, corridor. A small group of people were gathered around the corner to her right, pointing to something in another room and having what looked to be a disagreement. To her left the hall was clear.

She'd first thought to simply use her flame magic to start a fire and cause a distraction that way—problem being it was a violet-edged white in colour and risked someone realising it was a mage at work, and not an accidental fire.

So she'd planned for something a little more complex.

Settling back against the wall, eyes closing, she sank into her magic, using it to seek out the water running through a rudimentary piping system from an underground well into what she guessed was probably a washer-room for all the healing centre's linens. She'd mapped it out already while the others had been sleeping, then spent a long, exhausting hour using telekinesis to loosen the screws holding two sections of the pipe together.

Now all that was necessary was a sharp burst of her magic to yank the pipes apart and tear loose some of the ceiling tiles directly beneath.

Almost immediately she sensed the rushing flow of water as it flooded from both ends of the pipe and cascaded into the room below. A cry sounded, then running feet. She glanced around the corner—the group of healers were already disappearing in the direction of the flood. Their shouts echoed through the halls, hopefully drawing in anyone else who was around.

Grinning, Lira ran for the back door, grabbing her bags on the way. Garan was already lying in the back of the cart, Tarion clambering in beside him. Lorin now wore a jacket similar to Fari's and sat beside her in the driver's seat, reins in hand. The two horses hitched to the cart snorted at the sudden activity around them but otherwise made no protest. Presumably they were used to emergency trips to and from the healing centre.

Lira didn't hesitate to toss her saddlebag and duffel in, then clamber up to lie flat beside Tarion. She tied the mask around her face, pulled the covering blanket up as far as her neck, made sure it covered her bags too, then lifted a hand to signal that she was ready.

The cart immediately lurched into movement.

"Stay quiet, no matter what happens. If you hear someone approaching the cart, feign sleep," Fari called quietly. "Let me do all the talking."

While seeing the sense in Fari's words, Lira ill-liked lying vulnerable and still in the back of a cart, unable to see around her. Beside her, Tarion seemed utterly relaxed, while Garan snored softly. The masks hid most of their features, and what was visible was scruffy and dirty from weeks of travel.

It was clear when they approached the northern causeway gates, both from the sudden slowing of their progress, but also the crisp shouts of the guards ordering people to stop and submit to a search.

An interminable period passed, then suddenly Fari called out cheerfully, "Hey, Tellin. Nice to see you again."

"It's always a pleasure, Fari." He sounded thrilled to see her. Lira almost rolled her eyes—did he have a *crush* on the healer? "Another bad one?"

"They're actually not doing too badly, but all three had an odd rash appear overnight, and they're experiencing similar symptoms. I want to get Master A'ndreas' opinion and make sure we don't have anything infectious on our hands. You know how bad that could get in a city like this where everyone is packed so close together. Do you think you can wave me through?"

"I hope it's not what you think." He sounded horrified. "I won't come too close, just in case. Come on around. Hadins up top will let you through."

The cart lurched, and then their speed increased again. It wasn't long before a stiff breeze swept over the cart.

They were on the causeway.

"Fari Dirsk, you're a genius," Tarion murmured.

Lira was inclined to agree. A moment later, she risked pushing back the sheet and poking her head up a fraction. They were well out along the causeway, the northern gates of Karonan fading from sight behind them. A large carriage trundled a good distance behind them, but the line of people and vehicles looking to enter Karonan was slowed to a walking pace—the searching was slowing the amount of traffic able to move in and out of the city.

"Stay down," Fari murmured. "We don't want an idle glance to recognise one of you, and don't forget how far someone in Temari tower can see."

Warning heeded, they all stayed still and silent until a short time later, Fari called out. "All right, we're out of sight of the city and Temari," Fari reported. "You can sit up."

"We can't stay on the main road," Lira said instantly.

Fari merely rolled her eyes and pointed to an upcoming crossing, the main road continuing north while a smaller dirt road snaked out toward the west. Lorin took the turn, and soon trees closed in around them.

Nobody suggested waking Garan up—Dawn A'ndreas' telepathic strength was formidable and could likely still find him until they were at least several more hours away.

"Where do we go from here?" Lorin asked.

"We put as much distance as we can between us and Karonan before nightfall. Then we abandon the cart, make camp a good distance from it, *then* we plan," Lira said decidedly. "We're still too close to A'ndreas."

When darkness fell, they abandoned the cart in a ditch, covered it with brush, then took the two horses and struck off on foot over the countryside. Lira finally allowed them to stop just after midnight when Lorin spotted a disused old barn at the edge of a farming property. They didn't risk a fire but left the horses loosely tethered to graze and settled down inside with all the blankets they had. The night had turned bitterly cold.

Fari awoke Garan with a touch, and it took several minutes and lots of explanation from Tarion before he calmed down enough to listen to the full story of what had happened. Once they'd finished, his expression wavered between fury at what they'd done and overwhelming guilt. Eventually his shoulders sagged. "What Mama must think of me right now."

"I'm so sorry, Gar." Tarion looked just as guilty. "If you want to go back…"

"No." He shook his head. "It's too late now. Besides, I can only hope she read everything in my head, that she knows my intentions are good. Maybe she'll even try to convince the council that we're right about Underground kidnapping Uncle Dash and Aunt Alyx."

"Your hope is misplaced," Lira said sharply, remembering that night, Dawn A'ndreas leaving her to rot in prison. "She'll never believe Tarrick Tylender is a traitor."

A weary silence fell then, as if everyone was too exhausted to know where to begin discussing what to do next. It was Tarion that spoke first, almost hesitant. "I wasn't wrong, Garan. Not about Underground still being active. We know they are now, at least in Shivasa."

"No you don't." Garan rubbed a tired hand over his face. "Just because Lira spotted some of their operatives lurking around, even if she *is* telling the truth—"

"I *don't* know anything for certain," she said sharply. "Despite what you all think, I did not remain on Underground's membership roster after being imprisoned. I haven't seen the latest updates on their plans. But I am pretty sure."

"Maybe so, but you *are* keeping things from us," Fari pointed out.

"And that surprises you?" Lira countered. "Why would I trust you with anything?"

"What next?" Lorin interceded before an argument could develop. "If Duneskal was a dead end, then what do we do now?"

Silence fell. Nobody had an answer. Lira's thoughts returned to the tangle she'd been dwelling on throughout the day since leaving Karonan. Trying to decide whether it was time to leave them now, make her own way. She'd be better able to lose any pursuit on her own and they had nothing further to offer her.

It would be easy enough, too. She'd just wait until they all slept and slip out into the night. She'd be miles away before they even realised she was gone.

Problem was—she had no idea *where* to go.

Before she could come to a final decision, Tarion spoke, his thoughtful gaze on Lira. "Underground's interest in the letter from Duneskal to Uncle Finn ... are you sure that was serious and not just a way of testing your loyalty to them?"

"It was impossible to be sure of the truth where Lucinda was concerned, but my read was that yes, they were serious in their interest. And it's too much of a coincidence that they had the Darkhand spying on A'ndreas too." Lira rubbed at tired eyes. There *were* no coincidences where Lucinda was concerned, but it felt like an increasingly thin theory to rely upon, especially after her encounter with Duneskal—she was confident he'd not been lying. Problem was, without that theory she had nothing.

"Okay," Tarion said, "then let's assume you were right, Lira, and follow that logic to its simplest conclusion. There must be some aspect of Uncle Finn's project on Rotherburn that interested the

Shadowcouncil—we've established he wasn't working on anything else."

"What would the Shadowcouncil care about what happened to the people of Rotherburn?" Lorin said flatly. "We must be missing something else."

"What if we're not?" Tarion said patiently. "You're right: it doesn't make sense. But maybe that oddity is the key to everything ... we figure out why Underground is so interested in Rotherburn, and maybe we find the answers we need."

"That's an enormous reach," Garan said flatly, but then sighed and ran an agitated hand through his hair. "But I don't see what else we can do."

Lira felt very much the same way as Garan. She couldn't see why Lucinda would give a rotted carcass about A'ndreas researching Rotherburn, nor how figuring it out would help them find Egalion and Caverlock and what remained of Underground, but she had no other ideas. "Same here."

Fari lifted an eyebrow at Lira. "Does this mean you want to go back to Temari Hall and talk to Master A'ndreas?"

Lira shook her head. "He'll just tell us the same thing Duneskal did; details of his project on Rotherburn. It won't tell us *why* Underground is so interested in it."

"What else do we do, then?" Lorin asked.

"As the newest member of this rogue outfit, I'm inclined to think you never should have started in the first place without a better plan." Fari sniffed.

"You and me both," Lira snorted, speaking without thinking.

Fari flashed her a quick look, like she was surprised, and Lira immediately closed her expression.

Garan looked thoughtful. "What if we go to the archives in Carhall? We can..."

Lira tuned out their back-and-forth discussion, thinking through what Tarion had said. In any situation, the simplest explanation was often the right one—maybe she'd been a fool for dismissing it all this time. Assuming the Shadowcouncil's interest *was* in A'ndreas' project, to the degree that they'd placed their Darkhand at Temari to spy on him, then Rotherburn must impact them in some way, or be somehow critical to their interests, or...

Lira stilled. Thought about the razak, Lucinda's oddities, the too-neat and too-well-rehearsed explanations for what the Shadowcouncil's goals were. What if—

No. Lira shook her head; she was being fantastical. Surely it was too crazy. But still...

Her thoughts raced. There was one sure-fire way of figuring out whether her insane idea was right, and it had the advantage of moving them all well away from Karonan and any pursuit.

The downside was, to do this, she'd need a lot more than two mages, a healer, and a princess-consort—and she definitely couldn't do it alone. She'd have to stick with them for now. But it was highly unlikely the others would go for it. It only offered a slim chance of finding their precious missing mages. Also, it was crazy, and if she was wrong—which she probably was—she'd be wasting a lot of time and effort. Again. Her credibility was already strained with them after the Duneskal failure.

But what else did *she* have but time?

"Lira?" Tarion's voice broke her from her thoughts. "You've got an idea."

She hesitated only briefly. "We should go to Dirinan next. We need resources, and there might be someone there who can help us with that."

"Who?" Garan asked.

"Resources for what?" Fari asked at the same time.

"I'll tell you when we get there."

Garan's mouth thinned. "I've had enough with all the secrets, Lira. I'm not going anywhere unless I know why."

"Have I steered you wrong yet?" she challenged without thinking, then winced as the words came out.

"Only because you needed us. Don't think for a second I believe you'll hold to your word. We're useful to you, and you're only going to stick around as long as that keeps being the case."

"I—"

"So if you need us, then you need to convince me to come along with you." He crossed his arms over his chest.

Tarion's gaze flickered to Garan, and he opened his mouth as if to argue, but then closed it.

Lira's mouth curled in a snarl. She was so close to walking out her legs tensed, ready to push her to her feet. But then Fari chuckled, diverting her anger. "Ooh, he's got you nailed. And I'm going to side with him on this one. I'm willing to help Tarion and Garan, but I don't trust you for a second, Lira Astor."

"Then why did you break her out of prison?" Lorin asked Garan, surprising Lira. "If you're going to keep suspecting her every step of the way, then you should have just left her in there and done this on your own."

"I wasn't the one who wanted to break her out," Garan said stubbornly.

"Oh, I'm sorry," Lira snapped at Garan. "You thought I escaped jail, willingly remained with you elitist snobs, and endured talking to Mister Supercilious for fun? At this point, you can trust that I want to find Underground as badly as you do."

"Why?" Fari wanted to know.

"None of your business."

There was a moment's charged silence, then, "There's certainly an argument to be made that coming all the way to Karonan and threatening a council member was rather useless and got us nowhere," Tarion spoke in his quiet way. "Not to mention the longer we're on the run like this, the more council warriors, city guards, soldiers, and Taliath will be out looking for us. The amount of time we have to wander around looking for clues is shrinking rapidly. Now, trustworthy or not, Lira says she has a plan. Does anybody more trustworthy have an alternative to offer?"

A moment's silence fell as everyone stared at Tarion. Lira was grudgingly impressed—mostly by how many words he'd strung together without staring at his shoes—but supressed that and crossed her arms over her chest defiantly.

Garan let out a breath and shrugged. "Fine. We'll go to Dirinan. This is it though. If it doesn't pan out, we hand ourselves in. Lira, you can do as you like."

He looked defeated rather than accepting, and it made Lira feel bad for him for a moment. She gave him a glare. "Suits me just fine." Then she turned away, curling up on the floor. "We should get a couple of hours sleep then get moving at dawn before whoever runs this farm wakes up and finds us."

Nobody disputed that, and for a few moments the barn echoed with the rustling of blankets and stifled yawns, then the steady breathing of its occupants. Lira lay awake in the dark, gaze distant.

Returning to Dirinan after all these years.

Even now, she racked her brains, trying to think of some other option. But the only other one she could think of was tracking down Shiasta and following that lead to Underground—but finding him in a city as large as Karonan would take days, if not weeks, and by early tomorrow the city guard would be combing the streets for her. They couldn't go back there.

Not to mention trying to convince a highly trained Hunter to do what she wanted would be nigh on impossible.

No, if she wanted Underground, this was the only viable option. She sighed.

The last time she'd left Dirinan she'd been fifteen years old, abandoned by her crew, and hated by multiple rival gangs. This likely wasn't going to end well at all.

CHAPTER 15

The second largest city in Shivasa after Karonan, Dirinan sprawled outwards for miles in every direction from the harbour that saw the highest amount of shipping traffic on the continent.

This had been Lira's home from five years old to fifteen, the place she'd grown up in. Yet she hadn't been back since leaving for Temari Hall five years earlier. And since leaving, she hadn't allowed herself think about it very often. Had intended to *never* return.

Dirinan and her life there had been something she'd had to bury away in a box so that she could fit into the mould of what they wanted from her at Temari Hall. To fit in as a mage apprentice. And like a fool she'd worked tirelessly to force herself to be what they wanted because she'd thought it was the only way to make them accept her, the heir to the Darkmage, and see her as *Lira*, not Shakar.

That desperate hope had been fractured on her first arrival at Temari Hall, then had crumbled into a million pieces the day the council had locked her away in prison in Carhall for the rest of her life. But along with the death of that hope had come the freedom of no longer needing to pretend to be something she wasn't.

Now the sight of Dirinan in the distance brought a rush of homesickness that hit her with the force of a punch to the gut. Tears pricked her eyes. This place had welcomed her in its own rough way, had never pretended to be anything other than what it was, had been the only place in her entire life she'd experienced what contentment was.

She'd spent a long time thinking that contentment had just been an illusion, cruelly ripped away when Ahrin suddenly abandoned Lira and their crew—which had then precipitated Lira's departure and travel to Temari Hall. But it hadn't been an illusion after all. Not in the way she'd believed. Underground had taken that life from her, just like they'd taken everything else.

The thought of Ahrin, combined with the sight of Dirinan, had Lira's carefully buried grief and despair threatening to rise up and overwhelm her, so she quickly dismissed the Darkhand from her thoughts. If Ahrin was part of Egalion's kidnapping, if she'd truly gone back to Underground, then Lira would find out eventually. She would figure out what to do about it if or when that happened—and the longer off that was the better.

"This is a rough place." Lorin had ridden up beside her—they'd purchased three more horses two days out of Karonan—but his voice was low, so the others couldn't hear. Shiven-born and raised in a poor farming family, Lorin knew well what kind of city Dirinan was. She couldn't help the quick glance at her saddlebags as his horse shifted even closer, where her grandfather's sword was bundled amidst her other things. Nobody had asked about it since Tarion's query in Karonan, and she hoped they wouldn't for a little while longer. She could do without their inevitable freak out about it.

"Parts of it are, yes. But's it's also a thriving industrial and merchant city." It was that fact that drew the criminal overlords like Transk in like bees to honey. She forced her attention to Lorin and gestured to the others. "Worried they might get some dirt on their fine clothes?"

He glanced away, not able to entirely hide his smile. She hated that he understood, didn't want reminders of how she'd once believed them to be friends. How good that had felt. Anger surged. They'd never been friends; they'd walked away and abandoned her.

As long as it had been, Lira still remembered the streets like the back of her hand, even the tidier, richer area they entered after passing through the outskirts. Gaze ceaselessly roving their surroundings—her default behaviour inside this city—she led them to an unremarkable quarter that contained several lodging houses and inns.

"It's getting dark." Garan glanced up at the sky. "We should find an inn, settle down for the night."

Lira shot him a look. "Night-time is best for what I'm looking to do. But yes, we need somewhere to leave the horses and our things."

He opened his mouth as if to protest but seemed to think better of it and said nothing. She chose an inn that looked busy but was set back on a quieter street where there wasn't much foot traffic. She instantly felt better as they turned off the main road, not liking to have so many eyes on them. Still, nobody said anything or looked suspicious of their presence.

Garan organised for their horses to be stabled, and they convened in the room he, Tarion, and Lorin would share. By then it was dark outside. Lira's fingers curled and uncurled at her sides, no matter how many times she tried to still them. That lid she'd placed firmly over her emotions kept popping open and banging shut, like a bubbling pot.

She was excited to be here, couldn't wait to get out on the streets again. A foolish part wanted to just leave them now, forget about Underground, go back to the harbour and find a crew to run with. Do what she and Ahrin had always wanted to do.

But no … that could never be her again. She was Lira Astor, a mage, and she had scores to settle. That life wasn't for her anymore. She supposed it never had been hers.

"I need you all to stay here in your rooms and out of sight. Have a servant bring food up to you if you get hungry," she told them. "I'm going out, but I'll be back in a couple of hours."

Garan protested immediately. "You're not going anywhere on your own."

"And you and what army is going to stop me?" she asked coolly.

He surprised her when, rather than getting angry, he took a deep breath and visibly calmed himself. "You're right. I can't keep assuming the worst of you. Either you'll betray us or you won't, but at the end of the day I just want to find my uncle and aunt. Do what you need to do. We'll be good children and stay out of sight."

"Thank you." She hesitated, softened enough by his sincerity to offer, "I'm just doing some scouting to find the man we need to talk to, that's all." She held out a hand. "I'm going to need some coin."

Mouth drawn tight, he slid a hand into his tunic and passed her a handful of gold coins. "That's all I've got left."

She rolled her eyes—it was way more than what she needed—and handed back most of it. "If I don't reappear by morning, leave this inn, find a nicer one in the wealthier district, and wait a day. If I still don't show up, assume I'm dead and that you're in danger. You'll be on your own then."

"You're saying that the man you're going to ask for help from might kill you?" Fari lifted an eyebrow. "Good to know."

"I think we've already established that handing ourselves over to the council without my parents isn't a viable plan," Tarion said quietly. "So if you could do your best not to die, that would be appreciated."

"I know how to move in a place like this if you need some backup," Lorin offered.

"I don't," Lira said flatly, then she left.

She took the back stairs down to the kitchen and then through to where the inn workers' room was. Loitering in the shadows until it was empty, she ducked inside, opened one of the lockers, and rifled through until she found what she needed. Bundling it up under her arm, she slipped out the back door.

As expected, the inn backed onto a muddy, smelly alleyway. She took a deep breath, smiled, then set off.

Two blocks away from the inn, she turned onto a dim street, unfolded the ratty cloak she'd stolen, and shrugged it on over her shoulders. Then she un-braided her hair, shook it out, ran her fingers through it to make it messy. She looked different—older, better fed—than the last time she'd run the streets here, but she wanted to go unrecognised for as long as possible, so she drew the hood up over her head.

Then, cutting through back lanes and alleys of the merchant quarter—Silver Lord territory—she made her way steadily towards the harbour district; the patch controlled by the Revel Kings. A gang run by one of the most powerful crime bosses in Dirinan. Or at least he had been, five years ago.

Was Transk still undisputed leader down here, or had one of his rival crew bosses elbowed in on his territory? She doubted it. Transk hadn't been particularly old when she'd left, and he'd been a cunning and powerful man who held his crew's loyalty with an iron grip. He'd had expansion plans, too. No, if anything he was probably even more powerful now than he had been then.

And if she wanted to know whether her fanciful theory about Lucinda and the Shadowcouncil was right, she was going to need more than just the dwindling store of coin that Garan had. The only place she could think to get those kinds of resources without coming to the attention of the council was via underhanded means.

Transk would remember her, no doubt—Ahrin's crew had been one of his most daring and successful—but would he be willing to do her a favour? Not likely. She was going to have to make a deal, offer something substantial in return for his assistance. Making a deal with Transk that she couldn't guarantee making good on was beyond dangerous—his reach was wider than just the port city he ruled—but there was no other way to get this thing done. Lira shrugged. Anything was worth bringing Lucinda down.

Her knowledge of Transk's haunts was years old, so she headed for a bar in the harbour district where she was confident she'd find people inside who'd know how to access him.

Lira felt better than she had since breaking out of prison as she slipped through the streets of her old home. The unnameable despair wasn't gone, nor the crippling fear of re-capture, but she felt at home in her skin here. Comfortable at the prospect of a simple transaction where trust wasn't required, because nobody expected you to trust.

An hour-long walk brought her to a wide street across from a dilapidated but busy tavern. An earlier snowfall had turned the ground under her feet to slushy mud. The air was thick with the scents of salty ocean, seaweed, and refuse. She breathed deeply as she hovered in the shadows of the street and scanned the rooftops and corners within her range of view.

It didn't take long to clock the two spotters on corner rooftops and a runner loitering on the opposite corner, clearly keeping an eye on the entrance. Good. That meant the tavern was still one of Revel Kings' businesses.

As Lira approached the place, she appeared just like a denizen of these streets, her gaze watchful, shoulders slightly hunched. Stride confident enough to deter random attack, but not too confident to provoke a challenge.

It was easier than anything had been since the day she'd left these streets at fifteen.

The interior was no brighter than the street outside and smelled strongly of sweat, urine, and cheap ale. The curious gazes of the tavern's clientele flicked to her, assessing for threat, and moved away just as quickly when they saw nothing to make them suspicious.

Lira crossed to the bar, leaned against it rather than sitting on a stool, and kept a watchful eye as she waited for the barman to finish serving three men further along before coming to her.

"What can I getcha?" A tall, bearded man with intricate tattoos snaking out of the short sleeves of his shirt, he didn't seem to find her out of place. While he waited for her answer, he tugged a cloth from his belt and began wiping dry one of several empty glasses piled up nearby.

"Information." She leaned over the bar and dropped a single gold coin on its sticky surface. Then she lowered her voice, her voice slipping back into the rougher drawl she'd picked up on the streets. "Looking for Transk. Where's he at these days?"

Mingled fear and wariness flashed over the man's face and his gaze darted towards the back room, then back to the coin. He finished wiping clean the glass in his hands and carefully put it down.

"I'm not looking to hurt him, and this won't come back on you," she promised, though he'd be a fool to believe her. "I used to run in one of his crews, but I've been away for a while. I'm keen to get back in is all."

His hand flashed out to take the coin. It disappeared into a pocket in his apron, and he cast a casual glance around the bar. "Transk isn't the man running the docks anymore."

Rotted carcasses! Inwardly, Lira's heart sank, but she kept a curious look on her face, voice light and interested. "Really? Someone pushed him off the top spot?"

"Yup. Almost two years back now. He's long dead. Rotting at the bottom of the harbour, they say, though nobody knows for sure."

Lira considered that, then dropped a second coin on the bar top. If Transk had been deposed, then it had been done by either one of his lieutenants or a rival boss, either of whom would hopefully have at least heard of her. She could make a deal with them just as easily. "You have a name? A place I can find the new boss man?"

It surprised her when he hesitated rather than reaching out to take it. "New boss isn't one to be crossed."

"Like Transk was?" Lira barked a laugh. "I told you, this won't come back on you. I'm looking to make friends, not enemies. All I'm after is work."

"It's not me I'm worried about."

Lira scowled, leaned farther over the bar top. "Let's not pretend you give two coppers about my welfare. I'm offering you good coin for information. What happens to me after is no concern of yours."

He shrugged and reached out to take the coin. "It's your neck. The new boss used to run one of his crews. Ahrin Vensis."

A brief moment to freeze, that name ringing through her head, then...

Before even realising what she was doing, Lira had leaned across the bar, grabbed the man's shirt with both hands and yanked him forward. "Are you messing with me?"

"Why would I do that?" he asked in bewilderment, too astonished at being accosted by a slip of a girl to think about fighting back. No wonder he was running the bar rather than working for a crew.

"Where can I find her?" She tightened her grip when he didn't seem inclined to answer.

"Transk's old gambling hall," he gasped out.

Lira leaned closer, holding his gaze, and spoke so only he could hear. "Anyone learns I was in here asking about Transk *or* Vensis, I'm coming back to you. We clear?"

He swallowed, nodded, real fear flashing into his eyes.

She let him go, stood back from the bar, and sent a quelling glance around the room, one hand fingering the hilt of her knife. Then, she turned and strode out.

Three blocks away, when she was sure she hadn't been followed, she stopped and pressed a palm against the alley wall, legs trembling under her, breath gasping. Her blood was pounding in her ears, thoughts crashing over so fast she couldn't think straight.

Ahrin was here.

That changed everything.

CHAPTER 16

Lira had mastered herself by the time she returned to the inn. Sneaking in the same way she'd left, she returned the cloak to its owner's locker, then hurried upstairs. The others were still gathered together when Lira knocked and entered.

Garan stood. "You're back already. Everything okay?"

"Time to move."

"Now?"

She spoke briskly, hiding from them *and* herself how unsettled she still was. "Things aren't quite as I expected them to be, but for once the change might be a good thing for us." That was stretching the truth a little. Showing up on Ahrin Vensis' doorstep without invitation was as likely to lead to execution as welcome, especially after more than two years of silence, but Lira didn't mention that. Nor did she let herself wonder how much of her sudden urgency was about getting it done before she could talk herself out of facing Ahrin.

"What *are* we doing exactly?" Garan enquired.

Lira hesitated. If she told them her theory now, they would most likely laugh in her face and refuse to come, and where she was going, she might need mage backup. Begging favours from Ahrin would require a strong front. And showing up alone and dishevelled would immediately put Lira on the back foot. "We need resources, more than you can safely obtain. I have old connections here that can get us what we need."

Fari put her hands on her hips. "Yes, but to do what exactly?"

"Resources first. Then I'll explain. If we can't get them, then there's no point getting your hopes up, and we'll have to come up with something else." Seeing the objection on all their faces she lifted her hands. "That's the deal, right—this doesn't pan out, and we part company."

"All right," Garan conceded. "Let's do this."

She opened the door. "Come on. We'll take the back stairs."

They moved to follow her out without any further protest, but she stopped and pointed at their mage cloaks—both Lorin and Garan had put theirs on. "You sure you want to wear those?"

Garan shrugged. "They'll be a level of protection for us in a place like this."

Lira snorted. He had no idea. Although ... they could be a useful distraction. "As long as it's on the record that I recommended you leave them behind. You follow me and you say nothing, clear?"

A series of nods. Well, Fari's was more like a long-suffering sigh and rolled eyes, but it would do.

"Let's go."

"What exactly is it we're doing, and why are we doing it in the middle of the night?" Fari asked a while later as they made their way out of the respectable area of Dirinan and back into the harbour district. The healer cast a dubious glance at the ragged and wary appearance of those they passed. "Are we robbing a merchant house?"

All but Lorin were clearly uncomfortable in their surroundings. Lira enjoyed their discomfort. Every part of it was home—the bad smell, the rundown appearance, the man with the missing teeth watching them from the curb. "Something like that."

"I suppose we *will* need coin for a rescue mission." Garan shot a smile at Fari. She grinned back. Tarion appeared to be in his own world, eyes downcast, shoulders hunched.

Lorin glanced at Lira, his dark Shiven eyes glimmering. He knew this place too, probably guessed what type of people she was going to request help from. But he said nothing. She remembered that night at

DarkSkull. Him bleeding on the floor, his leg crushed. Her decision to sacrifice her chance at escape to go and help him.

She shook herself, returning her attention forwards.

She wouldn't make that mistake again.

"You said you would tell us your plan when you got back," Garan reminded her. "I accept that, but since I'm getting the increasing sense that this meeting we're about to have will be dangerous, can you tell me a little more so we can be prepared?"

She hesitated, then, "I have a theory about Lucinda and the Shadowcouncil, and if I'm right, we're going to need more than just your money to find Egalion and Caverlock. I have connections from when I used to live here that can help us. I scouted earlier to see who was still around. We're going to visit one of them now."

His eyebrows shot upwards. "Please tell me we aren't really going to rob a bank or merchant house?"

"You broke a dangerous prisoner out of jail and now you're worried about robbing someone?" she asked.

"She makes a good point," Fari said cheerfully. "We're essentially all dangerous criminals now."

"I'm the only son and heir of Lord-Taliath Egalion and Lord-Mage A'ndreas. I can't be a dangerous criminal," Garan said gloomily. "My parents will murder me. Right after King Cayr does."

"Maybe, but this is good news for Tarion. There's nothing more attractive to bored, stunning, princesses than a rogue criminal." Fari beamed. "I heard about your betrothal. Even in Karonan it was big news."

Tarion's shoulders hunched further. His throat bobbed as he swallowed. Fari's smile instantly faded.

"Isn't getting formally betrothed good news?" Lorin asked, clearly perplexed by Tarion's change of mood. Lira was equally puzzled. The only difference was, she didn't care.

"Of course it is." Tarion smiled at him. "I love Sesha more than anything."

"We're not going to rob anything, or marry princesses, anytime soon," Lira said, just to break the subsequent awkward silence. "At least, not if I can make a deal to get us what we need."

"Which is what, exactly?" Lorin asked.

"You'll see." She looked back at them. "All you four need to do is look intimidating and remain silent. You open your mouths even once and I will set your shoes alight. You don't know how things work down here and you could get us all killed with the wrong word."

"We get it," Garan muttered. "Silent and intimidating."

"The role Lorin was born for," Fari said with a smirk.

They all chuckled. Even Tarion cracked a smile.

The street outside the gambling hall—Transk's old base of operations—was filled with people and the raucous hum of laughter and drunken conversation. Music spilled out of its open doors, along with orange flamelight, cries of excitement or anger, and the almost tangible anticipation and bloodlust of its patrons.

It was celebration night. Lira shook her head at the coincidence of arriving on this particular evening of the year. The last time she'd attended celebration night she'd been barely fifteen years old, sitting in a rickety chair next to Ahrin and watching the most powerful criminal overlord in Dirinan preside over his kingdom.

The memories of that time threatened to crowd in—somehow, they were the most real of her memories before jail—and she physically shook herself to get rid of them. Facing Ahrin was going to require every shred of her composure. Anything less and the Darkhand would shred her to pieces, and Lira was already going into this needing a favour. Ahrin had the advantage, and she would use it.

"We're going in there?" Garan asked after she'd been silent for a few moments, his voice all kinds of dubious.

A nearby man, clearly drunk, lurched towards them. "What is it, pretty-boy, too scared to go inside a place where real men hang out? Or maybe you're worried about getting relieved of that fine cloak o' yours."

Those with the drunken man drifted towards them too, sensing an easy mark despite their inebriated state. One reached inside his tunic.

Lira moved before anyone else could, planting herself between Garan and the men, voice sharp and steel-hard. "You back up now or I use that knife in your pants to remove all future ability to bed a woman or bear children."

"Them kind don' belong here," he muttered, but didn't take any further steps forward.

"*Them kind* have business with the boss." Lira lifted an eyebrow. "You want to explain to her why you accosted them before they could even get inside?"

Fear flared in his eyes and he backed away, hands in the air. "Didn't mean no harm."

Lira held his gaze until he was well away from them, then turned back to the others. "What did I say about keeping your months shut?"

Without waiting for a response, she took the two wooden steps up to the porch and then walked through the open doors. She moved quickly, not missing the quick glances already coming their way from those outside at the sight of Lorin and Garan's mage cloaks.

Across the threshold, she paused. A long, rectangular hall spread out before her, packed full of bodies. The sight was so familiar it took her breath away. Gambling tables filled the right side of the room; people gathered around them playing cards, dice, and games of chance. Lira recognised all of them at a glance and she had to fight off the unexpectedly strong urge to forget about her mission and go join one of the games.

To the left against the wall was a long bar. In the space between the bar and the gambling tables was a haphazard arrangement of chairs and tables around which completely drunk, half-drunk, and nearly drunk attendees talked or danced to the loud music. Not many had noticed them, not yet, but the stares would start once more of the less-inebriated attendees registered the mage cloaks.

After only a minor hesitation, Lira stepped forward and began weaving her way through the throng. She kept her stride brisk and confident, knowing the others were following her by the looks, the turning shoulders, the slow silencing of the room.

They would be lucky if one of them didn't get stabbed before she reached her destination. Oh well. She *had* warned them.

She allowed her violet mage light to flicker around her hands and forearms just in case anyone got any ideas. After all, this hall was full of Dirinan's underworld: murderers, rapists, thieves, and worse, and they were deep enough inside now that there was no easy exit. Best not to give those beginning to crowd around any ideas that she was easy prey.

The farther she moved into the hall, the harder she struggled to maintain a calm expression while her heart thudded in her chest and her throat turned dry. Her stomach had curled into knots so tight it had become difficult to breathe.

It was a fight not to turn around and run back the way she'd come, disappear into the crowd. Particularly when the knots twisted tighter and tighter and sweat broke out on the inside of her palms and down her back.

The throng thinned out the deeper Lira moved into it, the tables becoming more spaced out—fancier, with the gambling tables to the right covered in velvet and surrounded by plush chairs for the wealthiest and most important players.

Transk had always portrayed celebration night as a gift to his crews. But he usually made more money that night than any other day of the year. Ahrin had taken note of that.

Ahrin.

Lira's feet slowed, until she realised what she was doing and forced herself to move faster.

The far end of the hall was cordoned off by golden rope. This was where the boss of this hall and the entire harbour district did their business. Where they sat and watched over their territory.

Only it wasn't Transk anymore.

Ahrin Vensis sprawled on a large, ornate chair, one leg bent, the other stretched out in front of her. Her hands rested on the cushioned arms of the chair.

Tall Shiven warriors stood protectively either side of her, though Lira doubted very much that Ahrin needed them. No, they were for show. Still, her eyes narrowed. Neither were Dirinan street criminals. They were trained soldiers.

"You have got to be kidding me," Garan muttered.

But Lira barely heard him. The hammering of her heartbeat in her ears had become too loud.

The instant Lira walked straight through the narrow gap in the cordon without stopping, Ahrin became aware of her, her cold gaze shifting straight to the incursion. When she saw it was Lira, her face hardened, eyes flashing dangerously, though her languid pose didn't change at all.

The muttering that had broken out by their procession had faded entirely by the time Lira stepped into the boss's private area without invitation. Avarice and anticipation, edged with violence and curiosity, filled the air. Lira could feel it crawling down the back of her neck.

They were ready for bloodshed.

"Hello, Ahrin." Lira spoke quietly, for her ears alone.

"Lira Astor. What a surprise." Ahrin's voice was cool, uninterested. "It's been so long."

"Years, in fact."

Men and women shifted restlessly behind them, clearly uncertain from the tone of this exchange whether Lira was a threat to be dealt with or not. Whether they were about to watch a bloodbath or a boringly mild conversation. Lira heard the rasp of a knife being drawn from its sheath and clocked the direction it came from but didn't tear her eyes away from Ahrin.

"What brings you here with your mage friends?" Ahrin sounded bored now, about ready to dismiss Lira as she would any underling. "Don't tell me your precious council has any interest in the crews of Dirinan."

"*My* precious council?" Lira's voice was ice-cold with banked anger. How *dare* she! Not saying anything further, she reached down and slowly, deliberately, pushed up the cuffs of her shirt, holding Ahrin's gaze the entire time. Once she was done, she lifted her forearms into the crime boss's eyeline.

Let Ahrin look upon the scars Lira had earned after the Darkhand had abandoned her to her fate in the interests of her own survival.

Ahrin held her stare for a moment longer before glancing down to look at Lira's wrists. When she saw the reddened scar tissue left by the manacles that had been locked around Lira's wrists every day for the past two years, her mouth tightened.

Danger abruptly rippled through the room, palpable, from that single, simple change in Ahrin's expression. Those near her chair took a half step back without even realising what they were doing. Any muttering faded abruptly. Another weapon was drawn. The air of anticipation changed to bloodlust in a blink.

Ahrin's gaze shifted back to meet Lira's, question and realisation both written in their depths. Her eyes had gone almost black. As if ... as if she hadn't known that Lira had been imprisoned. Had she not even *tried* to find out where Lira had gone? Anger and despair both punched a hole in her gut. "I just got out," she snapped.

In a single, graceful movement, Ahrin was up from her chair, fury blazing from her stance. Everyone nearby visibly quailed. "Take the mages and put them somewhere uncomfortable."

Lira stood aside as armed men and women closed in on them from every direction, reaching for the mages. Garan grabbed for his staff; Lorin's concussive magic flared.

"Don't." Ahrin's cold voice ripped through the room, stilling everyone in it. "Go quietly and I won't harm you ... yet. Try to fight and I'll have you killed where you stand."

"Lira, tell them to stand down," Tarion demanded.

"This isn't my house." She shrugged, inwardly enjoying their protests and discomfort. "I can't help you."

Garan drew his staff anyway. With a flick of her wrist, Ahrin sent it flying across the room. "Last warning, mageling."

"Garan, stop," Fari said. "Look at where we are. We won't win here. She's a killer, don't forget that."

"Sensible," Ahrin said, ice rippling through her voice. "Now get them out of my sight before I change my mind and spill their pure mage blood all over my floor."

Ahrin's gaze shifted back to Lira as her crew hustled Garan and the others out of the room. At a brisk gesture from her, the party and the gambling started up again, laughter and the clink of drinks filling the silence. "Come with me." It was the voice of effortless command as familiar to Lira as if she'd only heard it just yesterday instead of years ago.

So Lira followed.

She trailed Ahrin through a door leading to a dim, narrow hallway at the back of the hall. The crew boss opened a door at the end and went inside, waiting for Lira to enter before closing it behind her.

"My office," Ahrin explained, as if an explanation were necessary. "They know not to disturb me when I'm back here."

Lira nodded, staring around her. "I remember stealing Transk's take out of here one night." She'd come through the ceiling, small enough as a child to fit. It had been a good night. The manager's blood still stained the wood of the desk to her right.

Ahrin turned to face Lira. Her expression was inscrutable, her posture flawlessly relaxed yet coiled and ready to move in an instant. Lira forced herself to look away, not wanting to reveal anything of the emotional maelstrom boiling in her chest.

Rotted carcasses. It was so good just to see her face again.

"An informant in the local government offices brought me word almost three weeks ago that the heir to the Darkmage had broken out of a council prison in a dramatic escape. It was the first I'd heard any mention of you in years. I barely credited it. Was convinced it was a wild rumour." Ahrin paused. "How long have they had you?"

"Over two years," Lira said simply.

Ahrin's jaw hardened, and she exploded away from the desk, lashing out with a foot to send her dustbin flying across the room. "You never showed up in Karonan, so I..." She raked a hand through her long, raven hair. "Rotted damned fish carcasses. Those bastards."

"Right. I didn't show, so you came here and never thought of me again. Survival first, I understand." Lira couldn't look at her. Her heart had started thudding again. Ahrin was so close, the sound of her voice again, seeing her again, it threatened to overwhelm her hard-won equilibrium. She couldn't afford to lose that.

"Tell me what happened." The note of command was back in Ahrin's voice. It helped Lira reply without thinking.

"They took me the moment I reached Karonan after escaping Shadowfall Island. They drugged me and carried me to Carhall. I've been in their mage prison ever since, until Tarion helped me escape just under a month ago."

Ahrin was pacing again, her fury spilling into the space between them, a palpable darkness. So dangerous, this trained killer moulded to serve Lira's grandfather. Yet Lira had never been afraid of her, even when she should have been. "Rotting bastards." She kicked the bin again, and it crashed loudly against the wall.

Lira finally stepped towards her, instinctively reaching out to take her arm. Ahrin's murderous rage wasn't going to help the situation. They needed to shift to business. A discussion of what Lira needed; a deal made. That was the only way Lira would escape from here with her equilibrium intact.

Ahrin spun around unexpectedly, and they collided together. Lira's breath left her chest as Ahrin crushed Lira to her so fiercely she couldn't breathe. Without thinking about what she was doing, she held on just as tightly, burying her head in Ahrin's neck. It all rose up in her then, a tide of emotion that wanted to break out and explode all through the room.

She pulled away before that could happen, turning and ruthlessly quelling that rush of feeling before it could overwhelm her. She wanted to ask why Ahrin hadn't looked for her. Why she hadn't known Lira was trapped and unable to escape, but deep down she already knew the answer and thought hearing it might break her. So she said nothing.

A brief silence fell before Ahrin spoke again. "Your council friends look much scruffier than the last time I saw them, and what's wrong with Tarion Caverlock?"

Ah, so Ahrin had noticed it too, and so quickly. "I'm not sure, but he's been repressing his magic for the past two years."

She narrowed her eyes. "And why are you here with them? Why did they break you out now?" Her head cocked. "Don't tell me this has something to do with Councillor Egalion's mysterious disappearance."

"It does." Lira took a deep, steadying breath, making sure she was composed before turning back around. "Tarion and Garan got me out after we made a deal. Predictably, they messed it up, and Lorin and Fari saved their sorry carcasses—and mine—along the way."

"Tell me everything," Ahrin demanded, no inch of give in her voice.

Lira did, not leaving a single detail out.

Once she was done, midnight blue eyes searched hers. "You came here because you need resources to help find Egalion and her husband?"

"I—" It was on the tip of her tongue to say no, to admit that ever since the barman had told her earlier that Ahrin was in Dirinan, she hadn't cared whether Ahrin could help find Tarion's parents or not. But that uncontrollable emotion was threatening again, a weakness she couldn't afford. So she shrugged. "I thought I'd beg a favour from Transk, but finding you here is even better. You were in far deeper with Underground than I was. Maybe you can help me with a theory I have."

The flinch was imperceptible, but Lira didn't miss it. She never missed Ahrin's little tells; they were seared into her mind and heart. Largely because Ahrin didn't *have* tells. The Darkhand leaned back against the desk, crossed her arms. "I don't see why I should. I've got a business here now, a life, a crew. I don't have time for messing with mage affairs, and after what they did to you, I don't particularly care to either. Not to mention they're still hunting me. Once I step foot out of this city, I'm fair game."

"As much as I hate the council for what they did, Underground is even more to blame. If they're still out there, I want to burn them all, Ahrin."

Passion filled her voice, two years of bitterness spilling out. "I think they have Egalion and Caverlock, and if they do, then finding them means finding whatever is left of Underground. I'll worry about what to do with the council once Underground is dead and buried."

A cool smile spread over Ahrin's face, the flat look of a predator. "Revenge is a game I enjoy."

"I thought you might." A matching smile curled at Lira's mouth.

"All right. I can help, with supplies and coin too if you need it." Ahrin crossed her arms.

"I'm going to need more than that," Lira admitted

"What aren't you saying?" Ahrin's gaze searched hers. "What exactly *is* this theory of yours?"

There was no point holding back. So Lira hesitantly explained the crazy thought that had come to her back in Karonan. Once she was done, Ahrin let out a long whistle, then unexpectedly smiled that wicked smile Lira had always adored. Even now it made her heart flip in her chest. "I do love how your mind works, Astor. We have things to talk about, but first, what do you want me to do with your mage friends?"

"Let's go talk to them." Lira sighed. "I'll need their help if I'm to get to Underground."

"All right." Ahrin pushed off the desk and headed for the door. She was only a step past Lira when she paused, looked back. "Lira..."

"Don't." Lira shook her head, looked away. She needed to be clear-headed for what came next and Ahrin was just too much right now. "I can't, not right now. I just can't."

She started when Ahrin's hand closed around hers, entangling their fingers, before lifting their joined hands to her mouth. Her kiss was soft. "It's really good to see you."

Lira nodded, but she still couldn't meet Ahrin's eyes.

Ahrin dropped her hand, opened the door. "Let's go plan some revenge."

CHAPTER 17

They sat in Ahrin's office, a thick, sullen, silence filling the room. Ahrin sauntered over to the desk and dropped into the chair behind it, lifting one booted foot to rest on its surface. "Nobody will be listening in and we won't be disturbed. Shall we get down to business?"

The silence persisted. Lira stared pointedly at Tarion until he spoke, clearing his throat and staring at the ground. "Lira says she thinks you can help us with resources to find Underground. We think they're the ones who took my parents."

Ahrin lifted an eyebrow. "Really? I thought your precious council destroyed Lucinda and her people."

"Clearly not all of them," Garan countered.

Ahrin smirked. "I cut ties long ago, before they went down. I don't do sinking ships or losing causes."

"You were the Darkhand," Lorin said tightly.

"Indeed I was. So?"

"Then you can help them," Fari snapped.

"*Them?*" Ahrin pounced on the weakness. "What is it you expect to get out of this—that Egalion will be so overwhelmed with gratitude when you rescue her that she gives you a mage cloak out of pity?"

"Leave her alone!" Garan snapped.

"And there's our white knight, the protector of all." Ahrin leaned forward, dropping her voice to a dramatic whisper. "Just between you and me, lordling, I suspect Fari Dirsk is well capable of looking after herself."

"She's also capable of not rising to taunts," Fari drawled.

"Touché." Ahrin shrugged and leaned back in her chair. "I didn't kidnap the boy's parents, so what exactly is it you want my help with?"

"Information and resources," Garan said. "We need to know where to look for my aunt and uncle."

"What's my help worth?"

"We're not paying you any money," Lorin said coldly.

"Then we have nothing more to say to each other."

"Ahrin," Lira said pointedly. She was toying with them, and in normal circumstances, Lira wouldn't have a problem with it. But right now it was wasting time. Her muscles burned with restless energy.

Midnight blue eyes settled on her for a long moment, then Ahrin nodded imperceptibly and pushed off the desk. Five pairs of eyes tracked her as she went to one of the cabinets along the wall and pulled out a middle drawer. After rooting around inside it for a few moments, Ahrin pulled out a small leather bag, slammed the draw shut, and returned to the desk. Then, she looked at Lira. "Care to tell them your theory?"

"You told *her*?" Garan protested immediately, then shook his head, a rueful smile breaking out. "Why am I surprised? Go on then, tell us."

Lira took a breath. "I think Lucinda and her people, along with the razak and nerik, might have come from Rotherburn."

"You *what* now?" Fari's eyes turned wide as saucers.

"Nobody's from there anymore," Garan said.

"Any ship that's travelled there in the past fifty years never returned," Lorin added.

"My, my, they do teach decent history and geography lessons at Temari, don't they?" Ahrin drawled.

"I know all that. However, it would explain why the razak have never been spotted on this continent—because they didn't come from here," Lira said patiently. "Most of all, it explains why Underground were so damn interested in Finn A'ndreas's research project. They were worried he might stumble into their true origins."

"Rotherburn's people disappeared *decades* ago," Garan said in frustration. "But what ... your theory is some of them survived and decided to sail on over here to kidnap mages and do experiments on them? Why?"

Lira glanced at Ahrin. The Darkhand flashed her a smile, then, with a single movement, she upended the leather bag on her desk. Coins spilled loudly onto its surface.

Garan reached forward, picked up one, studied it, then passed it to the others. "I don't recognise it."

"That's because it's not from Shivasa. It's not Zandian, Rionnan, or Tregayan currency either." Ahrin dropped back into the chair, put both booted feet up on the desk this time. "When I cleaned out Underground's stash during my rapid exit from the organisation, I came across several bags of coin exactly like those."

"Where are they from then?" Tarion asked, looking curious despite himself.

Lira frowned, then grinned at Ahrin, unable to help herself. "Rotherburn?"

Ahrin picked up a dagger lying on the desk, began using its point to clean out her fingernails. "It fits with your theory nicely, no? How does this sound ... our friend Lucinda was never Underground, or at least, Underground was only ever a front. A ruse. She came here from Rotherburn for her own—as yet unidentified—purposes and used the poor bastards to get what she wanted. Then, when she was done, she set them all up to be taken down and sailed off into the sunset, mission accomplished, loose ends tied up."

They all stared at her. Even Lira. Her thoughts raced, putting it together. It all made a certain odd kind of sense. She leaned forward. "If that's true, then who took Egalion and Caverlock? And why did Lucinda even come here in the first place?"

Ahrin paused briefly. "I was the one who designed your kidnapping and carried it out, but Lucinda paid close attention." The mood in the room darkened, but Ahrin continued. "From what Lira told me about the circumstances of Egalion and Caverlock's kidnapping, I'd bet all these bags of foreign coin Lucinda is behind it. There's no other crew on this continent capable of taking a mage of the higher order without a trace, and trust me, I'd know."

Fari eyed her. "Except yours, I imagine."

Ahrin inclined her head in a nod. "Except mine."

Garan's face was tight with frustration. "Give me a plausible reason why Lucinda would come here from Rotherburn and go to such elaborate lengths to create Underground?"

Ahrin cocked her head, thinking about it for a moment. "Maybe they don't have many mages in Rotherburn. Maybe she wanted more. Maybe she needed to experiment on mages to learn how to make more of them." Ahrin dropped the knife with a thud, a smile curling at her mouth when they all jumped. "It's all just speculation. And I have no idea why they'd come back for mage-prince's parents two years later. I don't much care either."

"You're both either playing us, or you're crazy," Garan snapped. "Either way, I've had enough."

"Don't let the door hit you on the way out." Ahrin lifted a hand, waved. When nobody moved, she smiled.

Tarion placed a calming hand on his cousin's arm, then leaned forward. "Say you're right. Why did she leave two years ago? Why allow Underground to be dismantled?"

"If she's the one who took your parents, then she didn't leave, did she? Nor is the group entirely dismantled—grabbing up Egalion and her husband would have required some killer resources," Ahrin said.

Lira spoke before Garan could. "I've said it before, but nobody important was caught up in those arrests. Not Lucinda, not her mages, no other members of the Shadowcouncil. Unless something changed in the past two years, I take it nobody still has any idea who the other Shadowcouncil members even were?"

"That's true." Tarion considered. "The council ended the investigation under the belief the group was gone. And to be fair, there haven't been any activities linked to Underground since."

"Lucinda always thought twenty steps ahead," Ahrin said. "Those arrests happened because she wanted them to, I have no doubts about that. She was ready to leave here or something forced her hand. Either way, she went and took her people with her before the council could figure out where they were really from."

"So why come back and kidnap my aunt and uncle?" Garan asked helplessly, then lifted a hand when Ahrin opened her mouth. "I know, I know. You don't know."

There was a moment's silence, then Tarion spoke. "Can you help us, Ahrin?"

Ahrin glanced at Lira, who gave a little nod, then shrugged. "My runners keep a close eye on the comings and goings at the docks. Roughly a month and a half ago a ship without identifying flags departed in the middle of the night, *against* the tide, tacking west. Two long boxes, heavily guarded and locked, were carried aboard immediately before their departure. It picked up no other cargo while it was berthed."

Lira frowned. "Sounds like smugglers to me. It was probably illegal spirits or weapons in those boxes."

"Indeed, and that's what I thought too, until you came here tonight. Because there was one other interesting detail my runner provided about these smugglers." Ahrin smiled at her. "He grew up a sailor, you see, and he swore blind the ship was moving faster than possible given the strength of the incoming tide that night. He said there had to have been a mage on board, yet none of the crew wore council blue."

Relief flooded through Lira and she relaxed back in her chair. It was tenuous, circumstantial, but ... Ahrin had come through. Egalion and Caverlock had been probably taken offshore. Heading west. Her theory might be right.

Tarion and Garan shared a glance; it was full of wary hope.

Ahrin dragged her boots off the desk, stood up. "I can get you a ship, supplies, weapons. You leave my territory, board your ship on the evening tide tomorrow, and don't come back without an invitation. I don't like mages wandering about in my patch."

Garan stiffened, but before he could say anything, Fari waved a hand. "Yes, yes, and no doubt we'll be murdered horribly if we do. Understood, criminal boss leader."

Ahrin stopped by Lira's chair on the way to the door, voice dropping to a murmur. "You can come back anytime you like. It really was good seeing you." At the door, she turned to rake the others with her gaze. "Thus concludes our business."

"Wait, you haven't asked for anything in return." Garan demanded, suspicion written all over his face.

Ahrin winked at him. "No, I haven't."

She hauled the door open and left before he could respond. When one of Ahrin's people arrived moments later to escort them out, Lira rose to her feet and made sure the others did as well.

"Your girlfriend is an attractively capable sort, isn't she?" Fari muttered as they filed after the man through a narrow back corridor leading out to the street.

Lira ignored her.

They'd barely taken three steps down the hall when a deep, sonorous, voice yelled out from behind them. "Lira? Is that you?"

She spun, eyes widening at the sight of the tall Zandian walking towards her. "Yanzi?"

He let out a whoop and wrapped his arms around her before lifting her in the air and spinning her around. A delighted laugh spilled out of her and she hung on tight until he dropped her back to the ground. "Lira Astor." He grinned. "What a sight for sore eyes. I never thought I'd see you again."

"Same here," she said, the mirth fading from her face. "You weren't there when I came back that night ... just Timin. I thought you'd all left."

"We did." He nodded. "Timin sent us away when we found Ahrin's note."

"But you're back with her now?"

"She came looking for me when she returned, and I signed straight back on. I think deep down I was always hoping she'd come back. You too." He looked at her hopefully. "*Are* you back?"

"I ... no, just passing through."

"You look all grown up." His smile faded. "But you still haven't bothered with that rat's nest you call hair, I see. And the nose is still delightfully crooked."

"And you're taller but still just as irritating," she countered.

"No mage cloak." He frowned. "You're not one of them?"

"And I never will be." She straightened her shoulders. "Look, I'm sorry, but we have to go."

Disappointment flashed over his handsome face. "Will I see you again before you leave Dirinan?"

"No, probably not."

He reached out, squeezed her shoulder. "You take care of yourself."

"You too, Yanzi. It was good to see you."

"Come see us. Anytime." He looked sad that she was leaving so quickly. "I've missed you every day since you left."

"Yeah, me too," she said, so softly she was unsure if he even heard her.

They weren't much farther along the corridor when Tarion said, a look of contemplation on his face, "I've never seen you so delighted to see someone before. Not even close."

It wasn't a question, so she didn't answer it.

But she did glance back over her shoulder. Yanzi was already gone. She ignored the ache in her chest that followed and tried to focus on what lay ahead.

That life was long gone.

CHAPTER 18

T hey returned to the inn, well outside of Ahrin's territory, and slept for a few restless hours. Lira had expected extensive questioning on the way back, but the others seemed lost in their own thoughts—probably processing the fantastical idea that Lucinda and her people might have come from Rotherburn.

Lira wasn't sure how to feel. Although the theory had been hers, she'd never actually thought it would pan out. If she were honest with herself, she shared Garan's incredulity. It seemed crazy. Why had people from Rotherburn come here? And why now?

Exhausted emotionally as much as physically, Lira fell asleep the moment her head hit the scratchy pillow on the bed next to Fari's, despite the roiling of her thoughts. When she opened her eyes again, early morning sunlight shone through the narrow window between the beds.

Unable to lie still for more than a few moments, Lira tossed off the covers and opened the flimsy curtain, allowing more sunshine into the room. Then, after waking a very annoyed and sleep-dazed Fari, she dragged the girl next door to the others' room, knocking until an alert-looking Lorin opened it.

Garan was sitting on his bed, still rubbing sleep from his eyes, as Lira and Fari marched in. "I thought we had to wait for Ahrin's runner." He spoke through a yawn.

"Yes, but we also need to go out to buy new clothes. You can't keep wearing those cloaks around the place. The council searchers will reach

Dirinan sooner rather than later. And it's not like you can waltz into a strange country wearing them either, not if you don't want to be marked as outsiders the moment we arrive."

Fari lifted her hand. "Uhm ... what sort of clothing *do* they wear in Rotherburn?"

Garan glanced at Tarion. "You ever pay much attention to Uncle Finn rambling on about his project?"

Tarion gave a sheepish shrug. "I don't remember anything about clothing."

Fari put her hands on her hips. "What *do* we know about Rotherburn, exactly?"

The cousins shared another glance. Garan frowned in thought. "Not much that will help us. Uncle Finn was fascinated about the mystery of their disappearance ... not so much the details of how their society ran. At least, if he knew anything about that, he never mentioned it."

"He probably thought we'd get even more bored if he didn't at least try to keep it interesting," Tarion said ruefully.

"I don't remember any specifics either," Lorin said slowly. "When Rotherburn came up in classes at Temari, it was mainly historical stuff, references to when we used to trade with them. That sort of thing."

"What *did* we used to trade with them?" Lira asked.

"I don't remember."

"So ... we know nothing at all that will help us?" Fari clarified.

After a long pause, Lira cleared her throat. "We'll get sturdy but non-descript clothing. I'd also recommend leaving your mage staffs behind—they're too recognisable."

She had no idea where her mage staff was. She'd left it behind on Shadowfall Island when she'd escaped years ago. She doubted she'd ever get it back. Oddly, a memory of that night flashed strongly—of the moment Athira Walden had decided to turn back, to stay instead of escaping with Lira so that she too could spy for the Mage Council.

Lira hadn't thought of the girl with the mage ability to amplify the magic of those around her for years. She wondered what had happened to her after Lira had escaped Shadowfall. She was supposed to have gone back for her, but that had been impossible. The girl was either dead or still a prisoner. And after so long of being experimented on ... Lira hoped it was the former, for her sake.

"Athira." She said the girl's name out loud before she could think to stop herself. "Did the council ever find her?"

The looks they shot each other gave Lira the answer before Garan uttered a terse, "No."

"Do *you* know what happened to her?" Fari asked, unable to meet Lira's gaze, as if afraid of the answer. The charged silence that followed her question indicated the others felt a similar fear.

"No." Lira was going to leave it there. She didn't owe any of them answers. But ... maybe she owed Athira something—her bravery deserved people knowing about it. "But she was spying too. She could have escaped, but she chose to stay when I left, to try and help the council bring Underground down from the inside."

Hope spread over Garan's face. "So she's alive?"

"It's been a long time, Garan." Lira shook her head.

"Maybe if we find my parents, we'll find her." Tarion looked hopeful too, his face brightening.

"We've still got a long way to go before that happens." Lorin seemed to understand the slim likelihood of finding Athira alive as well as Lira did. "The first step being getting ourselves new clothes before Ahrin's runner gets here later."

Now it was Fari who brightened. "Clothes shopping. This dangerous and foolhardy mission suddenly became fun."

Ahrin's messenger arrived at midday carrying a note with the name of a ship and its captain, as well as the location on the docks where it could be found. The note signed off with instructions for them to be there at dusk. The girl also carried a chest the size of a large book. Inside were several bags of the foreign coins Ahrin had showed them the night before.

They were still peering through the coins, Tarion looking fascinated, when an older, broad-shouldered, man arrived lugging a large duffel bag across his shoulders. He placed it on the floor inside the door, gave them a single nod, and left as silently as he'd come. A quick investigation of the bag revealed weapons stacked inside. Daggers, knives, enough for a couple each, and a bow and quiver of arrows.

The sight of the coins, the weapons, booked passage on a ship ... it brought home the reality of what they were about to do. Lira bit her lip. The four people in this room had betrayed her, walked away without lifting a finger to help her, despite claiming to be her friends. They'd only helped her escape prison because they needed her.

The thought of going to a place completely foreign to her, unfamiliar territory, with four people she couldn't trust to have her back was an unsettling reality to face. But just as quickly as that thought came, another realisation flashed into her mind—faster now because of where she was, because the memories of her old life had been rising to the surface.

She didn't have to trust them as her friends. She just had to trust in their motives—finding Egalion and Caverlock. As long as Lira didn't threaten that, they were allies.

Garan, surprisingly, read her thoughtful silence accurately. "Yeah, I'm not any more thrilled at the idea of going to Rotherburn with you either, Spider."

"If we're not willing to put our grievances aside now, for the duration of this journey, then we shouldn't go," Tarion said. "We'll get ourselves killed."

Garan looked at him, expression thoughtful. "We could just let Lira go now. The council will eventually catch her, but we will have held up our end of the bargain, and we won't have to watch our backs against her anymore."

Lira froze as their glances turned to her. Frustration surged in her chest—this was the opportunity she'd been waiting for. The problem was, Underground was where they were going.

And she wanted to see Lucinda burn more than she wanted anything else.

That desire rose up, mingling with the thrill of anticipated danger, and it made everything startling clear. "I'm coming with you, because finding your parents suits my purposes," she said firmly. "And to that end, I'm willing to watch your backs if you'll watch mine. Not because we're friends, but because we all want to succeed in this mission. Once it's done, we never see each other again, but until then we're allies."

Tarion nodded instantly. "Agreed."

"Me too," Fari said. "Our chances of success are greater with Lira than without, and it's pretty clear she'd not been lying about how badly she wants Lucinda."

Garan held her gaze for a long moment. Eventually he nodded. "Works for me."

"I was never in any doubt that Lira should come along with us." Lorin sounded irritated. "Can we move on now? Like maybe sort out those weapons and get our packs together."

Lira distractedly watched Tarion and Garan divide the weapons between them, realising that with the decision she'd just made, there was one more thing she had to do. Still, she hesitated, even though the reasons for her hesitation were foolish, sentimental.

She slipped out of the room and went to the one she shared with Fari. There, she shifted her saddlebag from where it lay on top of the duffel she'd brought with her from Karonan.

Returning to the others, she placed it on one of the beds and looked at Tarion. Then she bit her lip, still hesitant.

Garan lifted an eyebrow. "You finally going to tell us what that thing is?"

"I..." She cleared her throat, cursed her foolish sentimentality, and stepped away from the bed, waving to the bag. "Tarion, given what we just agreed to, you should have this when we go. It makes us all surviving this trip more likely."

Curiosity flashing over his face, Tarion crossed to the bed and unbuckled the bag, revealing Shakar Astor's blade. He stilled when he saw it. "This is..."

"My grandfather's Taliath sword. Yes."

Fari gasped, lifting a hand to her mouth, eyes wide. Garan and Lorin both started, horrified fascination creeping over their faces. Tarion recoiled as if burned. "I can't wear that."

Lira scowled at him. "You're a Taliath and I have no idea why you're still pretending you're not. If you can't access your magic, at least you can still be useful to us if you carry this." When he continued to hesitate, her voice turned snappish. "Take the rotted sword, Tarion. My grandfather is long dead. Rename it, make it yours, I don't care. But you'll need it where we're going."

Lorin spoke up. "But Lira, that blade is yours by right."

"I'm no Taliath, and even if I was, it's too long and heavy for me. I can't wield it." She said those words with no small amount of regret, but if nothing else, Lira had always been practical. The sword wasn't meant for her.

None of the others said anything, and after a long hesitation Tarion reached out and closed his fingers around the onyx hilt. The blade whispered its quiet song as he lifted it easily and gave it an experimental swing. The sword was so dark it swallowed the sunlight around it, an odd visual dissonance. And possibly a useful distraction when fighting with it.

"It suits you, Tar," Garan said quietly.

"What did your grandfather call his sword?" Fari asked, staring at it in mingled horror and awe.

"I don't think anyone ever knew." Lira looked at Tarion. "Choose whatever name you like for it."

Tarion met her gaze, grave. "Are you sure about this?"

"Not a doubt in my mind," she murmured.

Without another word, Tarion sheathed the blade and then buckled it at his hip, fingers brushing gently over its hilt. That seemed to break the tense mood, and Lira went to pick up two daggers for herself from the pile remaining. The bow and quiver of arrows had been left for her too.

"She's certainly very helpful, your girlfriend," Garan admitted as he strapped a knife to the inside of his boot.

"Shame she's an evil crime boss who'd kill us as soon as look at us." Lorin flicked a little smile in Lira's direction.

"She's not my girlfriend," Lira said icily.

"He was just joking," Fari said.

"I'm not interested in joking around." Lira tucked a bag of the strange coins in her tunic, moved for the door. "Like I said, I just want to finish this so I never have to see any of you ever again. I'll see you at dusk."

Garan gave her a speculative look but didn't protest. "Understood, Lira. We'll be here when you get back."

She didn't have anything particular to do, she just couldn't bear being around them any longer. She wandered the streets for a while, purchased a roasted meat roll from a street vendor and wolfed it down, then headed back to the inn when the afternoon grew late.

Her stomach was tight with ... something ... by then. Anticipation, yes; she hungered for Lucinda's blood more than anything. But there was more to it, more she couldn't decipher. Being out of prison was wonderful, but it was also ... so much had been steadily building up inside her. Frustration, anger, betrayal, bitterness—and she didn't know what to do with it now she was free. Especially since she wasn't able to convince herself that she was going to stay free.

Arriving back at the inn, she paused at the entrance, thought about turning around and going back to the harbour district. Seeing Ahrin, saying goodbye properly.

It was too much. Far too much.

So she went inside.

They looked better than they had, Lira conceded as they headed downstairs from their rooms at the inn a short time later. Mage cloaks and staffs dispensed with, they wore the hardy, comfortable tunics, undershirts, and breeches they'd purchased that morning. In their packs, they all carried warm cloaks, a blanket, the money, a spare weapon, and a change of clothes. The boys hadn't shaved, which made Tarion and Garan look far less like young lords. Nobody passing them on the street would immediately recognise them as those the council was hunting. And hopefully they looked non-descript enough that nobody in Rotherburn would immediately mark them as outsiders.

Garan pushed open the inn's front door and waved them all out, but Lira came to a dead halt at the sight of Shiasta and his companion from Karonan waiting outside. If it hadn't been for the fact neither of them made a move towards her, instead performing two equally graceful bows in her direction, she would have had her dagger out in an instant.

"What are you doing here, Shiasta?" she snapped at him.

"Lady Astor, you remember me." He seemed a little pleased by this. "This is Therob, one of my warriors. We're here to escort you to your ship. Boss wants to make sure you all actually leave as ordered."

"You..." She hesitated. "You work for Ahrin?"

"We do." He stepped aside and gestured for her to join him.

She stayed where she was, ignoring the restless shifting of the others behind her. "If you work for Ahrin, what were you doing in Karonan last week?"

"Wait, *what*?" Garan demanded, interrupting. "You saw him in Karonan and didn't think to mention it?"

"I told you I spotted two Underground operatives." She dismissed him with a gesture. "What were you doing there, Shiasta?"

Calmly, Shiasta said, "Looking for you, Lady Astor. The boss heard a rumour about you escaping from prison. She thought if it was true you might go to Karonan to act on the address she'd given you."

Underground hadn't sent Shiasta and Therob to find her. *Ahrin* had. Lira wasn't sure what to make of that, of how stupid she'd been to assume so blindly. But if Ahrin had acted so quickly on hearing she'd broken out of prison, why hadn't she expended any effort trying to find her when she hadn't shown up in Karonan like she was supposed to two years ago? Surely a few simple messages sent out to contacts would have revealed that the Mage Council had imprisoned Lira? Maybe she'd been lying when she claimed not to know.

"And if you found me, what were your orders?"

"To provide whatever assistance you required." When Lira said nothing further, he added politely, "We should go, Lady Astor. You don't want to miss the evening tide."

"He's right." Garan pushed past her and started walking, which got them all moving. Lira trailed, blinking, trying to adjust to the shift in perspective Shiasta's appearance had brought. He paced silently at her side. Therob remained a distance away, clearly providing an outer layer of protective shield. He wasn't as tall as Shiasta, and his black curls, though neatly cropped as all Hunters, looked like they had a mind of their own if given a second too long before a cut.

"How many of you big strapping warriors does Vensis have under her command?" Fari asked curiously, lengthening her stride to join them.

"Enough."

Fari whistled. "Lucky nobody knew you were locked up, Lira, or I think the prison in Carhall might have found itself dealing with an armed assault on its walls."

Lira looked at her sharply. "What do you mean nobody knew?"

Tarion glanced back. "Your crimes and sentence were kept secret. Only the mage councillors and the four of us knew what really happened to you. The prison guards who knew your identity were sworn to secrecy and regularly monitored by a telepath to ensure they hadn't told anyone."

"Is that why—" *you didn't come to see me, because they wouldn't let you?* The words were on the tip of her tongue, but she didn't let herself say them. Or ask what everyone *had* thought happened to her if her imprisonment had been kept secret. Instead she cut herself off and said nothing more.

The remainder of the walk to the docks passed in a bit of a blur as Lira tried to process what she'd just learned and put all the pieces back together. Nobody had known. Even if Ahrin had gone looking for her—and maybe she had—she wouldn't have learned what had happened. Or where Lira was.

Lira had assumed the worst of Ahrin once again and been wrong. Did it change anything? No. Ahrin was set up with her crew in Dirinan, what she'd always wanted, and Lira wasn't going to be able to rest until Lucinda and Underground were razed. That clarity allowed her to settle herself so that by the time they arrived at the ship, she'd regained her focus. It wavered slightly when Shiasta and Therob bowed and bid her farewell—she'd missed him and his warriors, didn't want them to go—but she fought to hold it.

By the time she turned to face the ship, Shiasta and Therob had vanished into the crowded docks, and Garan and the others were already making their way up the gangplank.

Lira took in the tall, sleek ship, its rising sails, the fierce eagle of its figurehead ... and then took a deep breath and hefted her bags, starting up after the others.

It was actually happening. They were going to Rotherburn. And Lucinda.

Vengeance was finally in her grasp.

CHAPTER 19

The ship's captain, a woman named Rilvitha, welcomed them with a crisp nod. She was a tall, muscular Zandian, her raven hair in braids she'd bound loosely together at the base of her neck. A dagger rested at her hip, and a colourful tattoo of a serpent crawled up both forearms before disappearing under the rolled sleeves of her linen shirt. "We're about set to lift anchor. Which one of you is Lira?"

Lira lifted her hand.

"You'll bunk in the main cabin. The rest of you are belowdecks, two hammocks to a room. Grimmet will show you the way. Food is in the galley whenever you get hungry, and you'll find food supplies for your journey packed up and waiting in your cabins. I estimate four days sail to our destination. Please stay out of my crew's way. You need anything else, you come and find me, don't bother them."

Fari looked her up and down. "That's very accommodating of you. You work for Ahrin, huh?"

Rilvitha gave her a cool smile. "I work for myself."

"Why does Lira get a cabin to herself?" Garan asked.

"Because those are my orders. Any other stupid questions, or can I get back to my job seeing this ship off now?"

"Not the friendly sort, is she?" Garan commented as she walked off.

"I'm sure she's perfectly friendly when she's not dealing with privileged mage brats." Lira hefted her bag. "Enjoy your hammocks. I'll see you on the other side."

Lorin stifled a smile while Fari merely looked indignant.

"Lira..." Tarion tried to call after her, but she ignored him, quickening her stride to get out of hearing distance in case he called out again. Seeing Shiasta had unsettled her, and she desperately needed some time and space to herself.

The main cabin was only one level down from the top deck, the bulkheads of the corridor carved from pure oak and polished to a high gleam. Her bag hefted over one shoulder, Lira opened the door and stepped through, the floor rocking gently under her feet as the crew moved around above, calling instructions to each other.

She stopped dead after taking one step inside, her bag dropping to the floor with an unheeded thud. The door swung closed behind her, letting out a soft click.

Ahrin leaned against the bulkhead by a large porthole, long coat falling to her ankles, dark hair loose down her back. Her arms were crossed over her chest. "You took long enough. I was starting to worry you'd gotten delayed by losing your patience and killing the brats on your way here."

Lira's heart thudded in her chest.

"You really thought I was going to let you sail off to mortal danger without saying goodbye?" Ahrin cocked an eyebrow.

Lira cleared her throat, managed, "Mortal danger?"

"I think that's an apt description for Lucinda and her cronies, not to mention those pet monsters of hers. Who knows how many more like her there are where she comes from?"

"That's why you're here, to say goodbye?" Lira fought hard for a casual tone, hoped desperately Ahrin didn't hear the catch in it. "It wasn't necessary. Besides, the ship is about to weigh anchor. You should hurry and get off."

Ahrin was silent a moment. Then she pushed off the bulkhead and crossed the space between them. "Lira, I know that I'm cold and calculating, that I'm not the person that gives comfort or solace. I never learned how to be that person. But I do know *you*." She paused, as if having an internal battle with herself. "So I know that you're angry right now, you're furious, burning up with it. And I get that. But I also know you're hurting. You're hurting deeply. That's why you won't look at me, why you keep flinching away from my touch. You're afraid the dam will burst."

"Ahrin..." But she didn't know what to say. Ahrin had always known her so well, uncomfortably well. Better than she knew herself.

Ahrin lifted a hand, trailed her fingers with infinite gentleness down Lira's cheek. She wanted nothing more in the world than to lean into that touch, but she rigidly held herself back.

"Are you angry with me? Because you were in prison for over two years and I didn't know, didn't come looking for you?" Ahrin's gaze searched hers.

Lira's mouth twisted, and she looked away. "I know that it was a secret, that you couldn't have known. But I don't ... I can't talk about this. I can't. If I do, I'll..." She shook her head.

"That kind of denial is a weakness, Lira. It's a flaw in your armour, and you know that. You need to acknowledge what you're feeling, let it out."

"That's easy to say for someone who doesn't feel things," she muttered, staring determinedly at the floor, wishing Ahrin would just say goodbye and leave.

Ahrin dropped her hand. "It took me two months to get clear of Shadowfall—of Underground and the council both chasing me—to feel safe enough to come back to Karonan. You never came to the spot we agreed to meet and there were no messages from you there. I kept checking for a month, then I paid a boy to ask for you at Temari Hall. He came back and said he'd been told that you went to Carhall and wouldn't be returning."

"So you gave up and left. I know that already, and—"

"I *didn't* give up. I started frequenting one of the inns that the third- and fourth-year apprentices like to go to. I flirted with some of the boys, asked them about the rumours I'd heard that Shakar Astor's heir was at Temari Hall. They all told me the same thing when sufficiently motivated by drink and a pretty face ... that you were gone, on some secret assignment for the council. That the students had been told you had passed your Trials and weren't coming back."

"Oh." Lira blinked, not sure what to say to that.

"I figured, after Underground had suddenly been destroyed by council forces, you didn't need me anymore." Ahrin shook her head, letting out a long breath. "I didn't even *consider* that you'd been taken. I should have. When I heard the rumour that a dangerous mage had broken out of prison in Carhall, I sent Shiasta looking just in case, but I didn't truly believe it. We're so good at doubting each other, you and I."

It was true. They'd never trusted like they should have. So accustomed to their lives of wariness and betrayal, they'd never been able to get past that, even with each other.

The sound of the anchor landing on deck clanged loudly above, drawing Lira sharply from her thoughts. Rilvitha's deep voice sounded as she called orders to her crew. The ship rocked under her feet.

She cleared her throat, glanced over Ahrin's shoulder out the porthole. "You should go. They're leaving port."

Ahrin didn't move. Instead she shifted closer, leaning forward until their foreheads gently pressed together. Her hands reached for Lira's, tangling their fingers as she whispered, "You once said you'd burn down the world for me, Lira Astor. What makes you think I wouldn't do the same for you?"

Lira bit her lip, closing her eyes tightly to try and hold back the tears welling there. But she couldn't hold back the words that came spilling out, low and raw. "Come with me. Please come with me."

Ahrin laughed softly, fingers tightening on hers with almost painful intensity. "Why do you think I'm here, you fool?"

Lira lurched forward, wrapping her arms fiercely around Ahrin's neck, bringing them tightly together. "What about your crew, your business?"

"Yanzi and Shiasta will take care of things. It will all be here when I get back. And if it's not, I'll rebuild it." Ahrin murmured in her ear, holding her just as fiercely. "If you ever tell anyone I said this, I'll kill you *and* them, but ... I love you, Lira Astor, and right now I don't want to be anywhere but at your side. Two years is too long."

Those whispered words broke the dam. Lira's tears soaked Ahrin's neck, the collar of her shirt, the ends of her raven hair. They were silent, heaving sobs, nothing dignified about it as she clung to Ahrin and let it all spill out of her. Ahrin held on. She made no soothing noises, didn't rock her, didn't speak a single word of comfort. But she didn't let go, didn't loosen her hold, not even for a second.

When Lira finally came to the end of her tears, she pulled back, mortified, scrubbing the sleeve of her tunic over her face. "Do you still love me after that horrifying display of weakness?"

Ahrin grinned, wide and easy, almost entirely real for once. "You soaked my shirt, and I think you got some snot on my favourite jacket. But how about we make a deal, you and I? We show the world our strength. And we show each other our weakness."

Lira eyed her. "And what exactly is your weakness? You've never slobbered all over me."

"You," Ahrin said simply, then cocked her head, considering. She hesitated, shoulders turning rigid, but she said the words. "And dark, enclosed, spaces."

Lira smiled. For the first time in two years, she smiled. And it felt good. "I think that's a good deal."

"Then let's shake on it." Ahrin held out her hand.

Lira reached out, took hold of her hand, and then yanked Ahrin towards her, leaning up to kiss her like she'd wanted to every single moment of every single day of the past two years.

"I've missed you so much." Ahrin breathed when they broke for air, "So much." And then they were kissing again, and Ahrin's confident hands were unbuttoning her shirt, her tunic. Lira kicked off her boots, managed to wrestle Ahrin's jacket off her shoulders.

"Good work on getting the big cabin," Lira murmured as she dragged Ahrin onto the plush bed.

"I am a crime boss, after all." Ahrin's skin was hot against hers, feverishly so, and Lira's world faded to nothing but sensation and the first experience of joy she'd had in more than two long years.

"What was it like, prison?" Ahrin asked sometime later. They lay on their backs under the tangled sheets, candlelight giving the cabin a warm glow, rough seas out of the harbour sending the floor under them rocking sharply back and forth.

"Awful."

"If you ever want to talk about it—"

"I don't."

Ahrin turned to look at her. "I hear it's healthy to talk about things. With people you love and trust."

"Is that so?" Lira arched an eyebrow. "When will you be telling me about what happened to you, then? Before we met, I mean. When they were training you to be a Hunter."

"My life started when we met."

Lira snorted at that obvious deflection. "Rubbish. Also, romantic nonsense doesn't suit you."

Ahrin laughed, eyes bright. "You are the least romantic person I've ever met, Lira Astor. I made a grand declaration before and you barely miss a stride."

"I did cry embarrassingly into your chest."

"True enough." Ahrin hesitated. "Is it ... given I did just admit before that you are one of only two weaknesses ... do you...?"

"Do I what?" Lira grinned as Ahrin's words trailed off.

"Nothing," she grumbled and shifted away.

Lira frowned. "I've upset you somehow. What is it?"

Ahrin's face was serious as she lifted a hand to tuck a strand of hair behind Lira's ear. "Sometimes I find it hard to know where I stand with you. You're locked up so tight, so guarded, you always have been."

"So are you," Lira murmured. "You hide behind that cool mask of yours. Ever since we met. You even tried to convince me that you don't feel things like everyone else."

She frowned. "I don't. Not really. I—"

That awful rigidness came over Ahrin then, and Lira hesitated, trying desperately to think of the right thing to say to make it go away. But fortunately, at that moment, the ship hit a particularly powerful swell and rocked hard to starboard. Lira went tumbling to the side of the bed, the two of them tangling together as they fell. They came up laughing, kissing, eager hands sliding over bare skin.

"Talking later," Lira murmured, already breathless.

"Did you steal Lucinda's Hunter army?" Lira brushed her fingers absently over the tattoo on the inside of Ahrin's wrist. Three jagged black lines. Like claw marks. Ahrin shivered and pulled away, though Lira didn't think she realised she'd done it.

"It isn't her army. It's mine." Ferocity edged Ahrin's voice and sent a thrill through Lira.

Lira lifted an eyebrow. "You mean mine, don't you? They're my inheritance." She paused. "That night, when I escaped the island ... they ambushed me at one of the fishing villages. Timor was there. He said Lucinda knew about you being a traitor too. How did you get away?"

"Instinct. I went to wait at the top of the cliff path for Lucinda to return from her meeting with whoever had been on that ship." She paused, gaze narrowing. "The moment I saw her, I knew something was off, so instead of meeting her I hid in the shadows and followed her. She went straight to Shiasta, gave him orders to get his unit and bring me in."

Lira huffed a breath that was a mix of affection and horror. "Let me guess. Instead of leaving then, you gambled on Shiasta's loyalty, and waited for him to come for you?"

Ahrin shrugged lazily. "It was a good gamble. Shiasta and his unit came with me. When it came down to it, the brainwashing of our youth worked in my favour. Either that or the faint memory of sharing a dormitory since birth made him choose me."

"That's how you took down Transk so quickly."

"In six months." Ahrin stretched like a cat, eyes glowing with satisfaction. "No street thug in Dirinan is a match for a trained Hunter. Or my magical abilities."

Warm memories of running the streets with Ahrin filled her then, bringing with it a deep yearning that she tried to ignore. "And how do your Hunters feel about being criminals?"

"They do as I command them." Ahrin turned toward her. "We don't know how to want things. We were trained only to obey."

"But *you* want things. You came to Dirinan wanting Transk's spot, wealth and power of your own."

"I was different," she said, eyes going distant. "Don't, Lira." The warning voice was back, the implicit threat to back off and not ask any more questions.

"Fine." Lira scowled, then changed the subject, raising something that had been niggling at her. "Do you think Underground really is behind Egalion's kidnapping? I was sure of it because I saw Shiasta in Karonan and assumed that meant Underground were still active and hunting for me. But now … apart from the style of the kidnapping, there's nothing to connect Underground at all."

"I can't think of anyone else on this continent with the resources, *or* the motivation, to kidnap a mage of the higher order and her Taliath husband. And there's been no ransom note, no challenge to the council, nothing," Ahrin said thoughtfully. "So while I can't figure out *why* Underground would want to take them, they're the most likely culprit. I'm more confident in your theory that Lucinda and her people originate from Rotherburn."

"Good." Even if Lucinda hadn't taken Egalion, if she was in Rotherburn, that's where Lira wanted to go. The fierceness of that desire leapt up in her again, even clearer and more determined now that she had Ahrin at her side. "What do you think she came here for in the first place?"

"I'm not sure. Building mages was part of it, but that's not all." Her gaze narrowed. "I'd like to know before we walk into her home. It's dangerous, otherwise. I prefer to be more prepared than that."

Lira smiled, shifting closer. "Nothing is going to take us down."

"Confident, much?" Ahrin murmured, rolling them over so her hair fell like a curtain around Lira's face.

"You disagree?"

"Not for a second," Ahrin breathed as she leaned down to kiss her.

Hours later, Lira leaned against the bulkhead by the porthole, staring out at the endless darkness of the ocean. Shadows spilled across the floor of the cabin, the lantern long since burned out. The winds had calmed too, the ship's movement now just a gentle rocking under her feet.

Ahrin slept, still and silent, sprawled out under the covers.

Lira leaned forward until her forehead pressed against the wood, her eyes sliding closed, the invisible weight on her shoulders as heavy as it had ever been. She was glad of Ahrin's presence, relieved that Ahrin had chosen to come with her, but ... Ahrin was a crutch. Something that made the void disappear and the doubt fade away, but only for a short time. It didn't permanently remove any of it.

She'd tried, but failed, to sleep, tormented by the memory of being in that cell, of being abandoned by the Mage Council and thoroughly defeated by Lucinda. She didn't even know what she was anymore. There was no chance now of ever redeeming her name in the council's eyes, even if she'd wanted to, which she didn't. But there was no home to go back to either ... no place for her anywhere.

The need for vengeance sustained her now, but here in the darkness of night she knew deep down that once she'd achieved that, there was nothing. No next step. No hope for something more.

Lira was finally free, but she didn't *feel* free.

CHAPTER 20

T he sharp clanging of the ship's bell had Lira moving from where she'd been exercising on deck to head for the port railing, making sure to keep out of the way of Rilvitha's crew as she did so. The woman ran a tight ship, her authority clear and absolute, but Lira had her suspicions about their true nature. The scarred, tattooed, and well-armed sailors on this ship were no legitimate merchant crew.

Lira joined Garan and the others where they were already gathering, staring out to where blue ocean crashed against a visible landmass.

They'd reached the coast of Rotherburn.

Ahrin was there too, a step distant from the young mages. Garan had reacted predictably furiously to the sight of the Darkhand their first morning after leaving port, but when Lira pointed out that another skilled warrior and mage could only help them find his relatives, he'd subsided into unhappy silence. Tarion hadn't seemed bothered by the addition, nor had Lorin. Fari had merely let out a long sigh and said something about attractive killers. Ahrin had smartly kept her distance from them throughout the journey.

As glad as she was for Ahrin's presence at her side, Lira worried about the friction her presence might cause, especially if they encountered danger. She'd just have to hope that the Darkhand and Garan saw the sense in working together despite their differences. Pushing aside her worries, Lira stared out at what was revealed to them.

It was a cloudless, sunlit day, almost *too* bright in contrast to the dull weather in Shivasa, light reflecting off the water and making Lira's eyes water. She squinted, studying the distant land with curiosity.

The ship had dropped anchor several miles out from shore, Rilvitha presumably reluctant to move within range of any potential defences—not that any were visible. Lira's gaze narrowed on a gloomy, narrow gap between rugged cliffs, then followed the line of cliffs to the north where the land slowly inclined downwards to a flat, sandy, beach.

It wasn't just a lack of defences. There was *nothing* in sight that gave any indication people lived here.

What appeared to be buildings making up a village clustered not far back from the shore close to where the cliffs transitioned to beach. The area appeared empty, though. Utterly deserted. No people. No animals. No other boats bobbed on the sea. There were no signs of life at all.

To the south of the ominous gap, the towering cliffs ran as far as the eye could see before disappearing into the horizon. They were too high to give any glimpse of what might be up there.

"What are we looking at?" Ahrin asked tersely, glancing at the captain.

"This map says there's a port city right here." Rilvitha had the parchment unrolled and balanced on the railing, braced with one hand against the light breeze. She stabbed at a particular section of map with her index finger. They clustered more closely around her so they could see it. "This was the most recent one I could get my hands on at such short notice, but it's still decades old."

"That collection of rotting wood is not a harbour city," Ahrin said, staring across the water at the distant village. "So either the map is wrong or the city moved somewhere else."

Garan was frowning like the rest of them. "Or the distancing is out. Maybe the port is farther south or north along the coastline."

"Or never existed?" Fari suggested.

Ahrin waved a dismissive hand. "Then why put it on a map in the first place?"

"Enough with the tone," Garan snapped.

Ahrin spun on him, quick and dangerous. "Or what?"

"I can stand up for myself, thanks," Fari said before they came to blows. "And I honestly don't care how she talks to me. I only bother about people I like and respect."

Lira smothered a smile.

Fari continued, "But the murderous assassin has a point about it being on the map. So I concede that the map is most likely wrong."

Ahrin's cool gaze flicked to her. She gave Fari a single nod.

Lira moved away from the huddle, stretching tense shoulders before she spoke. "Either way, this is a good place to go ashore, where there's nobody around to see us. We can search for the nearest inhabited town on foot. And if we're not spotted coming ashore, it will make it easier to try and blend in and pretend we're locals."

"Assuming they speak Shiven, Zandian, or Tregayan," Tarion mumbled.

"I never paid much attention, but I'm pretty confident that if Uncle Finn had discovered a new language in all his research on Rotherburn, we would never have been able to shut him up about it." Garan shrugged.

Rilvitha rolled up the parchment, the dark skin of her forearms gleaming in the bright sun. "I'll give you one of my ship boats, but I'm not going any closer to shore. I have cargo to sail to Port Rantarin and no desire to lose it by running into an unexpected reef or a horde of antagonistic humans or mages who haven't had any contact with the outside world for decades."

"You'll circle back in three weeks?" Ahrin confirmed with a raised eyebrow.

"Presuming no bad weather or holdups at Port Rantarin." A sharp nod. "I'll be here, but I'll wait only as long as I judge it's safe. If you don't appear, I'll make two more runs, a fortnight apart as I move up and down the west coast, and then I'm done."

Garan pushed off the railing. "Let's get to it."

One by one, they hefted packs onto their shoulders and gathered the various weapons they'd brought. In addition to the food and water supplies in her pack—her bow attached to the outside—Lira slung a quiver of arrows over her shoulder, belted a dagger at her waist and a knife to her leg.

Her grandfather's sword had hung at Tarion's hip since they'd left Dirinan. When Ahrin had first caught sight of Tarion wearing it, she'd levelled a sharp look at Lira but said nothing. Whatever her thoughts were, the Darkhand was keeping them to herself for now. Or maybe she just didn't care what Lira did with her grandfather's sword.

Tarion hadn't named it or otherwise acknowledged its existence, but Lira hadn't missed how often his hand rested on its hilt, as if that was its most natural place to be. The sword suited him.

Once ready, they moved to where three of Rilvitha's crew were in the process of winching one of the ship's boats down into the water. It hit the surface with a splash, rocking from side to side before settling itself.

One of the crew quickly unrolled a rope ladder coiled on deck and tossed it over the side. After checking that it was firmly attached to the deck, he gave them a thumbs up.

Lira went first, swinging herself over the side and clambering down the rope ladder. Her progress was slower than she liked with the others watching her, and she almost fell at a couple of points, her movement made awkward by the heavy weight of her weapons and pack. The boat rocked hard when she landed in it, and she caught her balance before moving aside so the others could follow.

Being so close to so much water flooded her senses for a moment, and she took a deep breath, savouring the sensation. Her magic danced in her veins.

"You particularly enjoy the smell of saltwater, Spider?" Fari asked, landing next and catching the blissful look on Lira's face.

Lira shrugged. "So what if I do?"

Fari rolled her eyes so hard Lira was surprised they didn't pop out of her skull. "Are we really going to spend the rest of this ... mission ...

bickering at each other like children? I thought we'd agreed that we're allies for now."

"Mission?" Lira lifted an eyebrow, but then conceded with a sigh. The healer was right. "Yes, okay. Civility from here on in."

"That would be nice."

Lira almost smiled at the look on Fari's face, and something in her relaxed at their truce. She'd liked Fari so much, before. Not to mention constantly battling them, being on the defensive all the time, was tiring. She was glad for the excuse to end it. She needed all her energy for what came ahead.

Garan landed next, followed by Lorin, and then Ahrin. Tarion came last, and Lira's teeth ground at the sight of him climbing down the ladder rather than simply using his magic. Those bracelets were genuinely the stupidest thing she'd ever encountered. Not only that, but their existence was going to affect how useful he would be. Her gaze narrowed. Something to raise with Ahrin in private later.

"Garan and I will row," Ahrin said crisply. "The rest of you keep an eye out. You see anything untoward, any movement at all onshore, and you tell us at once."

Nobody seemed inclined to disagree with this plan, and soon the boat lurched into movement, heading steadily away from the ship. Lira leaned against the side, one hand reaching down to trail through the cold water. Idly, she let her magic out, using it to increase the force of the water flowing against the back of the boat, testing the strength of her ability.

Their progress quickened almost imperceptibly. Ahrin glanced back at her, as if noticing something had changed, but Lira said nothing. In minutes, she could feel the drain on her power, the increase in her heartrate, and let go of the magic. Like all new abilities, she was going to have to build up her strength in using it.

It wasn't long before the ship's boat scraped up against the sandy shore, and Tarion and Fari jumped out to drag it farther onto the beach. They climbed out and stared around them. It was a picturesque vista

... all blue ocean, sunlit sky, and pristine sand spread out as far as Lira could see. Grass waved lazily in a faint breeze where the beach ended.

Perfect. If not for the odd stillness of the place.

The empty remains of the village they'd spotted from the ship sat just beyond the beach, but nothing had moved at their arrival. Even so, Lira felt uncomfortably vulnerable standing out in the open with the midday sun glaring down and the open landscape rendering them visible for miles around.

"I'd like to make sure that village is empty before we continue on." Ahrin's voice was low.

"Agreed." Lira unslung her bow, slid it into her left hand, then reached back to make sure her arrows were within easy reach.

"Fari, Tarion, you swing around and approach from the south," Ahrin said, like a general addressing troops with the utmost confidence they would do what she said. "Lorin and Garan, you come in from the north. Lira and I will take the eastern approach from the beach. You run into anything or anyone that tries to eat or otherwise kill you, shout. Loudly."

Garan tensed, clearly not liking being ordered around, but gave a sharp nod. They split up, Ahrin and Lira continuing straight ahead. The sand turned into wiry grass under Lira's boots, then to the packed dirt of what had once been a road. The breeze whispered around them, toying with the loose strands of her hair and carrying the scent of salt and seaweed.

Part of her was glad of the clear and bright day for how it increased visibility—nothing was going to be able to sneak up on them—but the rest of her remained uneasy. They were still an open target to anyone or anything hiding inside the buildings.

As they closed in on the outskirts of the village, she and Ahrin instinctively slowed their pace, all senses attuned to their surroundings. Just like when they'd run the streets of Dirinan. The comfort of that slid over Lira like a warm cloak, dispelling any unease and making her feel on firmer footing than she had since breaking out of prison. This was familiar. This she could rely on. The thrill uncurled in the base of her stomach.

"What do you think?" Ahrin said as they moved warily along a wide street into the village.

"I think nobody has lived here for years and years." Lira padded over to stare through a cracked and grimy window, the first in a long line of buildings on their left. Similar structures lined the street to their right. She couldn't see anything through the glass but dust-covered furniture and cobwebs hanging from the ceiling. There were no footprints in the dust or marks that indicated anything had been moved or touched.

Ahrin appeared silently at her shoulder, her watchful gaze on the other buildings nearby, covering them. "The question is, why did they leave?"

"The port city wasn't where the map said it was." Lira cocked her head. "Maybe it was abandoned for some reason, and the villagers went with it? These buildings could be all that is left."

"Maybe." Ahrin didn't sound convinced. "But a village situated like this would have been a fishing village—their livelihood would have been the ocean, not a nearby port city."

"Unless the city moved too far away, making it too costly or time-consuming for them to sell their fish there?" Even as she said the words, Lira didn't buy them. Fari had been right. Nobody *moved* a city, and even if it had been the case, there would be other towns and villages in the area for these folks to sell their fish. Not to mention, if remnants of the village remained, then bits of the city should too. Yet nothing else was visible along the open coastline.

"No, I don't think that's it," Ahrin echoed her thoughts, her gaze coming to rest briefly on Lira's. "Do you feel it too?"

Lira nodded. The oddness. The prickle of danger even in the obvious emptiness of the place. "Back in Dirinan, this feeling usually resulted in you ordering us to abandon what we were planning and find another mark, on the grounds that the score wasn't worth the risk involved."

"That's not an option here. Rilvitha's well and truly raised anchor by now."

"Then we forge ahead." Lira shrugged. "Besides, it doesn't really matter why this town was abandoned. We're not here to solve the mystery of Rotherburn."

Ahrin gave her a look like she thought that was wishful thinking but moved on without a word. They made it almost all the way down the street, confirming every building they passed was empty, when running feet sounded from the north. Spinning, Lira had her bow knocked and raised in the next instant. A deadly looking knife materialised in Ahrin's right hand.

Lorin appeared seconds later, his dagger out and held ready. He didn't look panicked, just alert and wary. "You'd better come and see this."

Lira glanced at Ahrin, then set off after the Shiven mage. He moved fast despite the faint limp he still had, and his eyes darted around as he led them through the densest part of the village and out along a road leading north.

Garan waited outside a small house set just off the road, his dagger out too, shoulders tense. "Have a look inside," he said when Lira and Ahrin arrived. "Lorin, go and get Tarion and Fari. I don't think we should stay separated."

Ahrin was moving toward the front door before Garan finished speaking, and Lira followed, keeping her bow knocked and ready.

"You do have magic, you know." Ahrin gave her a look.

"Magic doesn't always work," she replied, gaze narrowing on the dark rectangle of the front door. "Remember that time you kidnapped us and set razak to hunt and kill me? I learned from that experience."

"I can't believe you're still holding a grudge over that."

Lira didn't reply. By then they'd stepped into the house, and she and Ahrin paused to let their eyes adjust to the dim interior. The main room to their right was almost completely dark; rotting curtains hung over every window so that only slivers of the outdoor sunlight made it through cracks in the fabric. Once her vision had adjusted, it only took a second for Lira's sweeping gaze to catch what had sent Lorin running to get them.

"That's creepy," Ahrin remarked.

Faint brown stains covered the floor; spatters ranging in size from tiny droplets to something more closely resembling a puddle, interspersed with streaks of varying widths and lengths. A couch in the middle of the room had a wide, circular patch of the same dark stain on the middle cushion. In Lira's experience, only one substance looked like that.

Old, dried blood.

A shiver ran down Lira's neck. Not fear, something else. Anticipation. Excitement. The long-buried thrill stirred more strongly in the pit of her stomach, and a smile curled unbidden at her mouth.

"No skeletons, so whoever was bleeding survived, or the bodies were moved." Ahrin turned and left, unlike Lira, completely businesslike, heading into the corridor leading away from the front door. "There are more bloody streaks along here." She called back a second later. "Very faint, but drag marks, by the look."

Eyes tracking the old blood, Lira crossed the living room and headed through into the room adjacent. Here a rectangular gap stood where a back door had once been, open to the day outside. A sea breeze whistled through a cracked window to her right, sending the mouldering curtain in front of it blowing back and forth. More dried blood spatters covered the path from hallway to back door, interrupted by drag marks, then led out into a grassy yard.

After making sure the room was empty, she crossed to the doorway and looked out the back. "No skeletons out here either," she called back. "Unless they were buried."

Ahrin appeared silently at her shoulder. "There's enough blood in this house to indicate at least three bodies. It's possible there were survivors, but I think there's too much blood for that."

Lira stepped out, bow raised again, and did a quick scan of the yard. "Do you see any signs of disturbed earth?"

"No. If they were buried, it was done a long time ago," Ahrin said. "Every curtain in this house is closed … whatever happened here, my guess is it happened at night-time, and nobody has set foot in the house since."

"The closed curtains also mean the bloodstains could have been there longer with no sunlight to fade them," Lira added. "Look here, where the light from the open door falls across the floor—those stains are barely visible compared to the rest in the house. There's no smell of rot either."

So why the prickling sense of existing danger?

"Whatever did this came through the doors, too." Ahrin looked at her. "No windows smashed or holes in the walls."

Lira frowned, crossed straight to the opening from the kitchen into the yard. No remnants of the door itself remained, but a close look at where the hinges had been revealed torn, splintered wood.

A whistle came from the front of the house. When Lira and Ahrin returned to the road, Fari and Tarion had arrived. Fari's dark skin was noticeably pale, and her hands trembled at her sides. Lira glanced from her to the grim look on Tarion's face and put the pieces together instantly: Fari's healing magic had a particular affinity with blood. "There are more houses like this."

"A lot more." Garan had a hand on Fari's shoulder, steadying her.

"I can sense it everywhere," she said, voice shaky.

"There's our answer for why everyone left the village." Ahrin sheathed her knife. "They were all killed. Any that weren't presumably made the sensible decision to flee."

"Killed by who?" Lorin asked.

"Or *what*?" Lira said.

"It might not be the villagers that died," Tarion pointed out. "Anyone who travelled here from home in the past decades completely vanished, right? What if some of them were looking for the same port city we were, came ashore here for shelter, and were killed when they arrived? That would explain why nobody ever came back to detail what they found here."

"Oh, that's just fantastic. So we'd be next on the list for murdering, then?" Fari lifted an eyebrow, then shook her head. "The blood is too old for that—at least it's too old for it to be anyone who travelled here in the last five to ten years. In some of the buildings Tarion and I searched where the windows were broken or curtains drawn back, the stains were barely visible. Years of sunlight had faded them."

Ahrin looked thoughtful. "Lira and I agree with that analysis. Besides, by the amount of blood you just implied you sensed, that's a lot of sailors being murdered, without a single one escaping back to their ship to return and tell everyone what happened. Not to mention all the bodies appear to have been taken away."

"Well there's the mystery to what happened to Rotherburn solved," Garan said with a hint of dour humour. "They were all brutally murdered in the night decades ago. Uncle Finn will be thrilled."

"We should have brought Master A'ndreas with us," Lorin said. "He'd have been able to make better sense of this."

"Sure. And add kidnapping a mage master to our list of crimes. Great idea," Fari muttered.

"Something *did* happen to those that sailed here over the years, though," Lira pointed out. "Even if this blood isn't theirs. Why did they never come back?"

"Good point. It's dangerous for us to remain here," Garan said. "We should head inland, look for a—"

"Better idea to follow the coastline until we find the port," Ahrin cut over him. "That's where we'd pick up the trail of Egalion and Caverlock; wherever the ship carrying them docked. That's what we came for, no?"

Garan's jaw clenched. "You don't—"

"She's right, Garan." Tarion touched his arm.

Garan shook his cousin off. "I know she is. Doesn't mean I like being cut off mid-sentence and spoken to as if I'm a child."

Ahrin studied him for a moment, then shrugged. "Fair enough. Question is, do we head south or north?"

Instantly, all six of them turned, shifting their gazes in unison north, then south, then back to stare at each other blankly.

"South," Lorin said suddenly, confidence in his voice.

Lira didn't have any particularly strong view against this, so she nodded. "We should move the boat off the beach first, hide it in one of these buildings. The last thing we want is someone stumbling across it and wondering who arrived in it."

She trailed after the others as they headed back to the beach, wondering how much danger they were heading into.

A smile curled at her mouth, that hot thrill rising through her and pushing aside all the uneasy despair she'd been feeling since escaping jail. That feeling had always filled the void inside her, and she let it come sweeping back in now.

Ahrin glanced back, saw Lira's face and gave her a pointed look. Lira scowled, not in the mood to hear another warning about controlling her recklessness.

She didn't need to. It would make her stronger. Harder. More powerful.

CHAPTER 21

Once the boat was safely hidden away, they checked their packs, ensured weapons were close at hand, and set out along a rutted dirt road heading south toward the ravine they'd seen from the ship.

They moved at a steady upward incline, the beach to their left slowly morphing into grass-topped cliffs high above the waves crashing against rock below. Their surroundings remained deserted. No sea birds swooping around looking to catch fish. No rabbits or other smaller animals, either.

Once they reached the highest point of the clifftops, where the road levelled out, they paused to look around. Back in the direction from which they'd come, they could see several miles farther along the coast beyond the village. There was no other sign of habitation, although the land curved sharply inward several miles north, leaving only ocean visible to the horizon. Ahead of them and inland to the west all they could see were empty, grassy plains.

"If this is what previous explorers travelling here found, then what could have happened to them?" Fari wondered aloud. "Presuming we're right that they weren't the source of the blood we found back there."

Lira glanced inland without thinking, a little shiver overtaking her.

"The same thing that happened to the people in that village?" Lorin suggested.

"I told you, I couldn't sense any recent blood." Fari looked unconvinced. "Besides, the blood we did find was decades old, it could be up to fifty, sixty years. Whatever killed the villagers would be pretty old by now."

Ahrin shot her a sharp look. "Fifty years ... you mean, the blood probably dates back to the time Rotherburn cut off all contact with the world and, for all intents and purposes, vanished?"

"Could be, yes." Fari shrugged. "It's impossible to know for certain."

"We didn't search every single building," Tarion pointed out quietly. "There could have been evidence of more recent deaths that we just didn't see."

"That's true." Fari glanced back uneasily. "Maybe we shouldn't have left so quickly."

Ahrin shook her head, started walking again. "Solving the mysteries of Rotherburn isn't our goal, remember? Besides, when we find this port city, wherever Lucinda came ashore with Egalion and Caverlock, we can ask one of the locals what happened to the village."

"Could it have been a razak attack?" Garan asked. "Especially if Lira's theory is right about the monsters originating here in Rotherburn."

"Unlikely," Ahrin said. "Razak drink human blood. They don't spray it about all over the place. Although..." She gave him a thoughtful look. "If razak killed any more recent travellers here, that would explain why Fari didn't sense any blood."

"Nerik, then?" he asked. "They *do* like to rip intestines out and slash up their prey. Not to mention they can fly. And, as vicious as they are, they're not too big that they wouldn't have been able to get through the doors of those homes."

Tarion flinched, looked away.

Ahrin shrugged, disinterested. "Maybe."

"We could be on the completely wrong trail," Lorin said, seemingly determined to be gloomy. "Wandering about a long-deserted island like fools while Lucinda and her cronies do who knows what to Tarion's parents back home."

"Even if that's true," Lira said sharply, "your precious council is searching the entire continent for Egalion and Caverlock—if they're back there, the chances of us doing a better job finding them are pretty slim."

Several glances came her way in grudging agreement.

"Besides, this place is unlikely to be completely deserted," Ahrin said. "Whoever—or *whatever*—killed those villagers is presumably still running around. If everyone who's travelled here in the past fifty years found only deserted countryside, they would have sailed safely back home to tell everyone about it. Yet not a single one did."

Fari sighed. "I can't decide whether I'm reassured or horrified by that thought."

"Definitely horrified," Garan said, a smile tugging at his mouth.

They chuckled, but Lira didn't join them. Her gaze had caught in a flash of sunlight from the bracelets on Tarion's wrists, visible since he'd rolled up his sleeves in the warmth, and now she lingered on them, thoughtful.

"Reckless move," Ahrin murmured at her side, catching the direction of Lira's thoughts.

Lira imperceptibly slowed her pace, putting some distance between them and the others. "We might need his ability. It could be a powerful weapon."

"If I recall correctly, his ability is strikingly similar to the behaviour of a nerik—didn't he tear up the guard dogs at Temari, a horse or two, and almost rip a mage apprentice to shreds? All while having no idea what he was doing."

"Yes. The change makes him stronger, bigger, a vicious fighter."

"If he can't control it, that's far more of a liability than a help, as likely to kill us as keep us alive." Ahrin said. "It's a completely untested result of Underground's experiments. As far as I know, Lucinda never even knew that was a possible outcome."

"His use to us is hampered without it."

"I've seen him use a sword. I'd say he's still useful."

Lira wasn't convinced. "I'm not so sure he can't control it."

"You confident enough in that you're willing to gamble all our lives on it?"

Lira smirked at her. "The only person's safety I care about is yours, and you can handle yourself just fine, Darkhand."

"Are you two back there flirting or plotting our painful demise?" Fari turned and called back. "Interested parties want to know."

"Not something I'd joke about, if I were you," Ahrin said coolly, and Fari's eyes went wide.

Lira swallowed a laugh.

Garan tossed an arch look their way. "The Darkhand thinks she's intimidating, but if there's one thing we know about her, it's that she's a survivor. She knows that killing us reduces her chances of getting off this island. We're safe enough for now."

Ahrin glanced at Lira, lifted an eyebrow. "The pretty lordling has a brain. You never told me that."

"It must be a recent development," she said dryly.

"Garan's always had a brain," Tarion said. "He just finds it too much effort to use most of the time."

"Hey!" Garan shoved Tarion. Tarion chuckled, and the two of them mock-wrestled for a few moments, laughing. Surprise flickered through Lira; the two cousins seemed closer than they had before, more comfortable around each other. They'd grown closer the past few years.

"Don't underestimate them," Lira said in an undertone. "I did for a long time, and it was a mistake."

Fari glanced back, a curious little frown on her face, as if she'd caught some of what Lira had said. But she looked away without saying anything.

"I don't underestimate anyone, Lira," Ahrin murmured back, then tipped her head towards Lorin. "What's his deal? He doesn't talk much."

"He never has. He's loyal, though, and solid. You can rely on him in a fight."

Ahrin made a face. "Loyal?"

"I saved his leg, and his life, back at DarkSkull Hall. He takes that very seriously." She paused. "He says that's why he's helping me."

"And you don't believe him?"

Lira thought about that. "It's hard for me to accept, but if nothing else, Lorin is a man of honour. He truly believes I saved his life, and I do believe he feels he owes me a rather significant debt."

"Oh, that's why he left you locked up in prison for the rest of your life?"

Lira lifted an eyebrow. "Just like you did?"

"The difference being I didn't *know* you were locked away in prison." Ahrin scowled.

Lira sighed, then nodded. "Yeah."

"If I had, I would have gotten you out," Ahrin continued. "I wouldn't have rested until you were out. My mistake was in assuming you'd left me. But if I'd known..."

It was as close to an apology Lira was going to get, closer than she'd thought Ahrin capable of. So with her next stride she leaned closer, bumped their arms together, and said quietly, "I know."

She'd thought that was the end of the conversation, but a moment later the Darkhand murmured, "I don't make the same mistakes twice, Lira. Not ever."

By late afternoon, they reached the gap in the cliffs that had been visible from the ship. At its opening, it looked roughly wide enough to admit maybe three or four ships the size of Rilvitha's sailing abreast. Waves crashed hard against its rocky corners, though, and Lira didn't think it would be a particularly appealing approach, even for an experienced captain. The gap cut the coastline in two, continuing inland as far as they could see in a rough westerly direction; a long, perilous, ravine.

"Maybe we should have gone north." Garan peered into the frothing ocean far below. There was no obvious way to get across to the other side, and the rocky side of the gorge was far too perilous to attempt climbing down without proper equipment.

"It's a waste of time to re-trace our steps," Tarion spoke. Lira strained to hear him around the whistling of the wind off the ocean. "Let's see how far inland it goes. It's a natural feature of the landscape—there will have to be a bridge, or some other kind of crossing, somewhere."

"Works for me." Ahrin set off.

Staying well clear of the crumbling edge, they turned west. The wind buffeted around them, stronger now, howling, tugging at hair and clothing. The occasional glance downward showed the water remained as far below as before, but the clifftop directly opposite to the south appeared to inch closer the farther they walked, the gap narrowing. The water looked rough, too, with tall rocks peeking above the surface in places. Even though it remained wide enough for multiple ships, it wouldn't be easy to navigate.

The map must have been wrong. Wherever the port city was, they hadn't landed anywhere near it. Hours passed, but no sign of a bridge or other crossing materialised. Ahrin continued leading, stride confident and sure, and the tacit agreement seemed to be that they'd come this far, they might as well keep going.

Lira suspected none of them wanted to go back to that village as night approached.

The terrain remained relatively flat, wiry grass under their feet, a few stunted trees dotting the landscape. At one point, Lorin, frowning, stopped. He squatted down and dug his hand into the soil, gouging out a handful and then staring at it.

Lira came to a halt without complaint, glad for the opportunity to rest her aching legs and shoulders. She gingerly lowered her pack to the ground and dug out her water flagon. Everyone else did the same.

"What's wrong?" Garan asked.

"The soil is bad. You wouldn't be able to grow much in it, if anything." Lorin let go of the dirt and stood, pointing around them. "It's been the same the whole way so far. And the grass isn't good enough for cattle or sheep."

"Hence the lack of any farms, I imagine," Ahrin said tersely, clearly impatient. "Look, my magic has been telling me that the whole way; the grass is of a type that doesn't need much water or sunlight to survive."

Lorin nodded. "That's my point."

Tarion was the first to realise what the mage was saying. "We haven't seen a single sign of habitation. No towns or villages since the beach. No main roads either. This land is flat, perfect for farming, and the lack of ruins suggests it must have been farmland at some point. Even if towns had been abandoned for some reason, the ruins would still be around, like back at the beach."

Lira didn't get it. "So what?"

"What flat, grassy land near the coast have you seen back home that *isn't* either built up or used as farmland?" Garan said. "It's how cities work. Access to waterways, flat land for building or farming to support the population."

Lira fought not to roll her eyes as memories rose of her most boring classes at Temari. "But Lorin just said the soil isn't good for farming."

"So if this area wasn't used for farming, why aren't there any towns built on it?" Tarion said.

Lira merely stared at him. "How should I know?"

"It's just odd." Lorin shrugged.

"Ahrin, if I recall correctly, one of the mage abilities Underground gave you allowed you to manipulate plant life, vegetation?" Fari asked.

"That, along with concussive magic and telekinesis."

"Right. So can you sense whether there's any forest, shrubs, or richer grass around?"

Ahrin huffed an annoyed sigh. "I can't feel anything like that within the extent of my range, though I haven't actually extended my magic actively outwards. I'd rather not draw any unwanted mage or monster attention."

"And your range is a mile, or a little more, right?" Lira asked.

She nodded.

"That's not so far," Garan said.

"No, it's not. Besides, everything here is odd. Can we keep going now?" Ahrin turned to walk off without waiting for them to follow. Lira hefted her pack back onto her aching shoulders and followed.

It was getting harder to fight the growing feeling that continuing along this path was a terrible idea.

The thrill inside her surged, and she smiled.

Bring it on. It had been too long since she'd danced with danger.

CHAPTER 22

Hours later, as sunset cast an orange glow over their surrounds, they came upon the first ruins since the beachside village. Two stone pillars rose from the ground not far from the edge of the ravine—the stone was weathered and chipped and weeds grew at the base of both. Rusted iron bolts poked out from the river-facing side, but whatever had been attached to them was long gone.

"I think we found the remains of the bridge we've been looking for," Garan said, after taking a closer look. "Though it must have been destroyed a long time ago."

Lira squinted across the gap—it was much closer now—and almost immediately spotted what looked like matching pillars on the other side. A glance down had her stomach swooping at the distance to the river below. There was only rushing water. No sign of any debris from a fallen bridge.

Ahrin let out a low whistle, and they all turned. She was a short distance away, hunkered down and studying the ground. "I think this was a road. It's grown over now, but you can see the surface underneath is much smoother."

Lorin glanced at her, then walked a bit farther. "It looks like it follows the ravine. So maybe this was the river crossing, with a road leading off the bridge and to the west."

"Roads usually lead somewhere." Lira shrugged. "I say we follow it."

Tarion glanced around. "Out in the open like this? We'll be visible for miles around."

"What a thrilling prospect," Fari muttered under her breath.

"We've been out in the open the whole way so far," Garan said. "And isn't the idea to find some locals so we can ask about Lucinda?"

Ahrin shook her head. "Tarion has a point. *If* there are still people here, they'd be watching a road, particularly if it leads somewhere populated. Maybe we should plan out how we're going to approach before—"

"Uh ... guys?" The trepidation filling Lorin's voice had them all spinning to look in the direction towards which he pointed.

Lira stared. The distant northern horizon had turned black, thick clouds boiling in the sky had cut off every bit of light in that direction. Even as she watched, bright forked lighting speared down between the storm clouds, and then the sunny afternoon grew appreciably dimmer. A shiver of instinct ran down her spine. *Danger.*

Fari took a step backwards. "That doesn't look like a regular storm."

"Even if it is, we should find shelter. We're exposed and that looks pretty bad," Garan said grimly. "Let's follow the road and hope wherever it leads isn't far away. Even more creepy ruins would be better than weathering a storm out in the open."

Ahrin hesitated, glancing back the way they'd come, before looking at the storm. "All right, then."

The storm closed in quickly. Not long after they'd started walking again, faster this time, a wind gusted up over the plains, sending Lira's short hair whipping about her face and her quiver swinging against her pack. She cast the northern sky a wary glance. Their pace sped up, almost to a jog.

When Lira felt magic prickling along her skin, her violet light flared in response. She swore and doused it immediately.

"Control yourself," Ahrin snapped at her, receiving a glare in return.

"I think there's magic in that storm," Tarion said.

"Either that or a mage is calling it; a mage with weather ability?" Garan suggested. "Maybe there is a populated town ahead."

Lira debated the merits of arguing that heading towards a potentially hostile mage might not be the smartest move but quickly dismissed the idea. If the oncoming weather was magical, then they were in more immediate danger if it caught them out in the open. None of them had an ability that would counter the destructive force of a storm.

Soon the magic in the air was so thick Lira could taste it on her tongue, feel it making the hairs on her arms stand up. It became increasingly difficult to keep a hold on her own surging power. Her magic wanted to explode out of her, join with that already vibrating in the air.

The thick clouds, racing toward them now, eclipsed the already lowering sun, taking all light with it. They kept walking, ignoring aching legs and panting breaths, until shapes grew visible ahead, shadowy in the moonlight.

Thunder roared then, a deep, rumbling sound that seemed to make the ground beneath their feet tremble. More lightning flashed, terrifyingly close, and the scent of charred earth drifted on the wind.

"I think we found where the road leads," Lorin shouted over the encroaching storm.

Lira instinctively moved to unsling her bow, then realised it would be useless in the powerful winds sweeping around them. She readied her magic instead.

"Maybe." Garan, in the lead, slowed his pace. "It looks bigger than the village—this could be a proper town."

"There are no lights coming from it," Ahrin said. "Keep alert."

"The storm is almost on us. We should hurry." Tarion urged.

Ahrin held out an arm to stop him running ahead. "I'm not running into a trap. A bit of bad weather won't kill us."

Almost as soon as she spoke those words, the storm reached them, the darkness becoming absolute apart from the random flashes of lighting. Thunder roared out overhead, and Lira had to place her hands over her ears it was so loud. It felt like the ground literally rocked under her feet with the force of it. Then the rain started. A torrent of water from the skies unloading on them. She was soaked to the skin in seconds.

When Fari screamed, it took a moment for Lira to figure out what had caused it. A lightning flash had momentarily blinded her. The healer was pointing at the ground, where the grass had turned to ash.

"It almost hit me," she yelled.

Another flash of lightning burned into the ground scant inches from Lorin's left foot, and the scent of charring became even more potent in the air. He hopped to the side with a shout.

"Run!" Garan bellowed.

Lira tried, but it was as if the wind sought to hold them in place so that the lightning could pick them off one by one ... the force of it curled around them, tugging at feet and hair and clothing, pushing at them, making each step forward a battle.

There was no time to approach the town cautiously. In the flashes of light from the deadly lightning, the place was large and looming, suggesting it had once been a big town. Smaller buildings spread out into the countryside to the north, while the main cluster sat near the ravine edge.

It had once been walled too—from stone, it looked like in the dark—though the parts of it Lira could see in brief flashes of light were crumbling and ruined. A lightning bolt slammed into the ground ahead of her, and she swore, jerking hard to the side as the scent of carbon filled her nose.

Ahrin, two steps ahead of everyone, put out a hand to halt them as they reached the walls. They pressed hard up against its remains, seeking cover from the lightning. "Fari?" the Darkhand shouted.

"There's blood," she yelled back, pushing sopping hair from her face as she looked at the sky. "Very old. Not as much as before, but enough that I can sense it despite its age. If there's new blood, though, the traces are either too small for me to pick up or too far distant. This town is much larger than the ruins on the beach."

Lira squinted back the way they'd come, but all she could see was the storm, which continued to howl around them, as if hungry for their blood. Even so, looking through the gap in the walls along what seemed to be the main street of the town left her feeling danger, the darkness heavy with menace. But they had to get out of the weather, and at least inside the walls they could find a defensive position.

"We'll find a building to shelter in," Ahrin shouted, as if reading Lira's thoughts. "Get a few hours' sleep, keep a watch, then as soon as it's daylight and the storm clears we move again."

"Agree," Garan bellowed back.

Another lightning bolt ploughed into the ground, as if reinforcing their decision. Ahrin took the lead, slipping over the wall and into the town.

Lira shivered, and not just from her soaked clothing. From what she could see in the gloom, the buildings were as empty and ramshackle as the village earlier. The road they'd been following led into what seemed like the centre of the town, with streets leading off from it. The wind howled through the nooks and crannies, a lightning bolt slamming onto a roof nearby and sending splinters of wood raining down on them.

Seconds later, a door torn loose from its hinges in the howling gale came flying down the street towards them. Lira caught it with her telekinesis seconds before it hit Garan. It had flown so fast he could have been completely taken out by it.

"Thanks!" he shouted.

"Stop using your magic!" Ahrin snapped.

Lira ignored her. Her magic hummed and surged in her blood, wanting to be let out. Whatever this storm was, whoever controlled it, she wanted them right there in front of her. An adversary to be fought and defeated. Her teeth bared in a snarl.

Another bolt of lightning slamming into the ground inches from Tarion's boots had them all running again, searching for a solid-enough structure to provide shelter. Lira's level of unease rose the farther they ran. Heading deeper inside this town wasn't the right move. Even with the storm forcing them into it. She clenched and unclenched her left hand, fidgeting. Ahrin glanced back at one point, her gaze searching out Lira's, and they shared a little nod.

Ahrin was feeling it too.

Lira leaned into the familiar rapport. The two of them had been in this kind of position before and always come out on top.

About three blocks farther along, a right turn led into a wide street with taller buildings lining it. Ahrin paused there. "Fari, what can you sense? It would be good to have a high vantage point. From what I can tell, that middle building might be tall enough to give us a good view across the town and anything approaching once the storm clears. It seems pretty stable, too."

"The old blood I can sense nearby is pretty faint." The healer frowned, rain running in rivulets down her face and dripping to the ground as she concentrated. "I don't think people lived in this area."

"All that tells us is that they weren't killed here," Ahrin pointed out, but even so she shot another look Lira's way. Lira shrugged. It was possible this had been the business centre of the town, and the killings had happened at night, like back in the village, when everyone was home. It didn't really matter right now. The priority was getting out of the storm. "Let's go."

Three more lightning bolts came flashing from the sky as they ran for the building Ahrin had chosen. One sent Lorin careening sideways, his bad leg tripping him up as he desperately sought to avoid being hit. Tarion caught his arm, steadied him. They were the last two to stumble through the broken door.

For a moment they all simply stood just beyond the threshold, gasping for air, dripping water onto the floor. The storm howled around them. Wind set the walls creaking and groaning and whistled through gaps in the windows. Lira couldn't escape the sensation that the storm somehow knew they were inside and was trying to get at them.

To distract herself, she looked around. The building had been abandoned for so long it was impossible to tell what had once filled it, although from the shelving and counter on the ground floor, she guessed it had been a store of some kind.

The entrance door had been ajar, meaning the floor and anything near the doorway was weathered by the elements. Beyond, everything else was covered in a thick, unbroken layer of dust.

If anything or anyone had been in here anytime recently, it hadn't walked on the floor.

When Garan went to slide his pack off his shoulders, Ahrin shot him a sharp look. "We search this place from top to bottom before settling down to wait out the storm."

Ahrin hunted around for a piece of kindling—broken from a rotted table—then used flint to light it. It gave off just enough light to see by, and she headed for the narrow stairs at the back of the room. Lira followed without thought, and after a moment, so did the others. The stairs creaked loudly and were rotted away in spots, forcing them to step carefully to avoid breaking an ankle.

The stairs led up to three more levels that were equally empty, the air musty and damp. The walls shook with the regular gusts of wind outside and rain hammered incessantly on the roof, providing a rousing accompaniment to the roars of thunder.

"Do we think a mage is causing this storm?" Fari asked.

"It certainly feels full of magic," Garan said.

"I didn't get any sense of direction from the storm. It felt chaotic to me out there." Ahrin frowned slightly. "But I don't have the same training you all do."

"She's right," Tarion said slowly. "Not that I've ever heard of uncontrolled magical storms before."

"Well I hope that's the case, because otherwise I'd worry that someone created the storm and used it to herd us into this creepy town," Fari said with a sigh.

Everyone turned to stare at her.

"What?" she asked indignantly.

Garan let out a chuckle. "Thanks for making sure I'll never sleep again."

"Enough chatter," Ahrin said in a low voice. "Tarion, Garan, you clear the first floor, Fari and Lorin the second, Lira and I will clear the top."

It didn't take long. Each floor only held a few rooms. Once they'd made sure everything was clear, they chose a room with no windows on the third floor. Lorin and Fari collected broken floorboards from other rooms as kindling, and without thinking, Lira used a touch of magic to get the fire going; wanting to get dry and warm as quickly as possible.

"No magic." Ahrin's voice snapped through the room. Fari visibly quailed at the tenor of it, and even Garan and Tarion froze in place.

Lira bristled instantly, *hating* the tone of command in the Darkhand's voice.

"Ahrin is right." Garan caught the look on Lira's face. "If there's any chance those bloodstains were caused by nerik, we need to be careful. They and the razak can track magic use."

"Thanks for telling me what I already know, but we haven't seen any sign of those monsters since we got here, not to mention the blood we found is *old*," Lira muttered, but it was half-hearted. Garan and Ahrin were right to be cautious.

They stripped off their soaking clothing, wrapped themselves in the damp blankets from their packs, and curled up around the flames to try and get some rest. Fari made a half-hearted attempt to clear away the dust on the floor, but eventually gave up with a sigh.

Ahrin took first watch, and Tarion offered to take the next one. He seemed unsettled, anxious, and Lira figured he probably wasn't going to be able to sleep. She instinctively felt for him, but when he caught her gaze across the room, she quickly looked away.

Right now there was no space for feeling anything but focus and calm. If they survived this little jaunt, Tarion would go back to his life in Alistriem and Lira would be on the run, spending the rest of her life hiding from the council.

If they survived. Listening to the wind and the thunder roaring outside, thinking about the bloodied ruins they'd seen, Lira wouldn't have put any money on that bet.

CHAPTER 23

L ira woke suddenly.

Everything was silent, as if the world had gone still. The storm must have blown itself out. She looked around, but nothing seemed out of place. Maybe the sudden ceasing of wind and rain had woken her. The fire still crackled, casting a violet-white glow over the room and providing enough warmth that their drying cloaks steamed softly.

She sat up and cast her gaze over the sleeping forms of her companions. Once she was sure they were all asleep, she rose quietly to her feet and padded over to her cloak. After a moment's concentration, she drew on her magic and used it to seek out all the water in the material and draw it out.

It was more subtle work than she was accustomed to, and sweat beaded on her forehead, the drain on her strength noticeable. But then water began dripping to the floor, more and more until her cloak was dry and a large puddle had formed underneath it.

A triumphant grin stretched over her face.

Putting the cloak on, she went upstairs to where Ahrin had taken watch on the top floor. It took a moment to spot the Darkhand where she stood perfectly still in the shadows by a window facing east.

"Can't sleep?" Ahrin asked quietly without turning around.

"Had enough." Lira moved to stand on the opposite side of the room to stare out the cracked and grimy windows. The storm had definitely cleared away; a watery moonlight shone down, giving her a dim view over the roofs and streets of the abandoned town. "You can go and get some rest if you like."

"I'm not tired."

Lira accepted that, and a comfortable silence fell. She studied the town more closely, but it was hard to see much detail. After a while, she grew bored of staring at nothing. "What do you think happened here?"

"I have no idea." Ahrin's voice floated back.

"The air feels ... wrong. I'll happily face down any known danger, but there's something entirely off about this place. And that storm ... it wasn't natural. Directed by a mage or not, it seemed like it was attacking us."

Ahrin let out a soft huff. "You love it, don't lie. I've seen that excitement creeping over you ever since we found the bloodstains in the village on the beach."

Lira said nothing to that. Ahrin was right.

"We could turn back at any point," the Darkhand said next. "I assume you've considered that *something* roaming these plains was enough to force a whole village, and probably this town too, to run and hide—*if* anyone survived. Rotherburn had mages back in the day, just like us, and presumably a standing army too. Yet now that all seems to be gone, and we're blithely strolling deeper into the countryside without knowing anything about what we might be facing."

"That's not fear I detect, is it?"

"You know it's not." That cold edge reappeared in Ahrin's voice. "I'm trying to temper that thrill-seeking side of yours by pointing out how unprepared we are."

"Have you considered that those mages and standing army you spoke of destroyed whatever was the cause of the bloodspill, hence the blood being so old? Or maybe the bloodshed was a result of a civil war, and maybe these places are empty because nobody wanted to come back and re-populate a town so many people were killed in." Lira's gaze narrowed when she thought she saw movement in one of the streets, but it was just a broken window shutter swinging in a breeze that had kicked up. It whistled through the broken glass in front of her, and she was glad of her dry cloak. The air had cooled.

"You make a good point, though none of that explains where everyone is now, or why no visitors to this place from our home have ever returned." A pause, then, casually, "Speaking of bloodshed, I heard you killed Greyson."

"I set him alight in his prison cell on my way out."

Silence fell, and Lira assumed Ahrin had no further interest, but a few moments later she spoke again. "I remember a time when you hesitated over killing a man in cold blood, even to save your life."

"And when that happened, you looked at me with contempt."

"I did. Killing is a necessary thing, for a wide range of reasons," Ahrin said. "You need to be capable of it if you want to survive."

"Is there a point to this little talk, then?" Lira asked, irritation beginning to grow.

"Just making conversation. Staring out the window at nothing is boring."

Lira chuckled softly. "Isn't it important for a trained killer like you to be able to stand still for long periods of time without getting bored?"

"It is. But I wasn't expected to kill by stealth often, Lira. I'm trained to murder your enemies in whatever way is necessary, but ideally in quick, efficient fashion."

Whether consciously or not, Ahrin's voice had placed emphasis on the 'your,' and it made Lira stiffen. A nagging worry that she'd never entirely buried rose up to distract her focus. She dismissed it, returning her attention to the streets.

She started suddenly when Ahrin's arms wrapped around her waist, her mouth brushing against the skin of her neck. "Didn't even hear me coming. Poor form, Astor."

"That's because my attention was *outside*, where we are supposed to be keeping a lookout," she grumbled, but it was half-hearted. She was already melting into Ahrin's touch.

"For what?" Ahrin kissed her neck, her collarbone, one of her hands sliding inside Lira's shirt. "This place is empty."

"We don't know—" Lira's self-control broke, and she turned to meet Ahrin's hungry kiss. After a moment she pulled away and made a face. "You're all wet and cold."

"We're all wet and..." Ahrin shifted away. "Why aren't you?"

Lira smiled and summoned her magic again, sending it into Ahrin's damp cloak this time, pulling out all the water she could sense until there was a puddle on the floor.

Ahrin looked at it in contemplation. "Another ability broke out?"

"While I was in prison. I can manipulate water."

"Just water? What about other liquids?"

"Not sure. Definitely water." Lira tensed as unwelcome memories threatened to rise. "There wasn't much opportunity to experiment in prison."

"Do the others know?"

"No."

"Good," Ahrin murmured, shifting closer again so that she could press Lira against the wall, mouth sliding along her jaw.

"They could all get murdered downstairs if we don't pay attention," Lira said half-heartedly, her hands busy unbuttoning Ahrin's shirt.

"And I care about that since when?"

"Fair," Lira mumbled, then, as Ahrin's hands found sensitive skin and a gasp escaped her. "I'm not doing this with you on that hard floor full of splinters and covered in dust."

"This wall is perfectly serviceable."

Smiling, Lira moved suddenly, spinning them so that Ahrin crashed against the wall. "Good, then *you* can get the splinters."

Ahrin chuckled and pulled her closer, always closer. They sank into another kiss, hands momentarily stilling in bliss. Then Lira pulled away, just enough to shift her head to press a kiss to Ahrin's jaw.

And they both froze.

Their breath was frosting as they breathed out.

"Rotted carcasses." Ahrin was swinging away from her and drawing her knife in the next heartbeat. Despite the situation, Lira's heart skipped a beat at the simple grace of her movement. "Razak."

"It has to be close. See if you can spot where it is," Lira said, then ran for the door, took the stairs swiftly while re-buttoning her shirt, and ducked into the room where the others were sleeping. She grabbed her bow and quiver of arrows, then knelt to shake the sleeping Tarion. His hazel eyes blinked open and stared into hers.

"There might be a razak out there. We're going to check it out. Keep an eye while we're gone, and don't use any magic. Put out the fire, too, just in case."

Sleepiness vanished from his face and he nodded, already sitting up and pushing his blanket off. By the time she got to the door he was reaching for the Darkmage's sword.

Ahrin met her on the stairs with a quick, "Nothing visible outside. Might be inside or hiding in the shadows of a nearby street."

A quick search of the rooms didn't reveal a razak hiding anywhere, though their breath continued to frost in the night air. Either a single razak was very close to their location, or there was more than one of them out there.

Once confident the building was empty, they returned to the ground floor and approached the front door cautiously, slipping outside and then stilling in the shadows of the overhang.

Lira glanced left and right, breath still frosting. It was hard to be sure, but the darkness two blocks away to their left looked different, *darker*, somehow. Her gaze narrowed—not sure if she caught a movement within the darkness or if she was just being paranoid.

"I see it too. Let's circle away from here, try and get around behind it," Ahrin said. "And be careful. For it to be so cold inside, there might be more than one nearby."

Lira nodded and together they inched to their right until they reached a corner. As soon as they turned, they moved into a swift run, putting several blocks between themselves and the building before circling back around until they came up two blocks behind the patch of darkness. There they paused, staring down towards it, confirming it was still there.

"Do you think it's watching the place?" Lira said, confused.

"Razak uncontrolled by a mage don't have that level of intelligence," Ahrin breathed. "But it could be that it scented your magic use earlier and tracked you this far—and now it's just waiting to sense it again so it can get a more specific lock on your location."

"If that's the case, other razak could have scented the same thing and be waiting nearby." Lira glanced at her Darkhand. "Draw them in?"

Ahrin lifted a palm, summoned a crackling concussion ball. The scarlet light washed over Lira's face, flared brightly for a few seconds, then flickered out of existence. At the same time, Lira allowed a trickle of magic to light up her hands in their familiar violet glow for a few seconds. Then, magic suppressed once again, they backed away, moving off the street and into the shadows by the wall of a building.

For a long moment, all was still. Nothing stirred in the night. Lira was just beginning to wonder if they were imaging the whole thing, if perhaps summer nights in Rotherburn were simply colder than back home, when the first rattle echoed through the street.

Her heart thudded.

She narrowed her gaze on the shadows where the sound had come from—the patch of darkness they'd already picked out—body utterly still. And then she saw the faint stirrings of movement. Lira's hand slid into Ahrin's, squeezed it once, then she moved away.

Slowly, inch by inch, she crept farther down the street, closer to the thing, keeping to the shadows the whole way. Another rattle, chains dragging over stone, rang out. This razak was curious, puzzled. And *much* closer.

In the next moment the monster moved into the street, a graceful slide of long, writhing limbs. A flash of silver eyes broke the darkness of its centre of mass. This one was larger than Lira remembered them being, its limbs stretching the width of the street, the inky tendrils blacker than night. It rattled again.

Once Lira was in position, Ahrin stepped out into the middle of the street and summoned another concussion burst. It spun bright scarlet in the palm of her raised hand, hissing and spitting with energy.

The monster *went* for her.

It covered the distance so quickly that Lira could barely blink before a long, scaled, limb was whipping out towards Ahrin's chest. The Darkhand danced away, rolled across the cobblestones, and came up slashing with her dagger.

Lira stepped into the street and lifted her nocked bow, allowing her violet light to surround her forearms and catch its attention. "Hey!"

It spun around, rattling, and she fired her first arrow. Having honed her muscle memory after hours of practice on Rilvitha's ship, her arrow unerringly buried itself in one of the creature's three eyes. It shrieked, lashing out at her so quickly that her second arrow flew wide—forcing Lira to dive away mid-loosing. Rotted carcasses!

She was back up on her feet in the next second, running with quick strides, ducking to avoid another blow. Ahrin, fearless, attacked from its other side, weaving between lashing limbs, trying to get to the creature's head. Lira managed to loose another arrow, but the creature was unbelievably fast and avoided the hit.

Swearing, she had to drop the bow, unable to lift and fire with any accuracy while ducking away from multiple thrashing limbs.

"Lira, no fire!" Ahrin bellowed just as Lira was about the set the thing alight.

Accustomed to obeying the command in Ahrin's voice, Lira drew her dagger instead. The two of them worked their way towards the monster's head, but there were too many flailing limbs to be able to gain any significant ground.

Sweat slicked her skin, and her heart raced. She still hadn't built up enough stamina after years of being trapped in a prison cell, and her lungs burned for air. Ahrin took more of the load, dauntless and fast, but the fight was at an impasse. Lira somehow doubted the monster would tire before they did.

Then she heard Tarion's voice bellowing, "Distract it!"

Lira moved, drawing the razak's attention away from the direction of Tarion's shout. Ahrin followed without hesitation. The monster let out a furious rattle, intensifying its attempts to catch its too-quick prey.

Lira ducked under a swing, came up slashing, then spotted Tarion dancing his way between several limbs to position himself behind the creature's head. Once there, the Darkmage's sword was up and swinging with unbelievable speed, a grunt of effort escaping him as it cut right through the middle of the razak's triangular head.

The shadowy tendrils vanished and the head dropped to the ground, the silver fire of the eyes going dark and dull.

"Nicely done." Ahrin spun, already checking the street for more razak.

Lira hunkered over her knees, swearing at herself, winded, muscles trembling from exertion.

"Why didn't you come back to get us?" Tarion asked, not even breathing hard. "It was foolish to take on one of those things alone."

"I prefer to fight with those I can trust at my back," Lira snapped, more irritated at herself than him. She needed to be stronger than this. To beat Lucinda she had to be at her best physically and mentally.

"And you trust her?" Tarion pointed at Ahrin. "I don't believe that for a second."

Lira's head snapped up to meet his gaze, surprised. "Are the others all right?" she deflected.

"They're all awake, waiting for us to go back and tell them what's going on."

"Go on and let them know." Lira glanced over at Ahrin. "We'll make sure there aren't any other creatures hanging around and meet you back there."

He hesitated, but then nodded and left, sword held loose and ready.

Lira walked over to pick up her bow, then adjusted the quiver on her back. Weariness tugged at her as she went to join Ahrin.

"I think there was just the one of them. Our magic would have drawn them in if there were more," Ahrin said quietly when Lira appeared. "This one might have just been out hunting."

"Then why was it so cold inside where we stood watch?"

"I don't know." Ahrin glanced around. "And wild razak roaming the countryside doesn't explain all the old blood everywhere. You okay?"

"Are *you* okay?"

Ahrin merely settled a look on her.

"Why'd you tell me not to use my fire? I could have ended that fight in seconds. Or have you forgotten the abilities Underground gave me can break through razak immunity?" Lira continued to be irritated, even though she wasn't sure why.

"Because not only would more magic use have drawn in any other razak around," Ahrin snapped, "a massive flaming bonfire in the middle of town on a dark night would have caught the attention of anything here with eyes in its head. Which you would have thought of too, had you not been so desperate to be in a fight and risk your life."

"I wasn't desperate to be in a fight. Will you stop with that!"

The Darkhand's jaw tightened, but all she said was, "Let's do a quick sweep of the area then get back. You need sleep."

"Thanks, but I'll be the one to decide whether I need sleep or not. You're not my crew leader anymore, remember? In fact, I'm the one who..." The words spilled out before she'd thought about them, a product of a tired mind.

"You're the one who what?" Ahrin asked sharply, her voice glacial.

"Never mind."

Ahrin stopped dead and looked her in the eye, that flat, killing look on her face. "Don't ever make the mistake of thinking you're the boss of me, Lira Astor. I don't care who your grandfather was."

Lira held her gaze, some stubborn, frustrated part of her refusing to reply, even though she should. Even though she didn't think she was the boss of Ahrin, had never *wanted* to be. So simple, to tell her that, yet she didn't. Because she was annoyed, and sore, and tired ... and didn't want to concede.

Ahrin's eyes darkened, fury snapping in them, and something else too, something that tugged at the part of Lira that had never wanted anyone but Ahrin. But she stayed silent, and instead of saying anything further, the Darkhand turned and strode away. After a beat of hesitation, Lira followed.

Tarion's words flickered through her mind on repeat, despite how hard she tried to block them out. *I don't believe that for a second.*

CHAPTER 24

They were almost back at the house, Lira staying two paces behind Ahrin to avoid conversation, when a shadow flickered in her peripheral vision. Ahrin caught it too and they instantly melted into the shadows of a nearby building before turning still.

A shriek ripped through the silence of the night, followed by a gust of air as something swooped low over the street, letting out another ear-splitting screech as it flew by. Even though she'd only heard it once before, Lira recognised the sound instantly. It stole her breath and made her want to close her hands over her ears.

A nerik.

She remained utterly still, yet poised for movement, as the creature swooped again. This time it came lower, and she could see its taloned feet, the sweep of its leathery wings. The moment it was out of sight, she and Ahrin surged back into movement, heading as quickly as they could towards the building where the others were.

As they moved, more shrieks echoed through the night around them; there was more than one nerik out there. At least two or three, Lira guessed. Every time one came close, Ahrin and Lira froze again, remaining still in the shadows until it flew away.

Eventually, they got back, diving through the doorway and heading straight up the stairs. The others were on the top floor, gathered by the windows. Their packs of supplies—including Lira and Ahrin's—were buckled up and waiting.

"This may not have been the best place to bunker down for the night," Garan said grimly when they entered, pointing out the window. "Braving the crazy storm might have been safer."

Lira looked out where he was pointing. Several dark shapes were visible in the moonlight, swooping over the city, clearly looking for something.

For them.

"There are razak too." Lorin pointed to a spot several blocks away where the spidery tendrils of inky black darkness crawled over the top of a small house.

"Too many to fight," Ahrin said. "The moment we use magic they'll be on us. We hole up here until daylight."

"And hope they don't find us in here?" Garan asked incredulously.

"You have a better idea, I suppose?"

He opened his mouth, but then let out a sigh, running a hand through his hair.

Lira hated the idea of staying trapped inside a building waiting for a monster to stumble across them. If the creatures *did* find them in here, they'd be trapped with no way out. "I'm with Garan. I say we slip out, move onto the streets where we have more freedom of movement. We can sneak around them, get out of this town now the weather has cleared."

"And go where?" Ahrin challenged. "We're the ones who drew the monsters in. There could be more roaming the plains outside the city where we'd have no cover and no defensible position to retreat to."

Fari made a face. "I really hate to do it, but I actually agree with the Darkhand."

"As do I," Tarion chimed in, his voice for once clear and audible. "I don't think the razak and nerik are pets managed by whomever lives here. They're wild, and the nerik might be the source of everyone abandoning these towns. We shouldn't leave the only cover we have."

He made sense, but Lira was still irritated with Ahrin, annoyed at being stuck with any of them, and just wanted to keep moving. "Fine. You all stay here. I'm going to go and try to draw the monsters' attention to a different part of the city, at least reduce the odds of them finding us in this building."

"Good thought. I'll come with you," Ahrin said instantly.

It was only Lira's unwillingness to fight with Ahrin in front of the others that held her back from a sharp refusal. Instead, she turned and left without another word, waiting until they were halfway down the stairs before snapping. "I don't need your protection."

"I'm not offering it," the Darkhand said just as coldly. "You think I want to sit up there with your council friends?"

"They're not my—" She cut herself off, refusing to be needled.

An icy silence settled between them as they continued down the stairs. Lira figured she'd make her way across to the opposite side of the town, use a bit of magic, then get clear before the monsters converged on it. It should keep the creatures busy searching for an hour or so at least. All they needed to do was buy time until dawn.

They were a mere handful of steps from the bottom of the stairwell when a low snarl echoed through the silence, followed by a thudding sound, like something heavy landing on the ground. Lira shared a glance with Ahrin then crept down to the bottom, pressed herself against the wall, and peered around it into the ground floor of the building.

Her breath caught. *Rotted carcasses!*

A nerik was nosing around the open front door, breath huffing. Abruptly its head came up and it let out a louder snarl that revealed two long fangs, saliva dripping from one onto the floor. Moments later a second nerik landed in the street behind it. The first nerik stepped into the building, wings furled so it could fit through the doorway, the claws on its padded foot scraping against wood.

She spun, pointed up, and Ahrin began moving back up the stairs. Lira followed quickly, both of them soundless. The creatures wouldn't find it easy to get up the stairs with their wings, and she hoped they would lose interest when they didn't find anything on the ground floor. She doubted it. Even if they couldn't sense magic, Lira had to assume they could scent the presence of humans so close by.

Garan spun to face them when they reappeared on the top floor, mouth opening, but Lira raised a finger to her lips, and they gathered in a huddle in the middle of the room.

"Two of them downstairs," she breathed.

Before anyone could respond, a loud thud sounded on the roof above them, followed by two more. A bloodcurdling snarl echoed through the ceiling.

"They know we're here," Ahrin said.

Lira swore inwardly. "They tracked my magic. Rotted blasted carcasses, I'm an idiot."

"It's just as likely they scented our presence," Garan said. "But we can't stay here now."

"We could barricade ourselves in one of the rooms," Tarion said quickly, "but then we'll be trapped with no way out. I doubt these monsters will just give up and go away." Another thump from above punctuated his words. "So we need to get out and find another place to hole up until first light."

"The ground floor is cut off, and the roof." Garan looked at Ahrin. "First floor windows?"

A shriek sounded, close by. Impossible to tell how close. The thrill uncurled, began spreading its seductive warmth through Lira's blood. She breathed in deeply.

"As long as the nerik down there haven't started climbing the stairs yet," Ahrin said.

"Then we'd best hurry." Lorin moved for the door.

They crept down the stairwell—Lira boiling with frustration at how slow they were going, even though she knew they couldn't afford to make a sound and alert the creatures to their presence. Eventually, they made it to the first-floor landing without running into nerik. They could hear them though ... the thud of their paws, soft snarling as they searched the floor below.

A creak sounded on the bottom stair just as they ducked into the first room they came to. The windows were all broken, and a glance at the street outside revealed it was momentarily empty.

"Be careful of the glass," Garan said.

Lorin went first, lowering his pack through the gap before lifting himself onto the cracked window frame and then dropping out of sight. Lira followed. She landed hard below, tucking into a roll to break her momentum.

Once they were all down, they hesitated, everyone looking to Ahrin for direction.

"If they can track our scent, we can't hole up somewhere to hide," the Darkhand said softly. "We'll have to keep moving. Stay out of their range."

"Until dawn, or longer?" Fari hissed. "Because the razak might go into hiding or hibernation or whatever in daylight, but we don't know if the nerik do."

"I—"

A long, bloodcurdling snarl sounded from inside, and seconds later, angry shrieks rang out from the roof above.

"Run!" Tarion said.

They ran.

"I think we're being herded towards the ravine," Tarion said suddenly, slowing up. "We need to change direction, before we're trapped there with nowhere to run."

Garan shot a worried glance in his direction. Ahrin clearly agreed, because she brought them all to a halt with a single raised hand. "Take shelter over there, and give me a moment."

They did as she bade, pressing up against the walls of the closest building, Ahrin moved farther down the street, wariness in every stride. Lira watched her, alert.

So far, they'd been creeping through the empty streets of the town, forced to constantly stop and hide, then change direction every time a nerik caught their scent or the air grew noticeably colder. Lira hadn't realised it, but Tarion was right: they'd been moving inexorably closer to the ravine's edge.

She glanced up. The night sky was still relatively clear, only a few wispy clouds concealing the stars. No sign of dawn on the horizon. It had to be an hour or two away at least.

It wasn't long before Ahrin re-joined them. "This way."

She led them across the street at a swift jog. Once in the shadows of the buildings there, Ahrin turned down a narrow alley, away from the direction of the ravine.

At the next cross street, Ahrin stopped dead before leaving the cover of the alley. Lira moved up to stand beside her, watching as a razak crawled along the thoroughfare, rattling softly to itself. They turned to stone, barely breathing, until the thing had passed.

As soon as it was gone the Darkhand was moving again, crossing the street until finding the next alley. In this fashion, they slowly began working their way towards the western edge of the town.

Eventually, she spotted the remains of the western city wall ahead of them. They slowed up, approaching carefully. Ahrin glanced back, gave Lira a look, made a familiar circular gesture.

Without hesitation, Lira turned and ran back several metres along their route, eyes scanning everything. There was no sign of pursuit. No nerik swooping in the air nearby.

They were clear for now.

When she returned to the others, they were all crowded up against a gap in the wall, muttering to each other. Their body language told Lira they were confused about something. "What is it?" she asked softly.

"See for yourself." Garan stepped away so Lira could worm her way in.

It took her a moment to make out what she was seeing in the dim light, but eventually realised she was looking out over fields spreading away from the western edge of the town—fields covered with crops. She couldn't name any of them, but the tall plants swayed gently in the breeze.

"Corn," Lorin said, as if reading the questions in her mind. "Wheat, too."

"So someone *is* living here," Lira said. "Razak and nerik didn't plant those."

Ahrin stilled suddenly, as if something had caught her attention. Lira tried to figure out what it was without success. A moment later the Darkhand turned and began jogging south along the dirt path by the base of the wall.

"I thought we were trying to move *away* from the ravine?" Garan muttered but didn't protest any further before following.

Soon they reached a wide road leading out of the city through a pair of broken gates towards the fields. Lira took a cautious look around but couldn't see any razak. The sky above was momentarily empty.

"Well, well, well." Ahrin's voice caught her attention. She'd stopped halfway across the road and was pointing at the muddy ground.

Lira's eyes widened. There were deep boot prints in the mud ... several pairs of them. She estimated six or seven people—likely men by the size of the prints. And they'd crossed this way *after* the rain had stopped, or they'd have been washed away in the torrential downpour.

Garan let out a whistle when he joined them and saw what they were looking at. Tarion immediately looked around, hand on the hilt of his sword.

"Maybe we weren't the ones the monsters were chasing?" Fari suggested.

"Maybe not the *only* ones, but they were definitely targeting us back there," Tarion said. "We might have finally found some locals."

A shriek broke the silence. Lira looked up; a distant nerik was swooping low over the roofs. It was closer than it had been before. "Let's get off this road. We're too open and dawn's still a while off."

Ahrin nodded. "How about we go and introduce ourselves to the owners of these prints?"

"It's either that or keep running endlessly around." Lorin shrugged. "Maybe whoever this is has a proper place to hide until dawn."

"They also might be able to direct us to the port city." Tarion shifted from foot to foot. "We've already wasted a lot of time."

"And if they decide to try and murder us when they realise we're foreigners?" Lira felt compelled to point out the flaws in this plan, even though she agreed with it. "You do all agree this whole place is weird?"

"We're going to have to talk to someone if we want to find your missing mages," Ahrin pointed out. "So while I agree it's not the safest of plans, I think it's the quickest way to our objective. And honestly, I'd rather be out of Rotherburn sooner rather than later."

"Agreed," Garan said, not looking at all reassured.

"I'm with the Darkhand." Fari sighed. "The sooner we're out of this creepy place, the better, as far as I'm concerned."

"Okay." Lira shrugged.

Ahrin nodded. "I'll take point. Tarion, you're in the rear. Lira, be ready to shoot anything that comes at us. Nobody uses magic unless their life is directly threatened. Clear?"

"Yes, sir!" Garan snorted.

Lira unslung her bow, nocked an arrow. Tarion moved to the back of the group. Ahrin set off at a swift jog, following the direction of the boot prints.

It quickly became clear that whoever had left the prints wasn't seeking to hide where they'd come from. They followed them several blocks before a right turn into a side street, then a left heading back in the direction of the ravine. Eventually the tracks led up to the closed doorway of a building situated among several others in the middle. Lira guessed the ravine was about two blocks behind it, maybe three at the most.

There was no visible guard out front.

After a brief pause, Ahrin palmed her knife, then set off towards the door. Lira followed, slinging her bow over her shoulder. It wouldn't be any use indoors. She drew her dagger as Ahrin pushed through the door, making sure to stay up on the Darkhand's left shoulder in case of unexpected attack. Tarion had moved up to Ahrin's other side.

She clocked a small room, the single lantern hanging from the ceiling providing a flickering light, and a man standing on the other side of it, astonishment spreading across his face at the sight of them bursting through the door.

Despite his shock, he reacted quickly. He let out a short, low whistle and swiftly drew the long dagger at his hip.

Within a heartbeat of the whistle, several men and women came pouring through a door on the opposite side of the room. All wore matching brown and gold uniforms, though they were well-worn and patched. Alarm and surprise in equal measure filled their expressions and they too drew weapons.

A palpable tension fell over the room as the two parties faced off. Ahrin stayed deliberately quiet, likely wanting to force the other party to reveal themselves first. Thankfully, the others followed her lead.

Lira counted their adversaries as the silence deepened—there were seven total, all carrying bladed weapons. The grips on their weapons indicated that they knew how to use them. But none had the watchful, shifting, gaze of criminals. Soldiers then. That meant Lira and her companions would be more likely to survive the encounter if they didn't appear to be an overt threat. No doubt Ahrin would be making the same read.

"Who are you?" the first man demanded eventually. From the way the others were looking at him, Lira placed him as their leader.

"You tell us first," Ahrin said. "And any of you take a single step towards me with those weapons, and you'll lose a limb. You stay where you are, and nobody gets hurt. Clear?"

A flicker of movement and Garan pushed past Ahrin. He had his arms raised and his tone was calm as he spoke in Shiven, the language the man had used, "My name is Garan Egalion. My friends and I are looking for someone who is missing, and we think they might be here. We mean you no harm."

If anything, the man's astonishment deepened. "Your accent ... you're not from Rotherburn."

"No. Now, how about you tell us who you are?" Ahrin asked. She hadn't lowered her knife an inch.

One of the women spoke to her leader, pointing outside. "Those things must be chasing them. That's why there are so many of them out there tonight." She turned to look at Garan. "Did you use magic?"

"Not since they arrived. We know it draws them in," Garan said, sending Ahrin a sharp glance. She ignored it, keeping her dagger raised and ready. "Like I said, we're not here to hurt anyone."

Another man spoke up, gaze darting nervously between the door and their leader. "It's nearly dawn. We have to go."

"We can't just leave them here, Rin," the woman said. "The First will want us to—"

"The First will be hiding away in his bed, likely." Rin cut over her with a contemptuous snort. "We should—"

The leader made a sharp cutting gesture and both went immediately silent. He looked at Garan. "My name is Barra. We don't want bloodshed, but you're strangers, so you understand we have to be careful. We can offer you safety, but you'll have to come on our terms. Weapons sheathed and wrists bound."

"Safety where?" Garan asked.

A grim smile spread over Barra's face. "Somewhere well away from here. I give you my word we won't harm you if you come with us quietly. Once we're safe, you'll be dealt with fairly." He shrugged. "Or you can head back out there and take your chances."

"We agree to your terms." Lira stepped forward before any of her companions could disagree. Barra and his people didn't need to know that she, Ahrin, and Garan could rip bindings away if needed. And, from the way they interacted and Barra's offer to take them to safety, she was increasingly confident in her read that these were likely soldiers with no immediate intent to harm them. She sheathed her dagger and lifted her hands clear of her body.

Garan shot her an exasperated glance, but Tarion sheathed his sword without a word, and Ahrin finally lowered and sheathed her knife. Lorin and Fari followed suit without complaint.

"Yarina." Barra nodded at the woman. She disappeared into the room they'd all emerged from, and he looked uneasily upwards. "We're just on one of our regular supply runs. It's close enough to dawn it should be an uneventful trip down."

"Down to where?" Fari enquired.

"Our boat. We'll take you to the city as soon as dawn breaks. Once we're there and safe you can tell us what you're doing in Rotherburn."

"It'll be a walk." Yarina reappeared from the other room, ropes hanging from both hands. "I hope none of you are squeamish about heights."

CHAPTER 25

Yarina hadn't been exaggerating. They led Lira and the others out of the back of the building and down a narrow street—so narrow they could only move single file—right up to the ravine's edge. In the dim light, she could just make out the first in a series of steps carved into the rock leading downwards.

"We go one at a time," the woman explained softly. "Stick close as you can to the inside of the steps and don't move too quickly, particularly until the light gets better. There are holes and cracks in the steps that aren't easy to see."

Despite *not* having a fear of heights, Lira's stomach still swooped alarmingly as she took the first step and realised how high above the water they were. Deciding not to look down, she focused her gaze determinedly on the rock at her feet and Garan's boots where he moved directly ahead of her.

Early morning light hadn't yet reached the surface of the water by the time they finally got to the bottom of the narrow, crumbling stairs. Early in the journey, a nerik swooping somewhere nearby had caused them all to freeze, pressing as far into the rock as they could in a desperate bid not to be seen.

Their escorts—each carrying a heavy, bulging pack—seemed even more terrified of the creatures than Lira and her companions were, which made her curious. Granted, the monsters were terrifying, but if these people lived here, surely they were accustomed to them? But no

... instead of paying attention to the strangers they'd caught wandering their land, their attention was firmly on the skies.

Lira was confident that if she wanted to, she could slip around the guards and head straight back up the path. She was almost as confident they wouldn't chase her for fear of catching the attention of a nerik.

At the bottom of the steps, there was no jetty, just a sleek, mid-sized boat tied up to a protruding section of rock. It bobbed up and down on the rough water. While the light was still dim this far down, the sun had crested the horizon above, and their guards seemed to relax, turning their attention more fully to their guests.

One man leapt the gap into the boat, then deftly handled the tiller to bring it closer to the rock without smashing it to pieces. Barra pointed to Lira and her companions, speaking in his rough Shiven. "In, please. Stay together in the middle and do not move about. These waters are dangerous to navigate, and we can't afford you distracting us."

They climbed aboard without protest, moving to sit on two long benches near the centre of the boat. It rocked wildly as all the guards jumped aboard. Yarina came last and brought the mooring rope with her.

Lira studied every detail of her surroundings. While she detested the rope around her wrists, she was willing to submit to the binding, curious to see where they would be taken, and to whom. Best case scenario: the authorities in this country knew of Lucinda and could provide information as to where she was, or where she might have taken Egalion and her husband.

Worst case: they had no clue who Lucinda was and liked to capture foreign visitors on arrival and question them before killing them. This seemed the more likely scenario given no traveller to this place in the past decades had ever returned.

Still, if that happened, Lira was confident she and Ahrin could fight their way out. With the others helping, they'd be fine. Probably. Her Darkhand was watching their surroundings carefully too, her relaxed posture belying how quickly she could explode into movement. There was still a coolness between them after their earlier fight, but that had been shelved while they faced a greater danger.

"You don't seem to be bothered by being tied up." Garan seemed intrigued by Ahrin's complete unconcern with their situation.

"I'm not."

"It's a good sign they let us keep our weapons, even though they're sheathed." Lira nodded to the sword at Tarion's hip, the bow and quiver still hanging over her shoulder. "We're not in any immediate danger."

"Did you see how terrified they were of the nerik?" Tarion murmured. "They were barely paying any attention to us for the first part of the climb."

Ahrin leaned closer to Lira. "Did you catch how Barra cut those two off?"

Lira nodded. "And whatever the First was a reference to, a handful of them looked displeased, almost angry at the word. And Rin was downright contemptuous."

"While Yarina's voice sounded respectful. Caught that too. It could be some kind of factional dispute. Have you noticed any signs that these soldiers have magic?"

"None." Lira shook her head.

"Me either. That's another advantage we have over them." Ahrin shifted away again. She was comfortable with their level of control over the situation. That gave Lira confidence too.

"Excuse me?" Garan spoke loudly enough for the soldiers around to hear. "Can I ask where you're taking us."

Barra glanced at him. "It's not far."

Despite how deeply they'd climbed into the ravine, the surface of the water soon glinted with the pink glow of dawn, brightening to gold as the sun rose higher above the horizon.

For the first part of the journey, they passed nothing but rocky ravine wall on both sides, their crew expertly navigating around the rocks in the water and through the rough rapids of some areas. Several times Lira had to grip hard to the side of the boat to avoid going over as they keeled hard to left or right in a sharp turn. She was extremely glad she didn't get seasick.

The river seemed to head in a roughly westerly direction, but after a few turns, Lira lost all sense of direction. Now that they were away from the nerik, their guards kept a much closer eye on them, their attention unwavering even when they sat still and silent and made no attempt to move or otherwise present a threat.

Interesting. When not terrified, these were disciplined soldiers. She wondered whether they were part of a national army, or a local fighting force. Whatever they were, the hint of discord she and Ahrin had picked up back in the city was absent here as they worked together to successfully pilot the boat.

Concentrating mostly on keeping her seat, Lira was thoroughly unprepared when they swept around a bend to see an entire city perched on both sides of the rocky ravine walls.

She straightened without thinking, eyes going wide.

The river here was much wider, and once they'd rounded the turn, the water calmed. Bridges spanned the gap over the water to join the two halves of the city in various places and at different heights. Lira counted four at first glance.

The ravine walls on either bank stretched upwards at a much shallower incline toward the ground above. Still steep, but climbable. Despite that, no part of the city reached higher than halfway up the gorge.

Fari glanced at them, eyebrow raised. "This would be the port city we were looking for then?"

"It's too far inland, surely?" Lira frowned.

"No ship the size of Rilvitha's or larger is getting this far along the river with all those rocks and rapids," Ahrin said tersely. "It might be a transport hub for smaller craft, but it's no port city."

"It's also the first sign of habitation we've seen, yet it's so far inland," Garan said quietly. "There's something we're missing here. Stay alert."

Lira merely nodded. Everything about the city was narrow and winding and, on first glance, seemed awfully precarious; streets, buildings, bridges, everything, all clinging to rock. Squinting, she could just make out where the city ended, a mile or so farther down the ravine. The gap seemed to close up there too; a dark, forbidding space.

A shadow passed briefly over them as they sailed under the first bridge—high, arching stone—but disappointingly, their boat didn't travel any farther into the ravine city. It tacked swiftly to the north, pulling up at a floating wharf.

Lira rose to her feet at a sharp gesture from the nearest guard and jumped lightly across to the jetty. Ahrin followed, their shoulders jostling as the crew crowded on after them. Garan, Tarion, Fari, and Lorin weren't far behind.

Ahead, a narrow stone path led into a dim corridor where a set of stone steps circled upwards. The city loomed high above them, making Lira dizzy when she tried to look up at it.

"You won't be harmed unless you make a threatening move, but we can't allow you to see too much, at least not until we know your purpose here." Barra spoke gruffly. "You'll be hooded and taken to a place where we can question you. You'll be allowed to keep your weapons as long as they stay sheathed and you make no move to touch them. Clear?"

Ahrin shot her a quick, questioning glance. Lira responded with a little nod. She instinctively rebelled at the idea of being hooded, but they'd come this far, and there was little point in balking now. Not to mention she had magic at her disposal if the situation turned dangerous. They needed information, after all, and her instinct wasn't to suspect the worst about these people—yet. For now best to let them think she and the others were completely cowed and didn't pose any threat.

She stood quietly while someone pulled a hood briskly over her face. A long walk ensued—there were multiple steps upwards at first, enough to make Lira's legs burn with effort, then several shorter sections also going up, and so many changes of direction Lira would have absolutely no idea how to find her way back to the wharf and boat, even if she could fight free.

Eventually the click of an opening door sounded ahead of them. The man holding her elbow pulled her along, then pushed her down into a chair, firmly but not roughly. She stifled the flare of anger that rose and, instead, readied herself for whatever came next. The door clanged shut.

Silence. Then booted feet passing outside. More silence.

Impatience gnawed at her. Sitting in silence with a hood blocking her vision made all the doubts come flooding back in. She was better on her feet, moving. Worse, it was obvious she'd been separated from Ahrin and the others.

Just as she was considering attempting to use her flame magic to melt through her bindings, and damn the consequences, the door opened again, and the hood was yanked off her face. She blinked, eyes smarting at the sudden bright light of the lantern in the corner.

The room was small, built into rock, and contained only the chair she was sitting on. A man stood opposite her, arms crossed, gaze openly curious. There was nothing remarkable about him; he had thinning brown hair, long limbs, a serrated knife at his belt. He wore the same uniform as those who'd captured them.

"Who are you?" he asked.

"Who are *you*?" she retorted.

"We don't get visitors this far inland, not ever," he said. "Any overly curious sailors who make landfall on the east coast don't usually make it far beyond the beach. You and your friends are quite the anomaly."

"You're referring to the deserted, blood-soaked towns we passed, I assume?" She eyed him. "Did your soldiers do that?" Those bloodstains had been left before this man had even been born, most likely, but she wanted to test him, maybe try and provoke a useful response.

His jaw tightened. "No."

"Then who did? Despite being chased by them last night, razak drink blood, they don't spray it everywhere. Was it nerik? Or humans?" She tried to sound casual, to keep the keen interest out of her voice. Were there warring factions in Rotherburn? Was that why they'd vanished, too caught up in an internal civil war? But surely not. If that were the case one or both sides would have reached out for an alliance at some point, or at least to buy arms or supplies from the continent. "Whatever it was happened a while ago. Why haven't you just killed the beasts?"

He laughed, and it was a bitter, desperate sound. "I ask again. Who are you?"

"My companions and I came here looking for someone. We don't mean you or your people any harm. As soon as we've found who we're looking for, we'll go home. If you can help us, perhaps we'll be gone even faster."

His look of mystification deepened. "Who would you be looking for here?"

Lira sat back in the chair, scanned the walls, the floor. There was no obvious escape, no weapon either except the knives in her belt. She wouldn't get far with this man until she told him something ... and while there was risk in revealing her intent without understanding their situation properly, impatience was clawing at her. "We're looking for a woman..." Lira tried to think of Lucinda's defining traits, something this man might recognise. "Someone with the magical ability to paralyse others, someone who I think is important here. Her name is Lucinda."

The man's face tightened, shifting quickly from confusion into wariness. Lira sat up straighter, eagerness leaping through her—he knew who Lucinda was. Her mouth opened to ask more questions but before she could, a sharp banging sounded at the door. Giving Lira a quick look, he strode over to open the door. Another man was outside, the same unease filling his expression. The two exchanged a whispered conversation. Lira's guard glanced back at her frequently.

Eventually they stopped talking, and her guard opened the door fully. "On your feet. We're taking you to the Seven."

"The *who*?" Lira's eyebrows rose.

"On your feet," he repeated. "You'll need to hand over your weapons now."

Lira stood but didn't move any further. "No way."

"We won't harm you, but you can't carry weapons in the presence of the Seven."

"Why exactly should I believe you won't harm me? What is the Seven?"

"You know Lucinda, but you don't know what the Seven is?" The man's face narrowed in suspicion. "Weapons, now. It's not a request."

Reluctantly, Lira unbuckled her daggers and handed over her bow and quiver, mulling over the man's words, the sudden change in his attitude since she'd mentioned Lucinda's name. Clearly she was somehow connected to this Seven. The situation was heading into more and more confusing territory, and the logical part of her wondered if it might be time to cut her losses and get out. But heading deeper into the unknown sent a hot thrill through her that she savoured.

Her smile widened a little at the sight of Ahrin standing in the hall outside, flanked by two more guards, these ones female. Ahrin flashed her a matching smile, quick, then her expression sobered. "You mention Lucinda's name?" Ahrin asked in an undertone as they began walking, all four soldiers closing around them.

"Right before guard number two came and banged on the door. You?"

A quick nod. "It elicited quite the reaction."

"Interesting. They definitely know who she is."

"Well, they know *someone* called Lucinda."

"So pedantic," Lira muttered.

"Assumptions get you killed," Ahrin said. "Have you seen the others?"

A brief flicker of worry went through Lira, which she quickly stifled. "No."

"I don't like that they've separated us. I take it you gave over your weapons too?"

"I did. I don't need them to get myself out of this if necessary."

Ahrin nodded approvingly. "Let's stay meek and non-threatening until we have a better idea of what's going on here."

Sunlight shone into their eyes as they emerged onto an external pathway that wound above a series of roofs roughly four levels above the rushing river. Wherever they were in the city, there wasn't much foot traffic. Nor any markets or shops that Lira could see. After following a short path, they started up another set of steps.

"You see or hear any birds since we arrived in this place?" Ahrin asked her.

"No. Why?"

"It's odd, don't you think?"

"I think every single thing about this place is odd." Lira glanced around them, lowered her voice even further. "Just to make sure we're prepared before we get wherever we're going ... at what point do we cut and run? I don't like the sound of this 'Seven'."

Ahrin stiffened slightly. "What?"

"They told me they were taking us to something called the Seven but refused to give me any details about what it was."

Ahrin was silent a moment, then her voice barely audible, "Don't tell me you missed those handful of occasions where Timor or Jora slipped up and called Lucinda 'Seventh'. Add that to Yarina mentioning something called 'the First'?"

Lira's eyes widened. "You think—"

"Let's just see how this plays out." Ahrin cast a warning look at how close the guards were. "We haven't learned anything yet. They haven't tried to hurt us, either. If things go south, we'll make a break for it. Otherwise we play along until we learn what we need to."

Lira nodded, changed the subject. "The ship carrying Egalion wouldn't have been able to get this far along the ravine."

"No, but she and Caverlock could have been transferred to a smaller boat like the one we came in on. By now Lucinda is probably a long way away though—she'd have been best off taking them further inland just in case anyone tracked her here."

"I hope she's here," Lira said, palms itching with the desire to close her fingers around the woman's throat.

Ahrin glanced at her. "Don't let your thirst for revenge lead you to underestimate her again, Lira. She's smart and calculating and has a powerful magic. It won't be easy to bring her down."

"I know all that," she snapped, loudly enough their guards turned to look at her.

Ahrin lifted her hands in capitulation, began whistling under her breath.

Finally, they stopped moving upwards and turned along a narrow path that headed through a gate which opened up into a paved square. The space was walled on three sides, with its northern side a large building reaching several stories high. Double-arched doors gleamed golden in the morning sun, and the same gold burnished the frames of every window peering down over the square.

Above the building was a steep ravine wall leading all the way to the top. They were on the highest level of the city, the river visible far below.

A soldier stood either side of the doors—one man, one woman—sheathed swords at their hips, wearing a red instead of brown uniform, edged in gold trim, every button polished to reflect the gleam of the sun.

Ahrin glanced at Lira. "Reckon someone important is in that building?"

Lira's mouth quirked. "It's very possible."

The woman's eyes shifted to Lira at their murmured conversation. There wasn't much to read in her expression, but she appeared focused, intent. And then ... a little shiver went through Lira's magic as their gazes held.

"They're mages," Lira said to Ahrin. "At least, the woman is."

Ahrin considered that. "From here on, we assume the red uniforms mean magical abilities."

Lira nodded but said nothing further.

Once through the double doors, they found themselves standing in a wide hallway leading away to the left and right, polished floorboards gleaming in the sunlight pouring through from high, arched windows. Directly ahead were another set of closed doors.

Two more red-dressed guards, who seemed to be expecting them, opened the doors without a word. It was possible their original guards had sent a messenger on ahead of them, but Lira instantly re-focused her mental shields. It was just as possible that one of these red uniforms was a telepath.

As the doors were opened, the original brown-uniformed guards left without a word, filing back out into the morning sunshine. The red soldiers remained silent as they gestured for Lira and Ahrin to enter the long, sunlit great hall beyond the second set of doors. Thick tapestries hung along each side of the hall, no gaps between them. It was a larger space than Lira had ever been in before. Although she was sorely tempted to stare in wonder and drink it all in, she focused her attention between the two guards following them inside and what lay ahead.

Aware of Ahrin just to her left, Lira held her magic ready, a thrill under her skin, one that grew to an almost burning level of intensity when she saw the seven people sitting in ornate chairs clustered on a dais at the end of the hall. She scanned those faces. In a heartbeat, she recognised the person sitting on the right-most chair.

"Rotted carcasses," Ahrin said, in the understatement of the day.

Lucinda smiled, rose from her seat, and opened her hands in a welcoming gesture. "Welcome to Rotherburn, Lira Astor."

CHAPTER 26

L ira froze. Fury surged hot and chaotic through her at the sight of Lucinda. Literally everything else in the room faded away. This was the woman who'd planned and connived to put Lira in prison for the rest of her life. Who'd experimented on her without permission. Who'd kidnapped her and hunted her with monsters.

Her vision hazed over, her hands moving of their own accord. She was going to—

"Lira, this might just be the stupidest thing we've ever done. Which is remarkable, really, because I've never done anything stupid before."

Ahrin's voice in her ear, low and familiar, brought her snapping back. To the reality of guards and likely mages arrayed all around them. Lira took a shuddering breath, forced her focus to the nearness of Ahrin at her side, the familiar and beloved hint of vanilla cigars in her scent. As she did, the fury faded to controllable levels. Reason took hold.

Lira glanced at Ahrin with gratitude. Their gazes caught and Lira felt back on an even keel. A little smile curled at her mouth. "On the bright side, our mission has been achieved rather sooner than expected. We found Lucinda."

"You make an excellent point. But when *haven't* we overachieved?" Midnight blue eyes held Lira's a moment longer before glancing away. Despite the light banter, there was warning in that gaze. Lira didn't need it. She knew how precarious this whole situation had just become. Rather than finding and approaching Lucinda on their own terms, they'd allowed themselves to be hand delivered to her. The woman was now in a position of significant power over them.

Her gaze swung back to Lucinda, as if drawn by a magnet, and it took all her concentration to again fight down the desire to launch herself at the woman and tear her face off with her bare hands.

If Lucinda was surprised to see them, she hid it well. They hadn't given the guards their names, so she couldn't have known who they were until this moment, only that her soldiers had found strangers asking for Lucinda and were bringing them to the Seven. Her composure was beyond impressive.

With an effort, Lira turned her attention to the six other occupants of the chairs, studying them one by one with a practised, assessing glance. Almost all of them looked much older than Lucinda. Only one seemed several years younger, and even seated, she was smaller in stature. All looked intensely curious. Lira's gaze lingered slightly longer on the man sitting to her far left. He appeared the oldest of them all, with a hunched back and wispy white hair. His curiosity was edged with wariness, and something ... weariness?

Reminded by Ahrin, memory flashed through Lira's thoughts—Jora and Timor referring to Lucinda as 'Seventh'. The title had always rung oddly to Lira. No longer. Whatever this 'Seven' was, Lucinda was a member.

Lucinda broke the silence first. "I can't say I ever expected to see either one of you ever again." She smiled then, that cold, flat smile Lira remembered so well. But there was a gleam of interest in her slightly frowning expression.

She wasn't upset that Lira was there. She was pleased.

Lira didn't like that one bit—it was never good when Lucinda got something she wanted. She hid her unease with a cool, uninterested, tone. "If that's true, then you're a fool. You framed me, you organised to have me put in prison for the rest of my life, yet you didn't expect me to get out someday and come straight for you?"

Lucinda didn't reply. Instead, her gaze shifted to Ahrin. "Darkhand, I'm even more surprised to see you."

Ahrin shrugged. "You never did know me as well as you thought you did."

"I know you like to think that." Lucinda walked slowly down the steps. She was dressed similarly to how she'd been back in Shivasa—every button, hem, and stitch of cloth perfectly in place. Behind her, the other seated men and women seemed content to let Lucinda handle this for the moment. It was an interesting insight into their dynamics, and one Lira filed away to consider later.

"We should start with apologies." Ahrin sounded anything but repentant. "You seem to hold some sort of power here. I had no idea, or I would have used your title when speaking with you."

Lucinda glanced back at the chairs of men and women. "The Seven rule Rotherburn."

Lira's chest tightened. Lucinda was one of the rulers of the entire *country?*

What in all rotted hells had she been doing in Shivasa?

Ahrin's eyes narrowed. "That makes me very curious."

"Does it?" Lucinda eyed her for a long moment. "You do like to think of yourself as clever, I recall."

"We both know I am. Just as we both know taunts don't work on me. And I'm not the only one who likes to think she's clever." Ahrin lifted an eyebrow. "Only, you don't know as much as you think you do."

Something rippled across Lucinda's face at her words. Whatever it was, Lira wanted to see it again, wanted to push open that minute crack in the woman's perfect composure. Wanted to see her control falter.

So she shifted a little closer, enough to get into Lucinda's personal space. Rustling sounded as guards moved, but Lucinda held up a hand to stop them.

Red anger hazed Lira's vision at their proximity, but she held it back with an effort. "You came looking for me in Dirinan, once, many years ago," she said. "You failed. Why do you think that was?"

Lucinda's expression didn't change, but her silence was telling. For once, she didn't know what Lira was talking about. She didn't have the answer. Satisfaction curled through her.

Ahrin glanced over, a little smile playing at her mouth, seeing where Lira was going instantly. "She might not have found you, Lira, but she found herself a Darkhand, didn't she?"

"She did indeed. Funny how that happened. Almost like you wanted it that way," Lira said idly.

Lucinda hesitated only briefly, but it was enough to show she *hadn't* known this—that Ahrin hadn't stumbled across Underground, that she'd gone to them deliberately after making sure Lira was safely away from them. The woman's gaze narrowed sharply, her mind clearly processing the new information.

Ahrin smiled that predatory smile of hers. "Still feeling clever, Seventh? By the way, I assume that title means you're the last one of the group? The least powerful, I'm guessing?"

A silence caught, held. It was like the entire room apart from the three of them had vanished. So much anger and tension and hate burning between them. Lira breathed it in, savouring the tiny win ... but it wasn't enough, not nearly enough. This woman had to burn.

One of the Seven broke the silence—the old man. His voice was sharp, with an escalating note of worry in it. "This is Lira Astor and the one you called the Darkhand, Lucinda? You said they'd been dealt with and would no longer be an issue for us. How did they find us here?"

Lucinda's demeanour altered subtly, taking on an aura of deference that Lira would have sworn was fake. "Burgen, I understand your concern. Would you grant me some leeway here, and I promise to explain everything in private afterward?"

He hesitated, but after a few others gave acceding nods, he sighed. "Very good."

Abruptly, Lucinda made a sharp gesture, shifting away and changing the subject in a blink. "What brings you to Rotherburn? You didn't come just to kill me, I gather. If you did, you've done rather a poor job of it."

Lira glanced at Ahrin, shrugged. Better to let her lead this interaction. She couldn't be confident of keeping her composure around this woman, whereas Ahrin was a master of manipulation.

Ahrin looked at Lucinda. "We're looking for a missing mage and Taliath and thought you might know something about it. Alyx Egalion and Dashan Caverlock. Ring any bells?"

Another silence shimmered through the room, and although Lucinda looked unsurprised by the question, several members of the Seven shifted in their chairs. Before Lucinda could respond, one of them—a tall man sitting in the middle—snapped out. "You assured us you left no trail of the kidnapping, Lucinda!"

Irritation rippled across Lucinda's expression, but she wiped it quickly away and responded calmly, "And if our visitors had any doubt at all, you've just confirmed what we did, Tallin. As Burgen agreed, please allow me to handle this. We can discuss the implications later."

Another one spoke, her long braids swinging in agitation. "We might not have time to wait. If we've been discovered, we'll need to implement emergency defences immediately."

"I didn't leave a trail, but I suspect the absence of a trail was what brought the Darkhand looking for me." Lucinda lifted a calming hand. "And the fact that these over-enthusiastic brats are here instead of a mage army tells me nobody else guesses we took Egalion and Caverlock. We are in no immediate danger."

"Even so." The woman with braids sounded severely unimpressed. "We will have to double our lookouts on the eastern coast, increase boat patrols. Put more lives we can't afford at risk."

"Indira, that is unnecessary." Lucinda remained composed. She had to be seething though, at having her authority undermined in front of others. Her control was masterful.

"*We* decide what is necessary, not you alone." Tallin said sharply.

Lucinda inclined her head. "Of course. May I suggest, again, that we discuss necessary measures in private where our visitors will not be privy to our affairs?"

All six looked in Burgen's direction. Lira's gaze narrowed at this—he had to be the First. After a brief hesitation, Burgen gave a nod of agreement.

Lucinda took a step closer to Lira, turning her rigid with a combination of anticipation and alertness. With a single touch of magic Lucinda could freeze them all to the spot and Lira wouldn't be able to do anything about it. The woman's words were softly spoken, dripping with malice, aimed to strike right at Lira's vulnerable spots. "They lock you up in prison for the rest of your life, and still your pathetic loyalty to the Mage Council has you trying to save their precious Alyx Egalion."

Lira smiled. "You thought I was spying on Underground out of some sort of undying loyalty to the council? I expected better from you." She shrugged. "I'm only here to kill you. Agreeing to help look for Egalion was my ticket to getting here. I don't much care what you do with her or her husband."

Lucinda studied her for a long moment, and when the woman shifted even closer Lira refused to let herself flinch. The calculation in Lucinda's expression was palpable, her sharp brain no doubt assessing Lira's every word and movement. "Prison made you harder instead of softer, I see. There's no mercy left in you, is there, Lira? Maybe now you truly would be the leader Underground needed."

"Shame you'll never find out." Lira ignored Ahrin's quick glance in her direction.

"I am impressed that you managed to figure out not only that we'd taken them, but where we came from." Lucinda blinked slowly. "Far less impressed that you basically handed yourselves over to me."

"How do you know that wasn't part of our plan?" Ahrin asked.

Lucinda merely smiled, clearly not believing that for a second. Looking over their shoulders, she made a gesture to the guards on the door.

A moment later they opened again. Tarion, Fari, Garan, and Lorin entered, escorted by another two red uniforms. Lira let out a hiss of annoyance at the relief that flickered through her. She didn't want to care about their safety. It would only split her focus.

The guards hustled them forward to where Lira and Ahrin stood, all looking angry and mutinous. As soon as they were close enough, Garan turned his attention to Lucinda. "I don't know what either of them has told you, but all we want is my aunt and uncle."

"You can even keep your Darkhand and heir to the Darkmage, if you like," Fari said with a little shrug. Lorin shot her an angry glance, which she countered with a lifted eyebrow.

"Ah, so you four aren't part of the murderous revenge team?" Lucinda smiled, looking genuinely amused. "Lira was telling the truth when she said you were a means to an end. Good to know."

Garan shot a furious look at Lira. Lorin just looked disappointed. Tarion didn't seem to have heard, stepping forward. "We have no intention of hurting anyone, even you," he said. "We just want our people, then we'll go and never return."

Lira almost scoffed aloud. Did either he or Garan genuinely think Lucinda would simply give up her hostages after being asked nicely?

Lucinda stepped back from Ahrin and Lira so she could survey the whole group. "We needed Egalion and her husband for a specific purpose. I honestly didn't think anyone would figure out where we'd taken them, and certainly didn't expect a rescue party to arrive so soon, but it suits my purposes rather neatly."

"*Your* purposes?" Lira asked, hunting for a chink in Lucinda's armour; the interaction earlier indicated there was some division within the Seven they might be able to exploit. "Or the Seven's? Given you seem to be the least important of the lot. Is that why you were the one sent to Shivasa to carry out their bidding?"

That *thing* rippled over Lucinda's face again. She glanced back at the men and women. They were listening intently, but none of them said anything, holding to their agreement to let Lucinda take the lead. From the look on the Burgen's face, she guessed he was amused by Lira's comment. "I lead the Seven's efforts in this particular matter. They have given me their trust."

"And what exactly is *this particular matter*?" Ahrin asked.

Lucinda merely smiled.

A second later, Tarion pushed between her and Ahrin, tall and angry. Lira blinked. In her battle of wills with Lucinda, she'd almost forgotten the others were there.

"Where are they?" Tarion's shoulders were straight and broad, his fists clenched, feet set firmly apart. Lira had never seen him so assertive.

Even so, Lucinda looked him slowly up and down, dismissing him in a way she never had Lira or Ahrin. "You're the son, I take it. The disappointing one. Your parents haven't returned from where we sent them. Yet. And they're behind schedule, too."

Tarion's left hand moved, only slightly, but Garan caught it, because he pushed forward, discreetly placing his hand on Tarion's wrist in warning. "Tell us what's going on, let us go, or kill us. We're not interested in game playing."

Lira shared a glance with Ahrin and then let them have the floor. Lucinda was unlikely to tell them anything they wanted to know unless it suited her purposes, but there was no harm in letting the mages try, giving her and Ahrin an opportunity to study Lucinda's reactions.

"I'm not interested in games either." Lucinda gave a rather suspicious shrug of capitulation, then made a sweeping gesture encompassing the space they were in. "This city holds all that remains of Rotherburn's people."

The words echoed through the hall, loud and stark in the silence that followed them. Lira shifted her gaze to the Seven, wondering if this was some lie or manipulation of Lucinda's, but her words clearly affected them deeply. And it made a grim kind of sense given what they'd encountered since coming ashore. Pained sorrow was written in all their faces. All amusement was gone from Burgen's face.

Lucinda was telling the truth.

The Darkhand's eyes were narrowed with interest. Garan and Tarion looked at each other, then back at Fari and Lorin. None of them seemed to know how to respond.

"Four hundred and twenty-two thousand people, give or take, packed into this ravine city which originally held about six thousand,"

Lucinda continued. "That many, from a population once as large as Shivasa's."

"Let me guess," Ahrin drawled. "You murdered them all in a bloody coup?"

"They died generations ago," Lucinda snarled, turning on Ahrin with violent speed. "And more have died every year since. We would *never* harm our own people."

Ahrin held her look. The air between the two women crackled with intensity. "Then what killed everyone and forced you into this city?"

As if it had never been, the fury drained from Lucinda's face. The calculated expression returned, and she shifted away from Ahrin, once again talking to all of them. "We had mages once, just like you. Many of them. And, just like you, there was a war between them. Only ours ended a little differently." Her gaze turned momentarily distant. "The magic deployed in our battles destroyed a large part of the country. About twenty miles inland of the east coast, the surface is mostly uninhabitable, poisoned and unable to support plant growth. Chaotic storms ravage the surface. Those who survived the war retreated here, to this city, and to the narrow stretch of land along the east coast that remained liveable."

Despite herself, Lira was fascinated—Lucinda's account explained why the people of Rotherburn had appeared to vanish completely. Almost.

"And that was fine, for a while." Lucinda's mouth tightened. "But not only did the magic used during the war destroy our landscape, it also created the razak, and the nerik. The razak drink human blood, as you know. The nerik just like to rip things apart and feed on the meat. Those who lived outside this city were slowly picked off in greater and greater numbers. Eventually we had to retreat from the only arable land in the country because we didn't have the numbers to defend it."

There was a moment of silence as they processed this, then Garan spoke. "You have mages. Why didn't you use magic to regenerate the land?"

"After the war only a handful of mage bloodlines remained—too many had died in the fighting. Worse, razak and nerik target those of mage blood, as you've experienced. Many more died trying to protect the villagers living up on the surface. The result is that our mage bloodlines have almost died out. Our warriors fight bitterly—we've learned and grown in skill over the decades—but the monsters are too numerous for us to defeat. We're trapped in a losing war."

Lira had no desire to feel any empathy for these people, let alone Lucinda. "Great story, but what does this has to do with any of us?"

Anger lashed over Lucinda's face. "Our nation's survival is at stake. We lose more to the monsters than are born every year. We have to find a way to destroy them entirely before they destroy us."

"Wait..." Tarion seemed to get there before the rest of them, his voice horrified. "That's why you took my parents?"

"I sent them to kill the razak queens," Lucinda said.

"Why my parents? Why not do it yourself?"

"Because no mage alive, either here or in your home, is as powerful as Alyx Egalion." Lucinda shrugged. "And her husband is a warrior of unparalleled skill."

"That sounds like a desperate plan to me, not a good one," Ahrin drawled. "And I suppose you want us to go after them, finish the job they either have already been killed doing, or have failed miserably at? What insanity is it exactly that makes you think we'd even consider it?"

Lucinda shifted her gaze to Tarion. "You find your parents, help them kill the razak queens, and we'll let you go home unscathed. That's all we want. We have no interest in hurting you, you family, or your home. We just want to survive."

Ahrin and Lira shared a glance. Utter fiction.

Tarion seemed equally suspicious. "Queens? Exactly how many are there?"

Lucinda sighed, glanced back at the rest of the Seven. "With a dwindling pool of human or animal blood to feed on, the razak have lost numbers too. They're hive animals and we track their population as best we can—we believe there are likely only two queens. Maybe three at the most."

"Then why haven't you just sent your warriors to kill them?" Lira asked quickly. "A mage of the higher order is still a mage ... equally unable to use magic against the razak."

"We've tried going after the queens and lost valuable lives doing it. The creatures are hidden deep and well protected. We don't have the numbers or pure magical strength to succeed." Lucinda paused. "And you, as a telekinetic mage, know well that multiple magical abilities can be used effectively in a fight—even when the magic can't touch your opponent directly."

Lorin spoke into the frustrated silence that followed. "You said the queens are hidden deep. What do you mean by that?"

"About seven years ago, the razak found a way down into this city. It reaches deep into the rock, down beneath the river—we had to keep expanding to fit a growing population. I don't know how the monsters got in, but now they haunt those deeper tunnels—in fact they seem to prefer it—and they took their queens down deep. We've had to bring everyone up to the higher levels, but even then we lose numbers each year as they encroach farther on our territory."

"Are the nerik underground too?" Fari asked.

"No. They've remained above ground; our theory is they prefer being in open air where they can fly."

Ahrin lifted an eyebrow. "Killing your razak queens doesn't help with your nerik problem, then, does it?"

"Claiming our home back from the more insidious problem of the razak gives us time to recoup and build strength. We will then be in a position to send warriors aboveground to begin hunting and destroying nerik. It will take time, but there will be hope." Lucinda's mouth tightened. "It's been a long time since we've had hope."

"Fine. We'll help." Tarion said.

"Tar—" Garan started, but Lira cut over him.

"No we won't." Lira swung to look at Tarion. "I've found your parents; our agreement is over. I'm going back home, not risking my life chasing down razak queens."

"Ah, but you have to go." Lucinda stepped closer. "You and Ahrin both."

"Why's that?"

"Because Egalion is either dead or lost, and unlike anyone else, *your* magic can hurt the razak—you were the one who killed them at DarkSkull, don't think I haven't figured that out. And the Darkhand?" Lucinda paused and settled her gaze on Ahrin, triumph kindling in her eyes. "Well, I've just learned that she goes wherever you go."

Lira swore internally, bitterly regretting their little cocky display earlier. It was never a good idea to offer information to Lucinda. They'd been fools to do it.

"That's a massive overstatement of reality," Ahrin drawled.

"Is it?" Lucinda settled a long look on Ahrin, and even though the Darkhand didn't flinch, didn't even betray a flicker, Lira could tell that they'd given too much away. Lucinda saw everything.

"And if we don't agree to go?" Lira asked, seeking to draw the woman's attention from Ahrin.

"Then I kill your Darkhand while you watch, frozen. And then I kill you." Lucinda shrugged. "Your choice."

A pause followed, and Lira took the opportunity to tear her attention away from Lucinda to settle on the Seven. None spoke out to protest Lucinda's threat, but Burgen and the woman with braids looked distinctly uncomfortable.

"That's the heir to the Darkmage you're talking to." Ahrin stepped closer to Lucinda, holding her gaze, that air of threat, of danger, rising into the space between them. "I wouldn't go threatening her if I were you."

"It's true." Lira smiled coolly. "You don't want to get me mad. You should ask Greyson what happens when I get angry ... except you can't, because he's dead. Died screaming, in fact, after a single click of my fingers."

"You do know her grandfather started two entire wars because someone killed his girlfriend?" Garan weighed in, astonishing Lira. "That kind of psychopathic insanity tends to run in families."

Lucinda's gaze switched to Lira's. "You think you can burn me before I freeze you in place?"

Lira's smiled widened. "I'd put gold coin on it."

Lucinda cocked her head. "There's no need for a gamble like that. Agree to what I want and we'll all be satisfied. You leave with nobody getting hurt, and I get my country back, a future for my people."

Ahrin turned to Lira, eyebrows raised. "Well, dearest, what do you think about a trek underground to rescue a rotted mage councillor and kill some murderous monsters?"

Her first instinct was to flatly refuse. But Ahrin's sudden shift from threatening to casual agreement checked her—if Ahrin was conceding to Lucinda, it was because she saw advantage in doing so. She shifted her glance to Tarion, who shrugged a little. "I won't ask, you've held to your word, but know that I would welcome your presence with us."

"As would I. I'd like to survive," Fari said firmly, levelling a pointed look at Garan when he seemed inclined to disagree.

Even then Lira hesitated. She wanted to rip Lucinda's head from her neck, not submit to her wishes once again. The anger still burned, the sight of the woman's face, the sound of her voice, enough to keep it raging. But that meant she wasn't thinking clearly.

She'd follow Ahrin's lead on this one. Lira shrugged. Levelled a smile at Lucinda. "All right. Let's go kill ourselves a razak queen or two."

CHAPTER 27

"This is rather a sticky situation we find ourselves in," Ahrin commented later, when they were alone.

When dismissing them from the Seven's presence, Lucinda had informed them that someone would be made available first thing the following day to answer any questions they might have about their mission. She further promised that supplies and weapons would be prepared for the journey. They did not have to leave until they felt ready.

It was far too accommodating behaviour for Lucinda, which made Lira itch.

They'd been taken to an apartment in a residential street a single level down from the Seven's building. Lira and Ahrin had been given a single room to share—Lucinda making a point she knew of their relationship in a way that made Lira extremely uncomfortable—while the others had been given a room each in the same building.

Before leaving, their red-garbed escorts had left strict warnings about wandering the streets after nightfall. "The nerik occasionally fly down into the ravine when they're extra hungry. Stay indoors and don't use your magic unless critically necessary."

Nightfall was at least an hour away though, and orange sunlight spilled through their windows. A narrow door out to a balcony was wedged open, letting in an evening breeze along with the sound of conversation from a group of people walking by below.

It was actually quite pleasant ... if you weren't aware of being sandwiched between dangerous monsters crawling the poisoned surface above and creeping through the dark lower levels beneath.

"Regretting coming with me now?" Lira straightened from where she'd been looking under the bed in an overabundance of caution, then turned to study the empty couch by the fireplace. A fire had been already lit when they arrived despite the warm air. Now it made the room feel cosy, safe. A dangerous way to feel whenever Lucinda was close.

"On the contrary." Ahrin was casing the room just as Lira had. Once she'd satisfied herself there were no listening ears or unexpected dangers, she leaned against the window by the balcony door and crossed her arms. "What's the plan now—we kill these razak queens, then sneak back into the citadel and murder Lucinda in her sleep before she knows we're back?"

"Something like that." Lira shrugged, crossing to Ahrin and lowering her voice. "Or we pretend to wander around the lower levels of the city for a little while, then double back and murder Lucinda in her sleep before she knows we're here. Less chance of getting eaten by razak that way."

Ahrin smiled that wicked smile of hers and reached out to draw Lira close. The argument between them earlier had been brushed aside in the unification of them versus Lucinda. "I do like the way you think. But I have a counter argument for you."

"Hmm?" Lira kissed her.

"If we kill the queens, that means no more razak."

Lira cracked an eye open and leaned back. "I see your logic there. It's clever. Really genius stuff."

"I mean, wouldn't we all be better off if there were no razak?"

"Since when do you give two coppers about the general welfare of the world?" Lira stared at her, irritated to be having this conversation.

"Rotted carcasses, Lira, *think*." Ahrin was annoyed now too. "If the razak are gone, Lucinda couldn't send them after us anymore. She'd be far more vulnerable."

"We could kill all the razak and there would still be nerik. You noticed she dismissed that problem rather easily, I take it?"

"Hmm. I can't tell if she truly believes the nerik would be a manageable problem if the razak were gone, or there's something we're missing."

"It's Lucinda," Lira said flatly. "We're missing something."

"Even so. Without the razak, she poses far less of a threat."

Lira eyed her, reluctantly seeing her point. "We shouldn't have bragged about Dirinan in front of her like that."

Ahrin shrugged. "Who cares what she knows?"

"You know she'll use anything we give her against us. That's how she operates."

"That's how *we* operate too. And at least now we know what she wants most, what her motivations are. We're the ones with the upper hand now, Lira."

"*We* are the ones about to venture into a deserted underground city to hunt monsters immune to our most powerful weapon, not her. As long as we're doing her bidding, she has the upper hand."

"Not once we kill the razak queens. You heard her—they barely have any mages left. A dwindling population. And you saw those fossils arrayed behind her calling themselves a ruling council. I'd eat my hat if she isn't working her way towards full control of the supposed Seven, even if they haven't noticed it yet."

"They did seem divided." Lira wandered over and dropped into the lounge by the fire, suddenly weary. "Aren't the razak just as much a danger to her as they are to us, though? I killed Dasta, remember? At least this explains how devastated they all were at his death."

"Maybe." But Ahrin didn't sound convinced. "His death was most definitely a blow, but that doesn't mean she didn't have other mages with the ability to control razak. And even if she didn't then, it's been almost three years. I doubt she's stopped her experimenting. It's just a matter of time before she creates another mage who has the ability to control the monsters. Maybe even more than one. She's desperate enough to be scaling up her little tests."

Desperate enough to kidnap Egalion and her husband, too. Lira eyed Ahrin. "You really think we have any chance of getting to these razak queens, let alone killing them and getting out alive? We don't even know how many razak there are crawling through the tunnels. The queens will be well protected."

Ahrin shrugged. "I think there's a very slim chance of succeeding."

"Then why suggest we do exactly what Lucinda wants? It's not like you." Lira watched her. Ahrin had to be planning something, seeing an angle Lira couldn't. It was what made her such an effective crew boss. But she clearly wasn't willing to share with Lira.

Ahrin looked away, the fingers of her left hand tapping unconsciously against her leg. "We have two apparent options before us. One is killing the queens and being allowed to go home. The second is fighting our way out of this place and then commandeering a ship to sail home. You saw the number of soldiers she has, even if she doesn't have many mages—and don't forget those soldiers are hardened from years of fighting monsters. None of us know how to crew a ship, especially through those rapids. Lucinda has most definitely prepared for us trying to escape. I think the first option gives us the highest chance of survival."

"Except that neither of us believes she's actually going to let us go home, even if we succeed in killing all the razak queens."

"Which is why, once we've done what she wants, we sneak back in and kill her, just like you said. She can't stop us from doing anything then."

"The Seven might take issue with us murdering one of their number."

"From the look on Burgen's face, I think he'd be happy if we took her off his hands," Ahrin said lightly. "Even if not, we'll have solved their razak problem. At worst, it stops them from sending monsters after us. At best, they're grateful enough to us for saving their country that in Lucinda's psychotic absence they let us go."

It was on the tip of Lira's tongue to suggest they go and kill Lucinda this moment. That would solve all their problems, and they could escape in the chaos that ensued. But Lucinda would be expecting that

... Lira had capitulated earlier because Lucinda held all the cards. That hadn't changed. But still.

What Ahrin said made perfect sense. It was what she did, calculate the odds of survival and choose the option with the highest odds. It's how she'd taught Lira to survive. But Ahrin wasn't meeting her gaze, which was unusual.

"You're holding something back from me," Lira accused softly.

"I'm not." Her tone was brisk.

"Now you're lying. You think I can't tell?" Lira said flatly.

Before Ahrin could reply, a sharp knock rapped at the door. It opened a second later, Garan not waiting for a reply before walking in. Tarion, Fari, and Lorin trailed in behind him.

"Visitors, how delightful," Ahrin said dryly.

Lira shot a glance her way, trying not to feel like the Darkhand was relieved to have been interrupted.

"I assume you've both ensured you're not being spied on in here?" Garan said.

Ahrin simply nodded.

"Don't assume there isn't a telepath nearby," Lira said sharply. "Shields up before you say a word."

"Done." He flashed her a quick smile. "Now, we need to talk."

Lira cocked an eyebrow. "About what?"

His expression hardened. "This is no time for your aloof stubbornness. Lucinda just fed us a handful of lies in order to convince us to go chasing monsters underground. Do you not think it smarter we discuss that as a group before marching into certain death?"

"He's right." Ahrin spoke before Lira could. "Let's sit."

"See." Fari gave Garan a look as they moved towards the couch and chairs. "I told you she'd listen to sense."

"Lira never listens to sense," he grumbled.

"I wasn't talking about Lira." Fari grinned in the Darkhand's direction.

Ahrin's mouth curled in a smile that looked almost genuine. Lira tried to ignore the hot sweep of jealousy that surged through her.

Once they'd all sat down, Fari was the one to get them going. "I don't know about you all, but I believe the story about the mage war, the destruction of the country, how it created the monsters."

"Agreed." Lira forced her focus to the present. "Even if Lucinda was only telling it to manipulate our sympathies, the looks on the faces of the Seven said it all. They're grieving. Desperate."

"It's also completely consistent with what we observed aboveground," Lorin added, "No wonder they were desperate enough to kidnap Tarion's parents."

"Nope, that's where she loses me," Garan said firmly. "Yes, Aunt Alyx is extremely powerful and has multiple mage abilities, and yes, it's true that many of those abilities can be used advantageously in a fight without needing to directly touch her opponent, but ... really? One single mage and Taliath, to take out more than one queen and any razak in their path?"

"Maybe they figure it's their only hope left," Tarion offered, but didn't look like he believed it.

For once, Lira was in firm agreement with Garan. "Sure, the desperation I believe, but *was* it their only hope left? Why not just officially approach the Mage Council and ask for proper help, a mage army?" Lira continued thinking out loud. "If the council says no, *then* start kidnapping people, but there's a good chance they wouldn't have. Egalion and Tylender are soft-hearted." Well, Tylender *had* been. Now he was Lucinda's puppet ... which only added weight to her argument.

"I guess some people just have trust issues." Fari shot a smile in Lira's direction, but then sobered. "In all seriousness, these people are scared and paranoid. Maybe it's just not in them to believe that the council would agree to help."

Lira shook her head, unconvinced.

Tarion clearly agreed. "On what would they base that lack of belief? Our countries were never at war. Admittedly, there wasn't much of a trade relationship, but what existed wasn't hostile."

"I think we're making more of this than we need to," Lorin said doggedly. "We came here to find Tarion's parents ... at least now we're on the right track. Once we find them, we leave; it's as simple as that. With our abilities combined with Councillor Egalion, not even Lucinda is stopping us getting home. We can worry about asking questions then."

"Abilities..." Ahrin said, thinking, then her gaze shot to Lira's. "What if the goal was more than just deploying Egalion against the razak. What if Lucinda injected her with razak blood, hoping for the same outcome she had with you, Lira?"

Lira nodded slowly, realising. "She tried to give Egalion the ability to break razak immunity with her magic."

"*If* the experiment worked, *and* didn't kill my aunt in the process." Garan frowned. "Lucinda had no way of knowing whether it would before kidnapping her."

"A mage of the higher order whose abilities could breach the monsters' immunity *would* be capable of destroying the queens," Fari said, realisation crossing her face. "The hope of that would be enough to risk what they did."

"The razak injections didn't allow my existing telekinesis ability to break their immunity—only my new flame ability can do that," Lira pointed out.

"It's a lot of gambles for someone as strategically brilliant as Lucinda," Ahrin admitted. "But maybe she saw the potential outcome as worth it."

Garan let out a long sigh and sat back. "I suppose Lorin had a point earlier. Our goal is clear, and we may just be complicating things for ourselves by trying to figure out Rotherburnian politics."

"We were promised a guide to talk to tomorrow." Tarion stood. "We can ask all the questions we need to then."

"Sleep, then, is it?" Fari rose with a relieved expression. "Good. I feel like I'm going to need it in the days ahead."

They trailed out without another word, all seemingly lost in thought, waving half-heartedly as they left.

Lira remained where she was, thinking furiously.

"You might have been right about them," Ahrin murmured, almost to herself, as she closed the door.

"Hmmm?" Lira blinked and looked up, before settling back in the chair. Weariness sank over her.

"Nothing. It's getting dark. We'd best close this up." She shut the balcony door and turned the lock with a soft click, then gave Lira a disgruntled look. "Are you going to come to bed, or are you planning on sleeping on that sofa tonight?"

Lira cracked an eye open, smiled. "These cushions are rather comfortable."

"You're serious, aren't you?" Ahrin stared at her. "Fine. Suit yourself."

Lira waited for a few moments, drawing it out, then held out a hand. "There's plenty of room on this sofa for two."

"Well, that's more like it."

Lira shifted to make room for her, waiting till Ahrin settled into the cushions before shifting to curl her body comfortably around her, forehead resting against Ahrin's neck. One of Ahrin's arms stretched out along the back of the sofa, her hand moving to slide idly through Lira's curls. In seconds, all Lira's tiredness, the depression that still lingered, her unease over being in Lucinda's clutches again, faded, and all she felt was warm contentment. "Ahrin, I honestly don't care which option we take. If you think the best bet is to do what Lucinda wants, then I'll do it."

Ahrin kissed her forehead, her other hand reaching over to take Lira's. "I know how badly you want revenge. And I'll help you get it, but you know as well as I do that we need to come at Lucinda from a position of strength."

"I do."

A long silence fell, and Lira's eyes drifted closed. Here, wrapped around Ahrin, their hands entangled, she felt safe. Ahrin's heartbeat under her ear slowed, relaxed, and her breath was warm against Lira's skin.

"Lira?"

"Mmm?"

"What do you want to do after?"

Surprised, she shifted, looking up to meet Ahrin's eyes. "After what?"

"After you get your revenge on Lucinda. On the Mage Council. Then what?"

Lira had tried looking ahead. During her time in prison, she'd attempted it often, trying to see past the culmination of her plans. But the future had always been dark. One big empty space not unlike the chasm of emptiness in her chest; it had only grown larger during her time in prison.

Her answer tumbled out before she could stop it. "Then *nothing*. There is nothing left. Not after..."

Silence followed her words, filled by the crackle and pop of the fire. Ahrin's gaze was distant as she stared into the flames. It was impossible to tell what she thought of Lira's words. A few moments later, Lira ventured. "What about you?"

Ahrin shook her head fractionally, still far away. Where was she? "I don't know either. I never had any of the things normal people have—home, family, a life. From birth I had weapons placed in my hands, combat training, a strategy teacher, and nothing else. I don't feel things like normal people do. I was created to be a tool, a weapon, and that's all I am."

"Not to me, you're not," Lira said softly.

Ahrin let out a bitter laugh. "Ah, but you're the one I was created to be a weapon *for*, Lira."

Deep down, Lira frowned at that, the unnameable *thing* in the pit of her stomach trembling with fear, worry. But before she could pursue it further, Ahrin's grip on her hand tightened, and she leaned down to kiss her. It was a fierce, hungry kiss, as if she were trying to hold Lira to her somehow. As if she were afraid Lira was slipping away. "You always have somewhere with me, you know that, don't you?"

Sometimes Lira thought Ahrin was the only thing that tethered her to this world. Right from the moment they'd met, she'd been a bright, shining thing lodged deep in Lira's heart, a solid, *powerful* connection to life, whether good or bad. But she didn't say that.

She didn't know how.

CHAPTER 28

Once Ahrin was asleep, Lira lay awake, staring up at the ceiling, her mind whirling restlessly. Their earlier conversation kept replaying in her thoughts. No matter how she tried, she couldn't turn it off.

She was *glad* that Lucinda was sending them off to hunt razak. Already the anticipation was building in the base of her stomach. The idea of tangling so closely with death, at winning that battle like she always had, filled her to brimming. It was an escape, and she knew it, but she welcomed it anyway. She was sick and tired of feeling that tightness in her chest, the bleakness of looking forward and seeing nothing beyond vengeance in her future.

And once the razak were dead, she'd finally have her shot at Lucinda. The woman would be prepared, of course; she knew Lira would eventually come for her. But once Lira and her companions were down in the depths, the Seventh would have no idea where they were, whether they even lived or died. Lucinda was taking a calculated gamble by sending Lira out of her control.

A gamble Lira would make her pay for.

But first they'd have to kill the razak queens. A close to impossible task, when she forced herself to be objective. Her flame magic could cut through the monsters' immunity, but none of the other mages going with her had that advantage. And Lira had no death wish. Her thrill—the headiness of intense danger—came from risking it and *surviving*.

And then there was the feeling Lira couldn't shake that they were going into this half blind. It was a recipe for failure. They needed more weapons to increase their odds of survival. And knowledge could be a powerful weapon indeed.

"*Lira Astor?*"

The voice slid into her head, smooth and effortless, and causing Lira to turned rigid with shock. Without thought she glanced around the dark room, body readying to leap out and attack, before she realised nobody was there—a telepath was reaching out to her.

"*Yes, I am a telepath. I mean you no harm. Relax.*"

"*Who are you?*" she demanded, angry at how the telepath had taken her off guard.

"*The Seven are meeting right now. They are discussing your arrival and the mission you agreed to. Would you like to listen in?*"

Suspicion must have filled her mind, because the voice let out a sigh. "*Your shielding is excellent, but even from quick glimpses of your surface thoughts I can tell you are a person that does not trust easily. I mean you no harm, Lira.*"

"*Why would you want me to listen in on the Seven?*"

"*I do not like the path that they are taking. I fear Lucinda will see us all burn if she is allowed to have her way.*"

"*Ah. So Lucinda is an enemy.*" Lira could use that.

"*Yes, you can.*"

Lira started, fear twining through her. "*You're powerful.*"

"*I do not want to see my people destroyed by bad decisions ... that's exactly what caused the mage wars and got us here in the first place. I want to help you, Lira, because I do not wish to see you and all your kingdoms' power turned against us.*"

"*Is Lucinda planning to betray us?*"

A hesitation. "*Not that I know of. Not yet, at least. But if she does, I would like you to remember that not all in Rotherburn share her views. That is why I'm reaching out.*"

"*And how do I know this isn't Lucinda trying to trick me?*"

"*What purpose would she have for that? You've agreed to do as she asks.*"

Lira was silent—trying to think through something complicated without the telepath in your head reading you was close to impossible.

"I will guide you safely to their meeting, to a place you can overhear, and then I will guide you safely back."

"What do you want in return?"

"Nothing but that you remember I helped you. That we all don't think as she does."

"Most of you do if you're giving her such free rein," Lira pointed out, but then conceded, *"What is your name?"*

"You do not need to know that." Impatience edged the person's voice. *"You will miss much of the meeting if you linger much longer."*

That checked Lira's instinct to keep probing. If there *was* a meeting happening, it would be the perfect opportunity to get some insight into what was really going on here.

Making a decision on the spur of the moment—ignoring the nagging voice that warned she just wanted an excuse not to lie there anymore, trapped in her thoughts—Lira rolled carefully out of bed and pulled her clothes back on.

"Leave via your balcony. None of the guards watching your building are stationed outside for fear of the nerik. I counsel you to stick to the shadows as you move through the streets and don't use your magic. It can draw them to you."

She did as ordered, slipping out onto their balcony without a noise so as not to wake Ahrin. Lights from the windows in the Seven's building drew her attention. Whoever this voice in her head was, it seemed they were telling the truth about a meeting happening.

"Move north along the street and take your first left."

Following a series of instructions from her new friend, Lira jogged through dark streets that took her toward the southern side of the building, making sure to stay in the shadows and frequently glance up at the sky to make sure there were no nerik swooping above.

Eventually the voice asked her to stop in a narrow alley that ended in the rocky ravine wall. *"You must climb the wall as high as the first level, then scramble sideways to the balcony on the far side of the building."*

The entire side of the building was shrouded in darkness, and the only sentries Lira could spot were the two red-garbed soldiers at the front entrance. Was it incompetence, laziness, or merely a lack of resources that had the building so poorly guarded?

"It is the latter."

Lira swore at the evident skill of this telepath to read her surface thoughts with such ease. She paused to reinforce her shields once again, then started climbing. Once she was through the balcony door, Lira paused inside the hallway she found herself in. It appeared to lead toward the northern side of the building. *"I'm in."*

"Follow the hallway to the end, where you will reach stairs. Go up one level."

Lira did as instructed, finding the next level dark and deserted. Following more instructions, she circled around to the opposite side of the building, went back down a level.

"You know the guard layout well," she murmured. She hadn't yet seen one.

"Go through the second door on your right."

The room inside was empty, but her gaze immediately snagged on the windows lining the far wall.

"This is as close as I can get you to the room where they're meeting. If you go to the windows and open one, you should be able to listen in. The windows in the meeting chamber are open."

Lira padded across the floor, gaze scanning the opening mechanism of the windows and then reaching out to open one. She moved painfully slowly, not wanting to create any noise. It opened outwards and she glanced down to see the lit windows below ... one of which was open, as promised.

She concentrated, listening carefully. Snatches of voices drifted up to her, but she wasn't close enough to make out the words. *"Are there guards below to see me if I climb out?"* Lira asked.

"Not on this side of the building. I had them re-assigned."

Lira filed away that detail for later. Whoever this person was, they had the power to move guards around and ensure a window was open in the Seven's meeting chamber despite the potential threat of nerik.

After a brief hesitation, she climbed out the window, shuffling along the narrow edge a short way before dropping down to the one below. Her feet scrabbled for purchase, and she almost fell, heart thudding, before she finally got her balance.

She went still, in case someone had seen her and sounded an alarm, but nothing happened. Relieved, she inched sideways, closer to the lit windows, and was able to shimmy almost right up beside the open one.

"We've been here hours, and we're only going around in circles. I think we've discussed this enough." Lucinda's voice was firm, showing no signs of weariness. Lira's heart leapt at how clear it was. "You've put your trust in me so far, so let me lead our efforts to save Rotherburn. There's no reason to stop now."

"You've potentially placed us in a position of war with the continent!" a man's voice said. While the words were angry, his voice had a slight shake to it, that of an old man. Lira guessed it was Burgen. "If they learn we kidnapped their beloved mage of the higher order—"

"They won't, as I've told you repeatedly," Lucinda snapped. "Panic-mongering doesn't suit you, Burgen, and it doesn't help us make a decision."

"We were all concerned about the risks of your plan from the beginning. Now they seem to be realised." Another voice, female. Lira placed her as the woman with the braids. "And yes, we keep going around in circles, but that's because you've yet to adequately address our concerns."

"Indira, we had no other choice. We *still* have no other choice."

A new voice joined in. Lira didn't recognise it, so she risked a quick peep through the glass. It was the youngest-looking member of the Seven. "Your efforts to create new mages were just beginning to pay off," she said. "You'd stabilised the subjects, started seeing real success. Why don't we just—"

"Nessin, you're the ones who *ordered* me to return here and abandon the program." Lucinda's voice was rife with frustration. "Because you were so scared—"

"You allowed a traitor in your ranks," Tallin cut in. "Your Darkhand knew far too much about us—proven by her ability to find us here. Not to mention Lira Astor. If the Mage Council had learned what we were doing there, using their citizens as experiments..."

"We should never have let you talk us out of asking the Mage Council and their kingdoms for help," another voice said in disgust. A man, but not Tallin or Burgen. "You used our fear and desperation against us and now it's too late. Now we face extermination either way."

"Verin is right, but it's not too late," Burgen said. "Maybe we should start thinking about going to them openly, admitting our misdeeds, asking for their mercy."

Indira sighed. "To succeed at that, we'd need a live Alyx Egalion to return to them. I—"

"Lucinda's plan is the right one." Another new voice, full of fervour. "Your squeamishness is understood but misplaced. We are in a desperate situation and it is our responsibility to save our people, no matter what we have to do. We have no choice."

"Thank you, Adellin. You have captured the key point perfectly. We cannot afford to be hesitant when it comes to the lives of our people. Please, I ask you all to hold to my plan." Lucinda spoke sincerely now. "We send Astor and the Darkhand after the razak queens. They have a chance of succeeding. Egalion is likely either lost or struggling to find the nests ... if they band together there is real hope."

"And if they don't? What then?" This from Nessin.

"I have another way out. Another way to save us."

There was a charged silence, filled with an odd mix of suspicion and hope. Eventually Burgen spoke. "Lucinda, tell me now that you don't have some ulterior motive in all of this."

"I want only to save our people. And I will succeed. I swear that to you."

"Lucinda has had many successes, far more than any of us," Tallin said in resignation. "Perhaps it is time to fully place our faith in her."

A frantic knocking sounded at the door before anyone could respond to that. It clicked open, there were murmured voices, then Burgen spoke. "There's been another possible incursion on the lower levels." He sounded exhausted suddenly. "We'd best go and make sure everything holds."

"How is it we got to this?" Verin said sadly as chairs scarped back and clothing rustled. "The ruling Seven of Rotherburn amongst the only remaining magebloods in the country with enough magical strength to hold back the razak."

"We will restore our power and our home," Lucinda said, voice ringing with conviction. "There is no doubt in my mind."

CHAPTER 29

"*J*ust wait a few moments, I'll let you know when it's safe to move.*" The telepath spoke once the meeting chamber fell silent, emptied out.

Lira waited patiently until getting the go ahead, then climbed back up on cramped and aching limbs and snuck back out of the building the same way she'd come in. As she moved, alert for any sign of being followed or noticed, she parsed through what she'd just overheard.

"*Are you there?*" She tried opening her thoughts to the telepath.

Silence.

The mission they'd sent Egalion on was genuine ... to the Seven at least, but it was clear Lucinda had another plan within a plan, one her fellow rulers didn't even know about. Her brain was formidable, and Lira no longer underestimated it.

"*Hello?*"

Still nothing. The telepath had gone. The fact they were so insistent on hiding their identity was understandable, particularly if they were an enemy of Lucinda's, but it made Lira itch. She didn't like relying on someone with unverifiable motives.

To win at this, to be ready for what came even if they *did* manage to succeed at killing the razak queens, they needed more than what they had. They needed every advantage they could get over Lucinda.

By the time she'd returned to their apartment, the telepath hadn't re-contacted her, and Lira had made up her mind. She climbed back up to her balcony railing, then jumped upwards, hands just managing to grab the bottom of the balcony immediately above. A few seconds to haul herself upwards, and she was over the railing and inside it. The glass door of this room revealed a snoring Garan, sprawled with limbs askew under the covers. After checking to ensure he was soundly asleep, she scrambled across from his balcony to the one beside it. Tarion's.

It took her the work of a seconds to pick the lock on his door and open it.

He slept on his back, looking far more peaceful than he did when awake, the constant furrow in his brow smoothed out. She crept on silent feet over to the bed, stopped to make sure her presence hadn't disturbed him, then shifted her gaze to his wrists. One hand was curled on the pillow by his head, the other resting on his stomach.

She was going to have to move quickly.

In one smooth movement, she swung into the bed, sitting lightly astride his sleeping figure. He began waking as she got the first circlet off his right wrist and started reaching for the second by his head.

He mumbled, still mostly asleep, "What are you—"

"Quiet!" she hissed, trying to ignore the numbing dissonance caused by touching the metal.

He was quick, only taking another second to realise what she was doing and yank his wrist away. But she already had the clasp undone and it wrenched off as he pulled away from her. She threw it onto the floor beside where she'd tossed the other one, then, before he could do anything more, she summoned her flame magic and set them alight.

"NO!" Tarion hurled her off him in one powerful movement and leapt out of bed.

Lira flew sideways, landing hard on the floor on the other side of the bed and rolling to break her momentum. By the time she'd regained her feet, he was standing over the melted pool of metal on the floor. Horror and despair filled his face.

In the next second, there was a banging on his door, Garan's voice shouting through it and demanding to know what was going on.

Tarion turned on her, eyes wild. "*Why?*"

She ignored him, scanned the room until she spotted an empty bowl, then yanked it to her hand with a touch of telekinesis. Bending, she scooped up the pile of melted metal as best she could without touching it, shuddering as its proximity interfered with her magic. Then she went to the jug of water near Tarion's bed and poured it into the bowl, filling it up. The water hissed, steam rising from its surface. Once she was satisfied that the metal was sufficiently diluted, she went to the balcony and tossed it over the edge.

Ahrin landed, catlike, on the balcony a second later, at the same moment Garan gave up on knocking and pushed through the door, Fari and Lorin on his heels. Ahrin took one look at Lira, the now-empty bowl in her hands, and her mouth thinned.

"What the magical hells is going on?" Garan demanded. "Tar, are you all right?"

Tarion's tall form vibrated with fury. "She destroyed my bracelets."

Garan paled, gaze turning to Lira. "Why? What were you thinking?"

"I was thinking that if you really want to get your relatives back, the six of us have to somehow sneak through a dark labyrinth infested with razak and kill multiple well-protected queens—something even the most powerful mage in the world doesn't seem to have succeeded at. I was thinking we need every advantage we can get, and Tarion willingly hobbling himself is stupid."

"What's stupid is setting me loose around all of you." Wrath pulsed in Tarion's words; anger born of fear. "I can't control the change. You'll be in just as much danger from me as you will from the razak."

"Have you ever tried to control it?" Lira asked.

"I..." He faltered. "No. It's too risky."

She let out an incredulous breath. She'd suspected as much, but hearing confirmation... "You mean to tell me that for almost three years you haven't even tried to learn your magic?"

"It's not magic." His jaw was rigid. "It's dangerous and turns me into a violent, mindless monster that attacks everything it sees. It hurts people, Lira. I didn't even know it was happening to me—how could I ever possibly control it!"

Lira opened her mouth to argue further, but Ahrin cut her off.

"You could stay here," she told Tarion. "That way you're no risk to us. They can keep you secured at night."

Lira shot her an angry glance. "What, and let Lucinda in on the fact that her experiments with nerik blood worked? Tarion can learn to control it, and when he does, it will help us. Don't you see, this is an advantage! Leverage we can use against her."

"Even if that's true, there's no time for him to learn anything." A nerve ticked in Garan's jaw. "What you've done is beyond irresponsible. More, it's dangerous and stupid. You've just torched our mission."

"Ahrin's right. I'll have to stay here," Tarion said miserably, sinking onto the bed. His anger seemed to have vanished as quickly as it had come. Lira fought the urge to snap at him. His self-defeating attitude was infuriating.

Until now, Fari and Lorin had faded into the background, clearly not wanting to get involved. But now Fari spoke up. "What's done is done. I don't know about the rest of you, but I'm not comfortable leaving Tarion here alone at Lucinda's mercy while we're gone. Maybe Lira is right and this is something Tarion can learn to control."

"That's an idealistic view." Lorin delivered these words with his characteristic hauteur. "Tarion has no time to learn anything, and as he himself said, he didn't even know when the change was happening to him. If we take him with us, there is no doubt he will turn and attack us. We will face an enemy within in addition to the razak."

Fari scowled. "That is dangerously close to the kind of black-and-white thinking I truly detest, Lorin Hester."

He looked a touch chastened, but simply said, "That doesn't mean I'm wrong."

Lira was surprised by Fari's unexpected support but didn't hesitate to use it. "You are wrong. Tarion *can* learn to control it. He can become a weapon we can wield."

"And that's all you care about, isn't it?" Garan said in disgust. "Surviving."

"And killing Lucinda, yes." She crossed her arms over her chest.

"The choice is Tarion's," Ahrin said coolly, breaking the tense silence of the room. "But if he turns into a monster and comes at me while we're down there, I'll slit his throat like any other threat." With that she turned and left, taking the door this time.

Lira didn't follow.

Fari looked between Lorin and Garan—somehow managing to look disappointed in both of them—then turned and left the room too, taking Lorin with her.

Garan took a breath, looking weary. "If one of us gets hurt because of this, Lira..."

Lira rolled her eyes. "I'm only here because you asked me to help you find your relatives. Don't blame me—"

"Don't give me that rubbish," he snapped. "You just said it. You're only here because you want to destroy Lucinda and we're your path to doing it. You'd even take down Ahrin if she stood in your way, and she's the only one of us you actually care about."

Denial rose hot and fast in her—then subsided as quickly as it had come, killed by the memory of Tarion's words to her, '*And you trust her? I don't believe that for a second.*'

"I *am* sitting here." Tarion said, some of his fire returning. "So please stop arguing about me like I'm a child."

"Sorry," Garan said sheepishly.

"Treating you like a child is putting a cage around your magic because nobody has any faith you can learn to control it," Lira said. "I know what it's like being in a cage, Tarion Caverlock, so don't even try and tell me you don't feel relieved right now."

A thick silence filled the room.

"Tar...?" Garan asked tentatively, shocked realisation crossing his face. "Is she right?"

"What?" she scoffed. "You thought the gaunt face, the paler than usual skin, the shadows under his eyes were nothing more than lack of sleep? For *more than two years*? You truly thought repressing the magic he was born with wouldn't have consequences?"

"I did it willingly." Tarion stood, facing his cousin, the two of them seemingly having forgotten Lira was in the room. "And I would have continued doing it willingly, because I never, *ever*, want to hurt anyone. But yes, having your magic hidden away from you is a horrible thing."

Garan nodded slowly. "It was the right choice, Tar. I still believe that, although I'm truly sorry it had such an effect on you."

Tarion's shoulders slumped, as if he'd hoped for something different from Garan. But then he straightened them. "I'm coming with you. I can't leave my parents alone down there."

Relief shimmered in Lira's chest. Garan seemed to waver, on the verge of arguing, but eventually he just ran a tired hand through his hair. "I think that's a mistake. But Ahrin was right; it is your choice."

Ahrin waited inside their room, pacing. The fingers of her left hand tapped restlessly against her thigh. Lira braced herself.

"I thought we were supposed to be making decisions together," Ahrin said, voice deceptively mild.

"I knew you'd stop me," Lira said simply. "And you're not in charge of me anymore."

"You like to keep throwing that at me, don't you?" Ahrin's tone was icy. "I came here for you."

"You came here because you have a purpose, like always, and you won't tell me what it is." Lira snapped back. "Don't think I can't tell."

Dead silence fell. Lira wasn't sure how to interpret Ahrin's expression, and it made her uneasy. But Ahrin said nothing. She merely walked past Lira and out the door, closing it with a soft click behind her.

Lira wanted nothing more than to pick up the nearest object to throw across the room—but a crash would only bring the others running, and she didn't want to talk to anyone again tonight.

Everything was so rotting tangled. She felt just as trapped as she'd always been, the weight on her chest a persistent, relentless anchor keeping her from the freedom she hadn't dared dream about in too many years.

She just had to see this through, she reminded herself. Kill the razak queens. Come back and kill Lucinda.

Then everything would be all right.

CHAPTER 30

When Lira ventured out early the following morning looking for breakfast—Ahrin had still been gone when she woke, and she had no desire to linger in the room alone with her thoughts—she found a sunlit dining room on the ground floor. The table in the centre of the space was laden with delicious-smelling food, surrounded by several empty chairs...

And one occupied by Lucinda.

The woman was perfectly attired as always, not a single hair or cuff or button out of place. Her hands were clasped loosely in her lap, back straight. A woman perfectly in control of herself and everything around her. There was no sign that Lucinda had any idea Lira had spied on the Seven's meeting the previous night, and her worry that the telepath had been leading her into a trap subsided slightly.

Even so, she lingered in the doorway, wanting to be sure. "How'd you manage to harvest all that with no farming land? The crops I saw outside your empty city didn't look nearly enough to feed the numbers you say are here." She pointed to the steaming porridge and large bowl of fruit. If nothing else at Temari, she'd learned the basics of how agriculture sustained a hungry population.

"We've gotten rather creative over the decades," Lucinda said. "But none of us eat like this all the time. Rarely, actually. Consider this largesse a thank you in advance."

Lira snorted. "Did Egalion and Caverlock get the same funeral breakfast?"

"They did." Lucinda cracked a small smile, then said smoothly, "We're genuinely appreciative of you agreeing to do this. Everything I did back in Shivasa was in service of this goal ... all I want is freedom for my people."

Lira leapt at the opportunity to test further what she'd overheard the previous night, Lucinda's willingness to be honest and open. "If that's true, then explain it to me, because I can't make any sense of it. You latched onto my grandfather's old network and their resources to ... what? Start a rebellion to somehow fix your problems back here. How does that logic work?"

Lucinda gave a graceful shrug. "We desperately needed more mages to hold back the razak and nerik, but to create them, we required test subjects for our experiments. We couldn't afford to lose any more of our own people, so we left home to find them. But your Mage Council, and your kingdoms? They're powerful. Well-resourced. If they'd learned what we were doing, they could wipe us out without any effort. Your grandfather's network provided me with both resources, and a cover that prevented the council from looking too deeply at *my* motivations. The council remains so scared of your grandfather's legacy, they didn't question that was what Underground was truly about."

Lira's instincts shivered through her. That hadn't been all Lucinda was doing—far from it, as plausible as it sounded. "So why the strikes? The secret meetings?"

Lucinda shrugged. "A necessary part of the charade. Your grandfather's network had certain expectations of us in return for the resources they provided. I couldn't afford for them to learn what we were really doing any more than I could afford the council learning of it."

"All that effort, and yet you just decided to abruptly sacrifice all of it and return here two years ago?" Lira lifted an eyebrow. Here it was ... the chance to see whether Lucinda would tell the same story.

"I was forced to do that when I learned of your duplicity, yours and the Darkhand's. The Seven were ... worried ... that you and the Darkhand knew too much, and over my objections they called an end to the experiments. So we neutralised you both and departed to regroup." Lucinda eyed her with interest. "You're the closest anyone's ever come to undoing me. Not that you were very close, but still."

Lira relaxed slightly. She'd been given the truth this time. How much more was Lucinda willing to give? "Tell me, after at least a decade in Shivasa doing your little experiments, pretending to foment rebellion on behalf of Shakar as cover for your activities … how many mages did you get out of it?"

Something like weary disappointment flickered on Lucinda's face. "Not as many as we'd hoped."

"That's a lot of time and effort wasted, then. That's not like you, Lucinda," Lira probed.

"We made some important progress in our experiments—enough to realise we'd never have a success rate fast enough to combat the razak losses. Not without a larger population." She shrugged, spread her hands. "But you're right. We invested significant time and resources and did not achieve anywhere close to the outcomes we wanted. So we pivoted, came up with a different plan."

"But you didn't pivot. You were overruled and ordered back here by your fellow rulers." Lira let that hit land, then pushed off the doorway and dropped into one of the chairs before starting to pile food onto her plate. "Why did it take you *two years* to decide that kidnapping Egalion and Caverlock and using them to do your dirty work was the way to go?"

Lucinda gave her a chilly little smile. "I know what you're doing, and I'm certainly not going to give you any further insights into the Seven or our strategies—you won't get the leverage you're seeking out of me. You will be told what you need to know to complete your mission, and that is all."

Lira leaned forward. "You mean you won't give me any more insight into *your* strategies. Because that's what's really going on here, right? You've gone to a lot of trouble to end up nowhere, your hopes for Rotherburn pinned on a handful of mage brats. The Seven might believe that's what you want. But they're not as suspicious and paranoid as me." Although at least one of them might be. Surely the telepath who'd contacted her the previous night was aligned with one of the Seven? The interactions of the soldiers that had escorted them to the ravine city had certainly suggested factional support for different members of the ruling council existed amongst Rotherburn's fighters.

A chuckle escaped Lucinda, an entirely unfeigned one. "If I can make a safe home for my people, you had better believe that's what I'll do, Lira Astor."

Lira forked some eggs into her mouth, chewed, swallowed, then nodded. Lucinda had an answer for everything, and there might be enough truth in there to be useful later. Time to focus on what came next. "How long have Egalion and her husband been gone?"

Lucinda straightened, voice turning businesslike. "Three weeks, give or take a few days. The commander of our guard will be here shortly. She can answer any questions you have. She has been given orders to provide you with anything you need."

"They the brown uniforms or the red?"

"The brown."

"So I'm right to guess the red ones are your mages? Used to protect your important personages rather than the poor citizens living in the lower level of this city being picked off by razak. I didn't notice any of them protecting the supply run the other night either." Lira raised an eyebrow.

Lucinda said nothing. The woman's ability not to react to any kind of taunt was impressive. And frustrating.

Lira shrugged. "If your commander is dropping by to tell us everything we need to know, why are *you* here?"

"To offer you a warning." Lucinda rose in a smooth, unhurried movement, shifted her chair closer to Lira, and sat down again, voice lowering. "I gambled on you being up for breakfast first. I'm betting you don't sleep much these days."

Lira lifted an eyebrow, trying her best to hide exactly how close to the mark Lucinda was. "You want to *warn* me? About what exactly?"

"Ahrin Vensis. I've been wrong on that score, all this time, and that doesn't happen often. I thought you understood she was your most dangerous enemy. Not me, Lira. *Her*." Lucinda's voice had lowered even further, and she sounded sincere. It was a flawless act.

Lira smiled thinly. "The list of things you've done to me makes that statement seem a tad ridiculous."

Lucinda cocked her head. "I keep an eye on events back in your home. I know she toppled Transk, took over his powerful Dirinan crew, the job she always wanted. Why did she give up all that to come here with you?"

"That's none of your concern."

"Ah." Lucinda sat back a little, looking pleased. "You hide your reactions well, but not when it comes to her. You've already figured it out, deep down."

Lira heaved a sigh and turned away, forking up some egg and shoving it in her mouth, faking disinterest. The rest of her tried furiously not to let Lucinda's words get under her skin.

"She was conditioned to follow your grandfather, obey his orders, and that carries to you. She has no choice in the matter." Lucinda's words were low, hypnotic, reaching right down into Lira's deepest fears and tearing them open. "She's here because you are. Not because she wants to be."

Lira managed to roll her eyes and huff. "Lucinda, I really—"

"We both know her well. We know how independent, how strong-willed, how capable and clever she is." Lucinda paused. "How do you think the conditioning she underwent as a child makes her feel? How much, deep down, do you think she resents it. Hates it. Rails against it. Against *you*?"

Conditioning. Ahrin had hinted at it, when she'd divulged her identity as a Hunter, told Lira that it kept her from telling people what she was. But ever since that moment, Lira had feared what else the conditioning had accomplished. She'd feared it so deeply she hadn't even been able to ask Ahrin about it, and now Lucinda was poking at those fears.

She swallowed her mouthful, took a deep breath, and turned to meet Lucinda's gaze. "You know nothing about Ahrin."

"She is your most dangerous enemy, Lira, and not just because she's your only weakness. I say this not to manipulate you, or to scare you, but because I want you to succeed in this mission. I want my people to have hope. And if you fail because you trust Ahrin Vensis too far..." Lucinda stood up. "How long do you think it will be until she takes out the one thing holding her back from true freedom? I warn you sincerely."

"Your intentions are never sincere," Lira said flatly.

Lucinda shrugged, pausing at the door. "When you get a chance, ask your Darkhand what happened to Athira Walden."

She was gone before Lira could process those words, and then, seconds later, Garan and Fari pushed through the door, casting suspicious looks behind them.

"What did she want?" Garan asked.

"To let me know the commander of their guard is on her way to talk to us." Lira turned back to her food, pushing away everything Lucinda had just said into a tiny box at the back of her mind never to be dragged out again. But the box had lots of little holes that kept leaking ... it sat like a weight on her chest and destroyed any appetite she might have had.

Fari looked all kinds of dubious. "She came to deliver the message personally?"

"I have little insight into why that woman does the things she does, except to never trust it," Lira said wearily. "I recommend enjoying the breakfast. It's the last bit of good food we're going to get for a while."

Ahrin came in next, scanning the room until she spotted Lira, then she came to take the seat beside her. She seemed relaxed, as if the tension of their conversation the night before had never happened. "Morning."

"Morning," Lira muttered. "Where were you all night?"

"Scouting, making sure I understand the layout of this place." Ahrin shrugged, then lifted an eyebrow at her. "Do you think you'll ever wake up one morning and be cheerful that a brand new day is starting?"

Fari dissolved into giggles on the other side of the table. "Lira? Look cheerful? *Ever*? Never going to happen."

Even Garan smiled.

Ahrin smiled slightly, then began piling food on her plate too. "What did Lucinda want?"

"Nothing interesting."

The Darkhand's mouth tightened, as if she knew this was a lie, but she didn't push any further. Lira thought about relaying what she'd overheard the previous night while spying on the Seven but decided against it. She couldn't be sure Lucinda or her people weren't watching them ... the information could wait until they were underground and alone.

A moment later, Tarion appeared in the middle of the room, startling everyone, who then proceeded to stare wide-eyed at him as if he might turn into a monster any second. When he didn't, the mood relaxed, but the topic of Lucinda had been forgotten. His gaze remained firmly on the floor, shoulders hunched, as he sat down at the table.

"How are you feeling?" Fari asked him carefully.

"Normal. Better now I can feel my magic, actually," he said reluctantly, then lowered his voice. "We should take chains with us, bind me while I sleep. And probably keep a watch too."

"I don't know." Garan sounded unconvinced. "How will we explain needing chains to take with us? If nothing else, I agree with what Lira said last night about Lucinda not learning what effects the nerik blood had on you."

Relieved to have their attention away from her, Lira went back to her food and let them carry on the conversation about Tarion, even though she'd completely lost all appetite. She had to eat, build up her strength. Tarion's words from two nights earlier, after they'd fought the razak, flashed through her brain. *"You trust her? I don't believe that for a second."*

Lira shook her head, pushed the memory away. Ahrin was her only ally in the world.

Ahrin would never be her enemy. Lira knew that. Didn't she? Damn Lucinda to rotting hells for her mind games.

What had happened to Athira?

CHAPTER 31

"From the river to halfway up the gorge, the city is divided into seven levels on both sides of the ravine."

The words of Commander Duriana, the one Lucinda had sent to answer their questions, echoed through Lira's thoughts as she followed the others down from their apartment level the following day. Their current guide was visibly nervous, beads of sweat sliding down from his forehead even though it wasn't overly warm.

While they walked, she went back over the conversation they'd had earlier carefully, making sure she'd absorbed all the necessary details.

"Below the river ... well, there's never been a proper map made, but we guesstimate there are another six or seven levels." Duriana had gestured out the window. "About two levels underground, the two sides of the city merge under the riverbed. Below that, there are likely tunnels down there that nobody has stepped foot in for decades."

"Do you have any idea where the razak queens are nested?" Ahrin had asked her.

"There have been a number of scouting missions over the past decades to try and find them ... none have returned successfully, most never returned at all. But we know they're down deep."

"How do you know that?" Ahrin had pushed.

"The missions that did make it back thought they'd gotten pretty close ... the problem was getting close *enough*. They lost most of their groups trying."

Garan had spoken into the grim silence that followed. "What other dangers do we need to be aware of down there? Tunnel collapses, bad air, anything like that?"

"The original builders and engineers who dug down there did it right. We've never encountered much trouble of that sort, though it's been a good ten years since we've been able to go farther than a couple levels below the city." Duriana had cocked her head, thinking. "There's an underground river that crosses from north to south, almost perpendicular to the ravine, about four levels down. It's rapids, mostly, so I wouldn't suggest trying to cross it, but it will be a source of fresh water if you run out."

"What about food?" Garan had asked next. He and Ahrin had dominated the earlier meeting, the others happy to leave the natural leaders to it. Lira had quickly grown bored discussing the details—she just wanted to get started rather than getting stuck bogged down in preparations—but did her best to pay attention, knowing it was important. "Anything down there we can eat?"

"Maybe some flat worms, cave spiders, millipedes, but nothing you can rely on. Any warm-blooded creatures that survived the mage wars have been hunted by the razak and nerik just like us, and there isn't a whole lot of wildlife living underground to begin with. You'll have to take enough food with you."

A door clanging shut behind them brought Lira back to the present, blinking. Their soldier guide was leading them along a long, dim hallway. There was an iron door at the end with three thick bars garrisoned across it.

Her pack was heavy on her back—enough food and water for two weeks if rationed out, plus her weapons. That meant she'd have to get this done in a week, giving her and Ahrin seven days to get back up into the city and sneak in to take out Lucinda before she knew they were coming.

Overgrown ivy crawled over the walls and the stone under their feet. They were only two levels above the river here, the sound of it rushing by on their left echoing loudly through the deserted hall. The water played against Lira's senses, light and playful, settling some of her unease.

"The last attack was here," the guide said, pointing at smears of dried blood on the floor with a trembling finger. "A razak grabbed the man outside his house after nightfall and dragged him away. Afterward, we moved out everyone who was still living on this level, just to be safe. That was six months ago."

"That's the only entrance to the next level down?" Garan asked sceptically.

The man glanced at him. "We sealed them all up."

Lira pushed, as dubious as Garan about the truth of that. "How did the razak that attacked your man get onto this level to begin with? I assume you had already sealed it up if you knew they were down there?"

He hesitated. "This city is a bit like a rabbit warren. It started out as a port city, but a rather disreputable one, a home for pirates and criminal gangs. Those who lived here liked to have tunnels and hidden places everywhere. There's always another way to get in somewhere."

Ahrin and Lira shared a glance. It sounded like they were heading into quite the labyrinth. It wasn't going to be easy to track down a razak queen, a creature presumably well hidden and protected somewhere deep down. But on the upside, if they could avoid the sealed doors and find an unguarded entry it would make it easier to sneak back into the city to fulfil their real mission here in Rotherburn.

They reached the door, and their guide lifted each of the bars, letting them drop to the floor with a clang. Then he drew a circle of keys from his jacket and worked at the stiff locks—three in total—unlocking each with a distinctive click. By the time he was done his skin had paled and he was sweating through the back of his shirt.

Ahrin and Lira shared another glance. Tarion seemed to notice the same thing they had. He cleared his throat and mumbled something to Garan.

"Are you planning on locking and barring that up behind us?" Garan asked sharply.

"Of course." Their guide swallowed. "It would be too dangerous to leave it unsecured."

Garan crossed his arms over his chest. "So how do we get back in once we've completed this mission of yours?"

"A soldier will be stationed here at all times," the man replied. "Merely bang on the other side and announce yourselves, and we'll let you back in."

Lira scoffed under her breath. This man didn't look like he'd be willing to wait down here another few minutes, let alone a full guard shift. If the other guards were like him, they'd be lucky if they checked on this door once a day.

Which was fine, she reminded herself. If all went well, they wouldn't be coming back this way anyway.

"That's reassuring." Fari threw her hands in the air. "How are we supposed to know that you're not just going to leave us down there to rot?"

"The Seven made an agreement with you." The solider looked offended. "We all want you to succeed."

"Let's just get on with it," Ahrin snapped when an awkward silence fell.

The solider straightened his shoulders and hauled the door open. On edge, they all had weapons out as it swung open, revealing a yawing darkness beyond. But nothing jumped out at them. The air temperature remained cool, rather than cold.

Staring into that darkness, Lira was struck by the reality of what they were about to do. Dealing with a razak was difficult enough on familiar ground with only a handful to manage. But they were about to descend into a maze of underground tunnels that sounded infested with the things.

She smiled, shot a glance at Ahrin, whose eyes glittered in anticipation. All the weight that had been riding on her shoulders for what seemed like forever slid away like it had never been. None of that mattered now. All she had to worry about was finding and killing the razak queens.

This was going to be fun.

"*Good luck, Lira Astor.*" The telepath slid into her head unexpectedly, their mental voice fainter than it had been the previous night. "*My range doesn't extend much farther, so I will be unable to help you from here. But when you return, if the guard does not answer your knock, lower your shields. I will find you.*"

"*Thank you.*" Having learned from the night before, she kept her thoughts still, not allowing herself to think of anything but the floor at her feet, until she could be sure the telepath was out of her head.

When nothing further came, she relaxed, turned her attention to the others.

Garan went inside first, Lira a step behind him, Ahrin coming last. Their guide didn't say a word before he began closing the door with indecent haste. It clanged shut behind them, instantly blanketing them in a darkness so profound it was hard to breathe for a moment.

The thud of bars falling into place echoed through the silence. Even Lira shuddered at the grim note of finality.

After a few moments, though, their eyes began to adjust. Watery sunlight from the river side of the street gave everything a greenish hue. Even though it was enough to see, Lira summoned her magic, using it to light the torches each of them held simultaneously.

Violet-edged white flame leapt to life and she let her magic die as quickly as she'd summoned it. "Remember, whatever you do, don't let them go out," Ahrin said.

They carried spares of course, and flint to light them; this would be a journey of several days, if not more. But if they ran out of torches, or the flames burned out, the only thing they'd have to rely on for light was Lira's flame, or Ahrin and Lorin's concussive magic. And using magic of any sort lower down, where the razak would be more likely to sense it, would draw the beasts to them like flies to a rotting carcass.

"Heard you the first time," Garan said peevishly. "Not to mention we know how the razak work, you know, from the time you sent them hunting us. We don't need you spelling it out repeatedly."

"Watch the tone." Ahrin's voice was mild but held that familiar dangerous edge.

"Not taking orders from you, Darkhand," he snapped back.

Lira sighed. Garan's dislike for Ahrin had only intensified the longer they spent together. Aside from the history between them, he was a natural leader who struggled to submit to anyone else's command. Ahrin submitted to nobody. It didn't make for an easy time.

If Lira didn't figure out how to head off the growing tension, it was going to become a problem. Ahrin would only tolerate Garan's noble-born high-handedness for so long. She dealt with threats and irritants quickly and decisively. Tarion seemed to sense this too, because he uncharacteristically spoke up to break the tension, waving his torch to light the corridor ahead. "Which way?"

"There's a blood trail." Ahrin pointed at the floor and began walking. "That seems like a good place to start."

Garan's jaw hardened, his grip on his torch turning white-knuckled, but at a look from Tarion, he said nothing, instead striding after Ahrin. Lorin set off after them, with Tarion close behind.

Fari tossed a look at Lira. "I can't decide whether it's a good thing the Darkhand is with us because it increases our survival odds, or whether I should be worried she'll eat us in our sleep."

"Ahrin doesn't eat people as a rule." Lira fell into step with her, casting a final glance back at the closed and locked door behind them. "But I wouldn't get on her bad side. She does enjoy slicing off fingers."

"Why is she even here?" Garan asked in irritation. "Lira, you made an agreement to help us in return for us breaking you out of prison. You gave your word, but she didn't. What has she got to gain from helping?"

Lira ignored the slide of uneasiness that rippled through her at his words and gave a shrug. "She estimates that our greatest chance of successfully escaping this rotted country alive is by doing what Lucinda wants. For now."

"Ah," Fari said knowingly.

"*Ah*, what?" Lira bridled.

"I begin to see where you get your 'survive at all costs' attitude from."

"That attitude is a requirement when you're homeless on the streets of a lawless city at six years old." Lira said. "As I've said before. Were you not listening the last time?"

"She was," Lorin said calmly. "Now she's just needling you."

Fari's grin flashed, confirming his words. Lira's mouth thinned. "How about we concentrate on staying alive rather than getting a rise out of each other?"

Fari smirked but lifted her hands in capitulation. "Funny, while the Darkhand terrifies me, I'm still not scared of you."

"I never wanted you to be."

"You could have fooled me."

"You still haven't answered my question," Garan pushed. "Explain why Ahrin even got on a ship to come with us in the first place. Am I the only one who thinks she must have some ulterior motive?"

Fari's eyes narrowed slightly. "As much as I am an ever-dying fan of true love, Ahrin Vensis isn't. She didn't get on that ship just for you, Lira."

Fortunately, Ahrin intervened before Lira had to figure out a response to that. "We should assume that the razak have functional hearing, so you might want to turn the volume down on your useless chatter," Ahrin called back. "It's not just magic that will draw the monsters to us."

Garan opened his mouth, and Lira could practically see the accusation that Ahrin was deflecting, but he then seemed to realise the truth of her words and closed his mouth, an expression of frustration on his face. The rest of them stayed quiet too, gazes warily scanning the darkness around them.

The space they were in was as wide as a road, with what looked like homes on either side. Daylight glimmered into the street through the river-facing homes on the left. A quick investigation revealed small, three-roomed residences with windows overlooking the ravine.

"Reckon one of those things could have gotten through an open window?" Garan mused. "Or smashed through one? When their limbs are in insubstantial form, their heads could probably fit through."

"That would mean one had crawled down from the surface, as opposed to creeping up from the lower levels," Lorin replied. "If that's the case, then sealing up the lower levels isn't going to save the city."

"An entire population reduced to a single remaining city, slowly being picked off one-by-one by terrifying monsters." Fari shuddered. "What a horror these people have lived through."

"These people kidnapped us, tortured us, and are now forcing us to risk our lives once again to save them," Lira said. "How about we turn down the sympathy?"

"Actually, Lucinda and her mages did all that to us," Fari corrected, casting a sidelong glance in Ahrin's direction. "I doubt the poor man who got eaten by a razak six months ago had anything to do with it."

"These people are not our problem, Fari, and if we start thinking that they are, we're going to die right along with them," Ahrin said, already heading for the door back to the street. "I don't care who gets eaten, as long as it's not me. Let's keep moving."

Lira gave a little nod of agreement and Garan scoffed. "She says things like that, you agree with her, and then you wonder why people are worried by your relationship to the Darkmage," he said in disgust, not waiting for a reply as he turned to follow Ahrin out.

Lira settled for a glare at his departing back, widened this to include Fari, Tarion, and Lorin as they all stared at her, then stalked after him.

The blood trail led all the way along the road, the spatters growing farther and farther apart until they reached the top of a set of wide steps leading down to the first level above ground. It was a massive space and looked like it had once been an atrium or town square of some kind. Maybe a marketplace? Or communal gathering spot for the residents.

The area was deserted, dust motes floating in the air highlighted by watery rays of sunlight shining down through arched windows high above. A body lay at the bottom of the stairs, partially skeletonised. More blood had dried in puddles under the bones, but not enough for an entire person, the razak having drained most of it.

"And there ends the trail," Fari said with a mournful sigh as they gathered around it.

"No scavenging bugs, which is unusual," Lorin commented. "It's cool in here, certainly not hot, so the state of the corpse is consistent with the six months the guard told us back there."

"I don't know about you all, but I'm not feeling particularly cold," Lira said.

"In the absence of any further trail to follow, we head down, like the commander said." Ahrin swept her torch around, then met Lira's gaze. "Point of no return. You sure this is how you want to play it?" She cast a pointed glance at Tarion as she asked that question, causing his jaw to tighten and everyone else to turn and look at him.

Lira stepped down off the final step. "Certain. We keep moving."

CHAPTER 32

A shiver of unease tangled inextricably with excitement rippled down Lira's spine as they ventured deeper into abandoned streets and homes that people had once lived in.

Furniture remained in most of them—in some cases belongings had been emptied out, chests and cupboards bare—but in others it was clear the residents had departed in a hurry, leaving their possessions strewn everywhere. In several places, dried blood dotted the stone floors, brown with age. There were more bodies too.

"You can tell roughly when each level was abandoned by how skeletonised the remains are," Ahrin said at one point, keeping her voice low. "I'd say the razak are moving upwards almost every six months."

Fari shuddered. "How terrifying."

"My point being, Lucinda and her people are running out of time. The monsters are going to have them within a few years if the incursion continues at this pace."

"That explains why the Seven are willing to go along with Lucinda's plans," Lira said. "They've become desperate. But I'm almost certain Lucinda has some alternate motive, and she's using their desperation to manipulate them into doing what she wants."

Ahrin whipped her head towards Lira. "You know something."

Lira nodded. It was time to tell them—they were far enough underground that they wouldn't be overheard. "I spied on them talking last night," she said, and related what had transpired. They gradually slowed to a halt as she spoke, listening carefully.

"How do we know we can trust this telepath?" Ahrin asked immediately. "That was a foolish gamble—you can't know whether it was a trap. Lucinda is twisted enough to set something like that up."

"I didn't trust them. I still don't. But they were offering an opportunity that we needed ... and I saw no signs at breakfast that Lucinda had any idea I'd overheard the meeting," Lira said. "It's more than plausible that there are those in Rotherburn who feel increasingly uncomfortable about what Lucinda is doing, and from what I overheard, that discomfort extends to members of the Seven."

Ahrin looked unconvinced, but said nothing further.

Tarion's eyes narrowed. "So the Seven had enough control over Lucinda two years ago that she was forced to abandon her experiments. But you think that's changed?"

"I'm confident it has," Lira said. "But I don't think they know it yet. They're increasingly afraid, and desperate, and they'll cling to any hope presented to them. Lucinda is preying on that."

"Whatever Lucinda's true goal is, it has something to do with Egalion and Caverlock," Ahrin said. "There is no way someone as smart as Lucinda pinned everything on the hope that a single mage of the higher order could kill the razak queens. She wants Egalion here for some other reason."

"Or she wants my father here, and Mama is a decoy for Lucinda to sell the plan to the Seven," Tarion said quietly.

Fari's mouth dropped open, eyes going wide. Ahrin gave him an approving look.

"If we follow that thought through to its logical conclusion," Garan said, looking grim, "then we have to ask ourselves whether *we're* here because that's what Lucinda wanted."

Ahrin's gaze narrowed. Lira felt a shiver of foreboding ripple through her.

"Lucinda isn't all-powerful." Lorin increased his pace. "I think we're overthinking things once again. Lucinda might be more ruthless in her actions than some other members of the Seven, but they all want the same thing. Survival for their people. How about we focus on what we can control right now, finding these queens and staying alive ourselves?"

Nobody disputed that, although both Ahrin and Tarion seemed uneasy. Lira shared a look with Ahrin—for a brief moment the tension between them forgotten—and tried to explain with her gaze, '*this is why I freed Tarion.*' Ahrin didn't respond, but when she looked away, her shoulders had relaxed fractionally.

"Something else to keep in mind," Lira said as they started walking again. "The telepath told me their range wasn't far, and their mental voice earlier did sound much weaker than last night, but Ahrin is right that we can't trust them. If they were faking their weakness, they could be monitoring us right now. So keep your shields up and focused."

"Marvellous," Fari muttered under her breath.

A moment later, they rounded a corner and were faced with a closed and barred steel door similar to the one they'd first entered through. A pile of skeletons lay scattered before it, the cloth of what had been guard uniforms mostly rotted through. Their weapons lay just as rusted beside them—there clearly hadn't even been time for others to retrieve the blades.

"Imagine having to live down in the dark because the world above was full of monsters. And then imagine having those monsters invade the one place you thought you were safe," Fari breathed, clearly lost in thought. "It would be like a nightmare coming to life. One you couldn't escape."

Ahrin and Lira shared an impatient look. What they needed to do was open the door and head down to the next level, not stand around waxing poetic about a pile of old bones. "This must be the main entrance down into the next level," Ahrin said. "So far, we've travelled what appeared to be the most straight-forward route from where we were left by that guard, but we know Egalion and Caverlock didn't come this way."

"How do you..." Lorin trailed off, then nodded. "The bars are on the outside of the door."

"We're lucky this didn't happen to us," Tarion murmured, biting his lip when curious gazes swung this way. Like Fari, he was still staring at the bones, similarly lost in thought. "Two wars with Shakar ... if he'd had more mages with destructive magic on his side, I imagine exactly the same thing could have happened back home."

"I wouldn't call it lucky," Garan said. "Thousands died in those wars. He destroyed entire cities, too."

Lira couldn't help herself, still irritated about his comment earlier. "Which makes the fact you broke me out of prison so much more foolish. It's only a matter of time before I wreak that same devastation. That's what you meant back there, right Garan?"

"You weren't imprisoned because people thought you were him," Tarion said quietly. "You were imprisoned because the council believed you were working with Underground to bring them down."

"Oh?" she asked, an edge to her voice. "And if my last name was Egalion, or Duneskal, or Walden, would I have been locked away absent any opportunity to defend myself or without a thorough and fair investigation?"

"No matter what your name is, membership of Underground was a betrayal of the council," Garan said grimly. "They had no choice."

She barked out a bitter laugh. "As far as the world is concerned, my name is the *only* thing that matters about me. Yet the irony is, I was only a member of Underground because the council asked me to be." The words were out before she could stop herself, and she swore inwardly. She didn't owe anything to these mages, certainly not an explanation.

"If you're going to say something like that, then you need to explain it!" Fari, wide-eyed, cut over Garan and Lorin, who looked about to demand the same thing. Only Tarion remained silent, expression calm, as if he wasn't entirely surprised.

"Quiet!" Ahrin hissed at the raised voices.

Lira ignored her, frowning at Garan. Her desire not to explain herself was suddenly outweighed by intense curiosity. "Your mother really didn't tell you?" Something inside her ached at that. She'd liked and respected Dawn A'ndreas, had trusted her. No matter what she'd ended up believing about Lira, she'd thought the lord-mage would have been honest with her son and nephew.

"She told me that she believed, truly, that you were a member of Underground. That you'd used them to get more magic for yourself, that you'd been turned against the council."

Lira bit her lip, turned away. "It was your mother who came to me and asked me to join Underground to spy for her. She knew I'd be a recruitment target for them."

Horror and disbelief warred for dominance in his expression. "When was this?"

"Years ago. When I was a second-year apprentice at Temari."

"You're lying. This is another manipulation. They said you can alter our thoughts, that you..." he trailed off, clearly uncertain despite his words.

"I wondered." Tarion looked at her speculatively. "I knew you weren't like Shakar, not really, and I knew you didn't want the same things he did. But I couldn't figure out why you'd joined Underground. Yet my parents, too, were utterly convinced, and I trust them implicitly. I didn't know what to think."

"So they told you *nothing* of the truth?" The betrayal stung, and she buried it with anger. She shouldn't be surprised. But she'd thought Dawn, at least, would have been honest with her son. "That's just wonderful. And none of you even thought about trying to talk to me, to hear my side of things?"

Part of Lira noticed that nobody was making a move to open the door, that Ahrin was a short distance away keeping careful watch on both them and their surroundings. But she was too caught up in the conversation to stop it now.

"We wanted to," Lorin said tersely. "But we didn't even know where they were holding you. The information was held very tightly. Only a handful knew that you even *were* in prison—the council members and us, that was all. The rest of the students and masters at Temari

Hall were told that you'd graduated early and were working on a secret assignment for the council."

Lira glanced briefly at the Darkhand—that fit with what Ahrin had thought too.

"They said you were spying on the Mage Council for Underground," Garan said. "That you and the Darkhand joined them when you were in Dirinan, and that's why you came to Temari Hall, to infiltrate the council. That's all they would say."

Lira stared at them, surprise and fury rising in equal measure. "And you *believed* them?"

"Why wouldn't we?" Fari's voice snapped with frustration. "They said Underground had given you more magic somehow, that you were trying to become as powerful as your grandfather. We saw evidence of that with our own eyes. And you hid things from us; you lied. What else were we supposed to think?"

"I did let them give me more power—partly as a way to maintain my cover as a spy, but not entirely," Lira said. "Is it a crime to want more magic?"

"It is not," Lorin said in his calm, haughty way. "But you should have told us what you were doing. If we'd known the truth, we could have challenged the council's version of events. We could have helped you, Lira. Instead we were left thinking you'd betrayed us."

She opened her mouth and closed it, taken aback by his words. She had no ready defence against them.

"And it was you that told us, over and over again, how you were no hero, that you weren't like us," Garan added.

"Yes, yes." Ahrin's tone was whiplash-sharp. She'd been holding back so far—because she would always let Lira fight her own battles—but seemed unable to resist at Lira's hesitation. "It's all well and good to hold to things like honesty, and honour, and blah blah noble deeds in your world. Try any of it when you have nothing to eat and no clothes on your back and you won't survive a day."

"Lira wasn't starving or clothes-less at Temari Hall," Garan insisted. "And there are still things that don't add up. Like her relationship with you, for instance. If the council is right about you, Lira, then these could be very pretty lies that you're spinning."

Fari glanced at Lira. "He's right."

"We tried to find out where you were," Tarion said, before Lira could say anything. "Because even though we believed what they told us, we *did* want to hear your side of things. But we failed."

"Yet you somehow managed to find me when you needed me to find your parents," she said bitterly.

"Yes," he said without hesitation. "For my parents, Garan and I were willing to break into the council's headquarters, the Magor-lier's offices, risking imprisonment ourselves, to find out where they were holding you."

Lira shrugged, suddenly completely fed up with this conversation. "The time I cared about your understanding is gone. For now we're allies, as agreed, so let's just get on with it." She ignored the little voice in her head that *did* want their explanations, wanted some reason to forgive, to let them back in. That voice was a traitor and listening to it would only bring more hurt and betrayal.

"What about her?" Garan pointed an accusing finger at Ahrin.

"Point that at me for another second and you'll lose it," she said coolly. "My reasons for being here are my own."

"The problem is, I don't trust you," he said.

Ahrin snorted. "I'm crushed. Really."

"Here we go again," Fari muttered, rolling her eyes heavenward.

"How about we *not* go again and be quiet instead," Lira snapped, scowling at both Garan and Ahrin. "Garan, you want my help in recovering your aunt, then you accept Ahrin's leadership here, because I'm sure as rotted hells not following your orders."

"I—"

She cut off his protest, spinning on Ahrin. "And you give your word now not to touch anyone in this group unless they threaten your life."

The Darkhand's eyes flashed, genuine fury hardening her beautiful face. "I don't take orders from you either, Lira."

"Then go back and leave us here. Ahrin, you know better than any of us that we're only going to survive down here if we work together." She held Ahrin's ice-cold gaze, trying and failing not to recall Lucinda's warning earlier. A tense silence settled over the group.

"Fine." She bit out the words, clearly still furious. Lira feared that *she* might be only seconds away from losing a limb if not for Ahrin's iron control over herself.

"And you?" Lira looked at Garan, refusing to let the relief show on her face.

"Provided I don't think she's placing us in unnecessary danger, I'll follow her lead," he said with equally bad grace.

"Three cheers to the concept of compromise," Fari said in a sing-song voice. "Now let us proceed into the darkened depths as distrustful and wary allies."

Lira glanced at Ahrin, but the Darkhand wouldn't meet her gaze, her shoulders rigid as she moved to open the door.

The door opened to more yawning blackness, Ahrin's torch casting flickering light on a set of stone steps leading downwards. Now they would be truly underground. No more daylight. Ahrin started down without looking at any of them.

Lira took a breath and followed.

CHAPTER 33

I t was eerie, walking through darkness lit only by their torches. The dark closed in around them, an almost palpable hush that filled every space they passed through. There was no sound at all apart from the echo of their footsteps, the rustle of their packs, and the crackling of the torches. The air temperature remained cool, but not cold.

As they walked, Lira's magical senses remained tethered to the massive body of water running through the ravine above, providing a helpful sense of where they were in relation to it. Each time they reached a staircase or a corridor winding downwards, Ahrin took that path. So far, the river remained roughly to the east of them.

At least they weren't going around in circles.

Gone was the mostly stone and wood construction. Now that they'd ventured down into the proper underground depths of the city, they walked amidst living areas that had been carved into bedrock. The ground under their feet had been smoothed out—presumably to allow the passage of carts or other means of transport—but the walls and ceiling were rough rock.

Eventually they entered a wide tunnel where water trickled down the rockface to their left, the damp supporting a vibrant fungal population. The weight of the river water had been growing steadily closer, and now, a moment's concentration told Lira that they were almost directly under it. It tickled against her senses, cold and sinuous, and she had to fight the urge to extend her magic into it and let it play. She glanced sidelong at Tarion—how had he gone two years without touching his magic? As wasteful as it had been, it spoke to a deep internal fortitude that she couldn't help but be impressed by.

"We must be under the river," Tarion murmured, the first time anyone had spoken in a while. His words whispered through the darkness.

Lira didn't speak up to confirm he was right. They didn't need to know the extent of her abilities. She wasn't even completely comfortable with Ahrin knowing—not that there was any rational reason to be concerned ... but Tarion's retort kept itching at her; *And you trust her? I don't believe that for a second.* She wished the words would stop playing on repeat in her head.

Without any further conversation, they stepped into the tunnel and continued along it, looking for the next route downwards. Ever downwards.

There was no way of telling time in the darkness, so they pushed on until weariness forced them to break. Though the mood remained tense after their argument earlier, they set up camp efficiently enough in a room that had once been part of a residence—Ahrin had picked one that had only a single entrance, in case razak came during the night.

In the middle of the bustle of settling in, Ahrin pulled Lira close, keeping her voice low so the others couldn't hear. "You trust them on watch?"

"I do. They might not always look it, but they're capable."

Ahrin nodded, then spun around to face the group. "We'll take turns on watch—we'll count the time by how far the torch burns down." As she spoke, she began making notches in the wood with her knife. "I'll go first, then Garan, then Tarion. Tarion, once it has burned down a notch, wake us and we'll get moving again. We'll keep one torch burning to preserve the others."

Fari sniffed, hands on hips. "I know we agreed you could be in charge, but maybe you could try throwing a please on the end of your high-handed orders."

Ahrin flicked a cool glance her way. "No deal."

Lira hid a smirk. She suspected both Tarion and Lorin of doing the same given the way they quickly turned away to hide their expressions.

"Fari, it's fine, she knows what she's doing," Garan capitulated. "And Lira was right earlier. Let's just get this done and we can worry about what comes next when it's over."

Lira shot him a surprised look. That scowl she'd seen on his face during the hours of walking had clearly been a sign of him thinking the situation over. He'd always been like that though, she recalled. Quick to anger but able to see the sense in things when given time to process. It was one of the things she'd liked most about him. His inborn noble arrogance didn't get in the way of common sense. Although it might take a little time, he was able to admit when he'd been wrong.

"You're more sensible than I first thought." Ahrin gave him an approving glance, echoing Lira's thoughts. "Right, let's eat and then get some sleep."

Fari scowled. "Just to be clear, I really don't like you."

"Consider me crushed by the weight of that knowledge." Ahrin turned away and began digging in her pack for her blanket.

"What do we do about me?" Tarion asked. "Specifically, what happens if I turn into a monster in the middle of the night and start trying to tear you all to pieces?"

"That's why Ahrin set a watch," Garan said before anyone else could. "If we notice you doing anything abnormal, we'll wake everyone and tie you down."

"And if it happens while *I'm* awake and on watch?"

"Did it ever happen while you were awake before?" Lira snapped, answering before he could. "No, it didn't. So let's assume that hasn't changed."

"If you do turn into a monster while you're on watch and start eating everyone, will you leave me till last?" Fari asked him with a little smile. "Give me time to run."

Lorin chuckled. Even Garan cracked a smile. Tarion scowled at them all, but after a moment he threw his hands up in the air and turned to his blankets. A moment later, Garan placed the ropes they'd brought in a neat pile beside Tarion, ready to use quickly if needed. Tarion rewarded the peace offering with a little smile.

Lira knelt next to Ahrin, lowering her voice into a teasing murmur. "You know you're not the boss of me, right?"

"I wouldn't dream of it." Ahrin smirked. "But at least you're sensible enough to know when I'm right. Most of the time, when you're not being stubborn, that is."

"Are you patronising me?"

"I would never."

There was a brief pause. "About earlier," Lira said hesitantly. "I had to do that. I know you didn't like it, but—"

"I get it." Ahrin cut her off. "I just wish you'd trust me enough to know that I wouldn't be stupid enough to attack one of them down here when we need all the help we can get. I'm the one who taught *you* about survival, no? And of the two of us, I'm not the one who has self-control issues."

"I..." But Ahrin was right. Lira *had* been worried that Ahrin might respond violently to Garan or one of the others pushing her too far. Even though she'd never seen Ahrin use violence unless it had been necessary, for a purpose. "You're right. I'm sorry."

"I don't want your apologies, Lira."

Lira snorted, dropping to the hard, uncomfortable ground and wrapping her blanket around herself. A moment later she felt Ahrin's mouth press a kiss to her cheek, and then the Darkhand moved away to take up her watch position.

Arguing voices—quiet but growing in volume—woke Lira sometime later. Her innate sense of the passage of time while sleeping told her it probably hadn't been much longer than Ahrin's watch period. She uncurled from her blankets instantly, glancing around to see Tarion's, Fari's, and Lorin's sleeping forms. Her next glance at the torch showed she'd been right—it had just burned down to the first notch. It didn't take long to locate Ahrin and Garan outside the residence, the source of the arguing.

Lira tried not to roll her eyes—the fight must have started when Garan awoke to take his turn at watch. He stood in his most stubborn pose, arms crossed over his chest. "I just don't think continuing to walk aimlessly downwards is the best course of action. We have limited food, we're already two days in, and yet we haven't found a trace of any razak."

Lira sighed inwardly. Garan's newfound patience hadn't lasted very long. She wasn't surprised—he looked tired and clearly hadn't gotten much sleep before waking to take watch. The constant glances he'd been throwing at Tarion all day indicated he was worrying over that situation like a dog with a bone. Stress and exhaustion weren't a good combination.

"We were told that the queens are down deep." Controlled anger filled Ahrin's voice. "So unless you have a better idea, we keep going down."

"I said I'd follow you, but not at the risk of our lives. If we run out of food and torches down here—"

"What is your better plan?" she cut over him.

Lira winced as Garan's voice shifted from angry murmur to an almost shout. "If you could talk to me like a normal person, rather than the dirt on the bottom of your shoe, maybe I could—"

"Enough." Ahrin turned to return inside. "Arguing will get us nowhere."

"No." Garan stepped in front of her. "I—"

Lira moved to intervene, but it was too late. In the next instant Ahrin's knife was at his throat. None of them had seen her move. "Get out of my space, lordling."

"Enough!" Lira hissed, stepping right up to them. "Ahrin, get that knife away from his throat, and Garan, stop pushing at her unless you do have a genuinely better idea. Can't you both see how this arguing isn't helping anything." She almost rolled her eyes. How had *she* ended up being the voice of reason?

Neither seemed inclined to listen to Lira, but it was Garan who moved first, stepping away from Ahrin with a tense jaw. Lira rounded on Ahrin. "You're supposed to be on watch. What if—"

Fari's scream from inside had all three of them running. A bloodcurdling snarl followed the scream, and Garan, in the lead, almost ran straight into Tarion's monster. Some instinct must have guided him, because instead of trying to dodge aside, he lowered his shoulder and charged, taking the creature by surprise.

He had enough momentum to crash Tarion into the opposite wall, but Tarion recovered quickly. Bigger, broader, interlocking scales covering every inch of exposed skin, he roared in fury, swiping at Garan with razor-sharp talons. Garan swore and ducked aside, his hold loosening. Lorin stepped unhesitatingly in to help and the two men fought to keep him contained against the wall. The creature's flamelit copper eyes were chaotic with fury.

Quickly internalising her shock at the sight of Tarion's change in favour of needed focus, Lira looked at Fari, pressed into the corner, eyes wide with horror. "Can you put him to sleep?"

"No magic!" Ahrin snapped.

"The sounds he's making are going to draw any razak within hearing distance anyway," Lira snapped back.

With matching grunts, both Garan and Lorin found themselves shoved away. Tarion's claws slashed at Lorin, who was closest. He managed to dodge the blow, but the claws sliced through the neat pile of packs nearby, spilling contents all over their floor, including one of their flagons of water. Garan slipped in the puddle of water it created as he tried to avoid the next below and went down hard.

Lorin stepped in to draw Tarion's attention, and Garan used the moment to scramble back to his feet, before kicking Tarion's leg out from under him. When the monster stumbled, momentarily off balance, Garan and Lorin both dived on him and managed to wrestle him to the floor.

"A little help please!" Garan bellowed.

Lira lurched into movement, straddling Tarion's neck and using both hands to press his head into the floor. His scales were sharp at the edges, cutting into her palms. He snarled and snapped, long incisors coming close to taking a finger off. Despite the fact he now had three full grown people sitting on top of him, he was putting up a vicious fight. Lira wasn't sure how long they could hold him.

Movement blurred at her peripheral vision—Ahrin approaching, knife in hand.

"No!" Lira met and held her gaze.

"I warned you," Ahrin said implacably. "He puts my life in danger and I put him down. This isn't on me, Lira Astor."

She swore. "Just give me a minute, I can—"

Abruptly Tarion went still, slumping into unconsciousness. The scales on his skin shimmered, faded, and he suddenly seemed smaller under them. Lira glanced over her shoulder. Fari was holding both his ankles, Zandian skin bloodless in the flamelight. "That took a lot..." she murmured, swaying.

"Wake him up!" Garan scrambled to his feet. "We have to relocate before any razak nearby track Fari's magic."

"I don't know..." Fari blinked, clearly trying to focus. "I think I'm almost all drained, I—"

"A deep breath, Fari." Lira said calmly, pushing the increasing urgency she felt out of her voice. "Another deep breath. That's it. You should only need a touch of magic to wake him. Just keep breathing until you've got enough focus to do it."

Nobody argued. Everyone stared, holding their breath, as Fari did as Lira instructed. Several tense minutes passed, but then Tarion's eyes blinked open, confused, their normal hazel colour. Abruptly he paled. "It happened, didn't it?'

"You didn't hurt anyone, and Fari put you to sleep to stop you," Lira said briskly. "But now we have to move in case any razak sensed her magic."

To his credit, though clearly shaken, he merely nodded and pulled himself to his feet. Everyone scrambled to grab their packs. They had to leave the shredded one where it was—there wasn't enough time to recapture all its contents either. Lorin helped Fari to her feet then wrapped a solid arm around her to help her stay upright.

They were all filing out the door when Garan swore.

His breath was frosting from his mouth.

CHAPTER 34

"Which way?" Fari glanced to left and right. Her voice seemed a little steadier now, the shock of the razak approach clearly bolstering her strength. Lira wasn't confident she'd be able to run far without a rest though.

Ahrin didn't respond, merely broke left, moving gracefully into a run. They followed without complaint, Tarion coming last, clearly still not quite back to himself.

The first warning they had of attack was the flickering of Ahrin's torch as an inky black limb whipped through the darkness, aiming for her head. She ducked to the side, and the limb almost took out Lorin, who was only a pace behind her.

A rattle echoed through the darkness, loud and angry. Another followed it, coming from behind them.

"Push forward," Ahrin ordered, cool and calm.

Lira dashed ahead, slicing anything that lashed at her, trying to get to the razak's head. Ahrin followed, faster and even more deadly, but it was Tarion, with his whispering Taliath sword, that took advantage of the space they were making to get to the monster's head and drive his blade into its brain.

It collapsed to the ground with a deafening shriek. The echoing shrieks of its colony gave them a good idea of where the rest of the razak were: behind them.

"We should head back up a level or two, get well clear," Garan shouted. "We can't fight our way through a full pack to get to the queens. We don't even know how many there are."

"You're right." Ahrin started moving again. "And I don't think we're deep enough to be anywhere near a nest. This might just be a scouting party."

They began running again, trying to keep to a route that led away from where they'd heard the shrieks. A single grim thought kept echoing through Lira's mind as they ran.

The creatures knew they were down here now.

They'd lost the advantage of surprise.

They ran for what seemed like hours but was probably less than one. Fari started lagging, and Lorin had to help her along. When he got weary, Garan stepped in. By the time Ahrin was finally confident they were clear, then found a residence that suited her purposes from a defensive perspective, Lira was sweating through her clothes, legs about to collapse from exhaustion under her. Fari sat where she stood.

Lorin lingered at the doorway, not taking his pack off. "We should keep moving, put more distance between us and the beasts."

"You need rest," Ahrin said in clipped tones. "All of you. If you keep pushing yourselves now, you'll get hurt or worse, Fari especially. We'll be fine here for a few hours at least—as long as nobody uses their magic."

Lira glared at both her and Garan. "We wouldn't even be in this situation if you two hadn't been arguing instead of being on watch."

"We wouldn't be in this situation at all if you hadn't destroyed his bracelets." Garan rounded on her, a frantic look in his eyes. "Lira, he turned into a monster the first time he fell asleep!"

"There's nothing we can do about that now," said Tarion. "From here on out, every time I sleep, someone has to be watching me the whole time. No distractions."

"The Darkhand is right about needing rest," Fari said wearily. "My healing magic will draw the razak like any other ability so we can't afford to get hurt."

"Tarion, the watch is yours. I'm not sleeping while you are," Ahrin said.

"Fair enough," he said gracefully.

"What are you going to do next time he turns?" Garan asked Lira. There wasn't any rancour in his voice; he looked strung out, stressed, exhausted. "He almost killed us just now. Not to mention we've lost a good chunk of our water and food supplies."

"I—"

"You should *never* have destroyed his bracelets."

"Finally, something we agree on," Ahrin muttered.

"I *am* right here," Tarion said in irritation.

"Look at him!" Lira had just enough presence of mind not to shout the words, despite her frustration.

"What?" Garan faltered.

"Have you bothered to notice how he's looking alert, talking more, how the shadows under his eyes have gone completely despite the situation we're in. Why do you think that is?"

"She's right," Fari said quietly when Garan's mouth tightened. "I can sense it. His life force is stronger."

Garan looked at Tarion, and his shoulders sagged. "I'm exhausted and worried about all of us, and I'm not thinking clearly. I apologise for my part in failing on watch, Lira."

She refused to apologise for what she'd done, but still, Garan's unbending made her want to give him something in return. "I know you can't trust me, but I do truly believe we're better off with Tarion able to use his magic. Have faith in your cousin, Garan."

He gave a weary nod, then dug his blanket out of his pack before heading over to curl up in the corner of the room beside Fari. He reached out as he passed Tarion, giving him a warm squeeze on the shoulder. Tarion leaned into the touch. "Sleep, Garan."

Lira glanced around. Ahrin had already curled up in her blankets, far away from the rest of them, her body language warning them all to stay away, Lira included. She sighed.

Best she get some rest too.

Tarion was still on watch when Lira woke, rested enough that the hard ground, in combination with her innate wariness given where they were, made falling back to sleep impossible. He noticed her waking and quietly made his way over to sit against the wall beside her, watchful gaze still on the front entrance. She shifted, sitting up as well.

He gestured to Ahrin's sleeping form. "She kept it well hidden while she was at Temari, but I spotted that tattoo on her wrist earlier, when she was lifting her torch in the air. I know what it means."

"Do you?" Lira kept her voice uninterested.

"Da talked about them once—I was a curious kid and he never hesitated to answer any of my questions. Unlike Mama, who wanted to try and protect me and Caria from the pain of the past."

Lira looked away. "Parental credit to your dad."

"How long have you known?"

She stiffened slightly. "Much longer than you."

Tarion's gaze never left Ahrin. "For decades, Shakar trained his Hunters to track and kill the most powerful council mages. And they did it without leaving a trace. All the council knew was that they were losing mages to some mysterious adversary."

"I've read the accounts too, Tarion."

"But she's too young to have been born while he was still alive." Tarion's jaw hardened. "Someone kept the program going, didn't they, in Shivasa? Who?"

Lira shrugged, again feigning disinterest, but also not sure how to respond. She wasn't willing to admit it to Tarion, but she'd very much like to know the answer to that question. *Who* had continued the program? Why had Ahrin been forced to escape? *Why* had the recruitment and training of children continued after Shakar's death? Ahrin either couldn't, or wouldn't, tell her. She'd bet Lucinda and her people hadn't been in Shivasa that long ... no, Underground had been a more recent development. Whoever Lucinda had tracked down, the people whose resources and cause she'd co-opted as her own ... they were responsible for training those children after Shakar's death.

"You think Lucinda knew what she was when she recruited Ahrin?"

"I think if she didn't, she very quickly found out," Lira said. "She made Ahrin the Darkhand for a reason."

"You know why." He wasn't accusing, just stating a fact.

"I do. And I have no interest in sharing the information with you." She certainly didn't want the Mage Council learning there was a small army of elite Hunters out there, now loyal to Ahrin, their general. Who, depending on the day and her mood, was allied with the Darkmage's only heir. That protective urge Lira had felt at Shadowfall Island surged strongly. Those Hunters were hers, too. Though neither they nor Lira had had a choice in any of it, they deserved Lira's protection. And she intended to give it to them.

He hesitated. "Lucinda really did recruit you while you were at Temari? You didn't go to them when you were in Dirinan?"

"It was Greyson that first recruited me. But yes, he came to *me*. After your aunt told me it was likely to happen and asked me to spy for her." She cocked her head. "You don't seem surprised. And you didn't look shocked either, like the others, when I said it earlier."

He paused another moment. "What makes you so sure that I can learn to control the change those experiments caused?"

She blinked at the change of topic, but shrugged, the answer easy. "You killed animals."

He let out a soft huff, part amusement, part exasperation. "Maybe you could expand on that a little?"

"You were roaming around inside a school full of people, and then a palace full of people, yet not once did you kill a human. Your good nature is so deeply embedded in you that when your ability manifested, even though the transformation was unconscious, you couldn't bring yourself to kill a person—the one time you attacked an apprentice, you let her live. Something inside you backed off before you could kill Neria.

That tells me you have a level of unconscious control already, Tarion. You just need to practice more. It's no different than with any other magical ability." She met his eyes. "I don't believe for a second you'd kill any of us. Hurt maybe, until you learn control, but not kill. Even me."

A long silence followed her words. Tarion stared at her like he was seeing her for the first time, and there was hope there too, like he believed she might be right.

"I love and trust my parents," he said a moment later, "so I believed that they truly thought you were a member of Underground, a traitor. But it didn't fit with what I knew of you. I decided there must be another explanation, and when you said it earlier, it made perfect sense. That's why I didn't look surprised."

She turned sharply, her turn to be shocked. "You're saying you believe me?"

"I'm saying I never thought for a second that you were trying to overthrow the council, though I admit I was unsure of your motives, and I could see why the council is so afraid of you." He settled back against the wall. "But now it's clearer ... you kept secrets because you didn't trust anyone not to misconstrue the truth, because of who you are. And you were so desperate to make a name for yourself with the council that you didn't want to risk being pulled off the assignment of spying on Underground."

Uncomfortable, she looked away. "That about sums it up."

He hesitated. "I did try to find where you were. I kept at my parents with questions about you constantly, trying to figure out what had happened. And when they were taken ... Lira, I broke you out for two reasons."

"Finally, some truth," she murmured, trying to hide how badly she wanted to hear what he had to say.

"First, I knew their kidnapping would give me a strong enough reason to convince Garan and Caria to help me break you out, and I needed their help to do it. I owed you that much at least, even if you didn't agree to help me find them, and I felt guilty for failing you so long."

She stared at him. "You thought you'd failed me?"

"I wasn't able to learn where you were or find out what had really happened, and I knew, deep down, that you hadn't done what they said you did." His mouth tightened. "But I couldn't do it alone. I'm sorry."

"What was your second reason?"

He stared at the ground, voice becoming almost inaudible. "I wanted your help. I knew that if I had you at my side, we had a real chance of getting my parents back. Because I think you're one of the most capable people I've ever known."

For a moment Lira didn't know what to say. She'd been so angry at all of them, and still was, for not believing in her, for not trying to find her—even at Ahrin. And now that Tarion had just told her the depth of his belief in her, she wanted to tell him he was a fool, that she wasn't worth the guilt he'd felt. That he should never have risked his entire life to break her out of prison. That it had been stupid.

That she wasn't worth it.

But he'd done it anyway. The memories of that night on the roof at DarkSkull rose suddenly strong ... memories she'd buried in her hurt and bitterness. Of Tarion stepping in front of a razak blow to save her life ... willingly almost dying to save *her*. Lira Astor.

Before she realised what she was doing, she'd reached out and taken his hand. "No matter what else happens, I'll help you find your parents and get them home safely, Tarion. I promise you."

He squeezed. Nodded. "Thank you."

"You didn't fail me. You tried." She hesitated, the words sticking before coming out. "That's all I ever really wanted."

They shifted closer together, shoulders pressing softly, sharing warmth and companionship. Some of the gaping chasm in Lira's chest closed over, the tightness loosening, even if only for a moment.

Tarion shifted, and he nodded toward Ahrin. "Is she really the best person for you to be with, if you want to separate yourself from your grandfather so completely? If you don't want to be him?"

"That's where I had it wrong." Lira's gaze was on Ahrin now, too. "I'm not trying to separate myself from him anymore. I *am* him, in many ways, and that's something I've finally accepted. It makes me stronger, less vulnerable, and it's leverage I can use."

"So you've given up on making them accept you?"

"I was never going to make them accept me. Understanding that was painful, but now that I have ... I'm free." That was mostly true, so she left it at that.

"Free? Or utterly lost?" he asked in a murmur.

She snorted. "Really?"

He grinned, that smile that always set her at ease. "I know what it's like, you know, wanting so badly to be something you can never be. It's a tough thing to accept."

"Have you? Accepted it?"

"No." Deep sadness filled his face. "But I know that I have to figure out a way to."

"Why are you still holding on?" she asked curiously. "It's not like your family minds who you are. They love you no matter what."

"That's not what I'm..." He shook his head. "Why did you hold on so long?"

She thought about that for a second. "I had to believe there was a way to change myself, to fit in with what the world wanted of me. Because if I couldn't, then I was going to spend my whole life getting those looks, never able to belong anywhere. And that thought was unbearable."

"And now?"

"Now I know I'm never going to have anywhere to belong," she said, sadness coming out instead of the bitterness she'd aimed for. "And I'm just putting one foot in front of the other till I figure it out."

A brief silence, then, "If I accept it, I lose the thing I love most in this world."

"Sesha?" She paused when he nodded. "I thought you were betrothed?"

He swallowed. "Cutting off my magic, deciding not to be a mage, it left me as Tarion Caverlock, a nobleman of the Rionnan court. Lord Egalion's nephew. It made me a more acceptable match for her, and when her father threw his support behind us, his court did too."

"I'm pretending like that made sense," she grumbled.

"It's everything I ever wanted." The words barely came out, they were so tortured. "And everything I never want at the same time. The thought of not having her in my life literally feels like a hot poker ripping through my chest ... but I can't be queen-consort, Lira. Especially if you're right, if I can learn to control this and be a mage again. It will make me miserable."

Lira nodded, her gaze lingering on Ahrin. "What would Sesha think of you doing all this?"

"She'd love me no matter what." Tarion paused, realisation crossing his face. "That's what Ahrin is for you."

"The only one ever," Lira agreed.

"Not the only one." He gave her a small smile. "Friends again, Lira?"

She nodded without hesitation. "I don't know if it will ever be fixed though ... with the others."

"Time will tell." He stood up. "You should get some more rest. There's still a little time before I need to wake everyone."

CHAPTER 35

L ira woke, gasping at Tarion's waking touch—her dream had been
so real it had felt like reality. They'd been memories. Of the time
before Ahrin, when she'd been at the orphanage, the night she'd run
away, followed the man that had wanted to take her. Even now they
played through her mind, as real as the cavern around her and the
blanket across her legs.

"Last time we spoke you were reluctant to give her up until she was older,"
the man had said.

"I get paid well by the council to keep an eye on her." The matron had
hesitated. *"But if she dies under my roof, they'll be severely unhappy. I could
lose everything. If you pay the fee I'm asking, you can have her. I'll just tell
them she ran away."*

"The fee is yours," a man's voice had replied. *"We'll be here to pick her
up in the morning."*

Lira had snuck out of the orphanage that night, waiting for the man
to leave, and then followed him...

Tarion's voice intruded. "Everything all right?"

She shook her head, let her current reality settle around her for a
moment, then pushed off her blankets. "I was dreaming of ... it made
me remember something."

"Something important?"

"I—"

"We need to move. Now!" Ahrin's voice cracked through the room as she stepped inside. She was awake and dressed—Lira assumed she'd been out scouting. "At least one razak is heading this way."

"How close?" Garan asked.

"Close enough that the nearest one will be on us in less than a minute if we don't run now. I can't tell if it knows exactly where we are, but it's definitely searching." Ahrin glanced over her shoulder. "Come on, I can lead us away from it."

"Rotted carcasses," Lira muttered. Her breath steamed, and she felt the bite of cold in the air. How long could the beasts sense the residue of magic? Had they tracked Fari to their location, or was it just a scouting party out looking now they knew humans were nearby?

Pushing aside questions for later, Lira reached for her pack, swinging it onto her shoulders as she came to her feet.

"Thanks for keeping an extra eye out," Garan murmured to Ahrin as he joined her at the doorway.

"Just trying to keep us all alive, mage boy."

Garan held her glance for a brief moment. "I believe you."

She gave him a single nod in return.

They were filing out of the door in under a minute. Lira ran at the back of the group as Ahrin led them down a dim tunnel, the single torch flickering ahead. The air grew even colder.

The creatures were close.

Lira glanced behind, uselessly. It was impossible to see anything in the darkness. Nothing loomed out at them though, and as they ran, the cold seemed to ebb.

"We're being pushed back upwards again," Garan observed in a murmur.

"It feels like they're herding us now, rather than the other way around," Fari agreed.

Ahrin glanced at her. "Maybe not herding us, so much as keeping us from getting anywhere near a nest."

"All we can do is get clear and try to head down from another direction," Lira said, though she shared this frustration. They were wasting much needed time. Maybe it hadn't been such a good idea to destroy Tarion's bracelets.

No. It had been the right decision. She was even more sure of that after their conversation the previous night. Still—they couldn't use magic to control him again if the change happened. They'd have to do it without.

Eventually the air warmed enough that they stopped for a brief break to dig out stale bread and cheese from their packs, swallow it down with some water, before setting off again.

The mood was subdued. Garan looked pale in the flickering flamelight, exhausted, the dark shadows that had recently decorated Tarion's eyes now hollowing out his. He kept glancing at his cousin, his expression a mix of guilt and fear. Lorin, too, kept looking warily at Tarion. Ahrin was silent, utterly withdrawn. Everyone's gaze darted around constantly, as if expecting a razak to slide out of the darkness at any moment.

She could almost feel the hopelessness descending over all of them. The slowly dawning belief that they might never succeed in this mission.

In contrast, after her conversation with Tarion, Lira felt better than she had in a long time. In an attempt to try and distract them, she broke the heavy silence, "Question for the group," she asked. "Did any of your important council relatives tell you whether they knew how long the Shadowcouncil had been in Shivasa?"

For a moment the tense silence held, nobody willing to engage. But then Tarion glanced over at Lira, seemingly sensing what she was trying to do, and gave Garan a little nudge.

Garan started a little, but a moment later replied, "Not specifically. Underground activities first started around the time I began at Temari Hall, I think. A year or so before you and Tarion arrived there?"

"That sounds about right," Fari said. "We heard nothing of the group in Zandia, but when I left home and joined Temari as an initiate, I heard the rumours about Underground straight away."

"We began hearing whispers of the group in southern Shivasa a year or two before I went to Temari," Lorin added.

Lira looked ahead, where Ahrin's back was visible as she led the group. "Ahrin and I know for a fact that Lucinda and her Rotherburn minions were in Dirinan for at least six months before I left to go to Temari Hall."

For a moment the Darkhand was silent, but then, "I'd put gold on the fact they were in Dirinan much longer. At least two years before you left."

Tarion asked, "What makes you so sure?"

Ahrin finally turned, looking at Lira as she responded. "Remember around that time the crew mages started going missing ... some of their bodies washing up onshore? Transk was furious, mainly because he couldn't tie the deaths to any of his rival crews. They were the first victims of Lucinda's experiments, no doubt."

"I think they were in Dirinan even earlier," Lira said. "I think they first came looking for me when I was at the orphanage, before we even met, Ahrin." Enjoying the surprise rippling over their faces, she relayed what she'd remembered in her dream, of the night she'd run away.

Garan gave her a look she thought might be admiration. "Six years old and you *followed* the creepy man instead of just getting out of there?"

"What exactly did you overhear?" Ahrin demanded.

Lira let out a breath. "I don't really remember. Soon after that merely surviving became my focus and I forgot most of that night. There was a woman there though."

"Lucinda?" Fari asked sharply.

"Maybe. I can't be sure."

Silence fell for a moment as they processed this, then Tarion spoke. "Planning what they did takes time, so it's plausible the Shadowcouncil spent a few years in Dirinan building their base before launching Underground."

"It is," Lira agreed. "But why take on the Darkmage's cause as a cover for their activities at all? Why not just start taking the homeless off the streets to experiment on without bothering with convincing my grandfather's network to help them? If we're right, Lucinda spent over a decade in Shivasa before kidnapping us."

"Coming from Rotherburn, they didn't know anyone there, didn't know how anything worked," Lorin said. "I assume Lucinda wanted to appropriate existing networks, resources. After all, they needed secure locations to conduct the experiments, materials to undertake them, local coin. Most importantly, they needed *cover*. If the council was running about trying to figure out why Shakar's cause was rising again, they wouldn't stumble across what Rotherburn was up to."

"Agreed—putting aside the question of *why* the Seven felt the need to do that rather than just asking for council help." Lira smiled. "But think about it, even now we're *still* missing the second underlying problem."

Tarion abruptly shook his head, smiling. "The fact that Shakar's old network was active and *had* resources when Lucinda and her people showed up in Shivasa. If they weren't already useful to her, she wouldn't have bothered with them."

Lira shot a nod of agreement in Tarion's direction, then looked at Garan. "Lucinda and her people aren't your only problem. My grandfather's network is still alive and well and has been since his death. I doubt their long-term goals have changed."

"You sound quite confident of that," Fari said. "Care to explain what you know that we don't?"

"No." Lira glanced involuntarily at Ahrin's wrist, at the tattoo that proved Shakar's network was still breeding and training Hunters, then away. Her shifting glance caught on Tarion, but he merely shook his head. He wasn't going to betray Ahrin's secret either. She gave him a little nod of gratitude.

Garan was frowning—the type of look he got on his face when he was genuinely thinking through something. "But Lucinda torched that network before she left Shivasa."

"No, what she *actually* did was frame Lira and sacrifice all of the unimportant pieces of the group," Ahrin said. "She and her people went free, and whoever fronts Shakar's network now wasn't touched in those arrests, I'm confident of it. Lucinda is careful and plans six steps ahead. She would have left that door open in case she ever needed to come back to Shivasa."

Fari glanced between them. "As soon as we're all back, we'll have to make sure the council knows about this. Leader Astohar is going to have some work to do hunting down the remnants of Shakar's network."

"I think you're worrying over nothing. Lucinda gave most of it up," Lorin said. "If there was anyone capable left, why aren't they doing anything? It's been over twenty years since the Darkmage was killed. If they posed a threat to the council, it would have emerged by now."

"The Darkmage planned for fifty years before re-emerging after the council thought they'd killed him the first time," Tarion said. "Maybe his people learned that same patience."

"What a cheery thought," Fari muttered.

"Either way, Astohar and the council would be better off addressing the underlying reasons people choose to join Underground," Garan said. "Remove their motivation rather than hunting them down and embedding their grievances even more deeply."

"That's rather enlightened of you, lordling," Ahrin said mildly. "And here I was stuck on Tarion's assumption that we're all getting back home alive to hunt anything down."

"You're a ray of sunshine, Darkhand." Fari sighed.

Everyone chuckled.

"Lira!" Garan's voice woke her instantly, and she was already rising to her feet as a faint growl rippled through the darkness. The single torch they'd left alight cast Garan in deep shadow as he hovered over the stirring form in Tarion's blankets.

Ahrin woke just as quickly, knife in her right hand.

"Don't," Lira said, quiet but firm as she stepped up beside Ahrin and curled her fingers around the wrist of the arm holding the knife. "Garan, stay where you are, keep still and calm."

"What about the ropes?" Garan asked her.

"He comes at me, and I'll kill you both if you try and stop me," Ahrin said calmly, breaking free of Lira's hold with insulting ease. "Look at that thing."

He was rising to his feet now, growing taller, broader, eyes flashing a fiery copper. Overlapping scales crept over the visible surfaces of his skin. A soft, threatening snarl escaped him.

They didn't have much time. Lira looked at Ahrin. "Wake the others and move them slowly out of the room. Don't make any quick movements and don't let Fari use her magic. I'll take care of this."

Ahrin didn't move. "You want me to let it kill you?"

"I want you to let me handle it."

Ahrin lowered her knife and stepped back. "The moment I think you're getting overwhelmed, I'm going to kill it. Just so we're clear."

Lira ignored her. Instead, she took a careful, slow step towards Tarion, keeping her hands high and palms open to show she was unarmed.

The change was almost complete ... she had maybe seconds before the monster took him over completely. They should be grabbing the ropes, tying him down before he could stop them, but instinct told her to try something else. "Tarion, it's me, Lira. Remember that conversation we had last night?"

Behind her, the sounds of Ahrin rousing the others and murmuring for them to gather their things brushed over her consciousness. She kept part of her attention focused on that, so she'd know when they were clear, and the rest firmly on Tarion.

He snarled, head lunging at her, snapping. She stilled. The fiery eyes were chaotic, filled with anger and hate. There was no reason in there she could see. But he hadn't made a serious move to hurt her yet.

She spoke again, quietly, not taking her eyes off the beast, "Garan, I could use your help for this, if you can handle it."

Garan must have moved towards them, because Tarion took a threatening step forward. He was quick as a blink, one hand lifted as if to strike, and a snarl reverberated through the room, deep enough that she almost quailed. Scales fully covered his skin now. Four long, vicious claws curved out from his knuckles.

Lira backed up, two slow paces, one arm reaching out to keep Garan from moving any farther forward. "Don't make any quick movements," she murmured. "Slow and steady. Calm. Anything could set him off right now."

"Got it." Garan appeared at her shoulder. His face was bloodless, jaw set, but he hadn't hesitated to help.

"Talk to him," she said. "I'm pretty sure he can still hear us even if he's lost to the change. We need to try and reach him. If he can summon any sort of reason, rational thought, he'll be able to control this. I'm confident of it, Garan. Will you trust me?"

Garan swallowed, his fear live in his green eyes. She knew what she was asking of him—to trust the word of one he felt had betrayed him. To risk his life on it. She didn't expect him to do it. *She* wouldn't have.

Eventually, though, he breathed out. "Tell me what to do, Lira."

"He needs to see you, his cousin who loves him, not your terror," Lira said quietly. "Think of him as you know him, use that to bury your fear where he can't sense it."

The young man took a deep, steadying breath, his eyes closing for a moment. When they opened, he wore his jovial smile, his tone easy. "Tar, I see you. It's me, Garan. Can you understand what I'm saying?"

Tarion said nothing, but a little shiver went through him. Lira gave Garan a nod. *Keep going.*

"I'm going to take that as a yes," Garan continued. "That's quite the new magical ability you have there. Just between you and me, I'm glad it was you that got this one, and not Shakar's spawn here. Could you imagine? There wouldn't be a student left alive at Temari."

"Well, I'd have left you four alive. I used to detest you all slightly less than the rest of them," Lira joined in, trying to keep it light. "And maybe Master A'ndreas. I liked him well enough despite his ridiculously protective rules."

Another shiver went through the monster, and he shook his head, the hand he'd lifted falling to his side. A low whine sounded. Lira let out a breath. At the very least, they were distracting it from its anger and need to destroy.

"Not sure what Sesha's going to think though." Garan had sunk completely into his easy, charming, persona, no trace of fear or hesitation. "Lira, what do you reckon?"

Lira smirked. "I think if she sees him and runs screaming, I'll happily marry her instead."

A snarl ripped through the room, violent and angry. Tarion stepped toward them, both hands lifted as if to strike. Even Lira took a half step back.

But Garan stood his ground.

Her heart pounded with adrenalin and she fought the urge to flee or attack, instead taking that half step back up to Garan's shoulder. They were in range of Tarion's claws now, and she wasn't sure she'd be able to move quickly enough to avoid them if he struck.

Tarion growled, his entire body shuddering, but he didn't move.

"That's right, Tarion. You don't want to hurt us. You just need to control what's happening," Lira said firmly. "Remember, this is just another magical ability. One you can learn to use. The first step is realising that."

"And don't worry, Sesha would never pick Lira over you. Have you seen how scrawny she is?" Garan chuckled. "And that rat's nest she calls hair? The crooked nose is, admittedly, a little charming, but you've got the handsome Taliath thing going for you."

"You're still you, Tarion." Lira's voice rang with conviction. "Garan and I know you're not going to hurt us. Why do you think we're still standing right here?"

"She's right, Tar." And in one incredibly foolhardy move, Garan Egalion took a slow step forward. There was no way he'd be able to move out of the way now if Tarion attacked.

A snarl tore from the monster's mouth and the moment hung heavy with threat.

And then, in a quick, breathless motion, Tarion spun and lashed out with his right hand, raking his claws down the wall as he let out a fury-filled roar. The strikes gouged deep into the rock, and he did it again, and again, before he stopped, shoulders shuddering. His breath rasped in and out. It was obvious he was locked in some kind of internal struggle.

"Tarion?" Garan said. "Come on, you're nearly there. You've got this."

Lira added, "Control, that's all it is. Focus and control. If I could learn how to control my anger to survive prison, you can too. You just have to focus on one single thing—whatever it is that means most to you. Sesha, I'm guessing? Focus on that. Think about how she smiles at you, how good it feels when you're with her, the sound of her laugh. Let it keep you in control. Then breathe."

The monster took a deep breath. Another one.

Then his form blurred, shifted, the scales sliding away.

When Tarion turned back around, the copper fire was already fading from his eyes, and they'd returned to their normal hazel brown. He looked pale, exhausted, upset, but he held Lira's gaze. "I could hear you both talking to me, just. It was hazy, indistinct, but there."

"Well, that's a good sign." Garan gave a shaky laugh, lifting a hand to run it through his hair. "Maybe Lira here is onto something."

"I felt so angry," Tarion said unhappily, eyes dropping to the floor. "I was burning like a furnace with it. It was only when I hit the walls that it faded enough that I could gain control over it like you said. I thought about Mama and Da, how badly I want to find them."

"Good. That's something you can keep practicing," Lira said. "If it's anger that feeds the change, then you can practice using that to bring it about consciously. Then you won't have to worry about it happening in your sleep."

"I don't like feeling so angry, so hateful," he mumbled.

"Yeah, well you can't change that. You can only learn to live with it ... and that's only going to happen if you stop hiding from it."

Fari suddenly appeared, sliding between Lira and Garan to pass Tarion a flagon of water. "Here. I'm betting you've got some serious magical drain after that—hydration will help. Drink it all."

"Thanks." Tarion took the flagon and drank in several long swallows. He looked a little brighter once he was done. "You don't seem scared."

"I'm not." Fari stepped away. "I think Lira's right about you."

"You brought me back to myself." Tarion swallowed, reached out to grip Garan's shoulder. "Thank you, Cousin. And you, Lira. You have no idea ..."

"I should have had more faith in you." Garan looked guilty. "Your parents, mine, they said the bracelets were the best thing. I didn't question it. I should have."

"I chose it willingly, Garan. This isn't on you. I should have had more faith in myself."

Lira shot Tarion a quick smile as Garan wrapped an arm around his cousin's shoulders and they hugged fiercely. Garan's eyes met Lira's, sober, and he gave her a little nod.

She returned it. "You trusted me."

"Thank you for not making me regret it."

"I'm going to scout the area." Ahrin's cool tones cut through the room, forestalling any reply Lira might have made. "You made quite a bit of noise just now and it might have drawn attention."

Ahrin didn't look at Lira once as she turned and strode out.

Lira followed, not missing the Darkhand's ire, waiting until they were clear of the others before demanding, "What are you angry about now? I told you we needed Tarion's—"

"And I told you you're wrong." Ahrin rounded on her, angry. "He's a liability, but worse, you haven't even been honest about your reasons for bringing him along."

Lira stopped, confounded. "What does that mean?"

"You *want* to help him. You trust him."

"I—"

"Do I need to remind you that they happily sat by and did nothing while you were imprisoned for the rest of your life?"

Lira's temper flared. "Tarion was the one who got me out! What exactly did you do while I was imprisoned for the rest of my life?"

"They will betray you again. You do know that? You aren't one of them, Lira, and you never will be."

"And again, I ask, how are you any different?" Her voice turned cold.

Ahrin flinched as if slapped. "You really mean that, don't you?"

"You forget how well I know you, Ahrin. You place your survival, your ambitions, over everything else, including me. I know you're here for a reason, one that you're hiding from me." Lira paused, held her gaze. "What happened to Athira?"

Now it was Ahrin who looked confounded. "What are you talking about?"

"After I escaped Shadowfall. What happened to her?"

Ahrin was quiet a moment. "You broke her out with you. That was your plan when you left."

"No. She volunteered to stay, to learn more about Lucinda and her people for the council. What happened to her?"

"I have no idea. I fled that night just like you, remember?" Ahrin shook her head impatiently. "Why are you asking about this now? Is Athira a bosom buddy of yours too?"

"Lucinda told me to ask you about her. She wouldn't have done that for no reason. What did you do to her?"

Cold fury descended over Ahrin's face. "This conversation is over."

"You can't just decide it's over and walk away."

"Yes I can. Because if you've started listening to Lucinda over me, then I have no further interest in talking to you, Lira Astor."

The Darkhand was gone in a blink, vanishing seamlessly into the darkness.

CHAPTER 36

W ater dripped somewhere in the distance, but otherwise the air was cool and still as they entered what felt like their hundredth hour of walking through the underground city. They were making another attempt to head downwards, taking a path they hoped would avoid any searching razak.

Tarion seemed none the worse for wear since they'd broken camp, and he and Garan walked close together, shoulders brushing occasionally. Lorin was in his own world, and Fari had sunk into a thoughtful silence. Lira wondered what they were thinking about.

Ahrin stalked ahead, the distance between her and the rest of the group not just a physical one. The Darkhand hadn't looked at Lira once since their argument the night before, and Lira was still angry enough that she was fine with being ignored. They'd never fought like that before.

Part of Lira knew it was her fault, that she'd probably gone too far, but the rest of her was annoyed and frustrated. Why couldn't Ahrin just tell Lira what she was up to? Deeper down, Lira feared the reason Ahrin hadn't told her was because whatever she was planning was a betrayal. And Lira *hated* that she suspected that.

"Here's the thing I'm wondering about," Garan said, bringing Lira back to the present. "This city is pretty extensive for what must have once been an inland port town. The construction along the outside of the ravine walls, sure, why not? But why dig so far underground?"

"Lucinda said the war happened generations ago," Lira said. "If they had to keep finding room for more refugees as the razak and nerik grew more numerous up on the surface, then it makes sense they had to keep digging."

"Right, but look around." Garan swept his torch in an arc. "The lower we go, the more established this place looks. If they were hurriedly digging deeper as the years passed to keep up with the inflow of refugees, it should look newer, less complete, rough."

A moment passed as they all realised he was completely right.

"Why would Lucinda lie to us about something like that?" Fari asked.

"Lucinda lies to suit her purposes," Lira said flatly. "She's never *not* manipulating. If she lied about the history of this place, it was for a reason."

Lorin said hesitantly, "Could the tunnels have been dug for protection during their mage war?"

"You're all wrong," Ahrin said, though she didn't turn back to face them. "Lucinda implied pretty heavily this was originally a hive of smuggling and criminal activity. The tunnels were dug for secrecy—because of the paranoia of those who lived here."

"Well," Garan said easily. "That's one mystery sorted."

Lira felt stung, even though Ahrin hadn't said a word directly to her, or even sounded accusatory. The Darkhand was right. It was something Lira should have figured out immediately but hadn't.

"One mystery down, about six hundred to go," Fari pointed out with a cheerful smile.

"We haven't found any trace of your parents either." Lira looked at Tarion, speaking aloud the words that had been playing on her mind for the past hour or so of walking. "This place is a maze, but even so..."

"It's odd," he agreed. A moment later, he slowed his pace until he was walking alongside Lira, then spoke so softly she could barely hear him. "Can I ask you something?"

"Sure."

"Were you serious, what you said about the Magor-lier working with Underground?"

"Very."

He sighed. "How?"

"I don't know." She'd been mulling on it for years, without any good answers. "The best I can come up with is that Lucinda or one of her people killed Tylender, then replaced him with a mage who has a strong illusion ability to take his place—we already know they have a mage with that skill. Or she placed a mage with powerful mind control ability somewhere in his orbit and they're controlling him that way."

Tarion's face whitened. "I don't know which of those would be more horrifying. I don't want to think of Uncle Tarrick dead ... but to have been trapped in his own mind all these years seems even worse somehow."

Lira shivered. She didn't give two coppers for Tarrick Tylender, but the thought of something like that happening to her *was* terrifying.

"If you're right about him, then it doesn't make sense the Seven didn't just approach the council for help—with the Magor-lier on their side, they would have been almost guaranteed of getting it."

"I know," she said quietly. "We're still missing something."

"Do you think the rest of the Seven even know Lucinda subverted Uncle Tarrick?"

She shot a surprised look at him. "Good question."

Before she could think on that anymore, Garan's jocular voice came from ahead. "What are you two whispering about? I hope you're not—"

"Guys?" Fari's voice called softly from where she'd wandered a little farther down the tunnel. "Anyone noticed how cold it's getting?"

Lira automatically shivered. The rolled sleeves of her shirt revealed goosebumps along her bare arms. Unconsciously she rolled them down for the extra warmth.

"We drop to one torch," Ahrin murmured. "And no more talk unless it's urgent."

Without hesitation, all but Ahrin smothered their torches, and they continued at a slower pace, senses straining to pick up any sign of a razak's rattle.

The air grew steadily colder, and as it did, their pace slowed even further, watchfulness increasing. The burn of anticipation spread through Lira's blood. As they crossed one wide avenue and started along another path circling downward, their breath began frosting in the air with every exhale.

When Lira concentrated, she could sense the ravine river far above them and, just to her left, a massive body of rushing water. But she could sense more water now, farther away, lower down—that must be the underground river they'd been told about.

Garan lifted a hand, catching Ahrin's attention. She halted, moving closer so he didn't have to speak loudly. "That torch is going to give us away to every razak in sight. And it's getting cold enough that they have to be close."

"If we blow it out, we won't be able to see a thing," Ahrin murmured back. "And the razak can see in the dark."

"They can *what* now?" Fari hissed.

Ahrin nodded. "We keep this torch going, at least we'll see them coming. If we douse it, we'll be wandering around blind in the dark and they'll be on us before we know they're there."

Tarion frowned. "There has to be a better way. We need the element of surprise if we're going to manage to kill a razak queen."

"You think of one, you tell me." Ahrin started walking again.

Halfway down, the path levelled out. The rocky wall to their left had been dug out into a square cavern surrounded by homes built into its walls. It was completely empty, holding the same air of abandonment as everywhere else.

"Let's make sure it's clear. I don't want to leave razak on our tail and risk being trapped between the creatures," Ahrin murmured. "Tarion, Lorin, you stand watch here. We won't be long."

Lira followed her into the square, Garan and Fari not hesitating either. When her breath continued frosting, she unslung her bow and nocked an arrow.

There were no rattling sounds, though, and as they carefully glanced into each ground-level home, no shadowy tendrils emerged, and the cold grew no deeper. Circling towards the back of the cavern, Ahrin's torch revealed a square hole cut into the rock between two housing levels—directly opposite where they'd entered the square. Garan walked over to take a look while the rest watched.

"Looks like a narrow set of steps leading into a tunnel," he called back softly. "Can you cast the light this way? I'll head down to have a look. If I'm not back in two minutes, please come save me."

The tall mage had to hunch over even to fit into the stairwell. At Lira's side, Ahrin's shoulders stiffened imperceptibly. Where her hand gripped the torch her fingers were white-knuckled. At the sight, some of Lira's lingering anger at the Darkhand faded … she couldn't help but remember Ahrin's flippant words thrown at her back on the ship, the one thing she was truly terrified of.

Garan was back a moment later. "Yep, about ten steps down there's a tunnel. Couldn't tell where it leads in the dark, but it's big enough for someone my size to crawl through. Might have been a smuggler's route once, I'd say."

"With its entrance out in the open like that?" Ahrin's voice was harsher than usual.

"I imagine when people lived here, they'd have just covered it up with a wall hanging or a stack of crates, anything really," Garan said. He seemed to have come to an acceptance of Ahrin's leadership, no longer pushing her on every single thing. Lira had to admit to herself that his ability to rise above his pride impressed her.

"Going that way might be a better option than wandering these wide-open halls where a razak could be hiding anywhere," Fari suggested. "The torch won't be as much of a beacon, either."

"You can do as you like, but I'm not climbing into a dark hole in the wall leading who knows where," Lira announced before Garan could agree with Fari. To reinforce the point, she turned and began walking back towards Tarion and Lorin. Ahrin was only a step behind, silent and withdrawn. "Let's hurry and finish clearing this area."

"I thought the Darkhand was in charge," Garan grumbled as he followed, but there was no real bite to his voice.

They were almost back to the square entrance when the cold turned frigid, burning Lira's lungs as she breathed in. Almost immediately they halted. Before they could do anything, soft footsteps sounded and Tarion and Lorin appeared out of the darkness.

"There's at least one out there," Tarion spoke quickly, quietly. "We heard a rattle coming up the tunnel. If they can see in the dark, we thought it best to retreat ... but it's likely already seen us."

Garan shifted restlessly from foot to foot. "Darkhand, what do we do?"

A rattle from the direction of the entrance cut over the end of his words. It was loud. And hungry.

It had seen them.

With a quick, graceful movement, Ahrin tossed the torch a short distance away, its light illuminating a wide circle. Then she turned and made for the nearest home at a run. The others followed.

As they'd passed each home, and Ahrin had shone the torch inside to illuminate its interior and make sure nothing was hiding in there, Lira had instinctively cased and memorised it. As had Ahrin.

Now the two of them led the way through the front entrance of one, moving around the obstacles inside all the way to the back. "Find cover. Hunker down. Stay quiet and don't use magic," Ahrin hissed.

And then she was gone in the dark.

Lira didn't move as far back as the others. She wanted to be able to see anything that came at them. So she moved around the mouldering remains of what had once been a sofa, flattening herself on the ground between it and the wall. From her spot, the torch still out in the square illuminated the front of the home just enough for her to make out.

There she waited.

The cold remained bitter, and she'd drawn her shirt up over her mouth to prevent it frosting. Keeping utterly still, she had to fight not to shiver as the ice settled deep into her bones. Her magic fought to be free, sensing the danger. She swallowed, memories of that night flooding back ... her mother never coming home ... then, years later, trapped under that bed in DarkSkull Hall as the razak hunted her.

Her heartbeat thudded. Her breath came faster.

And then the razak appeared.

She heard the rattle first ... chains rasping over stone ... then the flicker of darkness outside the door. It slid in like an inexorable force, inky black tendrils of darkness so complete it swallowed the glow from the torch.

Lira curled further into a ball, fists clenching, nails digging into her palms.

When nothing else moved or sounded, she risked shifting, moving closer to the end of the couch so she could see around...

The thing's triangular head was in the doorway, flamelit silver eyes eerie and menacing all at once. Swearing inwardly, she ducked back behind the couch, skin slick with sweat now despite the bitter cold.

Everything inside her urged her to move, to attack, to fight her way free, to flee the nightmare. But if she did that it would kill her. To survive she had to stay still in the dark.

For several long, terror-filled moments nothing moved. No rattles came. Then a flicker in her peripheral vision, a questing limb curling around the back of the couch. She lay still, staring fixedly at it, unable to move in case she made a sound it would hear.

Eventually it moved away.

Lira lay there, gasping, mouth dry, *hating* herself for the fear and panic she felt. Why this? Why, when in any other situation she welcomed the fear and danger.

Deep down she knew. It was being forced to sit still. Unable to flee or fight. That was what triggered her panic. Being hunted and unable to move. When a hand touched her shoulder, she started violently and came perilously close to loosing her magic in a blast strong enough to send the couch across the room.

"Just me," Ahrin murmured, voice distant and cool. "We move while it's deeper inside the square. Ready?"

Lira swallowed. She tried to respond but her throat was still dry, so she merely nodded.

They moved in a silent run, Ahrin swooping down to pick up the torch then leading them out the entrance and turning left. Nothing sounded behind them, but that didn't mean anything, so they moved quickly, listening hard for any sounds of pursuit.

Soon they came down a set of steps into a wide cavernous space. The violet flame of the single torch didn't illuminate far enough to be able to see the roof above and only broke the darkness a few yards ahead of them. Almost in perfect sync, they halted a few paces in.

"I don't like this." Ahrin's eyes narrowed.

Now that Lira was free and moving, the panic had faded like it had never been. The hot thrill of impending danger unfurled in her stomach, cleansing away her fear. Abruptly, the sense of danger was so sharp she could almost taste it. She let it in, welcomed it, desperately relieved the panic was gone.

"It's either go forward or go back and find another way down," Garan said. "That could take time we don't have. We should go back to that tunnel in the square—sneak past the razak if it's still there ... it's too big to follow us in."

"A space this big, we're visible to any razak close enough." Tarion sided with Garan. "It's still too cold ... they're close."

They were right. Lira didn't look at Ahrin, didn't need to. Before any of the others could think to ask the Darkhand's thoughts, Lira took a breath and unslung her bow again. "We go forward this way. Quickly, but carefully."

"I don't want you protecting me," Ahrin hissed low enough for Lira's ears only.

"I'm not," Lira said.

"Then you're letting your addiction to—"

"You can't go down that tunnel back there and we both know it," Lira said in a harsh whisper. "So we only have one option: go forward."

Ahrin reeled as if struck, eyes going wide with something Lira couldn't recognise. Lira ignored her and moved on, steps confident, bow nocked and ready.

This time it was her leading them into the darkness.

CHAPTER 37

They were several yards into the cavern, with no end in sight, when the cold deepened even further, burning the skin of her extremities.

"If anyone is using any magic, stop it now," Ahrin's quiet order rang out.

"We're not," Tarion murmured.

A wide sweep of the torch showed nothing but darkness surrounding them, but the cavern was massive—anything could be lurking beyond the small circle of light cast by the flames. Lira's magic surged, yearning to rise up and defend her. She fought it down, keeping it quelled but frothing inside her. "We need to push through until we get to a narrower space where it will be easier to defend ourselves."

They sped up to an almost run, the growing fear between them becoming palpable. Instinct warned her to douse the torch, but then they'd have no way of knowing where they were going. As much as she was comfortable operating in the darkness, getting lost without light down here would likely mean their deaths.

They'd moved another fifty yards or so when a rattle sounded behind them.

Without a word they moved into a quick jog. Lira's shoulders ached from the weight of her pack and her legs were beginning to protest. She tried to pierce the darkness ahead of them with her gaze, looking for a tunnel, an end to the expanse. But whatever cavern they were in, it was large, seemingly endless.

A louder rattle screeched directly ahead of them.

They slid to a halt, instinctively forming a circle. Ahrin waved her torch as widely as she could in an effort to see if anything lay to the left or right of them. But the darkness was too complete. Nothing but black was visible beyond the small circle of flickering flamelight.

Their breathing sounded too loud, echoing through the space like drumbeats. Air frosted with each exhale. Icy fingers of cold reached through Lira's clothes to slide like knives against her skin. She closed her eyes, took a deep breath, tried to sense where the creatures were. But they made no further sound.

"They're closing in ... the air is getting too cold too fast," Ahrin said.

"Tarion, now might be a good time to turn evil," Lira murmured. "I suspect your monster senses could help us here."

"I don't know how to do that."

"Try getting angry," she said tersely.

"I can't just turn on—"

The next rattle was louder, anticipatory, and frighteningly close. It came from behind them but was quickly echoed by another creature directly ahead.

"Go right, see if we can slip around them," Garan said, breaking abruptly in that direction.

He'd barely taken two steps when a scaled limb whipped out of the darkness towards his head. His loud cry of shock reverberated around them, and he swayed desperately to avoid the blow before stumbling backwards and falling to the ground. In the next instant Tarion blinked into existence in the space between Garan and the razak, hovering protectively over his cousin, the Darkmage's sword raised.

Urgency to *act* burst through Lira. Physically incapable of supressing her magic any longer, she lifted her free hand and let it explode. A hard exhale escaped her as she did, filled with the relief of no longer having to hold herself back. A large ball of violet-edged white flame roared into life high above their heads. Lira fed it heat and energy until it flared strongly enough to illuminate the cavern.

As soon as it did, she regretted her decision.

They were completely surrounded, razak closing in on them from every direction. She counted at least seven, though the shadows around the edges of the cavern could be holding even more of the blasted things.

"Rotted carcasses," Ahrin snapped. One of her hands held a knife, the other cupped a scarlet concussion ball, gaze searching for a way out.

Lira whistled. "Anyone else have a sinking feeling they've been waiting here for us?"

"An ambush." Fari sounded close to panicked. "Seriously? These things can *plan* too?"

Lira glanced at her. "Maybe not. It could be we've stumbled into a nesting site?"

"No." Ahrin was so confident Lira didn't doubt her. "They were waiting here. The monster back there probably intended to herd us in this direction."

We should have taken the tunnel. The unspoken words vibrated through the air between them, but Lira shook it off. She wouldn't make a different decision now even if she could.

"The light from my flame doesn't seem to be holding them back," Lira said to Ahrin. "Should I increase its intensity?"

"No, I don't think it will make enough of a difference, not with so many."

She nodded, unslinging her bow instead. The moment she fitted an arrow to the string, Lira felt confident, ready.

Let them come at her. She'd destroy them all. She kept the ball of flame high above their heads, monitoring to make sure it wasn't draining too much of her energy.

"We fight back to back, in a circle," Tarion said as Garan clambered back to his feet, daggers drawn. "We look for a gap and force it open to make a run for it ... then we keep running until we find a more defensible place to hole up, if not lose them entirely. Anyone disagree with that plan?"

"Works for me." Ahrin dropped her torch to the ground, the flame flickering eerily, and they moved into a circle around it. The Darkhand cast what might have been an envious look at Tarion's sword before drawing a second knife and flipping it gracefully.

"If we run, those things will move much faster than us," Fari pointed out. Both her hands held daggers too. "We don't know how far it is to an exit from this cavern."

"There are too many to stand and fight," Garan said calmly. "We break through. And we run."

"I can burn a path through, then cover our retreat," Lira said confidently. She itched to move, to fight, to set things *aflame,* unconsciously shifting her weight from foot to foot.

Ahrin was immediately at her shoulder. "I'll cover your back."

Lira glanced around at the others. "Be ready to push through behind us."

"Very happy to let you two be the heroes." Fari nodded. "I promise to do my best to patch you up on the other side. If I don't get eaten, that is."

Before Lira could respond, Lorin let out a furious bellow. One of the razak had rushed him, not bothering to wait for them to decide on their defence strategy. Tarion instantly flashed in and out of sight, sword slashing to take the writhing limb off in a single movement. The blade sang whisper-soft as it cut through the air. The creature screamed, setting off a series of echoing screams throughout the cavern.

And that was all Lira saw, because at that moment, a scaled leg swept out of the darkness, slashing down at her face. She ducked, rose, and instinctively summoned fire. The razak's limb erupted in violent flame. It screamed. The limb burned loud and bright, the stench of cooked meat filling her nostrils.

She'd used too much in one burst and the drain was staggering. Stupid! She had to let go of the flame above them, plunging their surroundings back into darkness. Only Ahrin's torch provided a single flickering light source now.

The second attack came from Lira's left, but Ahrin brought her knife slicing through the limb before giving the next one the same treatment. Behind them came the grunts and rattling of the others fighting too.

"We have to move before they separate us! Now, Lira," Ahrin ordered. "I've got you."

Lira glanced at Ahrin, then closed her eyes and summoned her magic from the deepest part of her, digging down into her reserves. She hadn't used her magic this way in so long, and now that she was letting it free, it exploded out of her, hot and rich and rapturous.

She set the closest razak alight, then weaved her way between its dying limbs as it screamed, Ahrin at her shoulder.

Deep breaths, quick movements, concentrated bursts of magic, distance gained with every stride. She set two more razak alight before she started losing strength. By then Ahrin had killed another, her knives like an extension of her arm, footwork so fast it was almost a blur.

"Go! We're almost through here," Lira bellowed, then summoned more flame to set another razak alight.

"Lira, there are too many!" Garan shouted back, voice strained.

Ahrin glanced at her, sent a concussion burst flying into the air. Its scarlet explosion illuminated the entire cavern and told them two things.

One: with a momentary gap in the cluster of razak, an exit was visible and approximately a thirty-yard dash almost directly ahead of where Lira and Ahrin stood.

Two: there were more than seven razak in the cavern now, and they were *joining* together, writhing limbs coalescing seamlessly, forming a larger monster that towered over them in terrifying fashion.

"What the...?" Fari's mouth was open, eyes wide.

"Rotted...." Lira stared, momentarily stunned into completely stillness. They could join together? Why hadn't Lucinda told them that?

"We have to move!" Tarion rapped out, voice clear and commanding. "Everyone behind me. Lira, keep using that fire of yours to help me force a way through."

He flashed out of sight, reappeared in front of her, and began running, sword slashing the air before him. Lira didn't hesitate. She summoned what remained of her magic and sprinted after him.

Whenever a slashing leg loomed out of the darkness, she set it alight. Ahrin ran at her left, knives just as deadly as Tarion's sword.

"Still behind us?" Tarion roared.

"We're here," Garan called back. "I'm at the rear, Fari and Lorin safe in front of me."

Garan Egalion is a brave man. That thought had time to flicker through Lira's mind as she gasped and burned and ran.

"Almost there!" Tarion called back.

Lira's breath rasped in her lungs, sweat slicking her skin, but she gritted her teeth and kept moving. More limbs reached for her out of the darkness. Magic draining quickly now, she drew her dagger, dodged around a leg, and slashed her blade at an eye that got too close. Two more strikes and it was dead with a loud scream. Soaked to the elbows in razak gore she turned to the next creature to find Ahrin had already killed it.

Dimly she was aware of the others behind her, of Tarion fighting just as fiercely ahead. But everything in her was focused. On breaking through, on forcing a clear gap to make a run for it.

Eventually they did it, killing another creature between them and finding only dark space ahead. With a flick of her hand, Lira summoned a ball of flame that lit up the way forward, revealing a dark doorway in a stone wall. Tarion had already reached it and was hauling it open.

"Quickly!" She slowed her speed just enough for Ahrin to reach the door and safety first, then Lira followed her inside. Ahrin reached back, grabbed her spare torch, and held it wordlessly out to Lira. She snapped her fingers and set it alight, and Ahrin turned and started up the narrow stone steps ahead of them.

Tarion lingered at the door while Lira began following Ahrin, glancing back every few seconds. Seconds later, Fari and Lorin raced through and started up the steps too.

When a turn in the stairs took them out of view of the door, Lira stopped, hovering, until she heard Garan's bellow. "We're all in!"

"Me too," Tarion echoed, and then the slamming of the door echoed through the space.

Together, they raced up the stairs, panting, light flickering from Ahrin's torch. A loud *crack* sounded below, something crashing against the door, and then they heard it slamming open. They redoubled their efforts, reaching the top of the steps and bursting into an empty hallway stretching away in both directions. To their left more stairs were visible leading upwards.

"Stairs," Lira said without even thinking about it. They needed to get clear of this grouping of monsters and find another way to sneak down and come at the queens. Rattling echoed up the stairs behind them, angry, hungry. They glanced at each other and ran left.

But razak were fast. So much faster than humans. And they were all tiring. Lira's legs burned almost as painfully as her lungs. Her pack had become a dead weight on her back, sending pain throbbing through her shoulders.

"Suck it up!" Ahrin snapped, noticing how they were slowing from exhaustion. She wasn't even breathing hard. "You run or you die. Go!"

"Yes, ma'am, Huntress, ma'am," Garan gasped out, a little smile on his face as he redoubled his pace.

"Rich noble brats have no stamina," Ahrin muttered, but her habitual hard expression had softened, and she dropped to the rear, sharp words cracking out occasionally to keep them all moving.

They made it to the stairs, but by then the razak were pouring out of the stairwell, streaming after them, long, deadly shadows gliding over the floor. The air was freezing, turning the sweat slicking her skin to ice, the crazed rattling like claws scraping over her brain. Lira glanced over her shoulder, frantically searching for anything she could use to throw at them, to try and halt their progress somehow.

There was nothing. The hall was empty, long since abandoned. She caught Ahrin's grim look, returned it. Their situation was dire.

Despite growing exhaustion, they sprinted up the steps, found more stairwells at the top spiralling away on both sides. In tacit agreement they turned left. The razak had already reached the landing below when they were only halfway up. Lira's heart pounded in her chest, trepidation growing with every inch the razak gained on them.

Struggling to the very top of the stairs, they emerged onto a wide rocky plateau and sprinted across it...

Before sliding to a halt at the edge of a precipitous drop.

Water rushed by hundreds of feet below them—the underground river they'd been told about. The waterway was fed by a crashing waterfall a short distance away, close enough Lira could feel the cool spray on her burning cheeks. The sheer amount of water crashed against Lira's exhausted magical senses, momentarily dizzying her until she could separate herself from it.

From somewhere far above, light shone down over the water; the silvery glow of moonlight.

"This is very bad," Fari observed.

"We're trapped." Ahrin's gaze was back on where they'd come up the stairs. "There's no exit."

"An apt analysis." Garan squared his shoulders, faced the darkness with his gore-covered daggers. "Which makes our options much simpler. We kill them all."

"What if we jumped?" Lorin asked, peering over the edge. "We all can swim, right?"

Ahrin tensed, said nothing. Lira looked at her, eyebrows raised, and she gave a little shake of her head.

"You ran the biggest criminal gang on the Dirinan *harbour,* and you can't swim?" Lira asked.

"I don't want to hear it, Astor."

"The drop is too high," Fari said decidedly, making moot the question of swimming ability. "Hitting the surface of the water at this height would kill us, even if it was deep enough that we didn't crack every bone in our bodies smashing into rocks at the bottom."

"Are you sure?" Garan was peering over too. "Because—"

"She's right," Ahrin said flatly. "There's no surviving that jump."

The razak reached the edge of the plateau, an inky black mass of rattling and flashing silver eyes. Instead of rushing their prey, the monsters slowly began to join themselves together again.

Lira drew an arrow, nocked her bow.

Ahrin tossed her torch into the space between them and the monsters, giving them light to fight by. Anger lined her expression and stiffened her shoulders.

Lira sympathised. She couldn't believe she was about to die underground without even getting close to taking down Lucinda. That woman continued to win, time after time. Hatred bubbled like acid in her stomach.

The monster loomed over them, its rattling turning deep and throaty. Lira drew back her bow, loosed her arrow. It hit where she'd aimed but did nothing. When joined, the creature's eyes were covered by a thick carapace.

Swearing, she dropped the bow and drew her dagger. Then she took a breath and reached into her magic. There wasn't a lot left.

And then it was on them.

Lira found herself shrouded in darkness and rattling and slashing, scaled limbs. She could hear the others fighting, shouting, but her visibility was gone. She wrapped the limb nearest her in flame, and the monster screamed, rearing back. The flame crawled higher and higher, and then faded and died.

She stared, chest heaving. Then she gritted her teeth, fury and determination winding through her. "Ahrin?" she roared her name. Somewhere in the distance Garan shouted in pain.

"Here." The Darkhand slid into the space at her side, splattered with dark blood, eyes fierce.

"Can you cover me for a few moments?"

"I can." Ahrin glanced around them. "Careful where you put your feet. This thing is pushing us towards the edge."

Lira took a deep breath, closed her eyes, and struggled to find a steady focus—that same focus and control she'd learned in hours upon hours of practice at Temari Hall, in even more hours and days imprisoned in Carhall.

She dragged up every single shred of magic remaining inside her, scraped the well of it dry. She ignored the rattling all around her. The shouts. Ahrin's quick breaths.

She took another long breath.

And she wrapped the entire monster in flame. The effort required tore through her, and she let out a hoarse scream, staggering forward with the force of what was exploding out of her. Her breath hissed out in a rasp. Something inside her weakened, cracked, almost broke, and her skin was too hot, her heartrate too fast.

But the thing was alight in violet-edged flame.

Fire wreathed almost every limb, burning through shadow and carapace alike. Fari became visible first, bloodied but alive, then Tarion, then Garan. Finally, Lorin, so close to the edge he gave it a look of horror and took a jumping step forward.

The razak screamed as it burned, remaining limbs flailing as the flame crept inexorably along them.

"Get back!" Ahrin shouted. "Get clear of its limbs. It's maddened."

But the monster seemed to know who was burning it. It screamed again, one of its remaining limbs lashing out of the darkness, its lethal scaled edge slashing right for Lira's face. She was too unsteady on her feet to move quickly enough to avoid it, barely even saw it coming in time to realise what was happening.

Then a boot landed square in her back, sending her flying forwards, out of the way of the swinging razak limb. She cried out, falling onto uncompromising rock and taking too long to right herself to see what had kicked her.

And when she did, it was only to see the flailing limb that had been aiming for her slam into Ahrin's side instead. The Darkhand hadn't been fast enough to recover her balance after lunging forward to kick Lira out of the way. The dying razak's blow sent her flying over the edge of the drop. Instinctively Lira lifted a hand, sought to grab Ahrin with her telekinetic magic, but she didn't have any magic left to use.

It was completely drained.

She grabbed on to the remnants what was left, tried to extend it towards Ahrin, but something burned inside her when she tried. Weakness engulfed her, and she lost her grip on it, couldn't summon the focus she needed to use her telekinesis.

Ahrin fell. Quicker than thought, she was gone.

"Ahrin!" Lira screamed, uncaring of whether it brought more monsters bearing down on them. She forced herself to her feet, swayed, and almost fell again, but somehow found enough inside her to stumble to the edge of the drop.

She couldn't see anything. The surface of the water churned far below, rough and choppy, the current swift. Garan appeared at her side, looking down, gaze searching frantically. "I wasn't quick enough. I'm sorry ... I could have, but I wasn't quick enough."

Lira shrugged off her pack and weapons. Yanked off her boots.

"Lira, no!" Tarion realised what was happening before anyone else.

She ignored him and dived out over the drop, air whistling past her face as she plummeted towards the surging river below.

CHAPTER 38

The impact was going to kill her.

It was going to crush bone and tendon and rip the life from her body.

This realisation came when Lira was halfway down, the air whistling past her ears as her speed increased, the river below approaching far too quickly. Deep down, she knew neither she nor Ahrin were going to win their dance with death this time.

She braced for the inevitable impact. There was just enough time to wonder how much it would hurt or whether she'd die too quickly to feel pain. Enough time for dread and fear and regret to rise up, sharp and strong ... only to be eclipsed by her terror, her need to get to Ahrin before...

The remnants of her magic reacted instinctively the moment she hit the river.

Water slid around her like a welcoming embrace, giving way at her touch rather than presenting a solid surface for her body to crash into. That alone took what was left of her magical strength, scraping her well dry. The impact, while not deadly, was shuddering, hard, painful.

She plunged deep underwater. It was dark. Cold. A heavy pressure on her chest tightened the deeper she fell, until eventually, her speed slowed, faded altogether.

Lira's survival instincts kicked in then, making her legs move, kicking upwards, dragging herself back up towards the surface. Her clothes were a dead weight dragging her down, and there was little strength remaining in her muscles. The current of the river wrapped her in its grip and dragged her ruthlessly along with it.

But she kept going. Lungs burning. Vision spotting. Desperate to suck in a lungful of air, the surface a faint haze of dim light above.

By the time she finally broke the surface, gasping, she only managed a single gulping breath before the current dragged her back under. Her struggles weakening, she broke above water level once more, her arms moving desperately, trying to hold herself steady.

Ahrin. She had to find—

The thought was gone as quickly as it had come. The water was too rough, the current stronger than she could manage even if she was at full strength, and it took every bit of focus she had just to try and get air.

While she knew the mechanics of swimming, Lira had never spent that much time in the water, and she was already exhausted from fleeing the razak, not to mention the overuse of magic it had taken to kill it. The current caught at her legs, swung her hard into the rocky wall of its banks. A rib snapped in what would have been an audible crack if not for how loudly the tumbling water roared around her.

She screamed in pain, and water flooded into her mouth. She coughed, gasping, curling up instinctively around the agony in her chest. She tried to swim, to steer herself, but she couldn't move her left arm, because it hurt her chest too much. The current sucked her back into the middle of the river, and she shot underneath a low gap in the cavern roof.

She didn't see the rocks on the other side until it was too late. The current smashed her right side into one, which propelled her straight into another. Her head cracked against something underwater.

Her vision blurred, darkness threatening. She kicked out frantically, her body instinctively still trying to survive, and her feet found purchase. A flailing hand touched slick rock and she grabbed it, anchoring herself against it. She was dizzy, shaking, unable to move her left side without unbearable agony. Trembling violently as water cascaded around her, she looked around and spotted a pebbled shoreline not far off.

She took a breath, gritted her teeth, and began struggling towards it. The current fought her every step of the way. At one point she lost her footing and was almost sucked back out into the main part of the river. She'd swallowed so much water she was convinced she was drowning. Fighting was no longer a conscious thing. Lost to pain and dizziness, she somehow, inch by inch, made her way into shallower water, dragging herself up out of the shallows.

There she collapsed, facedown, soaked and shivering. She had no strength left to move. No will. No interest in ever getting up again.

Ahrin couldn't have survived that fall, even if she *had* known how to swim. Lira had only survived it because of her magic.

For the first time in her life, Lira lost her battle with the yawning chasm in her chest. She didn't even try to fight it. She didn't want to anymore.

Ahrin was gone.

She let it swallow her whole.

"Is she breathing?"

Voices roused Lira back to consciousness, but it was a hazy kind of wakefulness. Her thoughts were dull, slow, and her body felt utterly limp, as if the connection between it and her brain had snapped.

A cool palm pressed against her neck. "She is, but her pulse is dangerously slow."

"How badly is she hurt?"

"She's got broken ribs, a cracked skull, and probably more injuries. But it's not just physical. I think it's magic overuse as well. Maybe hypothermia too, or shock." A hesitation, then, "Her body's energy reserves are so low ... she's barely holding on to life."

An indrawn breath from someone.

Warmth emanated from where the hand rested on Lira's neck. Her awareness grew a little clearer, enough to recognise the voices and be able to mumble, "Fari? What are you ... why ... you here?"

The hand pressed a little harder against her skin, as if in relief. "We came looking for you, stupid. Just lie still, you're in bad shape. I'll do what I can."

Lira faded out again. The next time she roused was when pain stabbed through her chest. She was being lifted. She cried out involuntarily.

"Sorry," Tarion's voice murmured in her ear. "I'll be as gentle as I can. We're just going to get you somewhere more protected—Fari had to use her magic on you so the razak might already be on their way. Rest, Lira. You're safe with us."

She closed her eyes, allowed the blackness to claim her.

She didn't want to be awake.

The next time she woke, her mind was mostly lucid. She'd been propped against a soft surface, half-sitting, two blankets wrapped tightly around her. Her clothes and hair were dry, and a fire crackled close enough she could feel its warmth. Despite that, she trembled uncontrollably, and she felt both parched and completely drained at once. Every single muscle in her body ached fiercely. But none of that registered beyond a dim awareness.

Everything was grey. Numb. Widening her awareness, she picked up movement around her; scuffling feet, two thuds as packs dropped to the ground. Her eyes blinked open of their own accord.

"No razak around," Garan said quietly.

"We went down two levels to make sure," Lorin added, barely audible.

"It's been quiet here, too," Tarion responded after a moment. "No movement since you left, and the air temperature has stayed normal."

"How is she?" Garan's voice again.

"She's just waking, I think." Fari shifted into Lira's line of sight, crouching down to reach out and press a palm against her forehead. "Hey, Spider. Good to see you. I can't feel any fever, which is a good sign. How much pain are you in?"

"It's fine," she said dully. Pain didn't mean anything anymore. She couldn't even really feel it, not from inside the chasm where it was all dull and flat and grey. Even the voices she heard seemed oddly distant.

Tarion appeared on Fari's other side, concern written all over his face. "Are you okay, Lira?"

She blinked, glancing around. The walls of the room were rock, and the space was small. Once her eyes adjusted to the shadows around the bright flames of the fire, she could make out Garan and Lorin standing opposite each other near the doorway. They were scruffy, shadows under their eyes, dirt creased in their skin. Lorin lifted a hand in greeting when her gaze fell on him. "Where are we?"

"The back room of what we think was a shop, a couple levels above where we found you," Lorin said. "The light from the fire can't be seen from the front door or the street outside. Tarion and Fari have been keeping an eye on you while Garan and I went scouting to make sure none of the razak trailed us here."

"How long was I out?"

"Almost a day."

Lira sank further into the blankets, tuning out from it all. She wasn't even sure why she'd asked. She didn't actually care. Habit, she supposed.

"What's her condition?" Garan asked Fari, giving Lira a worried look.

"Before we moved, I sped up the knitting of bone in her ribs and skull. The injury sites will be fragile for at least a few days." The healer was bone-pale, and her hands trembled too. "I did what I could to speed up recovery from magic overuse and stabilised her body temperature. Barring unexpected complications, she's going to be okay."

"Uncle Finn would be proud," Tarion said quietly, laying a hand on Fari's shoulder and giving it a squeeze.

"Thank everything for you, Fari," Garan agreed, then glanced around. "We'll lay up here for a day or two, at least, so you both can recover. We'll ration the food—we've still got enough for at least a week if we're careful—and Lorin and I re-filled the water flasks."

Lorin pushed away from the wall. "I'll go and scout a retreat location, just in case Lira takes a turn for the worse and Fari needs to use her magic again."

Lira tried to turn over, but bit down hard on her lip when pain stabbed through her side. Fari shot her a warning glance, but Lira merely curled back where she'd been. "Leave me here and go on after Egalion and Caverlock," she mumbled. "You can come back for me after if you don't get eaten."

"You're the only one who can use magic against those things. We need you," Garan said.

She shook her head, annoyed that he was making her *talk*. "You don't need me; you just need to find Egalion. We all know that. So go and do it."

She would wait here until she could move without stabbing agony, and then she would go back up to the city and hand herself over to Lucinda. The woman could let Lira go or kill her or chain her up forever. It didn't matter. None of it mattered anymore. Her trembling increased to shivering. Without a word, Tarion carried another blanket over, and added it to the ones already tucked around her. Garan gently tugged the swaying Fari down beside him and gave her his blanket.

Lira stared, unseeing, at the flames. The weight in her chest was so heavy she wasn't sure how she'd summon the ability to move ever again. "Please just go. I don't want you to wait for me."

"No," Tarion said. "We left you behind once already. I'm not doing it again. We go on, all of us together."

Tears pressed against her eyelids with the force of how much she didn't want to hear those words. "I'm not worth that, and you know it. Just leave me."

Garan shrugged and settled more comfortably against the wall, stretching his legs out in front of him. "We already broke you out of prison, Spider. We're all done. None of us are going to be mages anymore. You said I had to own my choices, and you were right. Here is me, owning what I've done."

"You did it for Egalion, your family." The effort to keep arguing was too much, her voice wasn't strong enough, and more tears pricked her eyes. She wanted them to go, leave her so she could be swallowed by the emptiness again. "They'll forgive you."

"No." Tarion said it again, clear and decisive. "I agree with Garan. For good or ill, I've made my choice, Lira. That is the end of it."

"Tarion—"

"I'm letting go," he said, holding her gaze without flinching. "I accept who I am now."

"Whereas I'm just stubborn." Garan's curious gaze flicked between them.

"Not sure if anyone cares what I think." Fari's voice was sleepy, emanating from where she curled up under Garan's blanket. "But even before this I was already an officially disgraced Dirsk. So I'm sticking around too. Pretty sure Lorin's not going anywhere either."

Lira merely shook her head. She had no energy to fight them anymore. A longer silence fell, and she hoped they were going to sleep, but instead Garan broke it again.

"Lira?" he asked. "Will you tell us what happened? Your side of things, I mean. Not to defend yourself, or explain, because you're right that you don't owe us that, but just because we'd really like to know."

The anger that had been there, that would have dismissed his question with a scowl, was gone. Warmth crept through her, her body slowly healing after Fari's work, but it did nothing to make her feel better. In the end she answered him because talking was better than staring at the flames and feeling the weight in her chest grow heavier and heavier with every breath.

She had to focus her still sluggish brain on remembering the details, on relating them correctly. She didn't leave anything out—there was no point in that anymore—finally coming to a hoarse stop at her conversation with Tarrick and Dawn after being imprisoned in Carhall. "They had me," she finished. "I'd lied to you all about having extra magical abilities, about"—she stumbled on the word, couldn't finish the sentence—"other important things. Underground did a good job framing me, but I helped them along." Without the resentment and defensiveness that always lived within her, it was easy to admit the truth. Her own actions had contributed to what had happened to her.

The fire crackled and popped into the thoughtful silence that followed. None of them seemed inclined to dispute her version of events. After a moment, Fari shifted under her blankets, shooting Tarion a look, and he rose, bringing a flagon of water to Lira. She took it and mechanically drank down several mouthfuls.

"Ahrin sacrificed herself to save your life up there on the plateau," Tarion said softly.

A shaft of pain stabbed through Lira, so blinding her breath caught and she almost turned and emptied her stomach onto the floor. She fled from it, searched desperately for that numbness so she could bury herself in it again.

Several glances were shared but nobody pushed any further. Lira's shivering had increased so much it was visible under the blankets, despite her warming body.

"We'll hole up here until you're recovered, then we move," Garan repeated. "And not because we need you, Lira, but because a few hours ago, you saved all our lives and put *your* life at risk in doing so. We want you with us. That's just how it is, whether you like it or not."

Those words might have meant something once. They probably would have made her angry. But she wasn't angry anymore. She wasn't anything anymore. "I told you. Just leave me."

Tarion glanced at Fari, who looked worried. "What's wrong with her?"

"Shock, maybe worse," Fari murmured. "Whatever it is, it's not just physical."

"What do we do?"

"I don't know. My speciality is blood, not the mind. Maybe if Garan's mother was here she could help."

Garan seemed to think keeping Lira talking was the best approach in the absence of his mother, because he cleared his throat. "Are you sure?"

he asked. "About the Magor-lier working for Lucinda? Tarion told us your theories about what might have happened."

"I saw the letter myself." She could still see it in her mind's eye. The Magor-lier's seal, his signature. The look on his face when he'd imprisoned her in Carhall.

"It could have been forged," Fari pointed out.

"Why would Lucinda have a forged letter secreted away in a safe in her office?" Tarion shook his head. "Besides, the way Lira describes her conversation with Uncle Tarrick ... it certainly sounds like he was instrumental in her imprisonment."

"Or he truly believed Lira was a traitor," Fari said. "*We* believed it, and we know Lira. She said it herself, Underground did their job well in framing her. Far be it from me to defend a Tylender, but he is one of the most honourable men alive, not to mention a powerful mage warrior. He was key to destroying the Darkmage and ending the war."

They were talking as if they accepted Lira's account as fact. As if they believed her completely. But even that failed to penetrate her numbness.

"What if Lucinda was trying to manipulate Lira?" Garan suggested, his gaze shifting to her. "To frame you like she did, that takes time and planning, so she must have been aware that you were a spy for a little while at least?"

"It's possible," Lira said, meaning it. She'd thought it over a lot, the fact Lucinda had been onto her for some time before she'd escaped Shadowfall Island. Lira's extraction from Aranan had probably been a result of Lucinda learning, or guessing, Lira was a traitor. By bringing her to the isolated Shadowfall Island, Lira had been completely contained while Lucinda and Greyson began putting the pieces in place to set her up.

The woman would have expected Lira to go snooping around, and it was exactly like her to have planted information she wanted Lira to find. She thought back to the night she'd been imprisoned, the anger and triumph on Tylender's face ... it *could* have just been the emotion of him thinking he'd finally dealt with the problem of Underground and

Shakar forever. "You could be right, but something about that letter …
I don't know."

Both Garan's and Tarion's shoulders slumped in relief. Neither
wanted to believe their beloved uncle was either a traitor or somehow
in thrall to Lucinda. Or dead. Deep down, she knew it was unlikely that
Tarrick Tylender still lived.

Tarion nodded. "We can figure it out once we're home. First we have
to get to these razak queens."

"Shouldn't we consider giving up and going back?" Fari suggested.
"We've lost our best strategist and Lira is badly hurt. Forcing her to go
on might make her injuries worse."

Lorin reappeared at that moment. "Found a good place if needed," he
said when all gazes swung to him. "And I heard what you were saying
as I came in. I'm not sure we have any choice but to continue. Lucinda
isn't going to let us go if we return."

Garan looked thoughtful. "Maybe our goal shouldn't be finding the
queens but finding Aunt Alyx and Uncle Dash. Together we'd have a
much better chance of succeeding."

Tarion brightened instantly. "That's a good idea."

"I don't want to be the downer here, and I'm really sorry to even say
it, but we don't know that they're still alive," Fari said gently.

The cousins shared a long look, then Garan smiled. "They're alive,
Fari. I don't know what happened to delay them, but they're still
going."

"All right." Fari conceded. "But even so, they're searching for the
nests too, right? I don't think we can do any different than what Ahrin
had planned—keep going down."

"True, but we'll stop using the wider streets and tunnels. From now
on we take the narrowest spaces we can find, where the razak can't
follow," Garan said. "Lira, what do you think?"

"I told you what I think," she said wearily. "Leave me here."

Tarion ignored her. "Fari, when do you think Lira will be okay to
move?"

"Another day at least of full rest." Fari looked at her. "How's your head?"

"It's fine."

"You should try and get some sleep. That will hasten your healing more than anything else."

Lira nodded. Maybe sleep would bring escape from this nightmare.

CHAPTER 39

They rested for another day. Lira spent most of it in a listless haze. It was safer inside the numbing chasm, but every now and then she drifted back towards its surface and splinters of pain stabbed through her so intensely that it left her breathless, terrified, and close to emptying her stomach.

She kept falling into short, fevered dozes, waking suddenly and feeling uncertain she was actually awake. Her sleep was plagued with images of the razak, limbs writhing, of Ahrin's boot in her back, the limb slamming into Ahrin's chest, sending her flying over the edge. Over and over again.

At some point, her magic slowly began trickling back, and she grasped onto it like a drowning fish, curling herself around it and letting its heat soothe everything else away. The weight on her chest hadn't lifted—it only seemed to grow heavier—but as her magic returned, she began to think about what to do next.

Her preference was to force them to go on ahead without her, then make her own way back up to the city, and—if she survived the journey—let Lucinda do whatever she wanted to her.

But she didn't have the energy for fighting them, or the will, not when they seemed so insistent on staying with her.

When Lira woke next, it was to the sound of boots on rock; Tarion and Lorin returning from somewhere. Garan had been on watch at the door, Fari keeping an eye on Lira. They both looked to Tarion, who gave a little shake of his head. Lorin looked defeated.

"What it is?" Lira sat up slowly. The stabbing pain in her ribs had faded to a sharp ache, which she felt only distantly.

To his credit, Tarion didn't hesitate in answering. "Lorin and I searched up and down the riverbank as far as we could. There were no tracks, no sign of Ahrin making it out of the water. I'm sorry."

Lira swallowed, turned away. Those words caused something inside her to want to scream and scream and never stop screaming, but the numbness protected her from that. "I already know she's dead. Nobody could have survived that fall."

"You did," Fari said gently.

"Only because..." She trailed off, shaking her head. Why keep hiding things from them? There was no point to that anymore. "I got another ability from being injected with razak blood. I can affect water."

"Oh." Fari blinked in surprise. "There hasn't been a water mage for decades."

Garan hesitated. "Is that all? Fire, telekinesis, water?"

"Lucinda told me I was given three injections of razak blood over a period of days when we were held at DarkSkull." Lira regretted shifting to talk when her chest tightened in pain. "But a third ability never broke out. It doesn't matter. I only survived the fall because I had just enough remnants of magic left to lessen the impact. And once I was in ... I only survived because I can swim. Ahrin never learned. One or the other would have killed her."

Tarion came over, resting a hand on her shoulder. "We wanted to make sure anyway."

"You shouldn't have. It was dangerous to go out there alone." She pulled the blanket over her head and closed her eyes.

"Lira." Tarion's voice was achingly gentle and she hated him for it. "We have to move."

"We're not leaving you here and that's final. I'll carry you if I have to." Garan's voice was unyielding.

She bit her lip, wanting so badly for it all to just go away that tears leaked from behind her eyelids and her heart ached with a desperation she'd never felt before. But some final remnant of pride, or that damned survival instinct she'd always been proud of but now resented more than anything, was enough to propel Lira upwards. She sat up, ignoring the distant tug of pain throughout her body. "Fine."

Garan led the way, now undisputedly in charge. Lira followed Tarion, Fari directly behind her to keep a close eye, Lorin bringing up the rear. She put one foot in front of the other, faintly surprised to find her limbs still working, the pain in her head and ribs a manageable soreness. Fari had done good work.

The heaviness tugging at her limbs felt ten times heavier than the pack and weapons on her back. It was too much effort to participate in the murmured conversation that floated around her, so she just followed wherever Tarion walked, gaze unseeing on the ground.

They headed downwards again, but this time they moved much more slowly, searching out the narrowest streets and closed in stairwells. Places the razak couldn't fit, let alone gather together to trap or ambush them.

It took what felt like hours to move down several levels to where they'd been before. The temperature began to drop again as they reached the bottom of the old city and moved into caverns and tunnels dug out of rock.

"I think Ahrin was right. These tunnels must have always existed in some form," Tarion said as they moved single file along a space so narrow the rock brushed against their shoulders. Lira shuddered, then quickly pushed the word *Ahrin* from her mind. "They're so extensive and many look natural."

"Old waterways perhaps?" Garan suggested.

"Yes," Lira said without thinking. The answer seemed right, and she could still feel the water, at a distance now, but there.

"Or maybe overflow tunnels?" Fari said with a shudder.

"Maybe something lived down here before the razak?" Garan said in a deliberately ghoulish tone.

"Something big and terrifying." Tarion smiled a little. "Big enough to carve through rock."

Fari snorted. "Bigger and scarier than razak?"

Lira breathed out, and her breath frosted in front of her mouth. The others noticed at the same time she did, and they slowed their pace.

"Exit coming up," Garan, in the lead, murmured.

The prospect of razak nearby caused a sharp spike of bitter hatred that pierced Lira's numbing despair. It gave her the first burst of energy she'd had since being dragged out of the river. Too short to see over Garan's shoulders, she pushed past him impatiently and dropped down in the hallway beyond. This one definitely seemed man-made; it was wide and the floor smooth.

"Pass me that." She reached for his torch. "And stay there."

"You're still hurt," Fari objected. "You—"

Lira cut Fari off. "I'm the only one whose magic works on the razak, remember?"

Garan passed her the torch without complaint, and she swept it in a wide arc. There was no tell-tale rattling, but the cold was enough to bite into her still-healing ribs. A headache thumped at her temples. The creatures couldn't be far off.

"I'm going to look for the best way down," she said. "You stay there in case it's another ambush."

"We'll stay here as long as your torchlight stays in sight," Garan countered.

She shot him a glare, but he was unrepentant.

Gone was the thrill facing impending danger or the fear of being trapped in a dark place by monsters. Now there was only a listless acknowledgment that she'd have to help the others get this done before they would let her go. All she wanted was to leave them and curl up somewhere and close her eyes until it all went away.

Lira moved slowly, sweeping the torch into the nearest caverns. There were no buildings or homes as such this far down, just caves gouged into rock.

She got as far as she could in one direction without losing sight of the others and then headed back the other way, passing them and continuing in the other direction. Shortly she came to a section where the original engineers had stopped digging at a natural opening in the rock. Dampness trickled down one wall, teasing her senses. Lira scrambled up a rocky incline, ignoring the stab of pain in her chest, and hunkered down at the top. "Found something," she called back softly.

Tarion reached her first, the others not far behind. A narrow tunnel, this one most definitely natural, stretched away into darkness. It looked like it was heading on a downward incline.

"That is a very narrow tunnel," Fari said, all kinds of dubiousness leaking from her voice. "Like, we'll have to crawl."

"Won't be able to hold a torch, either," Garan added.

"And if it narrows farther on, we might not be able to get back out. We'd be stuck," Tarion said.

"All correct," Lira said. "But the tunnel is also leading downwards, rather steeply. And no razak can touch us in there."

"I'll go first," Lorin volunteered.

"Good idea." Lira shifted aside. "You've got the broadest shoulders. If you get stuck, the rest of us should have enough room to scramble back out, and one of us can drag you if necessary."

Fari heaved a sigh. "Have we considered that there might be other living things down here? Like snakes, or spiders, or worse? Things small enough to fit in that. Things we won't be able to see in the pitch-black darkness?"

Garan gave her a reassuring smile. "I think we can safely assume the razak have eaten anything living down here."

"I am not reassured. Just for the record."

Seeming to have decided everything was sorted, Lorin dropped his torch and crawled into the tunnel opening. Garan went second.

"I'll bring up the rear," Lira said. "I'm the smallest."

"If we're going in order of size, you go next Tarion." Fari waved him in. "Anything to delay having to crawl into that tunnel."

For a while the light from the torch they'd left lit at the entrance was enough to be able to see where they were placing their hands, for Lira to see Fari's boots ahead of her. But soon enough they turned a bend and the light vanished completely.

"Everyone okay?" Garan called back and received a series of grunted assents.

"Tarion, if necessary, do you think you could teleport out of this tunnel?" Lorin asked curiously.

"Depends how far the next open space is. The distance I can travel is limited. If it was too far, I'd probably get crushed in rock."

"Best not try that then," Garan said hurriedly. "Damn, it's dark in here."

Their breathing was quicker than usual, and the sound of their movements had a frantic edge. They were scared, fighting not to lose their heads to it. Lira wondered if she would feel the same way if she hadn't lost the ability to feel things.

Ahrin would be terrified. '*You, and small, enclosed, spaces. Those are my only weaknesses*'. That stray thought had her freezing up in the tunnel, air gasping out of her chest, body turning rigid. And then it passed, and the fog returned, and she kept going.

The temperature grew colder and colder, until they began shivering despite the exertion of crawling through the tunnel.

"Definitely headed in the right direction," Garan said.

"Headed right for hypothermia too," Fari said cheerfully.

"Is it bad if I can't feel my fingers anymore?" Lorin asked, his teeth chattering.

"Probably."

"Lucky we've got a healer with us," Tarion said.

When a blinding flash of green light suddenly rippled through the darkness ahead, followed quickly by the roar of a concussion burst, they all froze in surprise. The blast was either powerful enough or close enough—or both—that Lira felt the force of it squeezing her chest before letting go as quickly as it had come.

The eruption of a magical concussion burst was so unexpected that it took a moment for them to realise what it was.

And that the mage light had been a bright emerald green.

"Mama!" Tarion said, hope seared into his voice.

And then they were moving, scrambling forward, heedless of scraped elbows and knees. As they crawled, the creak of rattling chains penetrated the space, growing louder the farther they went. The air deepened to a bone-chilling cold. Lira felt some of her fog fading, her senses sharpening at the potential of finding Alyx Egalion and her husband somewhere ahead of them.

"Slow down!" Garan bellowed suddenly. "I've reached the end."

Lira craned her neck, trying to see around Fari in front of her, but it was impossible. The progress ahead slowed, until finally she got close enough that Lira could see faint, silvery light ahead.

The tunnel grew higher, and Fari was able to move onto hands and knees. An opening yawned ahead. Tarion's arm reached around to help Fari, and then Lira scrambled forward, pushing herself out, before abruptly stopping herself as her legs swung out into open space.

"Careful!" Garan grabbed her arm.

The tunnel opened halfway up the side of an enormous cavern. High, *very high*, above, the cave must have been open to the sky, because watery sunlight shone down, casting just enough light that Lira's eyes, having grown sensitive in the dark, could see well enough without a torch.

"Look!" Lorin pointed.

The floor of the cavern below was crawling with the indistinct figures of multiple rattling razak; they surrounded what looked like a deep, sunken pit towards the far edge. Uneven spikes of rock rose from the ground all over the cavern floor.

It took only seconds for Lira's searching gaze to find Alyx Egalion. The woman was trapped halfway between the pit and the cavern's edge. Razak crawled over every inch of the space around her, barely held off by her staff and judicious use of her concussive magic's bright light to distract them.

Lira's gaze moved on from Egalion, searching for an exit and spotting two, on opposite sides of the cavern, to the left and right of where they balanced high above. Egalion wasn't close to either.

"Why isn't she flying out?" Garan asked.

Tarion studied the situation with a sweeping gaze. "She can't get clear enough to."

He was right. Several of the creatures had joined together to make a larger monster that towered above the mage councillor. If she tried to fly, she'd likely be caught by one of their writhing limbs.

"Can you go down and get her?" Fari asked him.

He shook his head, a faint edge of panic edging his voice. "She absorbed Da's Taliath immunity to magic. Mine won't work on her."

Lira barely heard him. Her gaze was on the sunken pit in the cavern floor. She counted fifteen razak at least, probably closer to twenty, in the cavern, yet only a third were surrounding Egalion. The rest surged in the space around the pit, clearly roused and angry.

Protective, even?

"I think there's a queen in there," she said. "Egalion must have been trying to get to it."

"What?" Garan asked.

"In the pit." She pointed. "Look how protective they are."

Anger curled suddenly in her gut, hot and powerful. Her mouth curled with the force of it. These things had killed...

So close. She was so close to stabbing a dagger through the queen's heart and killing every single one of her rotted creatures.

"Lira!" Tarion's hand landed on her shoulder, snapping her out of her daze.

"What?" she snapped.

His hazel eyes met hers. "Will you help me? Please."

It took a moment for the haze of sudden rage to fade enough to realise what he was talking about. And then it all dropped away, and she was tired and numb again. Another concussive burst went off, bright and green, squeezing her chest before letting go.

"Lira, please."

Alyx Egalion had been party to locking her in prison for the rest of her life. She hadn't come to visit Lira, hadn't given her an opportunity to explain anything. She'd cut her loose and left her to rot.

But Tarion hadn't.

He'd also risked his life to search a razak-infested underground city for Ahrin's body. He'd postponed looking for his parents to come and find her after she'd dived off a cliff to almost-certain death. He'd further delayed the search to wait for her to recover rather than abandoning her.

And she hadn't forgotten her promise to him.

"Do you have a plan?" she asked.

"No." His eyes were wide. "But I need to help her before she's overwhelmed. Please."

She hesitated still. But her magic surged, as if sensing there was an opportunity to be used, urging her to take it. Her body shuddered with relief as she sank into it. Then she looked at Tarion and nodded.

Without further hesitation, he stepped forward and wrapped an arm around her waist. She closed her eyes and breathed in, sinking into her magic. "What are you waiting for?"

The world blurred. Her stomach lurched. She was momentarily weightless.

And then solid ground was under her feet again and the deafening rattle of the razak filled her ears and senses. A limb slashed down at her head. She swayed aside instinctively. Tarion's sword cleared its sheath with a loud ring of steel, musical, like it was hungry.

"Tarion!" Alyx Egalion's shocked voice rang out. "*Lira?*"

Lira stepped forward, summoned her flame, and spun in a wide arc, letting it roar out of her. Magic sang in her blood, hot and heady and *hers*. And for that single moment she was herself again.

Violet-edged white flame lit up everything close enough for her magic to reach. Her flames licked around the monsters. They screamed in unison.

"Mama, fly!" Tarion bellowed. "Garan and the others are up there."

In the next moment, an arm wrapped around Lira's waist and the world blurred again.

CHAPTER 40

Alyx Egalion stared at Lira in something resembling shock and horror.

In any other circumstances Lira would have savoured the look on the woman's face. But far below them the razak seethed, none leaving the cavern, reinforcing Lira's certainty that a queen was in that pit.

They'd moved so quickly the creatures hadn't yet realised where the three of them had gone. Lira looked dubiously down the rocky wall, figuring the razak could probably climb it easily enough if—or when—they did figure it out.

They'd likely be able to trace the use of magic. It wouldn't take them long.

"I don't even know where to start." Egalion's expression was tense, skin pale under the dirt, dark shadows ringing her eyes. "What are you all *doing* here?"

"Looking for you, obviously," Lira said flatly.

"Mama," Tarion broke in before Egalion could respond to that. He was standing so close to his mother their arms were pressed tightly together. "Where's Da?"

"We got separated a few days ago fleeing from a bunch of them." Egalion lifted a hand to press against her forehead in what looked to be exhaustion. She had no pack with her, no weapons apart from her mage staff. "At least I think it was a few days. I haven't been able to find him."

"And are you okay?" Tarion's gaze ran over her. "We were so worried ... we thought Lucinda might have injected you with razak blood, or you'd gotten hurt down here, or..." All the concern that had been building up in Tarion over weeks now poured out of him.

"I'm okay Tarion." She wrapped an arm around him, holding his gaze. "She didn't inject me with anything, and I'm not hurt. I promise you."

Lira frowned, some inner instinct sparking at the woman's words. But it was gone as quickly as it had come. Tarion swallowed, leaning down to press his forehead to her hair. Garan wrapped an arm around her other side. She leaned into both of them, clearly exhausted and close to her wits' end. Far too familiar with that feeling, Lira turned away from the family reunion and stalked back to study the cavern below. Lorin and Fari followed.

"What are you thinking, Spider?" Fari asked.

Lira took a deep breath, but it did nothing to dislodge the weight dragging her down. She wasn't sure she cared what came next. It all seemed like too much of an effort. But then her eyes landed on the pit where she was sure a queen razak was.

"I'm thinking we need to end this. Now. Egalion has clearly been running for days without food, and we have minimal supplies left. We leave it much longer, and we'll be too weak to have any chance of getting that queen."

"I agree." Egalion came up behind them. Her composure seemed to have been restored and that noble aloofness had returned to her expression. "But not even all of us together could take on that many razak and win. Not once they join together. Even if we found Dash, we still couldn't do it." Her voice trembled momentarily on his name, but it was quickly hidden. "Now, somebody tell me why Lira Astor is here."

Garan straightened his shoulders. "We broke her out of jail to help us find you."

"You did *what*?" Egalion looked horrified.

"I figured out that Underground had taken you." Tarion spoke up, shifting to stand at Garan's shoulder. "And Lira knew more than any of us about the group. I agreed to help her escape in return for her help finding you and Da."

"Which proved to be the correct approach, because look where we are," Garan added, arms crossed firmly over his chest.

"Yes." Egalion barked a bitter laugh. "Here—to die alongside Dash and me. Which you know very well is the absolute last thing he and I would ever want. Not to mention releasing a dangerous prisoner you can't trust."

Her anger was deep and cold, and both young men flinched. Garan's arms dropped to hang by his sides. Lira thought about Ahrin pushing her away and taking that blow. Of Ahrin walking away from her in Dirinan in an attempt to save Lira from Underground. And a stirring of sympathy for Egalion flickered in her chest.

Fari and Lorin, clearly uncomfortable, had edged away from the discussion.

"The search for you was failing. We weren't going to do nothing. We couldn't," Garan managed, then cleared his throat. "Anyway, we're all here now, so let's figure out how to get ourselves out of this. You and Uncle Dash can yell at us later."

"And say what you want about Lira, but she's helped us. I trust her." Tarion held his mother's eyes, spoke firmly and audibly, and stood with his shoulders straight. Lira stared at him in amazement.

Egalion opened her mouth as if to deliver another stinging rebuke but seemed to see the sense in Garan's words. Her shoulders slumped and she lifted a hand to rub at her eyes again. "Fine."

"We need to draw them away from the pit," Tarion said then, his attention shifting to the writhing mass of razak below them.

Lira looked at him and nodded in agreement. "Long enough to get to the queen and kill it."

"You've got an idea." Fari nudged her with a smile.

"I might." She frowned and looked at Garan. She needed his infallible sense of direction. "How far is the river, do you think? I can sense the water, and it's close, but I couldn't tell you how close."

He hunkered down at the edge, studying the cavern, the tunnels leading out of it. "I reckon that exit there would take you in the right direction, but without going down the tunnel to take a look, it's impossible to know whether it would take you straight through or veer off in another direction."

"I'll go." Tarion promptly vanished.

"Tarion!" Egalion snapped, but far too late.

Abruptly the mass of razak below began rattling as they sensed his use of magic. Several of them scuttled toward the tunnel Garan had pointed to, moving in and out of dark shadow. But the majority remained.

"What happened to his bracelets?" Egalion rounded on Garan.

"Lira melted them." He happily shoved all blame in her direction. "He's only tried to eat us twice since she did that, and we managed to talk him down the second time."

"Don't!" Lira snapped as Egalion opened her mouth. "Your son has more strength than you give him credit for. He wanted to come here and save you, and he needs his magic to be able to do that. If you'd let him learn to control it instead of locking it away, we might all be better off right now."

Astonishingly, Egalion absorbed those words, blinked, then said nothing further.

The wait was interminable. Egalion stared at the spot where her son had disappeared. Garan paced. Lira didn't look away from the pit in the centre of the floor.

And then Tarion flashed back into existence, skin flushed, eyes bright. "We might have a bit of luck for once."

Garan opened his mouth to respond. "I—"

"*Where did you get that sword?*" Egalion's words were loud and reverberated through the space with shock and horror.

Tarion glanced down at his hip. "Lira gave it to me."

Her head whipped around to face Lira. Her face was bloodless. "Where did you get it?"

"Underground had it. I assume they dug it out from the ruins at DarkSkull," Lira said. "I stole it from them after I broke out of prison. Tarion needed a sword, so I gave it to him. It's too long and heavy for me to use."

Egalion's mouth tightened as she looked back at her son. "You know what that is you're carrying."

"I do." Tarion's hand caressed the hilt, a hint of protectiveness in his voice. "But it's mine now. Not his."

Garan cleared his throat. "What did you find, Tarion?"

"It's a good distance, several hundred yards maybe, but the tunnel is wide, and it leads through to the river." He shook his head. "Maybe the queen needs water to survive as well as blood, or something? Anyway, it's a straight shot through."

"How is that going to help us?" Egalion asked, looking straight at Lira.

Garan grinned at Lira. "I think I know where you're going with this. Have you recovered enough?"

"I'm fine." She just wanted this over with so she could go away somewhere, sit down, and just be left alone. "We're going to force the razak out of this cavern, through the tunnel, and down to the riverbank. Once that happens, you're all going to do your best to hold them there long enough for Tarion and I to get in here and kill the queen."

"How are you going to force them out?" Egalion asked sharply.

"I'm the dangerous prisoner, remember?" She held Egalion's gaze. "Can your big-deal mage-of-the-higher-order abilities hold that many razak when your magic can't touch them?"

"I..." Oddly, Egalion hesitated, her gaze shifting to the ground. But just as quickly the strange look had disappeared from her face. "I can hold them, but not for long, not that many." She glanced at Tarion, clearly worried for him. "Why do you need Tarion with you?"

"Because he's the best fighter I've ever seen."

Tarion looked at her, concerned. "Shouldn't I help the others hold the razak back?"

"I can't kill the queen without your help." It didn't even sting to admit that. She felt nothing.

"I don't trust you, and I don't trust my son with you," Egalion said flatly.

"I'll be fine, Mama," he said calmly. "Da taught me to fight, remember?"

She flinched at the mention of Dashan

"Do you have a better idea, Aunt Alyx?" Garan asked gently. "I know you don't trust Lira, but we do."

Egalion looked between her nephew and her son for a long moment, then let out a long breath. "I don't have a better idea." It was as close as she would come to agreement. "But if it goes wrong, we retreat instantly and come up with something else. I don't want your lives unnecessarily put at risk."

"Don't worry, the life most at risk here is that of the dangerous prisoner. Your precious son can vanish at will," Lira muttered.

Garan stepped in before Egalion could retort. "Let's do this. Tarion, start ferrying us down there."

He took his mother first, flashing a little wink in Lira's direction as he did so.

She almost smiled.

CHAPTER 41

A half hour later, they stood on the pebbled shore of the underground river, the water rushing by at a furious pace. Lira shuddered at the sight of it and deliberately turned away as memory threatened to rise and crush her whole.

"Lira?" Tarion frowned. Even Egalion was regarding her oddly. Cursing, Lira realised the woman was probably catching some of her thoughts with her telepathic ability. The focus Lira needed to reinforce her mental shield was more difficult than she liked. A successful shield was more about effort and focus than skill, and she was lacking sorely in two of those three areas.

She cleared her throat. "I need you all to move off to the side near the tunnel entrance and conceal yourselves. No matter what happens, remain still and silent. The razak are going to be here in a hurry, and they'll be angry and unsettled. You cannot move too soon—wait until they're all out here. Then, when I tell you, your job is to cut them off from going back into the tunnel. Tarion will take me to the queen, and you hold the razak here until we kill it. When it dies, they should die. Any questions?"

Fari lifted a hand. "I thought you said you had the most dangerous job. You want us to stand between upwards of twenty angry razak and their queen?"

"I do. Though I expect our resident mage of the higher order will do most of the heavy lifting."

"Without any magic?" Fari pushed.

"I'm accustomed to fighting dangerous adversaries who are impervious to my magic," Egalion said coolly, with a quick glance in Lira's direction. "And winning."

"What if we can't hold the razak, or you and Tarion can't kill the queen?" Lorin asked. "What happens then?"

"Then you do what Egalion says," Lira said simply. "Retreat and get clear. Find somewhere safe and figure out another plan." The relief that thought brought—of this no longer being her responsibility—should have worried her, but it didn't.

"How are you going to get all the razak out here?" Egalion asked again.

"You'll see," Lira said.

Egalion opened her mouth, presumably to push further, but Tarion touched her arm and murmured something inaudible in her ear. The woman's mouth thinned but she said nothing.

They quickly divvied up the remaining supplies between them, so that if they got separated each of them would have food and weapons. Only Lira refused to take any, claiming her healing ribs were too sore to take the extra weight. "And I need to be able to move freely if I'm going to kill a queen razak."

Once they were done, Egalion gave her a long, considering look. "If you're planning on betraying us, Lira, I—"

"She's not," Tarion cut over his mother.

"Not right now I'm not," Lira amended with a sharp look at Tarion. He didn't look away. "Now all of you get in position please."

She stood in the open ground about halfway between the river and the tunnel entrance, Tarion at her back, and waited while the others drew weapons and moved over to press themselves against the rock on either side of the yawning gap.

"We're ready, Lira," Garan called out. "Good luck."

"I've got your back," Tarion murmured.

Lira closed her eyes and sank deep into her magic. She'd been sensing the river at the back of her mind ever since they'd walked out of the tunnel, its force, its power, sliding against her magic like a caress.

Carefully, just like she'd done a thousand times before with a glass of water, only on a much bigger scale, she took hold of as much of the water as she could and lifted it *out* of the riverbed.

At first, she wavered, sudden doubt striking deep that she wouldn't be able to do what she intended. The water was moving so fast, sliding around and under her hold, making it extremely difficult to grab onto it. What if she lost control and drowned them all?

But she took a deep breath and tried again. This time, she moved slower, gathering more manageable amounts and joining them together. She poured more and more magic into her efforts, extending her hold over the river, sucking up more and more water, as much as she could manage. Then she made herself take even more again, forcing herself to keep going. It weighed almost unbearably on her, but she gritted her teeth, made sure she had a proper hold on the torrent...

Someone made a noise, maybe Garan. But she ignored them, close enough to losing her hold on the river that she couldn't afford any distractions.

Once she held as much as she could carry, the drain on her magical strength causing her legs to tremble underneath her, she began moving it, dragging it out of the riverbed and sending it flooding down into the tunnel. Once it was flowing in the direction she wanted it to go, she was able to loosen her grip, allowing her to suck up more water and send it after the initial rush.

The whole time she maintained her awareness of the water, keeping it shaped, drawing more out behind it ... the effort it took was immense. She swayed on her feet, but a steadying arm came around her waist, bolstering her. With relief, she forgot about her body and dived entirely into her magic.

And with that came instant relief. From grief, from numbness, from anger. All she felt was the sweet, seductive energy of her power. Something that could never be taken from her.

Her senses told her when the torrent of water swept into the queen's cavern. For a moment she thought about ignoring the razak and just trying to drown the queen, but she had no way of knowing whether that was possible, or how deep the pit was, and this was her only shot. This effort would drain her magic reserves for days, not to mention probably come close to incapacitating her again.

Instead Lira sent the water cascading through the cavern, picking up the razak as it flowed over the rock, gathering them in the current, then dragging them back out and down the tunnel.

The flood of water roared back towards her, as energising as it was exhausting, and exploded back out of the tunnel. She shaped it around her and Tarion, protecting the others as well, then threw it toward the riverbed.

Some of the razak went with it, rattling high and panicked as they were swept away with the current. Most of them crashed to the pebbled shore with the water, Lira finally losing her grip before she could get it all the way back to the riverbed.

"Go!" she screamed, eyes snapping back open.

If Tarion's arm hadn't been around her, she would have collapsed from the sudden energy drain. Her heart was racing too fast and sweat slicked her skin. Razak were everywhere, rattling furiously, apparently unharmed by the dousing. Even as she watched, some of them were forming together, becoming a towering monster.

Lucky she hadn't gone for the queen.

And then everything blurred.

When she could see again, she and Tarion were in the cavern, standing a short distance away from the pit. It was empty of razak, though the sound of fighting was audible from down the tunnel.

"You okay?" he asked.

She nodded around her panting breaths. "Mostly."

"How much magic do you have left?"

"Very little," she admitted. She was already trying to hide the fact that she was swaying on her feet, her legs feeling boneless from exhaustion. If they didn't do this now, she wouldn't get another chance. She couldn't afford for him to get noble and insist on resting first.

He drew his sword, slashed it through the air. The dark blade sang, an almost eerie sound that made Lira's magic ripple. "I'll cover you, no matter what."

She paused, looked at him. "Thanks, Tarion."

He gave her a little smile. "Let's do this."

Lira was only a step behind Tarion as they moved at a quick walk towards the pit, her leg muscles protesting as they climbed a slight incline and then reached the edge. She took one look down into the pit and knew instantly that the thing inside it had to be the queen.

"That's..." Tarion shook his head in awe. "This is going to be hard."

The razak queen was all physical form, no shadowy tendrils, and covered entirely in thick, sharp carapace. Her scales were a purply colour, rather than black, gleaming iridescent in the faint moonlight drifting down from above. She was at least three times the size of an individual razak, with what looked like double the number of scaled limbs. Their narrow ends were razor-sharp.

And the creature had sensed Tarion's use of magic bringing them in here. The rattle she let out was so deep in tenor it made the ground shudder, and Lira felt the echoes of it all through her bones.

The queen was angry.

Slowly but surely, she began to move, limbs uncurling into the air.

"No time to admire the problem, mage-prince," Lira said briskly. "You know what you have to do, right?"

"I don't think I can—"

"We've already proved you can bring yourself out of the change by focusing on Sesha, something good. Now, do the opposite. Think of something that makes you angry, furious, and remember how badly you want to save your parents. Then reach for your magic. We both know you can do this if you let go of your reluctance."

His eyes closed briefly, sadness and fear filling his expression. But slowly that cleared, replaced by resolve, and then anger. His eyes opened, and he stared down into the pit. He took a deep, focusing breath.

And he began to change.

Taller, broader, interlocking scales sliding down where his forearms and hands were bare. Copper fire with an edge of madness taking over those warm hazel eyes.

Tarion let out a low, bloodcurdling snarl.

Then he hefted his sword and leapt off the edge, landing inside the pit and immediately slashing at the nearest leg. The queen screamed. In anger, not pain. Tarion roared, his fury matching hers, and he swung again. And again. Fast and brutal and angry.

Gathering herself, Lira took a steadying breath and leapt in after him, her dagger in her right hand. She stepped in behind him, allowing him to lead the way, her feet dancing to ensure she didn't obstruct his sword arm.

His swordplay was a mesmerising mix of grace and chaotic fury, the weapon an extension of his arm, footwork so quick and powerful it made her vision blur, each move brutal and driven with fury. Lira stayed close, letting him cover her, lashing out with her dagger when the opportunity allowed. She made sure to stay out of his eyeline too—not wanting to become an unintended casualty.

Inch by fighting inch he got them closer to the creature's centre of mass, the Darkmage's blade slicing through limb after limb, the metal singing with each slide through the air. The queen rattled in fury, and Tarion matched each challenge with an echoing roar.

And despite the chaotic fury driving each of Tarion's blows, there was also purpose to his movement ... like he knew nothing else but the task of getting closer to the queen's centre of mass. The queen's rattling turned to shrieks, no doubt calling for her razak to come and protect her.

They didn't have much time. Egalion and the others wouldn't be able to hold so many desperate razak for much longer.

Sweat slicked Lira's skin, her muscles trembled, and her light footwork turned to stumbling she was so tired. But Tarion covered her—whether deliberately or not it was hard to tell—and he kept going, tireless and fearsome in his monster state, pushing closer, gaining inch by inch of ground.

And then Lira caught a flash of the creature's centre of mass, a rippling purple carapace. It moved, shifting towards them, and a glistening violet eye centred on her. Hate rippled in that gaze.

A snarl rumbled from Tarion, and for the first time it held an edge of weariness. Blood dripped from a cut on his cheek, and even more of it soaked the left sleeve of his jacket where a hard blow from the queen had torn through some of his scales.

She thought the sound held a questioning note, so she answered. "Not yet. You need to get me a little bit closer." She didn't have enough strength to cover the distance alone.

He took a deep, shuddering breath, then looked at her. Anger and frustration twined in that copper fire, and she watched as he let the anger take a firmer hold. A bellow of rage escaped him and then he was snarling as he began moving again, weaving the sword in one hand and slashing with the deadly claws of his other.

Slowly, inch by inch, he slashed and tore their way ever closer, until he got Lira where she needed to be.

She had to fight to call on her magic this time. It was slow and groggy inside her after her effort with the water, but she gritted her teeth and forced it to obey her bidding. With a grunt of effort, she forced it outwards.

And she set the queen's head alight.

The monster screamed shrilly, in pain as much as anger now. The enormous head writhed, limbs flailing. One clipped Lira's back, and she stumbled forward, nearly hitting the ground. It took almost more effort than she could summon to get back to her feet, and when she did, she swayed. She couldn't quite regain her balance.

Tarion roared in fury as another limb slammed into his leg. He ignored it and moved closer to Lira, his blade whipping around to keep her protected. She tried to help, but her vision was blurring alarmingly.

But the queen was burning.

Lira edged closer, staggering forward, determination and fury vibrating through her. She swayed to avoid another leg, stumbled again, then got another step closer. Her chest ached, her magic was burned dry, but her fury kept her on her feet. Beside her, Tarion snarled and tore entirely through a limb with his claws. Blood sprayed them both.

She lifted her dagger and drove it deep into the razak queen's eye.

The queen went still for an endless moment. Then gore exploded over Lira's hand and face. It burned fiercely where several drops landed in fresh wounds on her forehead, her right arm, increasing in intensity until it began to feel like her skin was burning away. A scream escaped her.

Then the agony was gone, and she felt only the stickiness of gore on her skin.

Seconds later, a new sensation swept through her, hot and atavistic, hungry. Her magic stirred, recognised something in it, before dying completely. Lira staggered, blinked, and then the rushing faded and stilled inside her.

The queen was dead.

A single, high-pitched scream came from down the tunnel, and then everything went quiet.

Breathing in frantic gasps, limbs threatening to collapse, Lira turned to Tarion. His furious copper eyes glared at her, mouth already letting out a threatening snarl. He lifted the sword.

She took a step toward him.

His snarl was louder this time, a warning. She took another step. He lunged, and she froze, holding his eyes. At the last second, he spun away, driving his left hand into the ground, claws scraping on rock.

Lira moved, for a moment forgetting the exhaustion dragging her body down. She dropped next to him, feeling how rigid his limbs and muscles were, and rested her forehead against his shoulder, her hand sliding around his where it held her grandfather's sword.

"Come back, Tarion."

And he did.

He took a long, shuddering breath, and then the scales were sliding away from his skin, the claws retreating. His head turned, and Tarion's hazel eyes met hers, glazed with the same exhaustion she felt. "You okay?" he asked.

She stared at him. The queen was dead. It was over. All she could think to say was, "You're bleeding."

"Got me good." He winced. "Fari will fix me up, though."

She nodded, her fingers uncurling to let her dagger drop to the floor. It was done.

He slumped, clearly as unable as her to stand at this point, and his gaze fell on the Taliath sword hanging loose in his grasp, the blade dark with razak ichor, but still gleaming underneath. It would never be a blade like *Heartfire* or *Mageson*, shining with its goodness and heart. But it was beautiful nonetheless, and it was Tarion's now. He seemed to realise that too.

"*Darksong*," he said, then raised his eyes to hers. "If you approve?"

A little shiver ran through her. "It's not for me to approve. The sword is yours now, not his or mine." She paused. "But I think it's right."

The sound of running feet made them look up. Tarion wrapped his arm around Lira's waist and transported them back up to the cavern floor. As they reappeared, he tried to stand, but sank back to his knees with a groan. Lira just managed not to fall too.

"Tarion!" Egalion flew to him.

"I'm fine. Just a few cuts and bruises." He smiled for his mother. "Fari, would you mind?"

The healer knelt beside him, pressed a palm over the blood-soaked section of his jacket. "You did it."

"Everyone else okay?" he asked.

"We're good." Garan stepped forward. He was covered in blood and razak ichor, they all were, but they were all upright and moving under their own steam. "Lira?"

"Magic drain and weariness. No major injuries." She waved off his concern. Now that the fight was over, the numbness was returning.

"You've got a nasty-looking gash on your forehead. Your arm too." Fari frowned in concern as she finished with Tarion. "No doubt with blood and other muck inside. I should clean them out before they get infected."

"We can clean up in the river," Egalion said. "Then we go and find Dash, locate the remaining nests, and get out of this cursed place."

Garan nodded. "There should only be one more nest, two at the most. And now we have a good strategy for destroying them. I think we've enough food supplies for a week."

All gazes swung to Lira, but she shrugged, not sure how it mattered what they did next. She'd killed a queen, the creatures responsible for Ahrin's ... she sucked in a deep breath. It didn't matter.

"You sure you're okay?" Fari left Tarion, now on his feet, to come over, rest a hand on Lira's neck.

Lira pushed her away, though as she did so, her vision blurred again. "You are just as exhausted as the rest of us, and I don't have any serious injuries." Maybe she could just sit down here for a while. Let it all go. They could come back for her after they found Caverlock.

Fari's frown only deepened, and her gaze searched out Tarion's. "I think something's wrong—"

A distant shriek cut her off.

"Everyone else hear that?" Lorin's gaze swept the cavern.

"I'm sure it's nothing, just wind through the tunnels," Garan murmured.

Lira frowned as something teased the edge of her senses. The sensation was like little pinpricks on her brain ... she absently lifted her hand to the cut on her forehead as the burning sensation flared again. But it was gone as quickly as it had come.

"All right. Garan, help Tarion to his feet," Egalion said briskly. "We'll head to the river, clean up, fill up our supply of fresh water. As much as I hate to wait, you could all use some rest before we head on. Lorin, you'll take the rear. I'll lead."

The little pinpricks in Lira's brain shifted, became more insistent. It was like they were ... stronger. No, that wasn't it. Closer?

"Lira?" Fari waved a hand before her face.

She focused her eyes. "Yes?"

"Something wrong?"

"No, I..." She shook her head, trying to dislodge the sensation. Maybe it was a symptom of her head injury. Lira shivered, realised the temperature was dropping. Rapidly.

"It's getting colder." Tarion's voice sounded stronger after Fari's work, and he was steady on his feet.

The pinpricks strengthened in intensity. There were so many ... she tried to separate them out. But she didn't have the energy or focus. "Fari, I think there's something wrong..."

"What is it? Describe what you're feeling." Fari looked at her, but before Lira could reply, the temperate dropped even more noticeably.

"That couldn't be ... not another nest this close." Garan turned white. His breath frosted.

Another shriek sounded. Closer this time. Lira winced, the little sparks in her brain growing more intense, the individual points coalescing into...

The shrieks became rattles. Louder.

"That way." She spoke without thinking, pointing to a tunnel entrance almost directly opposite from the one that led to the river. "Lots of them. Coming toward us."

Garan stared at her. "How do you—"

Egalion cut him off, her voice authoritative, calm. "We have to go. Now. Tarion, can you get Lira up to the ledge you rescued me from?"

"We can't go that way," Fari said instantly, voice firm. "The tunnel leading to it is narrow and pitch dark. Neither Tarion nor Lira can crawl that far."

"Then we'll head back towards the river. Hopefully it will deter them from following us," Egalion said. "Quickly now. We all know how fast those things can move."

"They shouldn't be running—"

"Fari, we understand your concern, but if we stay here, we're going to get eaten," Garan said. "Lira and Tarion, you're up front; the rest of us will cover from behind. Go."

The ratting was so loud now, and it was deathly cold. Lira's brain felt like it was burning. Fear raised tendrils through her numbness, prompting her to run after Tarion's long strides, ignoring the ache in her chest and the weariness in her limbs.

Razak were already spilling out into the cavern by the time they reached the tunnel entrance. Many of them. They made straight for the fleeing mages, unerringly following the residue of their magic.

Her breath burned in her chest as she forced herself to keep running, to put one foot in front of the other, gaze focused on Tarion's form ahead of her. They exited the tunnel, ran towards the shore.

Then, abruptly, Lira felt herself picked up, her legs swinging wildly as she rose higher and higher into the air.

Egalion.

The most powerful mage alive held them all in the grip of her flight magic as if it were nothing, carrying them over the rushing current and landing them with infinite gentleness on the other side of the swollen, tumbling, waters.

There, they steadied themselves, and turned to look behind them.

And stared in horror.

CHAPTER 42

L ira had killed a razak queen. Lit the monster up like a torch. All the razak connected to it had died, screaming ... but now she stood and stared across the river. The entire bank, the tunnel, the walls sloping down to the beach ... they were crawling with more of the monsters.

The burning in her brain, at their closeness, had become too intense to ignore. She closed her eyes and got swept away in it. Her mind, magic, whatever it was, spread outward, beyond the razak lining the opposite bank, finding the next little burning spots of razak, and then the next, and then the next, jumping from nest to nest, ever outwards.

Something sounded, and her focus wavered for a moment. She shook a little, dislodged it. Another sound, distant. Then searing pain across her cheek, enough to snap her out of her daze and come crashing back to the present.

Egalion stood before her, one hand still raised, green eyes looking almost concerned. Lira blinked, realising despite her fog of numbness what had just happened. Lucinda had lied to them. Or been horribly wrong.

Lira was sure it was the former.

"They're everywhere." Her voice came out as a croak.

"What?" Egalion snapped, then looked at Fari. "What's wrong with her?"

"Not sure, but I suspect she was using magic of some kind just now—she gets that look on her face whenever she does."

"Fari's right." Tarion shifted closer, a hand resting on Lira's arm. "Tell us what happened."

"Razak, everywhere," she managed, almost swaying on her feet. Too much magic. "Six nests, probably more, definitely more. They're everywhere, infesting the entire underground space."

His gaze held hers. "You can sense them?"

She nodded. "I don't know how, but..."

Silence fell, a bubble surrounding them that blocked out the furiously rattling razak still clambering along the opposite shore. A few were joining together ... at some point they were going to get large enough to cross the water.

"We can't do it." Tarion's voice was heavy, the words drawn reluctantly out of him.

Lira glanced at his mother, standing on Tarion's left. Her green eyes were distant, focused not on the cavern full of monsters, but on something else far away.

Lira had lost Ahrin on this foolish mission, but Egalion's husband might still be alive. *If* he wasn't anywhere near any of the crawling masses of razak her brain could suddenly sense. Her fingers curled and uncurled at her sides, torn between the numbing weight that made her want to curl up and never move again and a burning hatred of this entire place and everything in it.

"We'll go back up." Egalion seemed to be drawing herself together, shoulders straightening, clarity returning to her sharp gaze. Lira wondered at the effort it must have taken her. "Tell the Seven what we saw, and how much worse it is than they realised."

"The chances of Lucinda letting us leave Rotherburn are non-existent," Lira said dully, "especially now we've proven we can do what she wants."

"We can't though," Garan said grimly. "Not that many."

"Maybe Lira is wrong. How could so many hundreds of razak survive?" Lorin asked. "What are they feeding on down here?"

"Each other?" Fari suggested. "Or maybe they don't need much blood to survive. Don't forget these are magically born creatures—we can't assume anything about them."

Lorin waved a hand in frustration. "Rotted blasted hells. We were so close to finishing this."

"Here's what we'll do." Egalion was calm, her steady competence drowning the flash of despair threatening to spread through them all before it could take hold. "Lira is right about Lucinda. We don't have to leave, not yet. But if the Seven want all the razak destroyed, then we have to come up with another way to do it."

"Mama..." Tarion hesitated. "It's been days since..."

Egalion's expression darkened, the woman clearly refusing to entertain the thought that her husband was no longer alive. "We will go back up, and we will return with an army," she said doggedly. "And we will hunt down every single one of these monsters and destroy them, and we'll find Dash in the process. He's still out there. I know it."

"I'm sorry, Councillor Egalion, but I disagree with your plan." Fari stepped forward, expression nervous but clearly determined. "Risking more lives, especially yours, on this craziness is foolish. If Lira is right, then there are more than a hundred razak out there, rattling away ... six or seven queens? I don't even think an army could beat that, not down here in the dark where the razak have the advantage. Not to mention, if Lucinda was willing to give us an army, if they *had* an army, they'd have done that already. No, she lied to us, and we need to start thinking about what that means."

Egalion whirled on the healer, eyes flashing, but Garan spoke before she could. "Fari is right, Aunt Alyx. Lucinda can't be trusted, and we're pretty sure her plans aren't limited to destroying razak queens. You are the most powerful mage alive ... we need you to survive this so you can protect our home. Our priority has to be getting you back to Shivasa. Maybe we can help Rotherburn, but we need to do it from a position of strength."

Egalion visibly flinched at those words. Oddly, Lira understood what she must be feeling. Understood hearing words that cut to your soul and tore away any hope you had. For Lira, it was the constant comparison to her grandfather. For the councillor ... she'd probably heard this before, more than she ever wanted to, during the war against Shakar. She'd no doubt had to sacrifice those she'd loved because her power meant she was the only hope for saving everyone. The woman swayed on her feet.

Tarion moved swiftly to her side. He wrapped an arm around her. "They're right, Mama. You need to go, get out. I'll stay and find Da."

"No!" She straightened and threw him off. "I won't risk you too. He wouldn't want that. I—"

"Lira, what do you think?" Garan asked unexpectedly.

She blinked. "I don't know."

Even Egalion looked surprised by this response, and her gaze narrowed, roving over Lira's face. "Fari, is her magic overuse worse than we thought?"

"I'm not sure. It's the second bout in a short span of time though ... she suffered it the other day, saving us." Fari moved towards her. "She would have died, if not for..."

She trailed off. Tarion and Garan flinched. Egalion's gaze narrowed. "If not for what?"

Lira looked away as Fari pressed two gentle fingers to her neck, trying to drown out everyone's words, but it was impossible. Seeking distraction, her gaze caught on the mass of razak on the opposite shore. One creature was quickly growing large enough to span the width of the river.

"Ahrin pushed Lira out of the way of a flailing razak leg. Took the blow herself. It sent her flying off a cliff edge," Tarion said quietly. "She didn't make it."

Fari's fingers moved from Lira's neck to her forehead. "How do you feel? Anything hurting more than it should, any odd weakness, difficulty breathing?"

"I'm fine." She brushed the hand away listlessly.

"Ahrin Vensis?" Egalion snapped. "The Darkhand was here with you?"

"Stop!" Lira bellowed the word. They had to stop talking about her, making Lira *think* about her. She couldn't, she just couldn't. "We have to move. The razak over there are minutes away from growing large enough to cross the river to us."

They were all looking at her with expressions torn between pity and worry, but Egalion quickly moved on. "We go back up to the city, see how Lucinda responds, and plan what to do next. If we do decide to leave and return home, she can't hold me in this place. Nobody here can match my power."

Garan looked at Lira, eyebrow raised, but she merely shrugged. He sighed. "All right. We go back to the Seven."

Egalion led the way, Tarion bringing up the rear. After climbing up two levels, the bitter cold began to recede. When Lira concentrated, she could feel the little pinpricks in her brain fading too, growing less intense. But soon even monitoring them was too much—her magic died completely.

The rigours of overuse racked her: shivering, exhaustion, numbing of her thoughts. Combined with her injuries, it was a constant struggle just to put one foot in front of the other. She ignored the others' concerned looks.

Egalion was the only one who paid little attention to Lira—probably too caught up in her own internal pain. The woman glanced back at Tarion frequently, the look on her face telling Lira that losing her son after Caverlock might be the thing that finally broke her.

At one point, Garan fell into step beside Lira. It took some time for her dull thoughts to realise he was positioning himself so close in case she fell.

She didn't tell him to go away.

They marched for several hours, ever upwards, then Egalion stopped, ordering they all needed rest. "I'll take first watch."

"You need rest too, Mama," Tarion said quietly. "I should take watch—I still can't control turning into a monster while I sleep."

She hesitated, but Garan chimed in. "I'm confident we can talk Tarion down if he turns, but I think it's smarter to avoid it if we can. Tar is tired, but he can handle a few more hours awake. He's tough."

"Fari's help back there restored a lot of my strength," Tarion added. "I'll be fine."

Egalion glanced at the healer. "Fari?"

Fari looked surprised that Egalion wanted her opinion but nodded after a moment. "I think he'll be okay."

"All right," Egalion capitulated. "Tarion, you've got watch. Wake us in a couple of hours and we'll keep moving."

Relieved that she no longer had to do anything, Lira curled up in her blankets, closed her eyes, and allowed the world to disappear.

Coming back to wakefulness was hard. Lira opened her eyes at a gentle shaking of her shoulder and stared at the stone wall, everything flooding back before she'd barely taken a breath. For a moment she was paralysed by pain ... and then the numbness of the void settled back over her.

She rose without a word, gathered her pack, and followed the others out.

As they walked, Lira listened to Garan and Tarion filling Egalion in on their suspicions about Underground, about Shakar's existing network being alive and well in Shivasa.

"It's another reason we have to get back," Garan said. "We need to warn the council sooner rather than later."

"About Uncle Tarrick too," Tarion added after a hesitation.

"I appreciate that Lira has helped you both and you feel gratitude towards her. But I will never, not for a single second of my life, doubt Tarrick Tylender." Egalion's voice was granite. "You think I wouldn't have noticed if he was under some sort of telepathic mind control? He is no traitor. The girl is mistaken or lying. And knowing her history, I'd go with the latter."

"She was never a real member of Underground." The same granite crackled in Tarion's voice. "She joined them because you, the council, asked her to. They set her up, Mama, and you and the council let them do it."

Lira's head came up for the first time, and *something* wriggled underneath the numbness, threatening to dislodge it. Quickly she glanced back down, returning her gaze to the floor.

"She was a member long before we asked her to join," Egalion snapped.

"No, she wasn't. You kept the truth from us." Tarion sounded both angry and disappointed.

"Now is not the time for any of that." Egalion sounded weary suddenly. "Let's just get your father and get home. We can worry about all that once we're safe."

After what Lira guessed was another full day's travel, they reached the ground level, then trailed up the steps of the market square where the body lay. Following the old blood trail backwards this time, they got themselves to the main door through which Lira and her companions had originally entered.

Egalion, Garan, and Tarion had been talking in hushed tones for the past several hours, no doubt planning what they would do next. Lira hadn't paid much attention. Too weary. Too apathetic. Once they returned, Egalion and the others could do what they liked. Lira just wanted to be done with it all.

Garan banged on the door several times once they reached it, then announced his name loudly. Nothing.

"Told you," Lira said, finding some fire left at the befuddled looks on their faces. "We'll be lucky if they go near that door once a day."

"What about your telepath friend?" Fari suggested. "You said they promised to keep an eye out for your return if you lowered your shields when you got back."

Lira waved a tired hand at Garan when Egalion instantly opened her mouth. "Feel free to explain it all to your aunt. While you do that, I'll lower my shields and start thinking busy thoughts."

As she painstakingly brought down her mental shields, Garan's voice sounded soothingly in the background, telling Egalion all about the anonymous telepath who'd contacted Lira and led her to overhear the Seven meeting.

"*Lira!*" The telepath's voice slid into her mind, filled with surprise. Lira was equally surprised—she'd only partly believed that the telepath would be keeping a lookout for them. "*You've come back. Did you succeed?*"

"*Yes and no. We're all here, and we'd like to explain everything to the Seven. Could you please send a guard for us?*"

The telepath slid out of her mind, and Lira blinked her eyes open. "Guards are on their way."

"That was fast. They didn't press you for more details?" Tarion frowned slightly.

"No. Which tells me—"

"Your anonymous telepath is either one of the Seven or has direct access to them. They know they're going to hear your story shortly," Egalion said.

Lira merely nodded, not having enough energy to be annoyed at being cut off.

"Aunt, we got the distinct impression there are factions amongst the Seven. Some that side with Lucinda and others concerned about her influence over the rest," Garan said. "I—"

Egalion lifted a hand. "Dash thought the same thing, but let's not discuss it here. Lira's telepath could be reading our surface thoughts."

Garan immediately subsided into silence, and the rest followed suit. Lira sat against the wall, closed her eyes, and let the numbness take her for a while.

It wasn't long after that they heard bootsteps loud enough in the deathly silence that they were audible even through the thick steel door.

The bootsteps marched up to the door, then they all heard the thud of bars being lifted from their brackets and dropped to the floor. The door eventually creaked open, and a scared-looking soldier peered through the gap.

Egalion stepped up to it, shoulders back and voice at her imperious best. "We'd like to be taken to the Seven. Now."

CHAPTER 43

Alyx Egalion stood still as a statue before the Seven. Her blue mage cloak was torn and spattered with blood and dirt, her hair was wild, and yet she still looked somehow regal. Lira was her opposite—hollow, wrung out, barren.

She'd killed a razak queen; the creature's dried blood and gore still spattered her hands and clothes. But none of it mattered. It hadn't solved the razak problem. Their mission had failed.

And Ahrin was gone.

It had all been for nothing. Absolutely nothing. Not even seeing Lucinda before her, seated with the Seven, roused a shred of emotion in Lira; nothing like the bitter, corrosive hatred she'd once felt in that woman's presence.

"What a sight you all make," Lucinda marvelled, her sharp gaze taking in Egalion and Lira before widening to study the others arrayed behind them. As always, the Seventh was utterly composed. The other members of the ruling council had entered the chamber almost frantically, their expressions ranging from hope to anticipation, then to anxiety. They looked like the only hope for their future was about to be revealed to them, while Lucinda appeared as if she was about to hear whether she was getting eggs or oatmeal for breakfast and didn't much care which it was. "I count two of your number missing, though."

Egalion didn't prevaricate. "It's been quite the adventure, but we bring bad news," she said coolly, as calm as Lucinda was. From there, she went on to detail everything that had happened, pointing out the extent of the razak problem.

Lucinda listened with an expressionless façade, idly tapping the fingers of her left hand against the arm of her chair. Despite the weight of her numbness, Lira watched the Seven carefully as Egalion spoke, her instincts operating without conscious thought to ensure her survival.

One or two were almost as difficult to read as Lucinda, but most of them looked shaken and upset by the news that there were more than two or three razak queens, that they likely numbered closer to ten, a problem too big for even multiple powerful mages to solve.

As Egalion spoke, Burgen sank forward in his chair, both hands covering his face. His shoulders started shaking a moment later. The woman beside him—Indira, Lira placed her—reached out a shaking hand to lay on his back. She was as white-pale as a Shiven. Nessin and Adellin shared a glance that was easy to interpret; Nessin thought the other had been proved wrong on something. Adellin waved a hand in disgust and looked away.

Lira tried to figure out if one of them might be her anonymous telepath friend, but it was impossible. Apart from Lucinda, none had given any hint of their mage ability, so she couldn't even rule any of them out.

"If you want the razak exterminated, it's going to take more than an army," Egalion finished. "You'll need to come up with another way to deal with the problem—and in return for your help in finding my husband, I'm willing to remain for a short time to assist you in developing that solution."

Lira wasn't certain, but she thought she caught a glimpse of blinding fury break through Lucinda's iron control and ripple over her face. But it was gone as quickly as it had come.

A heavy silence settled over the room. Lira wondered whether she should have paid closer attention to the plans Egalion and her son and nephew had been making—she had no idea whether the mage was being genuine or if her offer was a ploy of some kind. But as soon as she thought it, the thought drifted away, taking too much effort to chase down.

After a long moment, Lucinda turned to glance at her fellow rulers. They seemed too shaken to say anything, and after a moment Burgen gave her a reluctant nod before sitting back in his chair, looking defeated. He was letting her take the lead. Those who'd previously seemed aligned with Burgen, including Tallin, matched his body language. Something cold rippled through Lira.

She has the Seven now.

The thought whispered through her mind, confident and sure. That realisation brought another one, something important, nagging at the edge of her thoughts ... but she couldn't quite grasp it, wasn't sure if she cared enough to.

Lucinda returned her gaze to Egalion. "We will need time to discuss and consider your report and your offer. You'll be escorted to rest and refreshment in the meantime, and medical attention if required. We thank you for your efforts."

She rose from her chair without another word, made a sharp gesture to the red-jacketed guards on the main doors, then she and the other Seven trailed out of the room together. Burgen shot a look backwards, something like sadness and regret on his face. The pre-numb Lira wouldn't have liked that look one bit.

As the door closed behind the Seven, the two guards moved towards them.

"Councillor Egalion, Lira Astor, will you please come with me?" The oldest of the two spoke politely, almost deferentially. "Anders will escort the rest of you to the apartment you had previously."

Lira noted the separation. Figured it didn't mean anything good. But struggled to care. Egalion shot a glance in Lira's direction but didn't protest either. When Garan crossed his arms and demanded to know why they weren't going together, Egalion cut in before the guards could answer. "It's fine, Garan. Take the chance to clean up and get some proper rest. Lira and I will join you as soon as we're done."

"Mama, no, this isn't a good idea." Tarion shook his head.

"Do as I say." A hint of magic shivered through Egalion's voice, reinforcing her command, and both young men conceded without another word.

Fari gave Lira a little smile as she turned to follow the others out, her eyes shadowed with worry. Lorin looked as reluctant as Garan and Tarion to leave but didn't dare gainsay Alyx Egalion.

Lira followed after Egalion. The woman vibrated with restless energy despite the fact she had to be exhausted. No doubt she was itching to go back and search for Caverlock.

They were led out of the Seven's audience hall and into the square outside. Lira fell into step without complaint—surely this would be over soon, and she could curl up in a bed and escape from the world for a time.

A short walk along a narrow, winding street brought them to a graceful home set amongst several others of similar size and obvious wealth. Torches lined the walls, but were unlit, presumably to avoid drawing in the nerik. Lira wondered why they bothered to keep them there at all. More guards stood watchfully inside.

Something about the situation stirred Lira's old instincts, and despite herself, she leaned in to ask Egalion in an undertone, "Can you read their thoughts?"

"Yes, but there's not much of use in them, apart from telling me this is Lucinda's home. They don't know why we've been brought here."

Lira wasn't surprised. Lucinda wasn't stupid enough to let Egalion near anyone who knew anything she didn't want the mage to know. "What about the telepath that contacted me. Have you managed to find out who it is?"

Another slight shake of Egalion's head. "I'm powerful, but I don't have Dawn's skill. The Seven all shield well, and I haven't even been able to pick up a hint of what their individual abilities are. The telepath could easily hide from me, especially if they're as skilled as you think."

They were shown through the front door and down a long hallway to a room in the back of the house.

"Please wait here. It won't be long." The guard spoke, again polite and deferential, before closing the doors behind them.

They'd barely clicked shut when they opened again, admitting a servant carrying a tray of steaming food and drink. He placed it on a table by the door and left. Lira caught the scent of herbal tea and warmed bread. Her appetite roused.

Instinct dismissed any thoughts about the food and focused her attention on studying their location instead. The room was large and rectangular, possibly running the entire back length of the house. It was well lit, with torches flickering in wall brackets and a crackling fire before a set of armchairs.

The wall immediately to the left of the entrance doors was covered with rich tapestries. To the right, at the far end of the rectangular space, two sets of polished wooden doors, no higher than Lira's waist, were set into the lower half of the wall. Each was closed with padlock hanging from the handle.

She was inside Lucinda's home.

Her numbness cracked open then, the furious hatred she felt for the woman breaking through, rising up, making her—

But with the anger came the pain. Ahrin was gone. Lira's breath caught and she went rigid. Instantly she shied away from the anger, ignored it until it subsided again, until the blessed numbness made it all go away.

To distract herself, she continued studying her surroundings. Tall windows ran the length of the back wall and a moonlit garden was visible through the glass. The back of the property was craggy rock face; presumably the ravine wall.

"Are you casing the joint or looking for escape routes?" Egalion asked dryly, breaking the silence.

"Both." Lira turned to her. "There's no obvious way out through the back garden unless you fancy climbing a good mile of precarious ravine wall and facing nerik and razak at the top. It's hard to tell exactly what time it is, but I suspect dawn is far off."

"So if we need to flee, it's through the door we came in." Egalion nodded. "Do you think you could find your way back to the townhouse where the others are if we had to break out?"

"Yes," Lira said confidently. "*If* that's truly where she took them. I'd recommend flying the distance to shake any pursuit."

"And from there down to the docks, steal a boat? Like you say, we don't want to be wandering around up on the surface."

"Agreed."

"Let's hope it doesn't come to that." Egalion looked around. "Given the situation we're in, I'd rather work with these people."

"Also agreed. It gives us the highest prospect of survival." But Lira's attention was already drifting, energy fading again.

The silence that followed was hesitant, and then Egalion let out a sigh. "Fari thinks there's something wrong with you."

"What of it?"

"I know we have our issues, Lira, but they can be sorted out when we get home. Right now we need to work together."

"I don't much care what you want, Egalion," she said with a trace of her old fire.

The woman's jaw tensed, but she didn't say anything further. Instead they waited in silence, not looking at each other, lost in their own thoughts.

Sometime later—Lira thought maybe an hour had passed—the telepath's voice slid into Lira's head, aching with regret. "*I am sorry, Lira Astor. We could not stop it.*"

She stiffened. "*Stop what?*"

"*I did what I could. Please remember that.*"

"*Wait! What are you talking about?*"

But the telepath was gone. Even though Lira deliberately lowered her shields for a moment, there was no more communication. She cut a glance at Egalion. "Well, that's not good."

"What happened?"

The door opened then, cutting Lira off. It revealed Lucinda, along with a single guard—a different one than the man who'd escorted them to this place. His uniform was brown, so presumably not a mage. He remained just inside the door after closing it behind Lucinda.

That was strange enough for Lira to frown. Lucinda had a powerful magical ability, but she'd just closed herself in a room with two powerful mages and a single guard who wouldn't last two seconds against either Lira or Egalion.

Logically, that meant Lucinda didn't fear them. There could only be two reasons for that. Either Lucinda had good news, or at least was planning to offer them something they wanted. *Or* she was confident enough in her leverage over them she didn't need to fear them.

"*Lira?*" Egalion's voice arrowed into her mind. "*What?*"

"*I don't know, but something bad is about to happen. The telepath just contacted me to apologise, then disappeared.*" Lira sent that, then re-raised her mental shields, turning her entire focus to Lucinda.

The Seventh stopped before them, hands folded in front of her body. Lira tensed—there was a supressed triumph about her. Something had gone the way she wanted it to. "Thank you both for waiting. I apologise for taking so long."

"What do you want?" Egalion's voice was flat, uncompromising; she was as unconvinced by Lucinda's feigned sincerity as Lira was. But she wasn't afraid. Egalion knew she was too powerful to be contained.

Lira's gaze wandered over the room, more carefully this time. The deep unease creeping through her was slowly pushing away the fog of despair despite her best efforts. Her survival instinct was stronger than anything else about her ... it was why she'd survived the orphanage, Dirinan, why even now when she no longer cared what happened to her, the instinct to survive forced her back to awareness, alertness. The thrill stirred in the pit of her stomach.

"That's the question, isn't it?" Lucinda smiled. "What do I ultimately want?"

A chill gripped Lira's chest at the look on her face, the faint realisation she'd had before returning to whisper at the edges of her mind. There *was* more. Lucinda's endgame hadn't been the razak at all. She just hoped Egalion realised what was going on here too. Neither Lira nor Egalion indulged Lucinda by speaking again. Silence filled the room.

A little smile of acknowledgment curled at Lucinda's mouth. "Very well, I'll get straight to it. Your news about the numbers and proliferation of the razak is not unexpected. I'd hoped for different, of course, but..." Lucinda looked away, shuttering her disappointment. "Well, I'm rarely wrong. Therefore, we have no choice but to move to my alternative plan. The Seven have just endorsed it."

Lira braced herself. Whatever was coming wasn't going to be good. "Another plan of yours, how delightful. What is it, exactly?" she drawled.

"The both of you are going to return to Carhall. You're going to bring the Mage Council under your control, ensure mages take the absolute power Shakar wanted, and then you will direct not only the mages, but the kingdoms of Shivasa, Rionn, Tregaya, and Zandia as *we* direct you."

Egalion laughed—the cool, contemptuous laugh of the highborn. "I hadn't marked you as insane, Lucinda." Her voice could have cut glass. "We did what you asked in good faith. I was open to helping you find a solution to save your people in return for your help to find my husband, but you're quickly reducing my willingness to do even that."

Lucinda considered them both, a little smile playing at her mouth. "You don't think we've spent generations trying to come up with an alternative solution? Your arrogance in assuming *you* can find one now is, frankly, insulting."

Neither of them said anything. Lira wasn't willing to give away anything that Lucinda could use, and it seemed Egalion thought the same way. Good.

Lucinda stepped closer, tone oozing self-satisfaction. "The only reason either of you are willing to stay and help is because Dashan Caverlock and the Darkhand didn't come back from the undercity with you."

A breath escaped Lira. Rage burned through her, pressing at her skin, making her heart race and palms sweat. She let it burn, grateful for the strength and focus it gave her.

"Help me find Dashan, let us go, and we will return with more resources to help you," Egalion said, voice tight with reluctance.

"No deal," Lucinda said simply. "I don't trust you, and I wouldn't even if I believed that mages could solve the razak and nerik problem. So I've changed our agreement."

"You do know the extent of my power, yes?" Egalion asked, gaze wandering the room. "I could bring this roof down over your head in a matter of seconds."

"Actually, yes, I do know the extent of your power. The *full* extent of it." Another smile flickered over Lucinda's face. "Why do you think we kidnapped you, Alyx Egalion, why we thought a single mage, even the most powerful one alive, might succeed against so many monsters? I know you—"

"Stop!" Egalion's voice snapped through the room. The expression on her face was one of almost panic.

Lucinda turned to Lira, gloating now. "Do you know the story of Cario Duneskal's death, Lira?"

Lira blinked at the apparent segue, taken aback by both it and the terror on Egalion's face, but the councillor was responding before she could even think to come up with a reply.

"Enough, Lucinda! You keep talking and I will kill you where you stand."

"If I didn't freeze you first," Lucinda lifted an eyebrow.

"Your magic won't work on me. I have Taliath immunity." Egalion's mouth was curled in a snarl.

"On the contrary." Lucinda made a small movement with her hands, sharp and contained, and Egalion turned rigid, clearly frozen in place. Lira stared in horror. After a long moment, Lucinda made another gesture.

Egalion took an abrupt step backwards, hissing out a breath, eyes wide. "How did you do that?"

"I think I'll keep my secrets to myself," Lucinda said lazily, then glanced toward the guard at the door. "Toster?"

He turned the knob and opened the door. Lira's dismay turned to shock as a long-familiar figure strode into the room. Egalion went equally still beside her.

It was Athira Walden.

CHAPTER 44

Athira's blonde hair was braided neatly, her clothing simple but fine, her aura radiating confident assurance. She said nothing, simply coming to a halt a few steps into the room. Toster closed the door with a click.

"You remember Athira's ability, I'm sure? It has been a little … upgraded … since the last time you saw her though." Lucinda cocked her head. "With my power amplified by Athira, I doubt either of you would be able to defeat me. But may I suggest that you hear me out before we put that to the test?"

Egalion ignored her completely, stunned gaze on the young woman. Whatever panic she'd been feeling had vanished in a blink. "*Athira?* Are you all right? What's going on?"

Athira said nothing, merely stood with her hands clasped loosely behind her back. Lira stared at her—trying to read something in her body language that would give her a clue as to what she was thinking or feeling. But there was nothing she could grab onto. The last time they'd spoken, she'd left Athira behind on Shadowfall Island to spy for the council, promising to come back for her.

But Lira had never come back, because she'd been locked away by the Mage Council. And Lucinda had had years to work on Athira. Manipulate her in whatever clever way she wanted.

Athira had to be treated as the enemy now.

When the young woman made no response, Egalion's gaze lingered on Athira a few moments longer before returning to Lucinda. "I'm losing my patience." Her voice was ice-cold, her fingers clenching and unclenching at her sides.

Lucinda waved a hand, a signal to the guard at the door. "In that case, allow me to demonstrate my point. Toster?"

The guard left the door and walked the length of the room, boots rapping on the hardwood floor, a set of keys jangling as he took them out of his pocket. When he reached the two rectangular doors set into the wall, he knelt between them. With quick, efficient movements, he unlocked both padlocks and let them thud to the floor.

Lira's heart began to quicken, sweat breaking out on her palms. Her instincts flared so strongly she almost turned and ran from the room. This time she knew even before Lucinda could reveal her trump card ... she'd won again.

"Open them," Lucinda ordered, that suppressed triumph back in her voice.

Toster opened both the doors wide, giving Egalion and Lira a view of what lay behind them. Two cages. Each containing a prone body.

Lira was running before she even knew she was doing it, dropping to her knees and sliding to a halt by the cage holding Ahrin's sprawled form. The Darkhand's eyes were closed, but the dark hair covering half her face moved slightly.

She was breathing. She was alive.

Lira bit her lip hard enough to stop the tears welling in her eyes, forcing herself to scan the bars of the cage, its interior, taking in all the details. It was barely big enough to hold Ahrin, certainly not enough for her to sit or stand, or even do more than turn over. It wasn't even high enough for her to get up on her hands and knees.

Lira dimly heard Egalion's anguished cry but ignored it, every single piece of her focused on Ahrin lying before her, only inches away. Ahrin lived. She wasn't dead or lost.

When Lira's hand touched the bars between them, her magic vanished, coming back the moment she let go. Uncaring, she thrust her hand back through, reaching out to touch Ahrin's hair, her face. "Ahrin!" The word tore out of her. "Please. Ahrin, wake up!"

"She's drugged. They both are." Lucinda spoke from behind them. She'd crossed the room without Lira being aware, though Toster was back at his post by the door and Athira hadn't moved. Her face remained expressionless.

It was only then that Lira realised the cage behind the other door held Dashan Caverlock, just as unconscious as Ahrin. Egalion's hands were curled, white-knuckled, around the bars, face bloodless, looking as if she hadn't even heard Lucinda as she stared at her husband.

Lira swallowed, looked up at Lucinda. "What did you do?"

"I obtained the best bargaining chips I possibly could in order to ensure your obedience," Lucinda said. "It was a mistake, bragging about how you and the Darkhand hid your relationship from me. The both of you were so stupidly cocky. For a long time I tried to learn your greatest weakness, your biggest vulnerability, something I could use effectively against you to bring you to heel.

"I was beginning to think you didn't have one—or at least I hadn't found it before I learned that you were a traitor to Underground's cause. But then you came here, and I saw how much Ahrin Vensis means to you. It was a surprise, but a welcome one."

Lira blinked, shook her head. "I don't—"

"I told you, I suspected the truth about the razak," Lucinda cut over her. "So I planned accordingly. I took Egalion's husband as leverage … we waited for the right opportunity and captured him. But imagine my utter delight when the Darkhand came staggering up to the higher levels a few days ago. Now I have both you *and* Egalion in my control."

Lira stared at her. That kind of planning, of preparation … it was staggering. Lucinda had always been ten steps ahead of Lira, and she still was. Worse, her magic could breach Taliath immunity.

How did she fight that?

"You fear Ahrin and me." Desperate, Lira threw the words at her in a snarl.

Lucinda barked a contemptuous laugh. "I don't fear anyone. I make sure I never need to. Yes, you and the Darkhand could be a potent pair, maybe even a true challenge to my mastery, but her mercenary disregard for anything but her own interests, and your complete inability to trust, means that will never happen."

"Let her go." Lira stood, violet light sparking around her hands as she gathered her magic. Egalion was still on her knees, staring at her husband, one hand touching his hair. "Now."

"I'll let her go as soon as you do what I ask," Lucinda said, as if requesting the most reasonable thing in the world.

"We won't do it." Alyx Egalion pulled herself to her feet, slowly, deliberately. "Not for anything."

"Then they die." Lucinda shrugged. "It's not a bluff. If they aren't enough to get you to do my bidding, they're useless to me. As are you. I'll send you back down into the tunnels. Maybe you can kill enough razak to buy me some more time to achieve what I want. That's the only use I'll have for you."

"You can't kill me without taking a lot of damage," Egalion said tightly. "And you'll be the first to die."

"I don't think so, not with Athira at my side. But even if you're right—we've already sustained a lot of damage. And your death won't stop me killing your husband. Or your son."

Lira's vision caught movement from Ahrin's cage, and she spun back to it, forgetting about everyone else in the room. She fell to her knees and reached for her hand. "Ahrin?"

The Darkhand blinked groggily, her midnight blue gaze taking a few seconds to focus on Lira. "Lira? What..."

"She took you." Lira squeezed fiercely, wanting more than anything to rip the bars off and drag Ahrin out and into her arms. Her magic clamoured fiercely inside her but using her flame to melt the bars would take too long ... Lucinda would paralyse her before she got close to freeing Ahrin. "I'm so sorry."

It took a few seconds for Ahrin's groggy mind to realise where she was, how she was completely trapped, and when she did, she went utterly rigid, her eyes darkening to black. Panic filled her face, and it made Lira want to tear her own eyes out. She'd never seen such horror on Ahrin's face before, never seen her so deeply afraid. She never wanted to see it again.

"Get me out." Ahrin swallowed, forcing the words out in a rasping plea. Each word tore at Lira's soul. "Please, Lira. I can't." Her breaths were short, gasping, desperate. "I can't be in here."

"She'd kill you before I could." Lira pressed as close as she could, letting go of Ahrin's hand so she could cup her cheek, stroke her hair. "She wants to—"

"Use me as leverage over you." Fury rippled over Ahrin's face, dispelling the panic momentarily. "Don't. Don't do it. Let her kill me. I won't be used against you like that."

Lira shook her head. "You know I can't do that."

"Lira—"

"What she wants me to do, I can do it. It doesn't matter to me." Lira held her gaze. "I'll do it, I promise you. Do you hear me? I'll get you out, Ahrin."

"Lira..." Ahrin gasped, panic and anger and helplessness radiating from her. Lira bit her lip, unable to bear it. "Don't let her control you. You can't ... I have to ... I have to get out of here." She slammed her forehead against the floor.

"Ahrin!" Lira cried out, reaching for her face, her hands. "Stop. I won't sacrifice you."

Ahrin was panting like a trapped animal, eyes wide and glassy. "Let her kill me if that's what she wants."

"I could never..." Lira's voice trailed off. "You know I can't."

Ahrin swallowed, shifted to hold her gaze. "Yes, you can. You're Lira Astor, and you know how to survive. I taught you how. You need to cut me loose. Beat her at her own game."

"I can't. I won't."

"I'm your blade, Lira, born to serve you in any way necessary." Ahrin held her gaze. "Let me do that."

Lira shook her head, ignoring the silent tears that slid down her cheeks.

"Shall I add a sweetener to my offer?" Lucinda's voice was silky, so confident in knowing she had Lira already. "You do as I ask, and not only will I release your Darkhand, I will give you the name of your father."

Lira scoffed, a barking laugh. "What do I care about him?"

"You *would* care. If you knew how much his identity could help you gain the power you crave."

Lucinda's words resonated through the room for a brief moment only. While there might have been a time that Lira cared about that, it paled in comparison to the terror on Ahrin's face.

Egalion, looking shocked, opened her mouth to say something, but Lira waved her off. "The world fears that I am like my grandfather, and the truth—what I've always run from—is that they're right." She paused, feeling the certainty slide through her. "I *am* just like him." She turned back to Ahrin. "I won't sacrifice you, not for anything. I love you."

Ahrin stilled, blue eyes darkening to almost black. "You've never said that before."

"I didn't know how. But it's true, you know it is, ever since that alley when I was a starving child and you saved me from those men."

"I'll get out." Ahrin swore, holding Lira's gaze. "I swear it. I'll free us both from this."

Lira gave her a little smile. "I know you will. And I'll do what I have to until then. You can trust me."

Ahrin glanced away, still breathing too fast, her hands clenching and unclenching until she had the panic briefly under control again.

"I need a name, to help me do what is necessary," Lira murmured.

Ahrin swallowed. "Yanzi."

"Thank you." She took Ahrin's hand again, lifted it to press a kiss to her knuckles, then let go and stood up, meeting Lucinda's gaze. Egalion was staring at her in horror, but Lira ignored her. "I'll do as you ask. But I'm going to need instructions a little more specific than 'take over the world, Lira'."

"You and Egalion will bring the Mage Council under your control, and then the kingdoms. You will succeed where your grandfather failed. And then we will use that power to take what we want of your home. Ours is almost destroyed. We want a better one, a *safe* one."

"You're going to invade our home?" Fury warred with grief in Egalion's voice. "You'll never succeed. You're not strong enough."

"Not now. But once you've taken control, removed all the dissenters, well … it's why Underground's manifesto suited us so perfectly, why we used them for our purposes. Your council will take over, and then we will come."

"I won't do it," Egalion said, determined despite her obvious fear for her husband.

"I will," Lira interrupted. "And I can do what you need without her."

"Lira!" Egalion snapped.

"What?" Lira rounded on her, angry and bitter now the numbness of grief had lifted. "How much do you think I care about your precious Mage Council? I don't. Nor do I care whether the council rules or Lucinda's people do."

"I—"

"You put me in prison with no hope of release when I had done *nothing* wrong," Lira spoke slowly, deliberately. "You made me into this. And now you want me to give a rotted toss about your precious council or your precious husband?"

"Are you really willing to let him die?" Lucinda asked Egalion curiously.

Egalion's gaze shifted to Caverlock, her shoulders slumping slightly, eyes sliding closed for a brief moment. "It's what he would choose. I respect that."

"Then I'll get your son in here and offer him the same deal." Lucinda shrugged. "He won't be quite as useful, but as your only surviving mage heir, he'll be able to get a council seat for himself, no doubt."

Egalion went white. "You wouldn't."

"She would," Lira said, impressed by Lucinda's mastery despite herself. "And if you don't agree to what she wants, Tarion will. He's too soft. And then you and Caverlock will both be held prisoner here to make him do what she wants and Tarion will have nobody to protect him." Tarion didn't need protection, but Lucinda didn't need to know that, and Lira needed to goad Egalion into agreeing to this.

A beat of silence filled the room. Athira hadn't moved. Toster was staring straight ahead as if paying attention to nothing but his post at the door.

"Toster." Lucinda spoke into the silence.

He crossed the room without a word, keys jangling again.

"No!" Lira cried as he moved to shut the door on Ahrin first. She got two steps before Lucinda's paralysing ability locked her limbs down. She watched, helpless, as the door closed on Ahrin; the Darkhand's midnight blue eyes holding hers to the last.

"I said I'd do what you wanted." Lira spun the moment the paralysis lifted. "Let her out of there."

"Once you have gone, she will be removed from the cage and held in more comfortable surroundings, you have my word," Lucinda said calmly. "The same goes for Caverlock."

Lira shook her head. "I want to see her out before I do anything for you."

"No deal," Lucinda said evenly.

Lira thought about negotiating, but eventually gave in. Lucinda held all the cards here.

"Egalion?" A hint of impatience edged Lucinda's voice. "Should I send Athira to fetch your son?"

"No," Egalion grated out. "But he and the others, all of them, leave here with me. You'll keep no other hostages. Agree to that and I'll do as you ask."

"All right." Lucinda smiled faintly. "But Athira will travel with you, to ensure you are following my instructions."

Egalion frowned. "How do you know we won't kill her the second we're away from here?"

"She will send me regular reports. I miss one, and ... well ... you can imagine the consequences, I'm sure. Besides, you'll find Athira can look after herself." Lucinda's voice turned brisk. "Your ship will depart in an hour, on the dawn tide—arrangements have been made. If I start to worry things aren't going to plan, I'll begin removing body parts from both my hostages." Her gaze focussed in on Egalion then. "Not to mention I might start letting slip information about you, a little detail that you've clearly been hiding from everyone."

Egalion paled. Lucinda let those words sit for a beat while Lira fought not to leap at the woman and tear her throat from her neck.

"Good." Lucinda smiled thinly. "Toster will take you back to your quarters to collect your things and your companions, and from there he'll escort you down to the dock."

Lira's eyes lingered on the door holding Ahrin the whole way out.

"Lira?" Lucinda's voice stopped her, mockery lining its cool edge. The woman waited until Lira's gaze shifted to her, shrugging slightly. "You are a fool. Sacrificing everything to save the thing most dangerous to you. Ahrin Vensis will destroy you."

Lira paused, cocked her head. "You are so confident in your hold over me that you're willing to goad me like that?"

"I am. I know you inside and out, Lira Astor. And I *enjoy* watching you fail over and over again."

Lira's gaze shifted to Athira, who remained expressionless. "I thought she was coming."

"She'll meet you at the ship."

Lira nodded, took a step towards the door, then paused again, thinking of the woman she loved more than life itself. "I'm not the one Ahrin Vensis is going to destroy, Lucinda."

Lucinda met her gaze, hard and flinty. "I suppose time will tell which of us is right. Although experience would seem to indicate that it will be me. Every single time."

Lira left without another word.

CHAPTER 45

A marvellous sunrise lit up the horizon as Lira joined Alyx Egalion where she stood at the prow of the ship. The breeze whipped the woman's long brown hair around her face and tugged at Lira's shorter curls. The coast of Rotherburn had finally faded from sight moments earlier, and the sense of wrenching devastation at leaving Ahrin behind was powerful enough that Lira had sought distraction.

Not that this conversation could wait, anyway. They had to have it before Garan or Tarion or one of the others started asking their inevitable questions. Their looks had spoken volumes when Egalion and Lira had been shown back to their shared quarters and informed them that a ship would be carrying them home on the dawn tide.

"She's letting us go? Just like that?" Garan demanded.

"Just like that," Egalion had said, and then refused to say any more. "Now, we're leaving in an hour. Gather your things and let's go. We'll talk when we're well out of the range of Lira's telepath."

Lira had avoided their questions by walking away and keeping her distance.

"What do you want, Lira?" Egalion sounded tired, worn. It made Lira uncomfortable, because she knew the other woman was leaving a loved one behind too, and she didn't want to feel any solidarity with her.

Lira glanced around before speaking—Athira was nowhere to be seen. That was another conversation that needed to happen. Lucinda would never have let the mage free unless she was confident of Athira's complete loyalty, and Lira needed to understand that better.

"Isn't it obvious? We need a plan. For starters, what to tell your son and nephew and the others."

Egalion gave a soft laugh, but there was no warmth in it, only a faint hint of contempt, mixed with resignation. "*We* don't need to do anything. The moment we get back, you're going back to prison while I help the council figure out what to do next."

Lira held her gaze, not entirely surprised. "You have no intention of doing what Lucinda wants."

"My son is now free of her control." Egalion's hands tightened on the railing, white-knuckled, before letting go, and she turned in an abrupt movement to face Lira.

Lira huffed a breath. "She underestimated you."

"Unlike you." Egalion regarded her coolly, not like master to student, but adult to adult. "Did you mean what you said to her?"

"Does that scare you? That I'm just like my grandfather?" Lira challenged.

"No. I defeated him. I have nothing to fear from his granddaughter."

"You're really willing to let your husband die?" Lira meant it as a taunt, another challenge, but part of her was genuinely curious to hear the answer.

"I thought him dead once before, you know. For five long years. I sacrificed him then in the war against the Darkmage." Egalion shook her head, grief making her seem older, worn, but also showing a glimpse of the woman's inner strength. "And I have no choice but to do it again. It's a choice he would want me to make. He would place the safety of our home and our people above his own life."

"What about this secret she's holding over you?" Lira's gaze narrowed, curiosity flickering at her. "You seemed even more concerned about that getting out than your husband dying."

"I will wear whatever consequences I must, but I will *never* do as she asks."

"Then we're at war, you and I," Lira said softly. Part of her couldn't help but shudder at the thought of that. How could she stand up to such a powerful woman and hope to win? But then she thought of Ahrin, in that box, and her resolve steadied.

Egalion didn't answer. Instead she said, "Ahrin's nothing like Dashan though, is she? She'd be happy for the world to burn, as long as she survived the flames. And you're no different. Willing to sacrifice thousands because your heart is broken."

That didn't sting Lira the way Egalion must have thought it would. She let out a chuckle, but not of amusement. "Like you, I'm simply making a choice. What does it matter to me who rules the Mage Council?"

"You think Lucinda won't fight those who try to stop her? You don't think she'll loose her razak and nerik on any mage or Taliath or soldier that opposes bringing her people to our home?"

Lira shrugged. "I've no doubt she would. But that doesn't have to be necessary."

"Then you're a naïve fool."

"No, I'm not. I'm talking about absolute power, Egalion. I'm talking about having a strong enough grip over the council, the kings, that nobody tries to stop Lucinda and her people coming to our shores. That's the way nobody gets hurt. You and I can achieve that."

"That kind of power is what I have spent my entire life trying to prevent *anyone* having," Egalion said. "I won't usher it in now, not even for Dashan's life."

"Then I will."

"Then there *will* be war between us, Lira Astor." Egalion stepped closer, her magic wrapping around Lira like a blade to the throat. "I defeated your grandfather, and I'll defeat you too."

Lira kept her shoulders straight, voice low. "Don't forget I can breach that invulnerability of yours. I hope you haven't lost your edge after all these years of peace. Because I have spent my entire life surviving." She paused. "Oh, and now I know that Lucinda has some powerful leverage over you, don't think I'm not going to do everything I can to ferret it out. I have a sneaking suspicion that whatever it is could bring you down, Alyx Egalion."

Egalion held her gaze for a moment longer, assessing, and then she strode away without another word.

Once she was out of sight, Lira stepped up to the railing and stared east towards home. She put her worry and fear for Ahrin aside—her Darkhand could and would take care of herself—and instead began thinking through what had to come next.

Lucinda needed to be dealt with. For what she'd done to Lira, to Ahrin. But the woman had given Lira an opportunity too ... her whole life, Lira had straddled the line between desperately wanting the Mage Council's acceptance and running from or denying how much like her grandfather she truly was.

It hadn't done her any good; it had only left her weak and confused. That first night she'd been locked away in prison, she'd chosen to stop running, to embrace the part of her that was the Darkmage's heir.

She'd chosen to learn from his mistakes, so she didn't repeat them. She'd be stronger, smarter. She'd do things differently.

And she'd come for Lucinda, in time.

But first. The Mage Council.

THE END...

The story continues in the final book of this series - out in late 2022

THE DOCK CITY CHRONICLE

Want to delve further into the world of Lisa's books?
By signing up to Lisa's monthly newsletter, *The Dock City Chronicle*,
you'll get exclusive access to lots of subscriber-only special content
including:
An exclusive foreword from the beginning of *Heir to the Darkmage;*
An ebook with a collection of short stories from *The Mage Chronicles*
world;
A novella from the *A Tale of Stars and Shadow* world;
Updates on Lisa's books, her writing process, the books she's reading,
and more!
You can sign up for the Chronicle at Lisa's website
lisacassidyauthor.com

Also by Lisa Cassidy

Heir to the Darkmage

Heir to the Darkmage

Mark of the Huntress

Whisper of the Darksong

CONSIDER A REVIEW?

'Your words are as important to an author as an author's words are to you'

Hello,

I really hope you enjoyed this story. If you did, I would be genuinely thrilled if you would take the time to leave an **honest** review on GoodReads or Amazon, or both (it doesn't have to be long - a few words or a single sentence is absolutely fine!).

Reviews can be absolute game changers for the success and visibility of a book, and by leaving a review you'll help this story reach others. Not to mention you'll also be helping me write more stories.

Thank you so much for reading this book,

Lisa

About Lisa

Lisa is a self-published fantasy author by day and book nerd in every other spare moment she has. She's a self-confessed coffee snob (don't try coming near her with any of that instant coffee rubbish) but is willing to accept all other hot drink aficionados, even tea drinkers. She lives in Australia's capital city, Canberra, and like all Australians, is pretty much in constant danger from highly poisonous spiders, crocodiles, sharks, and drop bears, to name a few. As you can see, she is also pro-Oxford comma.

A 2019 SPFBO finalist, and finalist for the 2020 ACT Writers Fiction award, Lisa is the author of the young adult fantasy series *The Mage Chronicles*, and epic fantasy series *A Tale of Stars and Shadow*. She is currently neck-deep in her latest series, *Heir to the Darkmage*.

As part of her writing journey, Lisa has partnered up with One Girl, a charity working to build a world where all girls have access to quality education. A world where all girls — no matter where they are born or how much money they have — enjoy the same rights and opportunities as boys. A percentage of all Lisa's royalties go to One Girl.

You can follow Lisa on Instagram and Facebook where she loves to interact with her fans. Lisa also has a Facebook group - The Writing Cave - where you can jump in and talk about anything and everything relating to books and reading.

If you want to learn more about Lisa and her books, head on over to Lisa's website - lisacassidyauthor.com

Printed in Great Britain
by Amazon